CW00485153

VOLUME I IN THE 'DAUGHT

EVER SONG

with love from A.C. Salt

A.C. SALTER

For my Scrumpy

First published by A.C. Salter, 2016

This novel is a work of fiction. Names, characters,
and events are products of the author's imagination.
Any resemblance to actual persons, living or dead,
is entirely coincidental.

Copyright © 2016 by A. C. Salter

All rights reserved. No part of this book may be used
or reproduced in any manner whatsoever without written
permission except in the case of brief quotations embodied
in critical articles and reviews.

ISBN 978-1-5272-0274-0

Other books in the *Daughter of Chaos* trilogy

Shadojak
Ethea

Printed and bound by S-Print

Prologue

The naked limbs of a willow whipped savagely at Norgie's body as the wind slapped rain against his face. Screwing his eyes tight against the weather, he searched for a way inside the derelict town house, seeking refuge from the relentless storm that battered the foul night.

Stooping low to avoid being stung by the tree, Norgie stumbled over the dilapidated lawn to a cellar window. He kicked it through with the heel of his boot, the sound drowned out by the watery night, then crawled through the gap. His belt buckle caught on the frame, holding him like a worm on a hook before he wriggled through and flopped to the concrete floor within.

Damn, if it wasn't the wettest night he had ever had. Struggling to his feet he shook the excess water from his heavy clothes.

Norgie wasn't a man for indoors, not even in the harshest of winters – yet this storm was something else. And, his age was beginning to show; living on the street will do that. It adds years to your face whilst stealing them from your life. Still, for a homeless guy, he wasn't doing all that bad and he had a couple of yellow teeth in his black gums to prove it.

A dank smell of mulch and turps permeated the cellar. Adding to the aroma was dust, mouse droppings and something unpleasant and pungent which he recognized yet couldn't put a name to. It tickled his nose and made him uneasy. It was a world apart from the fresh autumn air he should be relishing, as he lay merrily on a park bench by the river.

People would call him homeless, a bum, the dregs of society. He would call himself a 'free man'. No commitments, no dead-end job or boss to slave for, no debts, no responsibility. Just himself, the earth and sky. Waking up each day with no worries and the freedom to wander where his heart would lead. A free man; albeit a wet one.

Soft amber light from a street lamp filtered through the fractured window, casting a hypnotic effect against the far wall and creating strange shadows from objects on the floor. The effect would have been relaxing if it wasn't for the dead cat laid at his feet.

The feline had been torn open. Grey guts spilling out to the open air as dry eyes stared up at him, tongue hanging dark and limp from a gaping mouth

Norgie reached inside his coat and retrieved a bottle of Captain Morgan. He took a swallow of the rum to wash down the rising bile in his throat. That explains the stench then, he mused.

Smaller objects appeared as he grew accustomed to the dark. Scattered randomly about were dead mice that appeared to have succumbed to the same fate as the cat. They were gutted and crushed as if someone wasn't satisfied with merely cutting the poor creatures open, they'd felt they needed to stamp upon them too. Surrounding each tiny corpse was a circle of runes drawn onto the concrete with chalk. The cat also had its own circle, large enough to accommodate the limp body.

After swallowing another shot of rum, Norgie decided he would rather spend the night somewhere-else after all. It was then that he heard footfalls shuffling above him, before clomping heavily down the stairs toward the cellar.

Norgie was sure the place was empty, the whole street derelict. He got the unnerving feeling that whomever it was knew he was here.

The footfalls terminated on the other side of the door. He glanced to the window but realised he wouldn't get through in time and would be exposing his back to the stranger coming through. A second thought was to hide but apart from the scattered corpses, there was nothing to hide behind.

His breath caught as the handle turned, the spring mechanism inside making a metallic ping as the door swung towards him. Norgie's stomach clenched as he forced a smile upon his face but that quickly dropped, the eager greeting also died on his lips as a spindly creature, shrouded in shadow, shuffled into the cellar.

"Jim?" Norgie asked, gingerly.

The man before him resembled a guy he recognised as a fellow 'free man' who frequented the same soup kitchens as he did. Yet, he appeared older, frailer, as if something had sucked the life from him and left an emaciated creature which was more skeleton than man. It appeared a lifetime of debauchery had finally caught up with the old sod. Yet he was sure he had seen him only last week, looking healthier and decades younger.

"What the hell happened to you? You look like a prisoner of war or something."

Norgie took another swig from his bottle as Jim's sunken yellow eyes stared unblinking into his. His nose had been broken at an odd angle and split under the bridge, his mouth hung slack, jaw hanging low as if the effort was too great to close it. Tufts of white hair sprung from his head in patches, giving the impression he was suffering from alopecia or cancer.

Norgie offered him a drink, holding the bottle out but the gesture went unnoticed.

"You done this in here, Jim?" Norgie asked, gesturing about the cellar. "Not sure what the mice have done but the cat didn't deserve that."

Norgie realised his words were falling on deaf ears. Jim, didn't appear to even acknowledge that he was in the room. He took a step back and tried to peer into the darkness behind the decrepit man but the heel of his boot caught on something solid, knocking him off balance and it was all he could do, arms wind-milling, to keep upright.

He had stumbled over a brick. The sudden motion appearing to awaken something in the other man.

"She shouts!" Jim said suddenly, as if the quick movements before him jolted him out of his glum mood. His voice was shrill and desperate, startling a double-beat into Norgie's heart.

"Oh! How she shouts."

"Never enough, not nearly enough. I drew her fancy symbols didn't I? Got her the blood, nice and fresh how she wants it.

5

Squeezed every drop out of the mice's – lots. Sprinkled it all around just as she says."

Norgie watched as the frail figure before him clenched his fist around an imaginary creature, reliving the demise of the poor rodents.

"But still she shouts."

"Who, Jim? Who's been shouting?" Norgie asked, yet he'd an inkling that the 'She' was coming from inside Jim's senile head.

"Wasn't good enough, wasn't nearly good enough. Made friends with the cat – how it struggled when I killed it. Fresh, blood still hot; poor little thing, I didn't want to kill it." Jim shook his head, his gaze downcast, "Not good enough. I tried to run and found I couldn't; she had me. Tried to give her my own blood, thought that would be good enough, thought that might shut her yap – I thought wrong."

"You're not well, Jim. You need to see a doctor," Norgie said, gesticulating with his arms for the man to calm down.

"She's shouting. Still shouting!"

Norgie saw the keen focus return to Jim's narrowing eyes. Noticed the subtle shift in position: shoulders lowering, legs bent at the knee; noticed the dirty shard of glass, clenched so tight in Jim's fist that blood welled around the web of flesh connecting thumb and index finger. Then Jim leapt.

Reflexively, Norgie brought his arm up and felt the shard of glass bite deep into his wrist. His other arm was already in action, connecting the rum bottle with his attacker's head. It made a dull thud to the side of Jim's temple and the old man's body dropped to the ground like a discarded doll.

Norgie stepped back, clutching his injured arm and finding the glass imbedded an inch deep. His thick coat had taken most of the damage but he could feel warm blood running freely through his fingers to drip onto the floor.

"Crap," he muttered as he yanked the shard out, releasing a steadier flow of blood. It must have nicked a vein. He needed to get the cut seen to and fast. There was no telling what he would have picked up from the glass. He guessed it was probably the same thing used to kill and cut open the cat and mice.

Jim's body lay face down in the mouse blood. His arms and legs bent at odd angles.

"Jim?" offered Norgie, nudging the unconscious man in the ribs.

There was no response although he could make out the gentle rise and fall of his chest and a watery rattle from his phlegm-filled lungs.

The steady dripping sound of his blood focused him on the red patch it was creating as it slowly became a puddle. It fell into the centre of an empty circle of chalk scratched runes where it coalesced and spread toward the outer edges. The shape was roughly the size of a saucer and soon filled although his blood didn't run over the lines. Mesmerised, he struggled to look away as the entire circle turned black, reflecting his face back at him from an onyx surface. A layer of frost formed at the edges, the runes glistening white as they grew thicker.

Norgie shivered, a chill shaking through him as he watched vapour leave his mouth. The entire cellar fell icily cold. Steam began to rise from his hot blood as it dripped from the wound. It took all of his effort to squeeze the sleeve of his coat and cut the flow off but by then, the entire circle had filled and it appeared something was moving at its sticky centre.

A large insect struggled out of the blood. It dragged its elongated body from the puddle with long front legs, smearing blood across the white runes. It was spiky and black, like a strange hybrid of praying mantis and beetle. Standing tall on its back four legs, it clicked sharp pincers in the air as it wriggled free of the blood. It had a thick triangular head with red bulbous eyes that sat atop vicious mandibles. It stared at him as it worked its head along bent forelegs, cleaning the blood from sharp claws.

Ugly little thing, he thought, as it made several strange clicking sounds.

Tak … tak … tak …

There must have been a deep hole that he hadn't noticed, a trick of the light giving him the illusion that the creature crawled out of his blood. He bent down to take a closer look at the strange insect that looked like something from the depths of hell, yet Norgie felt as though it was himself that was being inspected.

Suddenly, the insect leapt at him, landing on his injured wrist and sinking its mandibles into the open cut.

Yelping, Norgie flicked the thing from his hand. It flew through the cellar and landed on Jim's back. Thin legs kicked as the insect righted itself before crawling to the unconscious man's neck and biting down.

"No you bloody don't!" Norgie growled.

He landed a kick on the creature which sent it hurtling against the wall where its body made a satisfying crunching sound, before dropping to the floor.

Norgie bent, thinking he'd drag Jim's body out of the blood but just as he slipped his hand beneath an armpit the unconscious man began to convulse. He was shaking like he had been attached to the electrical mains.

Norgie stumbled away, his heels caught on the same brick he had tripped over before and he fell onto his back, knocking his head against the floor and jarring his teeth.

Rising into a sitting position, he shook the fizzing white dots from his vision and saw that Jim had not only stopped shaking but was standing up. The old man flexed his fingers and arms as he rotated his head around, as if stretching after a run. In fact, he was even smiling. No, not smiling, grinning.

Norgie climbed groggily to his feet.

"You're looking brighter, you sick old git," he exclaimed.

Jim's eyes flicked to him. The strange grin widening and seeming not to belong to the Jim he knew but to a malicious being who had taken over the old man's body. He opened his mouth wide as if to reply but only a sharp clicking sound reverberated from him.

Tak … tak … tak …

Norgie backed away, accidently placing his foot on the circle his blood had soaked into. It didn't meet resistance and carried on through. His teeth jarred for the second time that night as he landed hard on his rump.

Using his hands, he scrambled back, dragging his leg clear from the hole which had swallowed it to the knee. God only knew what else might be down there ready to crawl out.

"Calm yourself, Gatekeeper," Jim said, stalking closer with the grace and confidence of a predator. "I'll be as gentle as I can. Unless you struggle."

"Stay away from me. You're sick, Jim. You need help," Norgie blurted, as he backed against the wall, feeling his bowels loosen.

He glanced to the window, seeking a way to escape but no sooner did he avert his attention, than he felt a vice-like grip on his injured wrist.

"What the hell do you want with me?" he screamed at the demented creature, as it dragged him with superhuman strength to the circle of runes, then held his injured arm above it.

Norgie struggled against him, throwing a couple of punches but it was to no avail. Jim, although the smaller between them, appeared to feel nothing.

"I only need you to bleed," Jim answered, calmly. An evil grin spreading across his face as his eyes followed the blood dripping through the inky black hole without making a splash or ripple.

Norgie felt weak. Like his body had burnt up his remaining energy and could do no more than sit there, arm held over the hole and watch his blood drip steadily into the black circle.

A coldness seeped into his body, paralyzing him as another creature crawled out of the hole within the runes. It was another praying mantis-like insect, dragging itself free and leaving a trail of sticky blood.

It preened itself before the wicked smile of Jim, making those awful clicking sounds that echoed through the dark cellar. Jim replied in kind.

"Tak … tak … tak … Welcome brother," he said. Then his attention returned to Norgie, an evil grin splitting his cruel face.

"More blood, Gatekeeper. My brethren have been patient for far too long."

Norgie sat in silence, any fight in him had disappeared. Any thoughts of escape gone with it as he watched almost dreamily as his blood began to run in a steady flow. His vision blurred, the images in the cellar becoming dark and unfocused, yet he felt more than saw the presence of another person shuffle into the room.

Struggling to remain conscious he let his head fall to the side, resting his jaw on his shoulder as he peered up. He could make out the silhouette of a hooded creature, its face hidden beneath the dark peak of a cloak.

"This one's blood will do nicely," said the newcomer. Its voice sounding dry and gravelly as if the words passed through a parched throat, yet the speaker was female. It brought to Norgie's mind an image of the old witch in a 'Hansel and Gretel' book that he had read as a child and which had given him nightmares.

"Let him bleed out. There's work to be done," she croaked.

"Tak … tak … tak …"

Norgie then gave in to unconsciousness, not wanting to remain in the present and longing for blissful sleep to steal him away.

1

The Song

The sky above Gloucester was dull and grey, much like the city itself and much like Elora's mood as she sat with her backside growing numb on a cold stone bench in the city centre. She fussed with the frayed hem of her denim jacket, working the thread loose.

The grating sounds of the tone-deaf busker nearby played on her nerves. Even the people passing by gave him a wide berth, as if he exuded a harmful disease instead of music. But in truth, he gave neither.

In search of distraction, Elora's violet eyes picked out a pale maple leaf as it tumbled across the busy street. At the mercy of the wind, it danced over the shoppers and tourists before catching in the frame of a coffee shop window, where it flapped about as if struggling to free itself. She could free it, she mused, concentrating on the leaf to take her mind away from the painful noise.

Air was the easiest of the elements to manipulate – that's what her uncle Nat had told her when she was a child.

Closing her senses to the city life, she focused on the leaf. Taking in its sharp edges, its brown stem, brittle skin and veins. Pursing her lips, she gently hummed the rhythm of the wind. She felt it on her bare arms, a light breeze playing in short waves and swirling randomly about the cobbled street. As she hummed, she matched the wind's rhythm, altering it imperceptibly and raising it ever so slightly in pitch. Never taking her eyes from her target, she enticed a thin tendril of air towards the leaf, picturing in her mind the leaf coming free, released from the window frame and dancing once more upon the breeze.

It took a moment for the leaf to react, and when it did the movement was subtle, a gentle tug in the opposite direction that may have been her doing or it could have been a natural eddy where the wind reflected off the glass. She was about to apply more pressure when a hand suddenly fell on her shoulder, snapping her out of her reverie.

"What's got your attention so hooked?" came a gravelly voice. Elora was so wrapped up with her attempt at freeing the leaf she hadn't realised that the singer had ceased his wailing and had come over to join her. A glance back at the window showed that the leaf had gone. Whether it was her doing or not she couldn't say.

"Nothing," she replied, irritated.

"So what do you think, am I improving or what? It can't be long before I'm spotted for the talent that I am." He slouched beside her, laying a battered guitar across his lap.

"It was definitely something," she reassured him – and it was something, just not the something he thought it was.

She had met Ben last summer, when she had first tried her hand at busking. He had stopped her halfway through a song and demanded that she find her own spot to perform. An argument had ensued but Ben had a permit from the council; she didn't. Luckily, she had stayed long enough to hear his dismal attempts at singing which sounded like a cat being strangled. If his aim was to sound that bad, then he had succeeded. She listned until he had finished torturing the song and his audience, then struck a deal with him: she would re-string his guitar and let him strum the chords while she sang and they'd split the takings. Doubtful at first, he had soon acquiesced when he found that they were actually making enough money to buy more than a cup of tea. But, a few months on he was still determined to go solo, refusing to give up his dream – and giving everyone else a headache.

Ben counted the change in his grubby cap, stubby fingers pushing the four copper coins around. "They're a bit on the stingy side today. Don't think we've even made enough for a custard slice." He stuffed the miserly change in his pocket. "Real shame them being so tight. I had plans tonight." He flicked the low E-string on the guitar causing a dull thrumming sound. It was out of tune again.

Elora nodded, waiting for the inevitable question. "Real shame," she agreed.

Ben scratched his unshaven chin. "Course, when we stick to the usual numbers, we never make that much."

It was true. The public could be hard-hearted when it came to buskers. The weather could make a difference. People seemed to be more generous when the sun was touching their faces. But those facts were obvious and she already had an inkling where Ben was going with the conversation.

"Unless … "

"No, Ben. Not happening," she said, before he could even ask.

"But we made a killing last time."

"No."

"We made more from that one song than we made all summer." He strummed the guitar, its sound grating through her and doing nothing to help his argument.

"*No.*"

It wasn't that she didn't want to sing the song: she enjoyed the thrill it gave her. It was the consequences she didn't like. The last time she sang it, Nat, her uncle and sole guardian, had found out and for some reason he had thrown a furious tantrum about it. The song was in a language only he understood and according to him, it had dangerous 'powers'. She couldn't say whether she believed it or not. It certainly had an effect on the people listening. They became silent and more importantly, generous. And, she did feel something odd when she sang it but 'powers'? What on earth did her uncle mean?

She turned back to Ben. "Why so desperate? We've had low takings before."

Ben glanced forward, picking at the guitar's scratchboard. "Gonna be a dad, aren't I? The missus told me last night. Said it was about time I got myself a proper job." He shrugged his shoulders. "Thought if I came home today with a tidy penny and some flowers, she might let me carry on busking."

"That's amazing, Ben. Congratulations. But you know she's right. Maybe it is time to grow up and move on."

"But … "

"Your singing is shocking and not in a good way."

Ben looked hurt and she felt a sudden pang of guilt yet he needed to hear it. He must realise, surely nobody could be that deluded? There was a long silence while he seemed to take in her words. Then he suddenly seemed to brighten. "What's up with you, anyway? You've got a face like a slapped arse."

"Nothing," she answered.

The truth was that Elora had worries of her own. Her uncle Nat was acting strangely – even more strangely than usual and he was an extremely strange person to begin with. However, she wouldn't discuss these things with Ben. She barely knew him and anyway, she wasn't planning on staying in Gloucester for much longer.

After a moment of awkward silence, she gave in. "Fine, I'll sing it but not here. And not to keep you in the job – your missus is right, you really need to get yourself a proper one. But, I do think you should take some flowers home." She smiled at seeing his scruffy face lighten up and felt her mood lift.

Elora's footfalls were light as she led the way from the busy city centre, the tarmac giving way to flagstones then to brick paving and finally to stone cobbles. This was the part of Gloucester she liked, away from the drab modern office blocks and shopping malls, towards the cathedral where the ancient buildings seemed to belong to a different world.

Passing through a narrow cobbled pathway, Elora caught her reflection in one of the quaint shop windows. Her long jet-black hair was tied back in a simple ponytail but the shock of blonde had somehow worked its way loose and hung beside her face in a single unruly lock. It never did as she wanted, always coming loose and falling beside her face as if not wanting to touch the black strands. People thought it was dyed – maybe some kind of Goth thing – but like her deep violet eyes, she was born with it.

The alley gave way to a small car-park and a neatly-tended green with trees and benches. Ahead of them, the cathedral suddenly filled the skyline. It was a beautiful building, although unsightly scaffolding clung to it in places where the stonework was being cleaned. Thankfully, the cathedral close was fairly quiet with only a few men at work on the scaffolding and an elderly couple eating sandwiches on a bench. Normally for busking, she would have chosen the busiest part of town, but for this performance she preferred it quiet.

Standing with her back against a wall facing the cathedral, Elora re-tuned the guitar then began to play a chord, picking gently at each string. The song was one she had learned from her late mother. She had only ever heard it once, years ago now, when she was back in her old village. She could only have been about two or three at the time, barely able to talk but somehow the song had sunk into her, every word, every syllable of it lodging deep within her memories although she had no idea what any of it meant.

When her village had been wiped out in the war, the local language died with it. Only Nat knew how to speak it and he thought it pointless to teach her. Why learn a language if there was nobody to speak it to? He had a point but it didn't stop her asking what the song was about. 'Nothing she need to worry herself about', her uncle had explained. So she never did find out what it meant but she sang it all the same.

The words tumbled from her mouth, matching the pitch of the guitar perfectly. The song had a gentle melody, rising and falling steadily like the rhythmic waves of the sea. The elderly couple sat up, their heads turned towards her, half-eaten sandwiches discarded and smiles forming on their faces. The workmen on the scaffold downed-tools and turned to look down at her. One was about to whistle something but the sound died on his lips as he turned towards her, listening intently.

Elora felt a tingling sensation rising from her stomach and a ripple through her lungs as she sang. It was the same thrill that she felt the last time she sang the song. It felt like static, like magic.

Another couple emerged from the alley beside her. Two women, their chatter silenced abruptly as they halted. They pulled their pushchairs to the side so they could listen, conversation forgotten. Within the short time it took her to reach the second verse, people had emerged from the cathedral: a small group of tourists escorted by a cathedral guide. All of them standing still, listening. From the corner of her eyes, Elora noticed Ben sidle around at the back, cap in hand, seeking offerings from the gathering crowd.

The words continued to spill from her, taking on a momentum of their own as she sang the familiar melody. The song was sweetly melancholy, a moody mix of doleful sounds that played on the emotions and danced upon the heart. She would give anything to know what it was about. Probably some sorrowful love song but you didn't need to understand the words to get the feel of it. Amongst the crowd, several people were dabbing at their eyes, even one of the workmen seemed to be affected. Elora held her audience captivated. Nobody spoke or moved. They were transfixed to the spot as if she had somehow hypnotised them. Even the seagulls that were a perpetual nuisance in the city had ceased squawking and remained silent, perched and observant from ledges and rooftops. Maybe there was some truth behind what Nat said about the song. She was glad he couldn't hear her. Luckily he would be on the *Molly* now, a Dutch barge moored up on the canal some five miles away.

Finally, the song came to an end and the last notes on the guitar gently faded away to nothing. A deep silence filled the air for several heartbeats before the sounds of the city returned and the small audience seemed to wake from their trance. People broke from their stares and seemed shocked to find themselves standing where they were, puzzled looks on their faces before they gradually drifted away. On the scaffolding work resumed, albeit in a more subdued manner. The tourists and guide went back inside the cathedral and the elderly couple began to chat once again, their sandwiches abandoned on the grass where they were soon spotted and pounced on by the seagulls.

Ben approached, jingling his cap in his hand. He was beaming now.

"That was brilliant! Thought it was good the last time I heard it, but that … that was something else. Made a tidy little sum too. Here," he said, offering her the cap. He always gave it to her to count out and share the money.

Elora shook her head. "Keep it, Ben," she smiled as his eyebrows furrowed. "With a baby on the way, you're going to need more than flowers."

"You sure? There's got to be more than a hundred quid here." He emptied the contents into his hand and stuffed the coins and notes into his pocket.

Elora nodded and handed him the guitar.

"So what now?" he asked, slinging the guitar over his shoulder.

"You get a job, become a dad and settle down."

"No, I mean with you. School's finished, so you got any plans?"

"Got a trip planned. Me and Nat are taking the barge over to France and across Europe. We're heading back to Croatia. The trip will probably take the best part of a year. The *Molly* plods along at a snail's pace."

"You sure she can take it?" he asked, scratching at his beard.

"She's a tough old skiff. Nat had the engine serviced in the summer so she's man enough for the job."

"Well, good luck with that. Gonna be a bit of an adventure for you."

"Good luck yourself. Having a baby, eh? Now that really is an adventure."

Ben leaned forward and surprised her by giving her a rib-crushing hug. "Gonna miss you," he said when he finally let her go.

"Same," she replied and realised that she meant it. Although she wouldn't miss his singing.

They said goodbye and she watched him disappear down the alley, giving her a mischievous wink as he slipped from view. She headed in the other direction, towards the docks that led to the canal.

The grey clouds had thinned, allowing the afternoon sun to spill through in patches, casting fractured patterns on the canal. Two swans glided gracefully on the dark water, keeping pace with her as she sauntered along the grassy bank, leaving the city for the quiet meadows and barley fields that surrounded Gloucester, thoughts of the trip at the forefront of her mind.

Elora had been pestering Nat for years about taking her to visit their homeland, even though her village in the foothills of Croatia no longer existed.

She and Nat had arrived in Britain as refugees from the troubles in Bosnia when she was five. Nat, her mother's brother, had smuggled them across the border on a cargo ship, hidden in a steel container. From Bristol docks they'd headed west for London. They got as far as a service station on the motorway, some thirty miles from Bristol before the authorities picked them up. After three months in a detention centre they were released with legal immigration status. Within a year, she had started school and Nat had found a steady job. A fresh new start, a new life free from the shadow of war. She even had a new name. After a mix-up filling in the papers, her second name had been replaced with the name of the service station. So she was now known as Elora Delamere. It was easier keeping the name than going through the trouble of changing it. Besides, Nat had never told her what her real second name was.

Her mind elsewhere and enjoying the sun on her face, she was startled as she suddenly felt a hand on her shoulder. Reflexively her hand clenched into a fist and she spun, pivoting on her heel.

A tall man staggered back, arms raised in defence and looking shocked.

"Sorry, didn't mean to startle you," he said, keeping his arms raised in surrender. Dressed in a dark suit and shiny shoes he looked out of place on the riverbank. Elora guessed him to be in his late twenties, maybe thirty.

"Can I help you?" she replied, still clenching her fist yet letting it drop to her side. She wasn't really a fighter and had never attended martial arts classes but she had a fiery temper and once released, somebody was going to get hurt.

"I heard you sing just now. At the cathedral."

Elora watched as he reached a hand into a pocket and retrieved a business card and handed it to her. She didn't recall seeing him amongst the crowd, but then again it was quite busy.

"Nice eyes, by the way," the man remarked.

"Contact lenses," she replied instantly. It was her standard reply. She got comments about her eyes so often that the lie came instinctively.

"The name's Reuben. I work for a man who would be extremely interested in hearing you sing. He's got good contacts in the music world."

Elora eyed the smartly dressed man suspiciously.

"Sorry to disappoint you, Reuben, but I won't be around for a while." She glanced at the card. On it was an image of the Earth embossed on a white background with a dark shadow overlapping one half. Underneath was a phone number printed in black alongside the name 'Silk'.

"That is a real shame. Mr Silk would have been smitten. Are you sure I can't persuade you … er … ?" There was an awkward pause while he waited for her to volunteer her name.

"Elora."

He flicked a silver coin with his thumb as he talked, catching it in his palm, then flicking it again. "Why not come along for an interview? You're exactly the kind of girl he's after."

"And what kind of girl is that?" she asked, watching the coin as it spun in the air.

Reuben smiled, but Elora noticed that his eyes were calculating, shining with an untrustworthy cunning that put her on edge. She was a good judge of character and her impression of him wasn't good.

"A voice like an angel. And the looks to go with it," he replied, slowly eyeing her over.

Elora laughed. "How many angels have you seen with black hair and violet eyes?"

"Maybe a dark Goth-angel then, I don't know. But I'm sure he's gonna love you."

She shook her head. "No, thanks. But if I come back I'll be glad to give you a call." She watched the silver coin flick end-over-end before landing in his palm.

"Tails," he chuckled. "Looks like it's your lucky day. If it had been heads, I wouldn't have taken no for an answer."

Elora raised an eyebrow. He would have been swimming in the canal if he hadn't taken no for an answer. "Really? What kind of businessman makes a decision on the toss of a coin?" she asked, slipping the card into her pocket.

"Always leave chance with a small hand in any deal." He gave her a wink. "I'll see you later then."

Elora watched him leave. There was a small shadow of doubt at the back of her mind. Had she been too hasty? By the time she had turned and continued on her way home, she had decided that she would prefer the trip over anything. Besides, if things didn't work out she had his business card.

As she neared the *Molly* she spotted her uncle out on deck, leaning against the cabin, hand resting on the tiller, waiting for her. A deep frown was drawing his wiry eyebrows together. She shoved her hands into her pockets, fighting to hide the guilt that rose from the pit of her stomach. Surely he couldn't have heard her sing? Gloucester Cathedral was more than five miles away.

He had gone ballistic when he heard her sing that song before, pleading with her never to sing it again. She couldn't understand why; it was only a song after all, and she'd sung it with good intentions. But, just by looking at the way he stood, frowning down, told her that he somehow knew.

"You heard me, right?" she asked, already knowing the answer.

Nat's solemn face turned to her, blue eyes alive with hurt and anger, yet he kept silent.

"I'm sorry, Nat. I know you asked me not to sing that song, but what harm can it do? It's only a song." She readied herself for the rebuke, waiting for the scorching words that when they came would pierce her ears, like the last time. Maybe if she kept quiet and didn't argue back it would be over in a few minutes. Let him have his say, show how sorry she was and then move on, job done.

After another minute had passed, Nat was still frowning down from the barge and she was still standing on the bank, waiting. Maybe he wasn't going to shout at her after all.

She folded her arms, the silence growing more uncomfortable by the moment. This was worse than him ranting and raving and she hated it.

"Say something then," she said finally. Breaking eye-contact but with a frown of her own, she stepped aboard the *Molly* and slipped past him to the cabin door. As she was about to disappear below, Nat grasped her firmly by the wrist.

"That song is dangerous, Elora. You shouldn't go meddling with it."

Nat's voice was firm but it wasn't the venomous outburst she was expecting. Elora turned to face her elderly uncle. He suddenly seemed frail in a way she hadn't noticed before. He was old, she knew that. He must be well past sixty, probably close on seventy. She wasn't sure exactly. They didn't celebrate birthdays and she wasn't even sure when her own was. Sometime in the spring was all Nat had told her.

"It's just a bloody song," she tried to pull her wrist free but Nat held it firm.

"You don't understand."

"I don't understand because you refuse to tell me anything. You don't explain why it's dangerous. You won't tell me why we live on this stupid boat. You won't even tell me about my mother or my life before we came here." She could feel her temper rising, her blood getting hot. She tried to calm herself. It would only make things worse if she lost control but there was so much she needed to say, years of putting up with her uncle's odd ways. He wouldn't even explain why she had violet eyes.

"Enough!" he growled, anger finally getting the better of him. He held her arm for a moment more before letting her go. Old fingers brushed through his grey hair as he took a deep breath and sat down on the cabin step. Once he had regained his composure he continued with a more soothing tone.

"Maybe you're right, Elora. I've gotten so used to you being my little Minu that I hadn't realised how much you've grown. I suppose I'm getting to that age where memories become a little harder to find. Harder to explain straight. Could be you're as ready as you'll ever be."

Elora struggled to believe what she was hearing. She kept quiet, anxious not to say the wrong thing and dissuade Nat from his apparent change of heart. She gave a weak nod, encouraging him to go on.

He remained quiet for a moment, the silence dragging out as it had before but with less of a charge in the atmosphere.

"But not now, not this minute. Let's enjoy the rest of this afternoon. Tomorrow will be the day of explaining. We can talk then but you might not like what you're going to hear. 'Ignorance is bliss', after all."

Elora opened her mouth, her words escaping before she had a chance to reel them in.

"Ignorance is for people who are too stupid or too cowardly to face the truth." She inwardly cursed herself. Crap, he would change his mind for sure.

"And the truth could ruin your life," Nat said. "Knowledge can't be undone, can't be forgotten. But you know your own mind Elora. The decision's yours."

Without missing a beat Elora replied.

"I want to know."

Nat rose back to his feet and put his arms out to her. She went to him and let him hug her. She hugged him back and rested her head against his chest, feeling his heart beating beneath his plain khaki shirt.

"Sorry I called your boat stupid."

He kissed the top of her head.

"I know you didn't mean it. Besides, she's as much yours as mine. Now go get some rest. We're leaving early."

2

Lies and Half-truths

It was early and the sun had yet to make an appearance above the mist that hovered over the canal. The *Molly* cut through the vapour as she meandered along at a leisurely speed, Nat's steady hand on the tiller and his gaze fixed directly ahead. Elora stood beside him, leaning against the bow, taking in the scenery and finding it hard not to smile. She had been waiting for this journey to start for a long time and now that it had finally begun she felt a thrill of exhilaration pulse through her. Nat however, obviously didn't share her excitement. When she looked to her uncle, his face was sorrowful. She didn't understand. He had wanted this journey as much as she had. It must be another of his odd moods. They seemed to be getting more frequent the older he got.

By mid-morning Nat was positively doleful, barely uttering more than a grunt when asked a question and avoiding eye-contact altogether. Elora had had enough. He was going to ruin the trip on the first day if she couldn't pull him out of it.

"What's up?" she asked.

Nat was silent. Thinking he might not have heard her, Elora was about to repeat the question when he cleared his throat.

"I've got things that I need to tell you but I don't know how to go about it," he muttered, his voice barely audible above the barge's diesel engine.

"If you've got to tell me, then it's probably best that you just say what you've got to say. No point sinking any further into your mood. It can't be that bad."

But secretly Elora couldn't help but feel a bit anxious. He had never held back from telling her anything before. Then a horrible thought struck her.

"It's not ... cancer?"

"No, I wish it were that simple." He gazed at her with his watery blue eyes.

"Then what?" she asked, feeling relief and dread at the same time.

"I need you to be patient, Elora. I've got so much to tell you. So much that needs to be said. So much for you to understand."

"You can tell me anything. Nothing that you say will ever change how I feel about you," she said, and felt his hand grasp hers tenderly.

"You've a good heart, Elora. A kind, sweet heart. And it took me a long while to realise it. You weren't the easiest child."

"I was a total bitch. It's OK, you can say it. I was."

She'd had a hard time fitting in at school. She found it hard making friends and too easy making enemies. With her freaky eyes and hair, she was an obvious target for bullies but the trouble was, she never backed down from a fight: her temper always got the better of her. Most weeks she was in detention and she was sent home regularly for fighting. In the words of her headmaster, she seemed to bring out the worst in people. One day after school she found herself cornered behind the bike shed. It was two girls she had fought with and hurt on a previous occasion but this time they'd brought their elder sisters along as reinforcement. It was four against one and they should have been able to give her a good hiding, but as always, her temper rose to the occasion. She put three of the girls in hospital, one of them in intensive care. The fourth girl ran off and came back with the school caretaker. He tried to restrain her until help arrived but by then he was on the floor, unconscious and with a broken nose. Elora felt tremendous guilt afterwards and vowed to control her anger. She managed to scrape though sixth-form without further trouble, largely due to people, including the teachers, either giving her a wide berth or avoiding her altogether.

Nat chuckled.

"Yeah, right. A total bitch." Then his face stiffened again. "And for a time I tolerated it. Told myself it was simply the tearaway actions of a girl who'd lost her mother. Who needed bringing up properly but at the back of my mind I had a choice to make. What if there really weren't no good in you? What if you grew to be an evil teen? Or into an evil adult? Thankfully, you grew out of it and you became the daughter I'd always longed for."

"And if I hadn't?" she asked, raising a mocking eyebrow.

"I'd have killed you," he said, deadpan. "To protect the worlds from you. Because of who you are. Because of what you are."

Elora let her hand drop. She was struggling to understand what her uncle was saying. For a moment she searched for the slow smile that would show her he was joking but Nat wasn't good at jokes. His face didn't crack.

"And what am I?"

Nat pushed his aged fingers through his hair and let out a heavy sigh. "You're powerful. More powerful than you have any right to be."

"I'm just a girl. How can I be powerful?"

"Because of who your father is."

The words hit her like an electric shock. She had never known her father and her uncle had always told her that he didn't know who he was either – that her mother had kept the secret with her to the day she died.

"So you do know. You lied to me. You told me you didn't, nobody knew." She felt an ache in her heart from the betrayal.

"I'm sorry, Elora. I never meant to hurt you but you needed to be protected from knowing who he was. What he was."

"And who the hell was he?" she demanded, hearing the anger in her voice and not caring.

"Later. I'll tell you later. The trouble is, there's so much I need to explain. So many lies and half-truths that need unpicking, I don't know where to begin." He stared ahead again, his lips forming a tight line.

"Damn it, Nat!" she said, slamming her fist against the cabin roof. "Tell me who he is. You've no right to keep it from me." She always wore her anger on her sleeve. It was always there, like a tight spring waiting to be released. Well, it had just sprung.

Nat put a hand softly on her shoulder but she pulled away, slapping it from her.

"How could you keep this from me?" she growled, the noise scaring a pair of wood pigeons that were nestling in a tree above the barge. "How many other lies have you told me?"

She read pain across his face as he answered.

"Too many to ever put right. But you have to believe me Elora, the lies were told to keep you safe."

"Safe from who? I don't know anybody."

"No, you don't. But that doesn't stop them from knowing who you are. There's a group of people who have been searching you out since you were born. Wanting to use you and bend you to their evil will. And the others who aren't evil, well, they want you dead so you can't be used. Either way, you can never be found. That's why I get so annoyed when you sing in public. It's like a homing-beacon to those that search for you."

"And that's why you chose to leave this morning? Because I sang in Gloucester yesterday? Ridiculous. It's all in your head Nat. You're going senile." She made to go below to her bedroom but Nat grasped her arm as she pushed by him.

"I told you I had some hard things to tell you and things that you must understand. It was never going to be easy, but please, Elora, hear me out." She pulled her arm free but stayed where she was, with her back to him so she didn't have to look him in the face.

"Your mother loved you very much. She was the one who asked me to bring you here. To leave Aslania and hide you away and to never go back."

"Aslania?"

"Where we lived. Where you were born. High up in the God's Peak Mountains.

"But we lived in Croatia."

"Another lie. We passed through Croatia when we fled Aslania. We used the war in the Balkans as a cover, so we could pretend we were refugees."

"And my mother? You told me she died when the village was shelled." She turned back to face him.

"She's still alive."

Meeting his eyes, Elora could see he was telling the truth – or at least what he believed was the truth. Whether it actually was true or just a fantasy, who could say? She felt a tear running down the side of her face and brushed it away with the back of her hand.

"She's alive," he repeated. "But you can never see her. She loves you with all her heart but if she saw you again, she would kill you."

"Nat, you're not making any sense. Why would she kill me?"

"I can't explain it now. Not yet. But I will, I promise. Just know that she loves you very much and she never regretted having you and still doesn't, even though she knows who your father was."

Elora was about to ask again who her father was but Nat held up a hand to stop her.

"These secrets I've been telling you – they were hard enough for me to keep and hard to tell, but there's something else I need you to know before we go on. Something more incredible and harder for you to learn, but something you need to understand before I can explain anything more."

"And what's harder to learn than the fact that my dead mother isn't really dead and I will never see her? Or that there's people out to kill me? You've lost the plot, Nat, you really have. Well, come on then, what's the next bombshell you're going to drop on me?" She sat on the ledge and folded her arms as she waited for Nat's reply.

"You were not born on Earth."

"What?" Now she knew he had lost his mind. "I'm an alien?"

"Not exactly. You were born on Thea, which is a twin of Earth. Taking up the exact same place and time but on different plains. That's where Aslania is, and where we escaped from."

Elora laughed. "And how did we do that? Catch a unicorn and ride it over a magic rainbow with the help of fairy dust?"

"No. We used the power from a charged star that had passed through both worlds and … "

"Enough, Nat. Cut the crap, I mean it. I can't take any more. I'm going to lie down."

She left him on deck and stepped below, slamming the door behind her before throwing herself on the narrow sofa in the cabin.

It took her a while to calm down. Suddenly she felt guilty for worrying that Nat was going to ruin the trip, when plainly she should have been worrying about his mental state. She needed to get him to a hospital. Taking a deep breath to calm her temper, she went to the tiny galley kitchen to make a cup of tea for them both. No doubt, Nat was feeling flustered by the argument they'd had; he never reacted well to her anger. But maybe she was the one who was driving him to this madness. She knew she wasn't the easiest. He had even admitted it himself. "Showing signs of evil … " It wasn't the first time he had mentioned Aslania. And hadn't he always told her that there was more to the world than she thought?

Faded memories tumbled through her mind. The two of them on a cart bumping down a dusty mountain trail feeling cold and afraid and crying for her mother. Her uncle's tender arm holding her close to him. She remembered nights cuddled up, sheltering under a heavy cloak from the rain, hands held out to an open fire and eating dry bread and cured meats. Another memory came back to her – of a boat trip on a lake, surrounded by hills and cliffs, but she couldn't remember any details, the flashback was too hazy. Her uncle pushing her into the icy water. Screaming as she tried to swim but her clothes dragged her down. Then Nat jumping in after her, holding her for a moment, telling her to hold her breath, to be brave; then ducking beneath the water and pulling her down with him into the deep where her screams allowed the water to fill her lungs. Next, she was coughing up water and sobbing into Nat's shoulder as he held her to him, singing softly to calm her, as tears ran down his worried face.

Why did all this come back to her now? Was it sparked by the conversation she had just had with Nat? Was she going crazy too? No, the memories were definitely real.

She finished making the tea and waited for a moment until she felt calm enough to go back on deck. Perhaps it was best to stay silent and let Nat ramble on about his falling stars and other worlds. It might sound mad to her, but it was obviously real enough for him. As long as she stayed calm, she could wait a few days to see if things improved. If they didn't, she would have to think again.

Nat remained silent for the rest of the day, keeping his eyes fixed on the waterway ahead and his thoughts to himself. Elora hoped their argument that morning was an isolated incident. She decided not to mention it for now but her uncle had other plans.

As the evening came on, they reached a quiet stretch of canal. Nat slowed the barge to a stop and killed the engine, letting the *Molly* drift slowly in the middle of the dark water, something he had never done before.

"What are you doing?" she asked, scanning the canal ahead for any oncoming vessels. The *Molly* would be an awkward obstacle to negotiate, especially since the engine wasn't running. They could drift into the path of another boat and collide.

Her uncle smiled as he leaned back against the railing, folding his arms.

"You're just like your mother when she was a girl. Stubborn as a mule. I've been searching my brains for a way to say to you what needs saying. For a way to make you believe. I can't explain in words, so I'm going to show you."

Elora's heart felt heavy. Was this going to be another of his crazy episodes?

"Don't be an idiot Nat. You're going to crash into something." She shook her head and made to turn the ignition back on but at that moment her uncle suddenly began to sing, causing her to pause, her hand hovering above the keys. His voice was beautiful. Deep rich tones reverberating on the water and echoing back against the boat. Elora wanted to join in, to harmonise with the rich melody but she couldn't. The words were sung in the same foreign language that Nat refused to teach her. She closed her eyes instead, letting the words and tones wash over her, gently stroking her nerves like a warm breeze.

Memories came to her again. Flashbacks to when she was a girl, when Nat had last sung this particular song. They had just bought the *Molly* and were taking her for their first trip. She smiled, remembering how excited she had been, pestering her uncle to steer the big barge and him finally relenting. How she'd found herself heading straight towards an expensive-looking yacht and panicking when she realised it was too late to alter course. It was then that her uncle had sung this song and somehow the *Molly* had banked on its side, drifting passed at a strange angle, a manoeuvre that even as a small girl she found impossible. As did the yacht's owners, whose horror-stricken faces froze as they watched them glide by, inches from their luxurious boat.

At that innocent age she guessed that somehow her uncle had used his singing voice to force the water to push them out of harm's way. She smiled. It was a memory she had long ago forgotten.

The barge suddenly jolted, knocking Elora off balance, she grabbed the handrail. Something had hit the *Molly* with enough force to propel them forwards. Gazing behind them, she expected to see a large boat but saw nothing which could have caused the impact. She checked ahead but the canal was empty. Confused, she turned to her uncle and realised that he was still singing and that they were moving through the water as if the engine was powering them along. But the engine wasn't running. Apart from the slapping noise as the hull cut through the water, the boat was silent. She leaned over the side-rail, feeling the wind in her face as she strained to see if there was anything hooked underneath, perhaps an unseen tow rope of some kind. There was nothing. Turning once more to look behind them, she saw that a huge wave was pushing them on and the *Molly* was riding on its crest like a huge surfboard.

"What the —" she exclaimed, unable to take her eyes off the huge wave. Her first thought was that it was the Severn Bore, the huge tidal surge of water that raced down the River Severn from the Bristol Channel. But that only happened in the spring and end of autumn, and only on the river. They were on the canal where there was no tide or current, yet a huge wave was propelling them and seemed to be gaining speed.

Elora stared at her uncle. "What's happening? How's this even possible?" She gripped tighter to the rail as the back of the barge lifted and they tilted forwards on a great wall of water. As their speed increased, Elora's black hair fell loose and floated free in the breeze. Impossibly the freak wave grew so immense its outer edges spread from bank to bank, spilling water onto the grass verges. Her grip on the handrail tightened as she fought to stay on her feet. The *Molly* was going so fast she was afraid the ancient vessel might begin to fall apart. She turned to Nat for answers but the old man seemed oblivious – standing there, relaxed and singing. Could he really be doing this? As she struggled to think of a rational explanation Nat's voice sank to a whisper, then stopped altogether.

As the song faded, the surging wave fell away, leaving the *Molly* to be carried along by the weight of her own momentum. The barge gradually slowed and her uncle broke the silence.

"Water is the second easiest of the elements to manipulate after air. I told you the order when you were small. It seems you have forgotten," he said, a playful smile curling the corners of his lips.

"But those were merely magic tricks you did. They were never real," she replied, gathering her wild hair together in her hands and tying it back in a ponytail.

She wanted to say more but her mind was still running over the extraordinary event that she had just witnessed. And hadn't she only the day before tried to manipulate the wind to set free the maple leaf in Gloucester? She had, yet it was nothing more than fantasy. A small daydream to distract herself while Ben was busking. She knew the order of the elements and the easier rhythms to touch them but never believed it to be real. Only tales an uncle told to amuse a child.

"Not tricks Elora. A gift," explained Nat, as he turned the ignition on and restarted the big diesel engine. "The same gift that you possess."

Elora sat back against the rail. "So all those things you said earlier were true?"

Nat nodded. "We'll moor up here for the night."

Elora folded her arms and opened her mouth to protest, to demand that he explain himself right away but she knew that he would only speak when he was ready and wouldn't be moved on the subject. She shut her mouth and stared into the water, her mind mulling over what had just happened and what Nat had told her.

The first stars began to appear in the night sky and she watched their reflection on the water, wondering if there were indeed worlds beyond the world she could see and touch and which she thought she knew.

It was a peaceful night. The secluded stretch of canal was far from any roads and only an unused pathway ran along the bank which was overgrown with grass and reeds. Elora brought her uncle a cup of tea as he sat on his favourite sofa, reading his old diary by the amber glow of an antique oil lamp. The book was one Elora was forbidden to read, even though it was written in the old language she didn't understand.

Noticing her, he put the book aside and took the tea gratefully, then patted the sofa beside him. Elora sat down, drawing her legs underneath her as she wrapped cold fingers around her own mug of tea.

As she gazed at the burning embers in the small wood burner, Elora wondered if Nat was going to tell her more. Questions had been plaguing her since the freak wave earlier. The revelation that she was being hunted by people who wanted to use her for evil ends, or by others who simply wanted her dead, was hard enough to believe. But even harder to accept was that her mother was still alive and that she would never get to see her. She couldn't get her head around it. What kind of mother would abandon her own daughter and promise to kill her if she ever returned? And her father – what kind of man was he, that people even feared his daughter, people who'd never even met him?

She couldn't wait any longer. She wanted to know. Needed to know. Somehow Nat must have sensed her unease and chose that moment to speak.

"I've been writing this," he said, tapping his diary. "Ever since we left Aslania. It covers everything from the trek through the mountain-pass to the lake. From the crossing between the worlds to the journey through Europe, right up until this evening. Not every day, but every important event. I thought it would help me to explain things to you when the time came. I was going to read you a page each day, let it sink in slowly. Make it less of a shock than hearing it all in one go. But … "

"I mucked things up by singing yesterday," Elora finished the sentence for him.

Nat nodded. "It's not your fault. I should have told you when you were younger. Explained things so you could understand. But I didn't. You're not to blame."

"You can explain things now."

Nat nodded and placed his journal on her lap. She put her mug down and opened the old book. She smiled as she flicked through the old pages and marvelled at her uncle's beautiful handwriting.

"I can't read it, remember?" she said.

"You can now. I'm giving it to you," he said with a loving smile.

"No, I can't. I don't understand it," she said, tracing with her index finger the flowing swirls and symbols that were like no language she had ever seen.

34

Nat chuckled and leaned closer, shifting so he could point down to the book. "I'll teach you. It's not that hard to understand."

"Oh really? Looks plenty hard to me." She flicked through the pages until she came to the back where she saw a small 'S'-like symbol within a circle. A phone number was beneath it. "What's this?" she asked, seeing Nat frown.

"The Shadojak. He's the person who helped us find refuge here."

"A friend, then?" She was puzzled. Nat had few acquaintances and no close friends that he had ever mentioned.

Nat's frown deepened. "No. Not a friend. Not somebody you'd ever want to meet, either."

Elora was intrigued. "Why not? If he helped us, then surely he's somebody we can trust?"

"You were only a small child then. He didn't know who you were. If he had … " Nat slowly shook his head.

"He would have killed me?"

Nat nodded.

"So why keep his phone number?" she asked, tapping the book.

Nat took a sip of tea before answering. "In case you turned out to be … different than you did."

It was clear to Elora that he didn't want to talk any more about this mysterious Shadojak character, yet her curiosity was stronger than ever. Maybe later.

"So are you some kind of wizard or something?" she asked lightheartedly, changing the subject in case he stopped talking again.

"No, not a wizard!" he snorted. "I'm just a good elemental manipulator. All Minuans can do it on some kind of level."

"Minuans?" Elora raised a questioning eyebrow. Nat had always called her his 'little Minu'; it was a special pet name for her. She had never thought about what it actually meant.

"You're a Minuan, as am I, and your mother, and our people of Aslania. We're descendants of the Goddess Minu who lived on Thea some few thousand years ago."

"Can they all do that thing you did with the water?"

"Probably not. It's rare to be able to work the elements to that level. Most go through life without even trying to do it. Those that want to must be trained properly and it takes a lifetime of study to master."

"Why wouldn't they want to? I mean, it's amazing. It's … magic."

"Not magic. Only a greater understanding of the elements yet most people choose to follow the path of the Eversong."

"Eversong?"

"What you were singing yesterday was a small part that makes up the Eversong. Now that is what you might call magic. It has great powers and Minuans are drawn towards that calling. It's more of a religion going back to the time of the small gods." Nat blinked and smiled. "But I'm racing ahead. We need to take this one step at a time."

"But if you didn't want me singing this Eversong, then why teach it to me in the first place?"

"I didn't. The song is in your blood. And when it's sung by a Minuan, it releases a power that can be felt by those sensitive to its tones and words. That's why I got so angry with you when you sang it. It alerted people that there was a Minuan. Singing it twice would bring them closer, like a homing beacon."

"And these people want me dead?"

Nat nodded. "Or worse."

"What could be worse than death?"

Nat tightened his lips, something he did when he was debating what to say without upsetting her.

"We'll talk more in the morning. I'll teach you how to read this." He tapped the diary, changing the subject. "Then you can read and understand it in your own time.

Elora was about to protest. She wanted answers now and couldn't see why he didn't translate directly from the book. But he held a hand up as if he expected what she was about to ask.

"There's no rush, Elora. We've got plenty of time. It's going to take us a couple of days to even reach Bath."

She realised he was right yet it didn't stop her wanting to know everything now. Frustration welled up inside her but there was no point arguing with him. If his mind was made up, it was made up.

Lifting herself from the sofa, she took her uncle's empty cup and her own and gave him a kiss on the cheek. "Night, then."

Elora went through to the galley, leaving the cups in the sink before heading for her bedroom. She was tired but sleep would be difficult with so much going on in her mind.

∞∞∞∞∞∞∞∞∞∞∞∞∞∞∞

The *Molly* dipped. Then dipped again. Somebody had stepped aboard the barge.

Elora raised herself onto her elbows, blinking the sleep from her eyes. Her room was in darkness, no morning light spilled through her curtains. Sleep must have found her at some point but she couldn't tell what time it was. Who the hell would be coming onto the *Molly* in the middle of the night?

The barge was still rocking as she got to her feet and paced out of her room, glad that she hadn't bothered to get undressed. Nat was asleep on the sofa, a blanket pulled up to his neck; when he was asleep, he went deep. The room was dark and in shadow, her uncle having blown the lamp out before turning in but she could still make out the silhouette of a figure through the frosted glass of the outer door.

She cleared the space to the door in three strides and unbolted it before wrenching it open, ready to give the intruder the benefit of her sharp tongue. She stopped when she recognised the figure.

"Reuben. What the hell are you doing here?" she barked, agitated. How had he known where to find her?

He grinned, dark eyes twinkling.

"Sorry, sweetheart. Afraid Mr Silk didn't take too kindly to your rejection. He insists on meeting you."

"Get stuffed!" she yelled, slamming the door in his face but he caught it in his hand and pushed through, forcing her to stumble down the steps. He followed her falling body and flicked on the light switch.

Her uncle sat up, flinging the blanket aside as he took in the man entering the *Molly* and the shape of Elora sprawled on the floor.

"What the hell — " He made to rise but was forced back down by another man who had squeezed through the doorway from the kitchen. That's right, remembered Elora, the barge dipped twice. He must have entered through the bow door.

The hulking mass who pushed her uncle down looked almost cartoon-comical, his size forcing him to duck his head within the narrow confines of the barge. Square and brutal with a fat nose, squashed tight to his face as if made from putty, he wore an expression as grim as an undertaker. Covering his thick forehead was a dark green tattoo of a fist, clenched as if about to strike.

"The boat secure?" asked Reuben, directing the question at the giant thug, who simply nodded, his face expressionless as if carved from granite. Elora noticed the small pig-like eyes light up, the hint of violence sparkling behind them.

Nat began to rise once again but the brute forced him back down, his thick hand closing on Nat's shoulder to keep him in place.

"Get off him, you ugly git!" Elora screamed, launching herself furiously at the thug. When her anger was up her body reacted before her brain and usually she ended up regretting her actions. But she was in motion now. Committed.

Grabbing around his neck with one hand whilst punching him with the other, she put all her strength into hurting him. It was like wrestling with a solid oak wardrobe. The giant didn't flinch. She changed tactics and raked her fingernails across his face, having to pull herself up to reach.

She was rewarded with a back-handed slap which sent her crashing into the wall and driving the breath from her lungs. Her knees struck the wooden floor and she crumpled into a painful heap.

Shaking the dizziness from her head she glanced up and saw angry red welts gauged across her attacker's face. She might have felt some satisfaction at that but for the cold stare he gave her, full of hatred, warning her that he would repay the pain with interest. She shifted her gaze to Reuben who smiled back, pleasantly amused.

"This here's Pinky. He's a bit messed up in the head but a mite handy with his fists. Now you can either sit down and wait like a good little girl or I'll let Pinky here make you."

Pinky's huge hand wiped delicately at the scratches on his face and Elora saw that he wanted to hurt her. Well, to hell with him. She wasn't scared for herself but Nat was fragile in comparison with the thug.

She got back to her feet.

"Tell your bitch to take his grubby mitts off my uncle," she spat at Reuben.

Reuben nodded towards the bulk who slowly let his hand drop to his side. Then, still smiling as if the whole situation was no more than a gentle amble through a park, he pulled a gun from beneath his suit and pointed it at Nat.

"Now be a good girl and come sit down next to him."

She did as she was told, feeling a stiffness in her neck and soreness in the knees that promised bruises later. She lowered herself down, Pinky backing away and folding his thick arms.

Reuben kept the gun trained on her uncle as he took a mobile phone from his pocket and pressed the speed-dial button. He put it to his ear and waited.

"I've got her … Yes … No … She's not going anywhere … An uncle." His gaze shifted to Nat. "What's your name?"

Elora gritted her teeth. There had to be more to this than just her singing.

"Don't tell him anything," she said, glaring at Reuben.

Reuben grinned, lowered his gun and squeezed the trigger.

The noise was painful, an explosion in her ears. She let out an involuntary high-pitched yelp but her uncle's scream was louder, the bullet having shot into his shin. He bent forwards, hands pressing over the bloody wound, face grimacing with the pain.

"You … " began Elora, as she prepared to hurl herself at Reuben but was pinned down by Pinky's hand at her throat, completely encircling her neck, the finger and thumb touching.

Reuben remained calm, still training his gun on Nat. Elora wanted to rip that infuriating smile off his face.

"Your name?" He turned to Nat, pleasantly.

"Nathaniel Delamere," Nat stammered through gritted teeth.

Reuben relayed the information over the phone and waited for a response.

"OK … No, we won't … You've got the coordinates. There's a big field adjacent to the canal, one of my men will meet you on the bank … OK, see you in forty minutes." Slipping the phone back into his pocket he sat back against the door. He gave Pinky a curt nod and Elora felt his hand release from her neck.

"You didn't need to shoot him, you arsehole," she blurted out as she slipped to the floor to inspect her uncle's leg.

The bullet had entered the outer edge of Nat's left shin, grazing his tibia and ripping a deep gash into his flesh. Mercifully it had missed the main artery. The copper smell of blood blended with the cordite that filled the room. Nat must be in excruciating pain yet didn't make a sound.

Reuben chuckled. "You're right. I didn't need to do it. Same as I don't need him to live. He's of no interest to Silk, so … " He flicked his silver coin into the air. "Heads he lives, tails he dies."

"No!" yelled Elora. For the first time since the thugs came aboard she felt blind panic. Reuben caught the coin and held it palm-out so she could see. It was heads.

"Best of three?" asked Reuben as he tossed the coin again, a smirk forming on his face. He caught the coin but held it in his fist.

"It's not up to fate if you keep flicking your coin until you get the result you want," Elora argued, eyeing his gun hand and wondering if she could reach it before he had time to react. She guessed she wouldn't.

"True. So maybe I'll keep playing until you behave. Now sit down," he demanded, shoving the coin back in his pocket.

Elora thought fast. Reuben was going to kill Nat anyway. So why delay unless he wanted to placate her? She decided to do as he said but would need to come up with a plan in the next forty minutes.

Sitting next to her uncle she leant down and placed a hand over his wound. "This needs a bandage and antiseptic, probably stitches too," she said tersely, searching for the bullet and seeing that it had disappeared into the sofa.

"I need a tall Scotch, ice and a nice Cuban but it just isn't on the cards."

Elora was silent as she sat beside her uncle. He squeezed her leg reassuringly yet she guessed he knew as well as she did that his chances were not good.

"Who's Silk?" asked Nat, frowning towards their captor.

Reuben remained silent as he took the coin from his pocket once again and gave it a flick. He caught it and glanced at the result. "Just a man, a very rich man who wants this little girl." He waved the gun in the direction of Elora. "Don't know why. Don't really care. As long as he's paying, he can have who he wants."

"So, you're mercenaries?" Nat asked.

"I prefer 'contractors'. It sounds more professional."

"But why her? She's done nothing wrong."

"Mine's not to reason why. But it's got something to do with what she was singing. Or how she sung it. I've spent the last six months hanging around this city, waiting and searching for a girl who could sing the way she did. To be honest, I thought I was wasting my time. Silk didn't give me a description, only said to hang about until I heard something special. That I'd know it when I heard it. I thought he was a bit crackers – he's a bit strange anyway – but the money was good and the job was easy. But after hearing her yesterday ... " He gave a satisfied whistle. "Well, that was something special."

Hearing his words, Elora burned with shame. This was her fault. If she hadn't sung that damned song, none of this would be happening. She was about to plead to Reuben to let her uncle go, it wasn't his fault, but Nat spoke before she had the chance.

"Please. You can't let him take her. There's a lot more at stake here than you think."

"I've been doing contracts for quite a while now. Always get my mark, never failed. It wouldn't look good if I didn't deliver the goods now would it?" Then changing the subject, he turned to his over-sized companion.

"Is it me or is it getting darker in here?"

"The lights are powered from the battery," offered Elora. "If the engine's not running, the battery won't charge. There's an oil lamp over there." She nodded towards the bookshelf. An idea was forming in her mind. She just hoped Nat would pick up on it. After all, fire was an element.

Reuben indicated for Pinky to light it and Elora watched his gorilla-like hands fumble with the glass cylinder, making the lamp seem delicate. Twice he came close to dropping it but eventually the room began to fill with a warm glow. Pinky smiled to himself as if he'd achieved some exceptionally hard task. Elora tapped her uncle's knee and subtly inclined her head towards the lamp. Nat's eyes narrowed to slits. He had got the message.

"You gonna rustle me up a cup of tea while we wait?" Reuben asked her, flicking his coin repeatedly. Elora wanted to shove that coin down his throat.

"No, she stays with me," said Nat forcefully, laying a hand on her lap to still her as she began to rise.

She thought she could have been more help from the kitchen, maybe come at them with a frying pan or knife but her uncle had placed his hand on her knee. He wanted her where she was.

"I'll make you a cup of tea, alright. How many spits do you want with that, two?"

Reuben chuckled. "No, it's fine. I can wait until you're gone then make a cup of tea myself before I torch your boat."

Elora wanted to say something clever but couldn't at that moment think of anything, so kept tight-lipped. Next to her, her uncle had already begun to hum a tune under his breath.

"What's he doing?" asked Reuben, amused. Elora didn't reply. She was getting a strange sensation from her leg, beneath where Nat's hand was placed. She turned to him but his eyes were closed tight, his brow creased in concentration. The feeling in her leg was similar to what she felt in her stomach when she sang the song that had got her into this mess in the first place. A crackling sensation, like static that pulsed through her body in time with her heart beat. She realised Nat was drawing energy from her, like a torch pulling volts from a battery. He may have been weakened from his injury and needed her for the magic but as the room suddenly brightened she realised that he had something else planned. She needed to distract Reuben.

"That's an interesting tattoo your bitch has got on his face. A fist? What does it mean, that he's a knucklehead or something?"

Reuben grinned, but it was Pinky who replied.

"Sometimes I can't make up my mind if I want to punch somebody or put the nut on them." His voice was deep and throaty with the hint of a Scottish accent. "But with this ... " He pointed to the tattoo on his forehead, "I get to do both."

Suddenly, a bright flash exploded from the lamp and Pinky fell to his knees, cracking the polished floorboards and sending a jolt through the *Molly* that ran from stem to stern. His big hands were rubbing at flames that suddenly sprouted from his scalp, even though there was nothing for them to burn upon. He screamed as he patted frantically at the top of his head.

"Put it out! Put it out!"

Elora watched as the huge thug stumbled back into the coffee table, catching behind his knees and falling over, kicking his legs in the air as he went down. Reuben's mouth was agape and she couldn't help but notice that the gun was still trained on her uncle, his finger, looking ever twitchier, as it hovered over the trigger.

"Now Elora, run!" Nat shouted as he let go of her leg and fell forward against Reuben. Grasping his gun arm with both of his hands, he pushed it away.

For the length of a heartbeat, Elora remained rooted to the spot, dazed by the connection she had been released from and the thought of leaving her uncle behind.

"Go!" Nat shouted as he struggled with Reuben. Elora scrambled to her feet and with one last glance at her uncle, bolted for the kitchen door and pelted down the narrow corridor to the stern of the *Molly*. If she could just get away, she could get to a phone and ring the police. Behind her, Reuben was screaming at Pinky, so she guessed the flames must have died when Nat lunged at Reuben. But by now she was at the stern door and once she was on the canal bank, there was no way Pinky could catch her.

She flung open the door and ran straight into the arms of a third man who grabbed her about the waist and shoved her back inside the *Molly*.

"Having problems?" he asked, a tone of sarcasm thick in his voice as Pinky gripped her by the shoulder.

"Shove it, Kitch," Pinky replied, fighting for breath. "This little bitch is as vicious as a pit bull."

There was a clatter from the living room. A glass smashing, Reuben cursing and then a gunshot that silenced everything.

"No!" Elora screamed. She thrashed against her captors but couldn't break their hold.

"Guess the old man won't be causing us any more trouble," Pinky chuckled.

With another scream of fury laced with frustration, Elora stomped her heel down hard on top of Pinky's foot. He yelped with pain but held fast, shoving her against the wall with a brute force that jarred every bone in her body.

Reuben appeared, blood trickling from a gash on his forehead. "Lock her in her bedroom. Make sure she can't climb out of the window." He turned to Elora. The amused tone was absent from his voice now, replaced by anger and hatred. "Carry on, you little bitch and you'll get what your uncle got. Silk maybe paying well but I may not be able to help myself."

Elora met his eyes and spat in his face. "I'm going to kill you," she said. And meant it.

3

All Teeth and Claws

Bray was being followed. He had been aware of it for the last thirty minutes and if he had to guess, he would say that his pursuer wasn't being all that careful which led him to believe that he was a random target. Nobody would follow him if they knew who he really was and what he was capable of; and if he was the intended target, they had greatly underestimated him.

Bray took a sharp turn down an alley. Behind him, heavy footsteps echoed down the empty street followed by a click, as if talons or claws struck the pavement. He paused to let his pursuer catch up before moving on, drawing whoever or whatever was stalking him into a quieter part of the city, away from people and CCTV cameras.

Behind him Bray could hear laboured breathing, the light rasping sound of a creature with huge lungs, sniffing the air and tasting him upon it. The footsteps quickened, suggesting the beast was close and eager to reach him. Bray pressed on, into an industrial area and across a patch of waste ground. A large disused warehouse loomed ahead of him, the silver moon hovering above, silhouetting the square frame and throwing him into shadow. Not that the creature wouldn't already have a clear view of him. If he guessed right, its eyes would be extremely keen in the dark and its nose would have capabilities beyond that of any bloodhound.

The warehouse was a hangar-like affair, built of breeze block and steel with a corrugated iron roof. The large sliding doors were unlocked and he slid them open wide enough to slip through. He let his hand linger on the cold metal frame, deliberately leaving a scent so that his pursuer would be in no doubt where he was.

A vast dark space opened out before him, empty and deserted. A fractured skylight allowed a sliver of moonlight to penetrate the gloom. A musty smell coated the air, the copper and plastic tang of old wiring mingled with more than a hint of rat droppings. The place had been empty a while.

Bray wasted no time. Moving swiftly passed long-abandoned aisles of rusting machinery, he clambered on top of an ancient-looking generator and swung himself onto the steel girder above. Half-upright, his arms outstretched for balance, he edged silently along the narrow beam just as a large wolf-like snout poked through the gap in the shed door. Bray crouched low to the beam, keeping still and watched his pursuer enter.

The creature sucked in the air hungrily and sniffed the spot on the door where Bray had left his handprint. Straining to locate its prey, it heaved the doors open with its razor-sharp claws. Once inside, it dropped to all fours and began to follow the trail towards the machinery, moving with the stealth of a seasoned predator, its dark grey fur merging into the shadowy gloom but occasionally picked out by shafts of moonlight from the fractured skylight.

Bray narrowed his eyes and dropped to the concrete floor behind the beast with the dexterity of a lithe cat.

His orders were simple. Find the creature that had been roaming the city and eliminate it.

For weeks the news media had been full of tales of a madman roaming the streets of London, apparently choosing random victims to mutilate – a savage killer of superhuman strength who had left a trail of disemboweled and often limbless corpses behind him. The killer seemed to prey on lone individuals who were careless enough to find themselves alone at the early hours. Bray knew better. Bray's master knew better, and that was why Diagus had ordered him to seek and destroy. And to mete out justice.

The creature was a bulworg. Part wolf, part bull, part rock troll. All teeth and claws and bred to kill. Bray had seen plenty back home on Thea. They made good guards, protectors, even first-wave soldiers. A single bulworg could rip through an enemy platoon in moments, without fatigue, without fear. A pack of them could change the outcome of a battle. He had heard of bulworgs being taught to read and write, but it seemed unlikely. Bulworgs had little more intelligence than the average wolf and could only follow the simplest orders. He had never heard of one on Earth. He couldn't guess how it had penetrated the barrier between the worlds. It had to belong to someone. Either way, the bulworg must die.

Bray trod carefully in its footsteps, staying out of range of its vision until he felt he was close enough. With his left hand he opened the smuggler's pouch, an invisible pocket that hung in the ether between worlds, and pulled his sword silently free. To an outsider it would have seemed that he pulled his sword from thin air, the pouch being undetectable by eye or touch. But the sword was solid enough. He could feel the weight of it.

He adopted a defensive stance, legs shoulder-width apart, his left foot planted slightly in front, balancing his weight on the ball of his right foot. Both hands grasped the hilt of his sword as he levelled the grey steel point-first at the creature.

Bray's voice was calm but edged with authority. "By the order of the Shadojak, I command you to yield."

The creature halted and rose back onto its hind legs until it stood upright like a man, albeit a man of eight foot with a mass of grey fur, muscle and twisted sinew. Its claws made a click-clack sound on the floor as it slowly turned to face him, yellow eyes full of hatred, snout pulled tight in a rictus grin, canines on either side dripping hunger-driven saliva from needle-sharp points. It sunk lower, its leg muscles bunching up, ready to pounce.

Have it your own way, thought Bray. It wouldn't have made any difference if the beast had yielded. It still had to die.

The bulworg came at him, bursting forward with a speed that belied its bulk. Bray dropped to his knee and rolled to the left, feeling the impact of the bulworg's front paws as they slammed into the ground where he had just been. Before he finished his roll, Bray spun around, leaping into the air with his body parallel to the ground, narrowly missing the beast's tail as it whipped by. Landing deftly, he immediately went into a forward roll, letting his reflexes propel him out of harm's way as a large clawed foot hit the ground beside him.

The bulworg howled in frustration and punched a steel support, causing the building to shake and leaving a massive dent in the inch-thick steel. It was fast, but Bray was faster.

He changed his grip on the sword, grasping it in one hand and bringing it above his head whilst extending his leg forward to form the scorpion stance. The bulworg began to pace around him, sizing him up, searching for a weakness. Bray didn't flinch as the beast's yellow eyes drilled into him. The creature's fury burned brighter at being thwarted by a mere man. Bray felt a flicker of sympathy. It was true, he was a man – but only partly.

The creature grunted, then sprang. This time Bray pivoted on his heel, dropped low and brought his sword down, swinging it in a lethal arc. The blade caught the beast's thick wrist joint as it came down, severing the paw. In the same fluid motion, he grasped the other wrist with his free hand and spun to the side, using the creature's own momentum to fling it face-first into the floor. He followed it down, landing on its back and driving his knees into its kidneys. As the bulworg raised its head to scream, Bray reached under its jaw and pulled it back, exposing the vulnerable neck, then slipped his blade across it, feeling the cartilage and windpipe give before his cold steel.

An ugly hiss escaped the beast's throat as blood bubbled from the gash. It struggled momentarily, fighting to draw air into its lungs but Bray held the jaw firm, refusing to allow the beast a final bite. The creature bucked and writhed in a futile attempt to dislodge him before finally going limp and sagging forward. Bray held tight for a few moments more, ensuring the beast had succumbed to death before relaxing his grip.

He stood and walked to the open door and scanned the wasteland beyond. Empty. You couldn't be too careful. He had dispatched the bulworg swiftly yet he knew that his master,

Diagus, would have berated him for not being swift or silent enough. If any witnesses or passersby had been present, he would have had to eliminate them too. Secrecy was paramount.

He returned to the dead beast, wiping the blade of his sword with a cloth he found on the warehouse floor, before returning it to its scabbard in the smuggler's pouch.

Throwing the bloodied cloth down beside the body of the limp beast, he circled it, checking for any identifying marks. A gurgling sound belched from its gut as he pushed it onto its back with his foot. The slash at its throat opened wide like a second mouth, blood trickling from the corners. Bray lifted a paw, admiring the size and sharpness of the claws. There was nothing to indicate the owner. Yet it was highly unlikely that the bulworg was a free agent, roaming as it pleased. No, this creature was either brought to this world, or sent.

Eventually, having given up his search of the body, Bray found the severed paw and was about to toss it onto the carcass when he discovered a coin-sized tattoo below the calloused knuckles. It looked like a rough kind of circle with eight tentacle-like appendages – an octopus, maybe? He had never seen it before. He stared at it for a moment, letting the image lodge into his mind before dropping the paw on top of the body.

Taking a step back, he retrieved a small glass vial from the inside of his jacket and held it up to the moonlight. Inside was a black powder that filled the bell-shaped base and came partway up the slender neck. Carrion spore. He removed the stopper and tipped half the contents over the bulworg, then pushed the stopper back on, put the vial back in his jacket and took a step back.

Wisps of grey vapour began to spiral from the black powder as it reacted with the creature's body. The carrion spore lay dormant in the glass vial, yet once in contact with dead flesh it began to feast on it at a microscopic scale, devouring flesh and bone until there was nothing left. Guessing that a creature the size of the bulworg would take about half an hour to be fully consumed, he returned to the door.

He leaned against the frame with his arms folded, scanning the barren patch of ground. Apart from the odd rat darting amongst the brambles and the piles of rubble and brick, he was alone. In earlier times he would have relished any opportunity to stand still and do nothing. Such moments had been rare growing up in the Imperial army; even more so as he progressed to blade-master and then transferred to the Shades, the Emperor's special forces. After he took the black cloak, standing still was not an option. To be a black cloak, a Shaigun, you had to give yourself body and soul to the Shadojaks, the highest-ranking mortals on Thea. The eight Shadojaks ranked higher than any king and only one step below the Emperor himself and were answerable to nobody but themselves. And each had an apprentice like him, a Shaigun.

He cast his eyes back to the bulworg. The carrion spore was working well and the carcass was beginning to smoke as the micro-organisms devoured its flesh. The heat reached him where he stood and an acrid methane smell filled his nostrils. He snorted it out and returned his gaze to the night.

Three years he had spent here on Earth. Learning how people lived, how they went about their lives and communicated with each other. It didn't take him long to blend in, to hide amongst them while he and his master, Diagus, kept watch. But there was a change coming – a shift in the ether that had the Supreme Shadojak worried. It was the job of the league of Shadojaks to bring balance and stability.

A fox scurried between a gap in the bramble and rubble, pausing briefly to sniff the air before moving on. In the pale moonlight he could make out its matted coat, mottled with stains and midges. It was gone in a moment, leaving the ground undisturbed and no sign of its passing. Bray couldn't suppress a brief pang of envy. No responsibilities, no orders to follow. Free to come and go as it pleased. Of course, it had a family to feed – but families also meant fellowship, warmth. Love.

Bray could control and suppress his emotions well. It was one of the first lessons he learned when he took the black cloak. Hatred, anger, fear, jealousy, empathy, even love: these were emotions that he had shed willingly and easily. In the Imperial Guard or even as a Shade, a wife and family would have been a possibility. But once you followed the path of a Shadojak, you relinquished all human attachments. You were stripped of anything that could be used against you. To be a Shadojak was to be above mortal life and mortal things. To be a balancer of things, your mind had to be perfectly aligned. Good and evil were merely concepts created by man to identify the things they favoured or opposed. One man's good was another man's evil. It was the same for gods, but the effects of their actions were more far-reaching. It was the Shadojaks' job to step between the two. To intervene in order that the worlds remained in equilibrium. If one side upset the balance, oblivion would threaten all. Life, be it mortal or immortal, would cease to exist. Or so the theory went. It wasn't his job to question. The principles were thousands of years old, the code written down by the founding fathers of the League of Shadojaks, the original eight who had killed Solarius, the God of Chaos, and taken his sword: a soul reaver and those of his seven knights. Eight soul reavers for eight Shadojaks.

Bray returned to the bulworg – or what was left of it. The carrion spore had worked well, dissolving the flesh of the beast until a small pile of dust remained. The residue would have been unrecognisable to anyone on Earth, but he kicked the pile of dust anyway, scattering it into a more random pile before leaving the warehouse.

A short walk later and he was back beside his motorbike, parked behind a skip on a side road, a sheet of old tarpaulin hiding it from view. He pulled the sheet back to reveal the Ducati Diavel. The engine was a 1198cc V-twin, mighty enough to produce 155 brake horsepower. He had added some refinements: nitros, a turbo-charger, racing pipes and brakes.

It wasn't road-legal, but then, he didn't have a license or insurance anyway.

Strapping on a matching carbon-black helmet, he swung a leg over the seat, pulled the bike from its stand and pressed the ignition button. He couldn't help smiling as the engine growled to life. Of course, Diagus would have disapproved. Even a smile was a display of emotion. But Diagus wasn't here and he wouldn't have been able to see beneath the tinted visor.

He kicked the bike into gear and let the clutch out as he applied the throttle. Bray's grin spread across his face as he accelerated into the night.

4

Silk

Captive in her room on board the *Molly* , Elora perched on the end of her bed, clutching Nat's journal. Her fingers were stiff as she held the book to her chest, her eyes red and swollen with grief and fear. For the past half an hour she had been desperately casting around for a means of escape, while trying to rid her mind of the image of her uncle lying bleeding or dead on the floor on the other side of the thin partition. The clatter of an approaching helicopter jolted her mind back to her present danger. She had to get out of here. There would only be minutes to get away from the *Molly* before Reuben handed her over to Silk.

She heard Reuben order one of his thugs to go up on deck. "Bastard!" she muttered under her breath as she jammed her wooden chair beneath the door handle. The door wouldn't hold for long, especially with Pinky battering against it, but all she needed was a precious few minutes.

When she was younger and liked to play tricks on Nat, she had discovered that the wall between her room and the bathroom was only made of thin plastic-coated plywood panels screwed into place. Hiding in her wardrobe, she had unscrewed the back panel and squeezed into the bathroom, confusing Nat. She smiled at the memory. She just hoped to God the screws were still loose.

Glancing at the door a final time, she squeezed into the wardrobe between her clothes, the plastic hangers clattering as she pushed them aside. Cursing and trying to keep as quiet as possible, she searched with her fingers for the screws that held the panel in place. It didn't take long to find the ones she had loosened as a child, but she wasn't a child anymore and she wouldn't be able to squeeze through a gap that small. She would have to find a way to unscrew the other side as well.

Suddenly she heard the metallic ping of the spring in her door handle. Somebody was trying to get in.

"Little pig, little pig, let me come in," came Pinky's gravelly voice as he repeatedly twisted the handle.

Elora swore under her breath. No time to unscrew the panel. She slid on her bottom so her back was against the wardrobe doors and pushed her feet against the thin wall. She felt the thin plywood flex.

"Open up, you awkward bitch!" shouted Pinky, as he began to put his shoulder to the door.

Elora pushed against the panel with all the strength she could muster, timing her efforts to coincide with the thumping on the door. If Pinky heard her in here, the game was up.

A final push and the plywood gave with a snap. There was no time to waste. She slid through the hole on her belly and lowered herself onto the cold bathroom floor.

Pinky still hadn't broken down the door to her bedroom – she could hear him raging in the corridor. She would get them back for what they did to Nat. But first she needed to get away and ring the police.

Unlike the rest of the windows on the *Molly* which were of the small round porthole kind, the bathroom window opened wide. She eased it open as softly as she could. Warm air poured in and the sound of the helicopter grew louder. The black shape was hard to make out against the night sky, but it was clearly heading for the adjacent field and she could see the red flashing light beneath. She didn't have long.

A quick glance out of the window told her the coast was clear. That didn't mean she couldn't be seen. But it was a risk she had to take.

As she climbed over the toilet and placed a leg through the window and a foot on the outer ledge, she heard a splintered crash from her bedroom. Pinky had broken down the door. Time had just shortened dramatically.

Swinging her legs over the side of the boat she dipped a toe in the black water. It was icy cold compared to the warm night air. Struggling not to gasp out loud, she transferred her weight to the steel handrail and lowered herself into the canal.

A moment later the bathroom window was flung open and Pinky's head poked out. She released her grip on the handrail, took a deep breath and let the weight of her wet clothes drag her below the surface. She prayed she hadn't been spotted.

Feeling her way across the cold metal underside of the barge, she groped towards the canal bank. Trailing weeds snatched at her legs but soon she felt solid concrete ahead of her and hauled herself to the surface, to emerge gasping into the night air.

A gap of a few inches separated the barge from the concrete side of the canal. Above her, the boat's rounded hull gave her enough room to lift her head out of the water and still remain hidden. She tried to slow her breathing as she sucked in the night air.

On the bank, the rattle of the helicopter blades had died away and Elora could hear Reuben's voice welcoming the mysterious Mr Silk.

"She was a right handful, that one. Fought like a bloody vixen."

Beside Reuben, Elora could make out a thin, elderly man in an elegantly tailored black suit. His face was expressionless, his cold, dead eyes fixed on the *Molly*. A third man, plainly a bodyguard and even bigger than Pinky, stood some distance apart, his eyes darting about in all directions.

"The uncle wasn't all that easy either. He needed quieting," continued Reuben. "We had to lock the girl in her room until you came."

Silk turned and fixed Reuben with an icy stare. His voice was dry, rasping and thick with menace. "I sincerely hope you didn't leave her unguarded."

From her hiding place, Elora felt the barge dip with the weight of someone moving around on deck. Then Pinky's panicked voice rang out.

"She's gone!"

"What? That's impossible!" said Reuben. "Find her, she won't have got far." He turned to Silk and was about to speak when the older man slapped him hard across the face.

Reuben stumbled back, almost knocked off his feet with the unexpected force of the blow. Pinky stepped forward, arms raised as if about to lunge at Silk but thought better of it when the bodyguard slipped between them.

"You bloody fools, I told you not to let her out of your sight."

"But she's just a girl," argued Reuben, dabbing at a trickle of blood where Silk's blow had broken the skin.

Ignoring him, Silk turned to his bodyguard and appeared to make several strange clicking sounds from his mouth. Tak-tak-tak. They sounded like the noises an insect might make, something other than human. The giant responded with clicks of his own before stomping towards the *Molly*. Elora felt the boat dip in the water as he stepped aboard.

"That girl is capable of tearing you and your men to shreds. It's a wonder you're not dead already," said Silk.

The remark puzzled Elora. Did he have her confused with someone else? Hadn't Reuben explained, she was just a girl?

A moment later the bodyguard reappeared with the body of her uncle over his shoulder. In her hiding place, Elora struggled to lift her head closer to the top of the bank, desperate to get a view of Nat. The bodyguard directed more of the strange clicking sounds at Silk, who clicked back. Nat was lowered to the ground where he sat, head slumping forwards. At least he seemed to be breathing, but his breath sounded slow and laboured. Elora longed to reach out to him.

"Where is she?" asked Silk. Nat lifted his head, a trickle of blood dripping from a split lip, one eye swollen shut.

"She's long gone, takwich," he said, locking his good eye on the elderly man. Silk knelt down with surprising agility. He gripped her uncle's long hair in his bony fingers and pulled his head back. Elora fought hard not to scream.

"I will find her, Minuan. The barrier grows weaker day by day, and more and more brothers join my army. She will be ours very soon."

"Never!" Nat spat out the word in a voice that Elora hardly recognised. "You'll never find her. And I'll welcome death with open arms before I tell you anything. She's probably halfway to Thea as we speak."

Silk grinned.

"My dear friend, I'm not going to kill you. I have something far more exotic in mind. And I will find her, have no doubt about that. I very much doubt she's bound for Thea. Only death would await her there, as you well know. You should have killed the girl when she was a child. Now, she will be mine, and there will be no stopping His coming … "

Turning to his bodyguard, Silk gave several more clicks. The huge man hoisted her uncle on to his shoulder again as if he was nothing more than a child and headed towards the helicopter.

"Where the hell's Thea?" asked Reuben.

Silk ignored the question. "Find the girl," he ordered.

"We need to leave. She'll have found a phone by now and called the police," said Reuben.

"I hope she has called the police. I've already warned them. They're expecting to hear from her."

"You've got people on the inside?"

For a moment Silk didn't reply, but stood in silence, his gaze turned skywards. "You've failed me once already. That was a mistake. You make the same mistake again and that's a problem. I deal with problems … severely. Do you understand?"

"We won't fail a second time, Mr Silk," said Reuben, a nervous tremor slipping into his normally smooth voice.

"No, you won't."

Still clinging with numb fingers to the slimy canal wall, Elora watched the old man walk back towards the helicopter. After long minutes in the icy water, she was frozen and exhausted.

Her teeth were chattering uncontrollably and she was terrified that Reuben or one his men would hear.

"Come on. We better find this bitch. I don't think Mr Silk issues idle threats."

She watched as Reuben and his two thugs set off down the canal bank. As soon as they were out of sight, she dragged herself along the bank, clear of the *Molly*. With great effort she struggled onto the grassy bank and lay still for a moment, legs curled beneath her wet body as she tried to decide what to do next. Going to the police was not an option.

For the few remaining hours of darkness, Elora huddled in the corner of a shed on a nearby allotment. It wasn't comfortable, but at least it was safe. Nobody was going to come looking for her here.

Fearing to stay on the *Molly* in case Reuben or his men returned, she had quickly darted back on board and snatched up a few belongings: a change of dry clothes, all the money she had – which wasn't much – and Nat's journal. That was when she had found herself glancing at the name 'Shado-jak' with the telephone number scribbled underneath. Could this person help? Nat had warned her that he wasn't somebody you'd want to meet, but from what he had told her, the Shadojak had helped them once before. Wasn't it worth giving him a call? By the time the sun came up and filtered through the dusty shed window, she had made up her mind.

Coins bounced noisily into the phone box as she fed it a handful of coins and then dialed the Shadojak's number.

The phone rang for almost a minute before being picked up. There was no sound at the other end, but Elora had the feeling that somebody was there, listening.

"Hello? I need to speak to Shadojak." A long silence followed. Elora's fingers clutched the receiver anxiously. She was on the point of putting the phone down when a stern voice spoke at the other end.

"Who gave you this number?" The man's accent was hard to place, slightly foreign-sounding.

"Is that Shadojak? Please, I need your help."

"Who gave you this number?" The voice was as stern as before.

"My uncle. Nathaniel Delamere. He's been kidnapped."

"I don't know the name," cut in the voice.

By now, Elora felt a growing anger but fought to control it: she had to keep calm. There was no point upsetting the only person who might be able to help.

"Your telephone number was in his journal."

"I can't help you. You must have the wrong number," came the curt reply.

"Please," she begged, before the speaker had time to hang up. "He's been taken by a man called Silk. A takwich."

There was a pause.

"How do you know he is a Takwich?"

"I – I don't know. That's what my uncle called him. But Silk – or the takwich or whatever he is – has him and now he wants me. Please, I've got nobody else to turn to." In the silence that followed, Elora realised how true that was: she was totally alone. Nat had been her only family.

"Have you a pen?" the man asked finally.

"No."

"Then you'll need to remember this address. Unit 27b, Chadwell Heath Industrial Estate, North London." Elora repeated the address to herself, committing it to memory. "Be there at two this afternoon." There was an audible click followed by the disconnection tone. He had hung up.

Did she really trust this person? She had never met him and he sounded rude as hell. But what choice did she have? None. She checked the time on the telephone display. It was a little past eight am. If she caught the train she could be in London in two hours. That would give her time to find the address. It wouldn't be cheap. She took out the money stuffed in her jeans pocket. She had a little under ninety pounds. It should be enough for the train but there wouldn't be much left over.

○○○○○○○○○○○○○○○○○○○○

Bray hung up and put the mobile back in his pocket. The call had come totally out of the blue. Nobody had dialled that number in his three years on Earth. And according to Diagus, nobody had used it in all his five-year duty.

He had never understood why he had to have a phone at all. Only a handful of people on Earth even knew of his existence. For security reasons, the number was linked to a landline on the other side of the city, and calls – if there were any – were automatically redirected to his mobile. Never mind: it paid to be careful. In theory it was easy to trace a call on the landline, but almost impossible for anyone to locate his mobile. That's why he had instructed the girl to meet him at the industrial estate, at a place and time of his choosing. It would give him the perfect opportunity to check out if she was genuine or was leading him into some kind of trap. Maybe she was being followed. Diagus was always telling him to be vigilant. He never explained why. But if there was one thing he had learned about the aged Shadojak, it was that he always had his reasons, and they were usually good ones. Right now, the Shadojak wasn't here and so it was his responsibility as Shaigun to take whatever action was necessary. Yet if the girl spoke the truth and there really was a takwich involved, then Diagus needed to be told. Like the bulworg he had dispatched the previous night, some creatures didn't belong on Earth.

Strapping on his helmet, he fired the bike to life, put it into gear and roared down the street and back towards the city. He needed to prepare and get into an advantageous position to study the girl.

61

5

Heads or Tails?

Chadwell Heath Industrial Estate was a concrete maze of huge factories and smaller units that lay on either side of a heavily potholed road, on the outskirts of London. Standing beside the entrance, Elora gazed at a map, trying to locate Unit 27b. A steady stream of articulated lorries pulled out of the gates onto the uneven road, airbrakes and suspension hissing as they thundered past, putting her already frayed nerves on edge.

The train journey to London and the subsequent taxi ride to the estate had been uneventful but Elora had scarcely relaxed for a moment, constantly on the alert for any signs of Reuben and his thugs. Guided by the map, she located the unit, a small service garage by the name of TimeScale Motors. Taking a deep breath to calm herself, she approached the entrance.

The building was sandwiched between two unused units but the garage itself was open. A large roller door was up and from inside she could hear the sound of a car engine running.

Elora stepped inside the dimly lit workshop. A car was up on a ramp and a tall man in an outsized boiler suit and tanned rigger boots was working under it with his back to her. He appeared to be alone.

Despite the gloom she could see that the place was in serious need of a clean. The windows were cobweb-strewn and filthy and the bare brick walls plastered with faded pinups and calendars displaying naked women. She passed a steel welder's bench, full of dents and scratches. On it was a stripped-down engine, with parts, belts and bolts strewn around it haphazardly. How could anybody run a business like this? How would they know which bits went where? But then again, what did she know about cars?

She checked her watch: nearly two o'clock.

"Excuse me?" she said, raising her voice over the noise of the engine. The man appeared not to have noticed her. Then she saw why. He was wearing headphones – probably listening to an iPod or something. Elora approached him and tapped him on the shoulder.

His shocked face showed utter surprise as he turned to look at her. She guessed him to be a year or two older than herself, tall with dark, unruly hair. His face was heavy with acne and a large angry boil sat beside his nose, looking ready to burst at any moment. He popped his headphones out and let them hang loose from the top of his greasy boiler suit.

"Sorry to disturb you. I'm meeting somebody at two, Shadojak. He told me to come here." She tried hard not stare at his boil, but it wasn't easy to ignore.

The mechanic wiped his chin absent-mindedly.

"Don't know anyone by that name," he said in a thick London accent. "What's wrong with your eyes?" His face screwed up in the puzzled expression of somebody dimwitted.

"Nothing, they're contact lenses. Maybe I got the place wrong." Yet this was unit 27b, exactly where the man on the phone had said.

"Hang on a bit, let me check the diary. The gaffer booked somebody in for a service this afternoon." He sauntered over to a metal bench laden with tools, car parts, magazines and manuals. It took him a moment to find what he was looking for, shifting boxes and other items out of the way before he flipped open an oil-stained diary. He flicked to today's page and frowned.

"Says here there's a Mr Shadojak booked in for two." He glanced to a clock on the wall. "Should be here any minute."

Elora nodded. So she had come to the right place after all.

"Would it be OK if I waited here?" Ever since last night, she had had been looking over her shoulder constantly in case somebody was following or watching her.

"Suit yourself," the mechanic shrugged. He was about to put his earphones back in and get back to work, then he stopped.

"Fancy a cup of tea, coffee?"

Elora hadn't eaten since the night before and was sure it would make her feel a little better.

"Yes, please."

"Great. Kettle's over there," he said, nodding towards a darkened corner of the room where there was a sink and small unit with a kettle and a mess of unwashed cups. "Mine's a coffee, white, two sugars." With a wink, he wandered back to the ramp.

Elora couldn't believe the cheek of him. Well, if making him a cup of coffee was the price of being able to wait inside, so be it. At least he seemed friendly enough.

She filled the plastic kettle and washed a couple of mugs which she doubted had ever been clean. There was no cloth, so she rinsed them under the tap and used her fingers to rub the grime off, hoping that the boiling water would kill any remaining germs. The milk was powdered   and judging by the trail of small white paw prints along the lid, some tiny creature had been burrowing in it. OK, maybe black coffee then. Elora put a heaped spoonful into the mechanic's mug, along with two spoons of clumped-together sugar, took his coffee over to him, then leaned against the bench as she drank hers. Without milk or sugar it wasn't great, but it was better than nothing.

She checked the clock. It was almost twenty past two and the mysterious Shadojak hadn't shown up. By three, he still hadn't made an appearance and she was debating whether to ask the mechanic if she could use the phone to ring him, when three men stepped into the garage. Elora's heart suddenly jumped as fright took a hold of her. She recognised the trio.

"Hello, Elora," said Reuben smoothly, as he drew out his gun. "You gave us a bit of a fright running off like that. Didn't think I'd ever get chance to see those pretty eyes of yours again."

She looked to the mechanic for help but he was oblivious, under the ramp, bobbing his head to the music on his headphones. On a nod from Reuben, Pinky gave him a savage kick in the back of the knees and he fell in a painful heap on the concrete floor, yelling as he went. The cry was cut short as Pinky grabbed him by the collar of the boiler suit, dragged him out and roughly hauled him to his feet.

"What the bloody hell's going on? Get outta my garage before I call the police," he said, looking as petrified as she felt.

"Who's this?" asked Reuben, levelling the gun on her. "Relation, boyfriend?"

Elora stared at the gun that had shot her uncle, fear making her stammer.

"I – I don't know him. He's just a mechanic. He works here. Leave him alone, he's got nothing to do with any of this. Please." If he got hurt, it would be all her fault. Why had she insisted on waiting inside with him?

Reuben raised a sceptical eyebrow. He took out his coin, tossed and caught it then checked the result. He nodded again to Pinky who, holding the mechanic by the scruff of his neck, drove a fist into his stomach.

"No!" screamed Elora as she watched the man double over. Pinky pulled him back up straight and she could see pain on the poor boy's face as he struggled to draw in breath.

"Please, Reuben. I'll come quietly – leave him alone."

Reuben grinned, his dark eyes sparkling menacingly. He was enjoying this.

"You could have done that last night. What d'you think, Pinky?"

"Think this ugly sod's got a nice big boil that needs bursting," said the thug, as he smashed a fist into the boy's face.

Elora could feel the thud of the punch from where she stood. It was amazing the mechanic was still conscious.

"Reckon that's popped it, laughed Pinky, his tattooed face beginning to look positively demented.

The other man, Kitch, joined in the laughter and went to roll down the shutter door. Elora felt dread in the pit of her stomach. They were going to kill him. They wouldn't leave any witnesses. A sense of helpless fury overcame her. In truth, she had killed the boy by coming here.

Reuben took out his phone and put the phone to his ear. Elora guessed he was calling Silk.

"I've found the girl ... Unit 27b, Chadwell Heath Industrial Estate ... No – Just a mechanic ... I'll ask." He held the phone away and his gaze locked with hers.

"Why here? Were you meeting anybody?"

Elora was silent. Realising that she wasn't going to reply, Reuben nodded at Pinky, who immediately landed another brutal blow in the boy's ribs.

"Shadojak. I was supposed to meet a man called Shadojak," she blurted out, not wanting to look at the mechanic, but feeling that she owed it to him to at least witness his suffering.

"Some guy called Shadojak," Reuben relayed.

Elora couldn't hear what was being said at the other end of the line but saw the frown that crept upon Reuben's face.

"Understood," he said before hanging up. Then he turned to Kitch. "Keep her quiet."

She flinched as Kitch came behind her, snaked one arm about her waist and the other over her shoulder, placing a hand over her mouth. She could smell his foul body odour and onion breath.

"What's up boss?" Kitch asked Reuben, who had wandered over to Pinky.

"This Shadojak. He's trouble. He's got Silk's knickers in a right twist."

"Don't matter. We can take him. Ain't nobody better than me in a fight. And you're one nasty piece of work yourself," Pinky grinned, but Elora saw the doubt on Reuben's face.

"Well, whoever he is, he's got Silk worried. And if Silk's worried, we need to be careful, that's all. He'll be here in a few minutes; we've just got to hold the fort until he arrives."

"And this ugly git?" asked Pinky, shaking the boy.

Reuben shrugged and grinning, took out a coin and flicked it in the air.

"Heads or tails, heads or tails?" he said, levelling his gun first at the boy's head then at his groin. "Heads or tails?"

Elora saw the panic in the mechanic's eyes and prayed that he wouldn't suffer any more. But she refused to look away.

oooooooooooooooooooo

Bray slowed his breathing, weighing up the options and probable outcomes until he found the right course of action.

The girl Elora was certainly a strange one and not at all what he was expecting. From the small time he'd had to study her, she seemed genuine, but there was something about her he couldn't fathom. The strange violet eyes indicated she wasn't Earth-born, but she didn't seem of the other world either. It was clear she was stressed and frightened – and that was before this ugly trio walked in.

He watched the silver coin spin end over end as it ascended in the air, while he took in every detail of the scene around him. The big man called Pinky was behind him and a little to the right, one hand gripping his collar, the other weakly grasping his wrist. Currently his attention was on the coin. Bray judged the man's weight and posture and guessed that he was undisciplined and ill-trained in close combat. He would be easy to deal with.

Reuben to his front, less than two feet away, had the gun trained on him, but was constantly shifting position, aiming first at his head, then his groin. His grip on the weapon was loose, his wrist weak and although he was the leader and mildly more intelligent than Pinky, he also had allowed his attention to be distracted by the glinting silver coin.

Kitch, the final one of the three, was out of reach behind the girl. Clearly he was no brighter than Pinky. But he had need to be dealt with too, before he hurt the girl.

The silver coin reached its zenith and began to descend as Bray chose his next move. He closed his eyes and held his breath, running through the sequence in his mind.

His body had already adopted an offensive stance with feet firmly planted shoulder-width apart, knees slightly bent and arms hovering above his waist, hands slack and ready to snap into fists. His oversized boiler suit hid his intentions from the untrained thugs, even though they probably wouldn't have noticed his preparedness even if it was spelt out for them – all they could see was a scared boy facing an inescapable death. Surprise was the best weapon in his arsenal, but not the only one.

Snapping his eyes open, Bray launched himself into action.

Dropping low, he shifted his weight onto his right foot whilst kicking back with his left leg. He felt his boot drive through Pinky's kneecap, snapping bone and cartilage and bending the man's leg backwards as if he was double-jointed. In the same fluid movement, he reversed the grip on his wrist, twisting his own so that he now grasped Pinky's. Forcing it down and under him, he stepped back and snapped his hand forwards. As the bigger man was flung over his shoulder, Bray gave a final sharp twist. A wet, popping sound let him know that he had dislocated the thug's shoulder.

Before Pinky's body hit the ground, Bray's left arm was already descending on Reuben's gun. Grasping his hand, he twisted the 9 mm Sigsaur to the left, forcing the barrel down slightly. All the time he kept his eyes firmly locked on Reuben, who had barely begun to register what was happening. Feeling for Reuben's trigger finger, he forced him to fire the gun before his own middle finger found the magazine release catch and flicked it, releasing the clip before another round could be chambered.

The thunderclap sound of the fired gun coincided with the sound of Pinky's body slamming face-first into the floor. Bray saw Reuben's eyes widen, his brain only just beginning to take in what was going on.

With his free hand, Bray caught the falling coin, closing his fingers over it and feeling the queen's face press into his palm.

"Heads," he informed Reuben, with a wink. Then brought his forehead down into the man's face, feeling the satisfying crunch of cartilage and bone before his body crashed against the roller door.

A heartbeat later, Kitch screamed and Bray heard his body collapse to the ground at the same time as Reuben's. Echoes from the gunshot still resonated around the garage.

Seeing that the threat had been eliminated and the three men immobilised, Bray let out the breath he had been holding and turned to the girl. Her mouth drooped open and she was staring at him with a dazed expression, although fortunately she had had the foresight to step away from Kitch, who was struggling to his feet, snatching a clasp knife from his pocket.

Bray looked at the blood leaking from the man's thigh. He had missed the pelvis which was the target. With a shattered pelvic bone, he wouldn't have risen. If he didn't suppress his emotions, he would be cursing himself.

"Stay back, you freak," stuttered Kitch, brandishing the clasp knife with a shaky hand.

Bray saw fear in the injured man's eyes. He took a step towards him, reaching for the smuggler's pouch.

Both girl and thug watched in disbelief as he appeared to draw a sword out of thin air. He put the point against Kitch's neck and twisted it, as if inspecting its razor-sharp edge. A sudden smell of urine hit his nostrils. Kitch had emptied his bladder.

Bray raised an eyebrow as a dark stain spread down the man's leg. Bullies always made the weakest victims.

He was about to flick his blade down, severing the hand that held the knife and finish by driving the hilt of the sword into the man's face, when the girl slipped up behind and struck the back of her attacker's head with a crowbar. The man sank to the floor, the girl watching wide-eyed as he went, her hands trembling as they gripped her weapon. She looked to him, as if unsure of what to do next.

The buzzing of a phone broke the silence. Bray returned his sword to the smuggler's pouch, walked back to Reuben and retrieved the phone from his inside pocket. He put it to his ear and pressed the answer button.

"Reuben?" said a dry voice. "Are you there? Have you still got the girl? Reuben!"

Enraged, the voice changed from human-sounding to the typical insect-like clicking of a takwich. The clicking went on for several seconds until the owner of the voice regained control. There was a pause, then the human voice resumed.

"Shadojak. Leave the girl be, do not harm her. Leave her there and be gone by the time we arrive and I'll forget this happened."

"And what's the girl to a takwich? Why's she so important?"

"Do as I say, or I'll tear this city to shreds. Then we'll see who does the balancing."

There was a moment's silence before Bray spoke. "You will be judged." There was another furious burst of clicking, then he hung up.

It was clear to Bray that the takwich wanted this girl for something more than just possession. What her importance was, who could say? He dropped the phone onto Reuben's body and turned back to the girl. She was staring down at Kitch and looking horrified at what she had done.

"It's alright," he told her. "You didn't kill him."

Elora unlocked her fingers and let the metal bar fall. It clanged as it struck the concrete floor, the ringing nose echoing around the workshop. Relief flooded over her. She hated these men, but she had no desire to kill them.

"How did you do that? Are you Shadojak?" she asked.

"The Shadojak. It's a title, not a name. And no. I'm his Shaigun. My name's Bray."

Suddenly, the London accent seemed to have vanished. In its place was the curious, faintly foreign-sounding voice she recognised from earlier. This was the man she had spoken to in the phone box.

"What's a Shaigun?"

"An apprentice." He seemed keen to change the subject. "Why do they want you?"

"I don't know. But they've got my uncle. I need your help, or Shadojak's, or the Shadojak's or whatever. Please."

He regarded her for a moment, then in one fluid movement pulled his face off.

"What the … ?"

"Latex," he said, holding the mask in his hand.

Elora's shock quickly gave way to curiosity. The face under it was smooth and without blemish. He had a strong jawline and cleft chin. His green eyes were piercing. She guessed they had probably melted the hearts of many girls.

Approaching sirens in the distance brought her back to earth with a jolt.

"It's him, Silk. He's got people on the police force," she said hurriedly, feeling the familiar fear return. "We need to get out of here."

Calmly, Bray slipped the boiler suit off his shoulders and tied the arms of it around his waist. He wore a plain black T-shirt underneath that clung to his wide shoulders and thin waist, showing that he wasn't at all as skinny as she first thought.

"I want answers. This Silk is a takwich and he wants you badly, but all I can see is a little girl with odd eyes. Maybe my best course of action is to leave you here," he said, his green eyes drilling into hers.

"But I came to you for help. Isn't that what the Shadojak's supposed to do? Help those in need?" she argued.

"No, you're confusing him with the Samaritans. The Shadojak doesn't help, he judges and restores the balance." His voice was deep and full of authority and lacked the tiniest bit of compassion.

Elora felt her face flush.

"Well, can you at least take me to him? I've nobody else to turn to. Maybe he can rebalance this takwich."

"Silk will be judged, there's no doubt about that. Earth is no place for his kind. But be under no illusions, Elora. The Shadojak will also judge you. You're no more Earth-born than I am."

By now, the sound of sirens was coming from directly outside. At least two cars had skidded to a halt although Elora couldn't see them as the roller door was down. Reuben's body still slumped against it.

"I'll take the risk. Please." There was a deafening rattling sound as somebody attempted to force the door.

Bray regarded her coldly.

"Coming with me could still mean death," he warned.

The commotion at the front of the building grew louder. It sounded as if the police were using a battering ram. Angry voices could be heard yelling at anyone inside to open up.

"How are we going to get out? They've got us cornered," Elora pointed out.

"Always have an escape route. Now make your choice," said Bray coldly.

Elora preferred him as the mechanic. He seemed friendlier than this heartless Shaigun. Good-looking he may be, but he was harder than coffin nails.

"I'll take my chances with you."

He nodded once. "Follow me," he said, stepping passed her and going over to a man hole cover that was on the floor beneath the sink.

He pulled it up and slid it to the side revealing a circular black hole. Elora guessed it must be part of a drainage system but she couldn't see beyond its rim.

Without a second glance, Bray dropped into the hole. Elora waited for the sound of him landing but there was nothing. It seemed unreal as if he simply jumped into a silent vacuum in space. Could it be a vortex or something? A hidden gate between worlds. She doubted it as she stepped closer to the hole, but her vision still couldn't penetrate the blackness.

The roller door rattled again making her jump and she was sure she heard Reuben begin to murmur as if waking from unconsciousness. Time for a leap of faith. She edged closer so her toes were over the rim, folded her arms so she wouldn't bang them on the sides of the hole and readied herself to jump.

"Use the ladder. I'm not going to carry you if you break your legs," Bray said from the darkness below.

Elora bent down and could barely make out the dull grey metal of a rung, bolted half a foot below her. She wasted no time in lowering herself, putting one foot on the rung and climbing down. What an idiot she must have looked, about to jump blindly into the hole.

"And pull the cover back over," he ordered as she was a few rungs down.

"Yes sir," she whispered under her breath as she climbed back up to pull the cover back over and block the light out completely.

The rungs were cold and wet to the touch as she climbed down to the bottom, her feet splashing into what must be a stream of water less than an inch deep. It didn't smell like the sewers, more like a run-off for the drains that most likely fed into the sewer system someway ahead. She guessed they must be about ten feet below ground and was glad she used the ladder and didn't jump. It would more likely have been her neck that would have broken as well as her legs. How had Bray dropped down and landed in the water without making a sound?

The darkness was impenetrable, there wasn't even a sliver of light from the opening above and she wondered if Bray had left her alone to find her own way. Judging by his rudeness, she wouldn't be surprised.

She pressed the wall with the fingers of one hand whilst reaching out with the other, trying to build a mental image of her surroundings. The tunnel was circular with a diameter of about five foot, meaning that she would need to bend over to make her way along. That is, if the water level didn't get any deeper.

She took a few steps along the tunnel, her left hand trailing the one side, like the boy in the labyrinth of the Minotaur and having no idea if Bray was in front or at the end of the tunnel. He already proved how silent he could be, but she wasn't going to give him the satisfaction of seeing her ask for help and so plodded on determined to reach the end. She would show him she wasn't just a little girl with odd eyes.

After what must have been about ten minutes, yet seemed more like an hour, the tunnel walls abruptly ended, the hand trailing it meeting empty air and making her lose her balance. Almost about to topple over into the water, a hand grasped hers as it flailed wildly.

"Nearly there. Keep quiet," came Bray's voice from beside her.

She could feel his warm breath brushing her ear. Had he been that close the entire length of the tunnel? She squinted, trying desperately to see him through the blackness but failed. His hand felt warm and gave her reassurance as he pulled her down a different direction. She put out her other hand to the wall for guidance waiting for him to let go of her, but thankfully he held on and so she followed with a more confident stride.

Grey shadows slowly began to appear along the roof and she could make out the top of Bray as he walked in front, bending over so as not to bang his head. But it didn't stop her from walking straight into his back when he halted.

"Wait here," he said, then began to climb up a ladder to the side which she hadn't noticed.

A painfully bright crescent of light shone down as Bray scraped back a cover at the top of the shaft. A moment later and the crescent was a circle and she could see the silhouette of him climbing out. Then the shape of his head, his face hidden in darkness as it peered down again.

"Come on up."

6

Diavel

They emerged from the tunnel onto a street surrounded by red brick houses. The top of the tall grey silos of the dairy producer could be seen poking above the roofs of another street behind them, so Elora knew they were still close to the industrial estate, but at least they would be harder to find.

Bray didn't waste any time sliding the man hole cover back into place before leading her off down a path between the dwellings. Luckily there was nobody about to see the strange scene of the pair of them emerging out of the road.

The pathway led behind the street and across a back lane to a row of garages that must have belonged to the homes. Bray paced along the front of them until he reached one with a steel door. He unlocked a padlock and swung up the door before gesturing for her to enter, all the time scanning up the road for any signs they were being watched. Once inside he shut the door and flicked on a light.

Elora took in the small garage. A roll mat and sleeping bag lay unrolled on the floor – had Bray been sleeping in here? A large double-breasted wardrobe stood against the far wall with shelves clinging to either side. It appeared to be more of a bedroom than a garage, although the huge black motorbike standing in the middle and taking up most of the room, proved otherwise.

She had never seen a bike look so mean; with huge exhaust pipes and a rear tyre thicker than on most trucks. Ducati was spelt out in silver letters along the sleek fuel tank. It faced the wardrobe, leaning to the side and resting on a side stand that looked too thin to hold its weight.

"This is where you live?" she asked.

Bray shrugged "Sometimes," he replied as he stepped out of his rigger boots and pulled the boiler suit completely off revealing blue jeans. He tossed the suit over a chair and put the riggers back on. Then stretched his arms out. Elora heard a grating sound as Bray winced.

"What is it?" she asked.

"Think I've broke a rib," he replied as he wandered over to the wardrobe and pulled it open, revealing a mirror on the inside of the door.

He put his back to hers and pulled his t-shirt over his head. Elora found it hard to pull her eyes away from his muscled back as he lifted an arm and pressed a rib that was red and ready for bruises. She looked away before he caught her staring although he didn't seem to notice that she was even there. He pressed the injury a couple more times before taking a fresh t-shirt from the wardrobe and sliding it on.

"Is it broken?" she asked, knowing that if it was somebody the size of Pinky throwing punches then it probably was.

He nodded. "Nothing much I can do about it though. It'll heal by tomorrow."

Elora frowned. It would take more than a day for a rib to heal. More like several weeks, but didn't say anything. She sat on the chair and tried not to get oil from the boiler suit onto her vest and wished that she had brought her spare clothes from the *Molly* .

"So where's the Shadojak?" she asked, feeling anxious. Surely he wouldn't kill her, it wasn't as if she was dangerous although Nat had warned her that there were people searching, wanting to kill her. Maybe the Shadojak was one of them.

Bray leaned against his motorbike and folded his arms. He stared at her for a moment, making her feel on edge. Those big green eyes, deep as forest moss, sparkled with an intensity that made her want to shrink back into the chair. Eventually he spoke.

"He's out of the country. Should be back in the next day or two," he said.

"I thought you were his apprentice. Shouldn't you be with him?" she replied, wanting to look away from his stare but forcing herself not to do so. It was one thing to feel intimidated, it was another to act as such.

"Shaigun. And no, there was a task that needed to be done here."

"Judging?" she enquired sarcastically. But he ignored the question. This boy took his job far too seriously. Had he actually killed somebody before? She guessed he must have by the way he handled Reuben and his thugs. Maybe it was his line of work that made him so stern and rude.

"I need you to tell me everything that you know. Everything that has happened," he said.

She told him what she knew: that she was Minuan and that her uncle had brought her from Thea and it was the Shadojak that had helped them to hide in Britain. She told about the events of the previous day right up until she walked into his garage. Then a thought came to her. She took her uncle's journal from her pocket and handed it to him. He opened it and flicked through the pages before glancing up.

"I can't read this," he said, handing it back.

"Why? It's written in your language isn't it?"

Bray shook his head, "There is a common language on Thea that's spoken in the Empire and surrounding countries, but that's not it. I've never seen it before. The Minuans are a small group of people that keep themselves to themselves. I doubt even the Shadojak could decipher it."

"So who can?" she began, but Bray held his hand up to silence her. He cocked his head to the side as if listening to something although she couldn't hear anything other than the distant traffic.

"They've found us," he said. A moment later and she could make out the sirens of approaching police cars and the thudding of a helicopter.

"How could they know where we are?"

"You must have a tracker planted on you. It's the only way they would have found us so quickly."

77

Elora felt a wave of guilt wash over her, mixing with her rising panic as she struggled to come to terms with the thought that she had been bugged like something out of a spy movie.

"There's no point in leaving until we find the tracker and destroy it," he said as he wandered over to the garage door and double checked it was locked.

"I don't know what it looks like, even if I knew where it was," she said, rising from the seat.

"Think. Did they slip something into your pockets or pin something to your jacket? It could be as small as a coin or a card, anything.

"No. I changed my clothes after they had left ... wait a sec." She took out Mr Silk's business card from her pocket, "Reuben gave me this."

Bray snatched it and tore it in half, revealing a thin circuit inside. He crushed it in his hand before letting it drop to the floor.

"Now we can leave," he said, as the sirens arrived on the other side of the garage doors.

Too late, they're here," said Elora as the wriggly tin roof began to rattle with the down draft from the helicopter.

"Get on the bike," Bray said, as he opened the wardrobe up wide and retrieved a leather jacket. He threw it at her, "Put it on. And the helmet."

Elora slipped her arms into the thick biker's jacket, surprised at how heavy it felt as she struggled to swing her leg over the huge bike. She was afraid the whole thing might topple over as she struggled to find somewhere to place her feet, yet the bike didn't budge. Taking the helmet, she pushed it down on her head. Immediately her breath fogged the visor up so she flipped it open. Surely he didn't expect her to ride the bike, she worried.

The door suddenly rattled as somebody tried to get in. She couldn't guess what Bray had in mind. But wished he would hurry up about it.

"Open up," came a voice from outside, having to shout to be heard above the noise of the helicopter. It wouldn't be long before they came in; the door wasn't that strong.

Bray swung his long leg over the bike, forcing her to shuffle back yet the shape of the seat caused her to slide down against him.

"You ever been on a bike before?" he asked, as he pushed a pair of sunglasses on.

"No, never," replied Elora, who wondered why he didn't have a helmet. Maybe there was only one and he felt that she had more chance of banging her head. He was probably right – motorbikes were scary.

"It's simple: lean with me, not the bike he explained as he pressed the ignition and fired the engine. He gave a twist of the throttle and the roar hurt her ears. "And don't fall off," he added, kicking the stand away and letting the clutch out.

Elora yelped as she flung her arms around Bray's waist. The huge rear tyre squealed as it spun, causing dark plumes of smoke to engulf the back of the garage. She felt her body pull back with inertia as the bike surged forwards. Tightening her grip around Bray, she locked her arms together as he gunned the bike straight at the open wardrobe.

Where was he taking her, Narnia?

Elora shut her eyes and braced for an impact yet all she felt was a thump as the bike dropped down suddenly whilst the smashing of splintering wood reached her ears.

They'd driven through a false wall made of thin plywood and were now accelerating down a narrow alley that ran behind the garages. They travelled so fast that the wall beside her appeared to be a red blur, the single bricks and mortar becoming one as the bike headed to a dead end.

Her body was suddenly flung forwards, her chest crushing into Bray's solid back as he harshly applied the brakes. She fought not to close her eyes as the wheels locked up, Bray leaned hard to the left and the back wheel skidded around. She leaned her body with his, as he had instructed, putting her trust fully into his ability to handle the powerful machine. The bike skidded sideways, almost parallel to the wall they headed for and now faced a side street. Her mind had only just taken in the details of the road ahead when her body was flung back once again, the bike lunging forwards, tearing from the alley like a ball from a cannon.

The alley fed into a busy street and Bray didn't pause to check for crossing traffic, instead pushing the bike on blindly and narrowly missing a passing bus as he cut across two lanes and turned them into traffic heading away from the city.

They accelerated along the white line that separated the lanes, Elora squeezing her knees as far into Bray as she could, fearing that they might clip the cars to either side which they passed as if they were standing still.

Hurtling passed a large glass building Elora caught the reflection of the black helicopter that had caught them up. She couldn't hear it above the noise of the motorbike but knew they had little chance of escaping its sights.

They were going so fast now that the cars around them appeared to be going backwards. If one decided to change lanes at the wrong moment they would hit it like a torpedo, probably killing those inside the vehicle as well as themselves. She gripped tighter but couldn't take her gaze from the way ahead. Further up was a junction, the traffic lights glowing red and the cars they passed began to slow down.

The shadow of the helicopter suddenly passed over them, she realised it had pushed ahead to cut them off as they slowed for the traffic lights. Yet, as they approached Bray kept his hand firmly on the throttle, their speed a constant suicide cruise.

Elora felt an involuntary scream rising from her chest as they cut across the junction, passing between a white van and a truck in a gap barely wide enough for the bike. The helicopter descended low enough for her to see a man leaning out of a side door, rifle tucked into his shoulder as he a prepared to take a shot, but they were moving too fast for him and rode beneath the helicopter before the pilot had time to react.

The way ahead was clear and Bray squeezed more speed from the bike, leaning hard into bends that would barely have been noticed if travelling at a normal pace. A second later and she was thrown into his back again as he braked. The front of the bike dipping down and her chest crushing the air from her lungs. He leaned hard right, almost bringing her knees into contact with the road before accelerating again down another side street.

Above, the helicopter banked with them and she could feel the eyes of the gunman as he stared down his scope. Bray's erratic manoeuvres were the only thing stopping her from being shot.

Bray swerved the bike suddenly, decelerating as he turned towards the pavement and mounted the curb, going straight over and down a set of concrete steps. The bike took the shock hard and Elora's teeth crashed together as it bottomed out before Bray twisted the throttle again, racing them along a narrow footpath that cut through a park.

Reaching the park exit, Bray slid the bike again so when they were out they were already facing down the road and she was thrown back once again, holding tight around him to keep herself from toppling off.

Racing on they came to a large roundabout that connected with the M25, they leaned over as they went around then rocketed down a slip road to join the motorway. Elora only registered that they were heading into oncoming traffic as her gaze fell onto the huge grill of an articulated lorry.

They swerved between it and a car, cutting between lanes amongst startled drivers and leaving them in a chorus of horn blasts. She wondered what Bray was doing when her gaze fell on what was ahead. They were about to enter the Dartmouth tunnel.

The wide mouth of the tunnel swallowed them as they drove into the oncoming traffic. Elora noticed that a line of curved tiles that made up the tunnel walls, had begun to pop and explode beside her and realised that the gunman, in a last desperate effort to stop them, was shooting.

Every shot missed, but she had little time to dwell on it as once again the Ducati's tyres locked up and she was squashed up against Bray's body. He dragged his left foot on the floor and did a 180-degree spin so they were now facing back towards the tunnel entrance; or exit, now that they were heading in the right direction of travel.

He waited a moment, revving the engine but not releasing the clutch.

"You alright?" he shouted over his shoulder.

"I'm still alive."

He let go the clutch causing the back tyre to squeal. They emerged back into daylight, leaving the safety of the tunnel. She expected the helicopter to be hovering above, waiting for them to appear.

"Where's it gone?" she shouted through the helmet, unsure if Bray could even hear her over the roar of the engine.

He tilted his head to the side, checking in the wing mirror. "It went ahead to the other side of the Thames. They expect to ambush us when we come out."

Elora's shoulders let go a little of the tension she had being feeling as the pursuit carried on. But it didn't effect Bray who accelerated back up to top speed. She guessed if they carried on like this it wouldn't be long before they got far enough away from their pursuers that they'd be safe. Yet it seemed Bray had other plans.

He steered the bike down the next junction and powered around the roundabout and headed down a country road that was signposted for Epping Forest. A moment later he slowed and took a detour down a bumpy lane that had once being made of tarmac but was now mainly potholes and mud. The back wheel of the bike tried to spin every chance it got, the tyres too slick for this kind of terrain, yet somehow Bray kept them upright and riding at a terrifying speed.

The lane ended at a field which contained a large wooden hay barn and stables. Two chestnut coloured mares lifted their heads to regard them curiously. Bray stopped the bike at the steel gate that led to the field.

"Open it," he ordered.

Cramp threatened her inner thighs as she swung her leg off the bike before hobbling over to the gate. Lifting the rope over the post she gave the gate a shove inwards and closed it again after Bray rode the bike through. Then went to join him in the barn.

"What now?" she asked, removing the helmet and letting her dark hair fall.

Bray was busy pulling an old horse rug over the bike, his back to her.

"We need a new ride. This one's been compromised and it's too risky to stay."

Elora watched him move to the open door and search the sky.

"They're back in the air. Will most likely follow the motor-way for a while, thinking we tried to make a clean get away. He turned back to her, removing the sunglasses and hung them from the neck of his t-shirt. "We need to go back into the city."

"Why?"

"I need to get you to a safe house. If this takwich has people in the police, he'll have them scouring all exits out of the area. He may even have the CCTV's monitored too. We need to be careful. And we need to keep moving before they work out what we've done and head back."

He scanned the air a second time then gestured for her to follow as he set off jogging across the field. By the time she caught up with him he was through it and waiting for her beneath tall conifers that skirted the lane. She no sooner joined him than he took off again. Sweat had already begun to stick her vest to her back, the heavy leather jacket didn't help as she tried to match Bray's pace. Yet he seemed to speed up, hugging the tree line and rolling over the uneven ground as smoothly as a cat, where she felt cumbersome, bounding on behind him, her feet finding every hole and tree root whilst her face found the thin branches.

At the end of the lane was a bus stop, Bray was leaning against the post studying the times printed on the wall as she arrived, out of breath. He checked his watch then gazed down the road as a red double-decker bus rounded the corner.

"Right on time," he said, then looped his arm through hers as he held out his other to stop the bus. Then under his breath muttered, "Calm your breathing. You're going to get the driver wondering what we've being up to down this quiet country lane. And put these on." He handed her his sunglasses.

Elora felt her face redden as she slipped them on, thinking about his words as the bus pulled in and the door swung open. She let herself be pulled aboard as she tried to control her breathing, but the more she tried the worse it got. She really needed to get fitter.

She was relieved when Bray paid their fares and led them to a seat near the rear of the bus although they could have sat on any of the seats as it was empty. He sat beside the window and surprised her by putting an arm over her shoulder, pulling her close to him. He leaned in closer, putting his mouth towards her cheek as if leaning in for a kiss.

Elora's body went rigid, her eyebrows came together as she struggled to comprehend his intentions.

"We need the driver to think we're lovers." His breath was warm against her ear.

Her mouth fell open.

"You mean, like boyfriend–girlfriend?" His lips tenderly brushed against her cheek and she felt her face flush.

"Sooner or later they'll find the bike and track our movements to the bus stop. They'll interview the driver. But instead of picking up a pair of panicked looking individuals, one of which had violet eyes, the other badly riddled with acne, he picked up a couple who hadn't a care in the world but each other. With any luck he'll have forgotten us completely."

"Oh," was all she could think of saying as he relaxed back into the seat, pulling her in close. She rested her head on his shoulder and gazed out of the window, watching the black dot of the helicopter hovering above the motorway and trying not to think about the close contact with Bray.

For some strange reason it gave her butterflies in her stomach, a phrase which she had never understood until now. But why him? She'd had a couple of boyfriends before; nothing solid, just a bit of fun and her temper usually put an end to the relationship. This feeling she was experiencing with Bray was something new and she had only known him for the last couple of chaotic hours. Unless it was the fact that he had saved her life at least twice. Probably that and the fact that he was the most gorgeous boy she had ever seen.

Without realising it she found that her gaze had slipped to his face as he stared out of the window and was glad she was wearing his sunglasses. It wouldn't be too hard to act like they were lovers.

Half an hour later they disembarked the bus holding hands. Their fingers interlaced as Bray led her along a busy street to a parked taxi. He opened the door for her to climb in.

"Enfield, please mate," Bray said, using his London accent once again. The driver nodded, barely giving them a second glance before pulling out onto the road.

Elora turned to Bray, about to ask him what was at Enfield when he stole the words from her mouth by kissing her on the lips.

The movement was so sudden and unexpected that her mouth was still open and he ended up kissing her teeth. She felt an overwhelming wave of embarrassment as he chuckled, putting an easy arm around her.

"Relax. There's nobody following," he said.

Elora nodded and forced a smile. "I'll relax when my uncle is safe."

After Bray paid the driver they set off walking down a high street full of betting shops, off licences and closed takeaways. The majority of people they passed were Asian and didn't give them the slightest acknowledgement. At the end of the row of shops was another bus stop and Bray picked up the pace to catch the red lion bus before it departed.

The driver was about to set off but noticed them at the last moment and let them on. Bray paid once again and led them to the only available seats, passing a couple of female college students whose eyes widened as they watched him squeeze by.

As the bus joined the traffic they kept glancing at his reflection in the window and whispered to one another, giggling. Elora couldn't help but feel a pang of jealousy. She narrowed her eyes at them; didn't they see that he had a girlfriend? Even if it was only pretend. Leaning in close she pulled his face towards hers before planting a kiss on his lips and holding it longer than she had intended.

Bray seemed surprised at first but he kissed her back and smiled when she pulled away. Her eyes went back to the students whose expressions took on a sullen quality. They got off two stops later but not before one of them turned to give Bray a smile, all white teeth and makeup. Elora thought she was attractive and fully expected Bray to smile back but instead he looked the girl up and down indifferently. The girl, at seeing his reaction, stormed off the bus to join her friend. Elora couldn't help but feel a tinge of satisfaction as he leaned into her and gave her another kiss. This one more passionate than before. It left her feeling breathless, her heart thumping in her chest, she had to remind herself that it was only pretend. The girls glanced at them as the bus passed and Bray chuckled making her laugh too.

They got off the bus at the next stop at a more residential part of London although Elora couldn't guess where they were, apart from it was somewhere towards the north of the city.

Bray led her through housing estate after housing estate, each one looking like the other. A labyrinth of red brick and pavements. Yet Bray led the way as easily as if he had lived here all his life, although his accent told otherwise, that was if his accent wasn't another act.

Eventually the well cared for properties began to look a little tired as they progressed. The high-end German cars parked on well-kept drives giving way to dated run-arounds squeezed together on the road. The occasional shop changing from a Waitrose or wine shop to a corner shop or bookies.

As the sun began to sink below the roofs of a block of flats they turned down a dimly lit road where there were no cars parked, or shops or even signs of life. Bray led her to the end block of terraces that were set slightly back from the rest. The street lamps were unlit and cast no light into the shadows that seemed to consume the buildings.

He turned down the garden path to the middle house, its gate hung on one hinge, the wood rotted. The front lawn was overgrown, the grass gone to hay and poking through the cracks in the stone path. An ancient willow loomed over them, forcing her to duck low to avoid being whipped in the face and as she cast her face aside she noticed that a cellar window had been smashed through and was boarded up. Like the majority of houses on the road, the place seemed derelict and unfit for human habitation. So Elora was surprised when Bray knocked heavily on the front door.

7

Gurple

As they waited under the canopy of a porch, its paint peeled back and blistered, Elora noticed that she couldn't hear anything from the houses around: no televisions, nobody chatting or music and nothing to indicate that there were people living in the street. It gave the area an ominous quality. She shuffled closer to Bray, expecting him to place his arm over her but he didn't. So the pretence of boyfriend–girlfriend was now over.

What had she been expecting? That they carry on the facade even when there was nobody about and now that she glanced at him, his face in shadow, she could see that his features returned to being stern. It brought back the loneliness she had felt since Nat's kidnapping.

Folding her arms, she stepped away from him, acting like she didn't care but feeling the opposite. He was a cold hard killer, she reminded herself. He slipped on different faces and changed personalities like a schizophrenic chameleon. He was probably incapable of feeling affection towards others.

A pale face suddenly appeared on the other side of the door's frosted window, staring at them briefly before a bolt was slid back. The door swung in until stopped by a thick chain, an angular face with thick cheek bones peered through the gap. He regarded her accusingly before he turned his attention to Bray and his face broke into a warm smile.

"Now there's a sight for sore eyes," the man said as he slid the safety chain off the door and swung it open.

He was tall with narrow shoulders, dressed in khaki trousers and vest with a thick tartan dressing gown tied loosely over the top. He was of an age with her uncle yet his face appeared more weathered as if he spent most of his life outdoors.

"Norgie," Bray said and gave a single nod as he stepped into the house leaving her outside on the door step.

The other man shook his head and chuckled.

"Shaigun he may be, but that lad's got less manners than a hermit crab. Come on in lass, don't dawdle out there on the step. We don't want too much of the darkness coming in."

Elora stepped through into the already dark hallway wondering how the darkness from outside could possibly follow her in.

The door closed behind her and the man turned on a lamp, filling the gloom with light. A fine dark mist, she hadn't noticed until the light came on, began to slowly sink to the floor, curling around her ankles as it drifted under the door. She wouldn't have believed what she saw until the man remarked.

"That damned darkness always tries to get in every time I open the door. It's supposed to be gloomy outside, not in here."

"It's there for a reason. You'd soon miss its protection if it went," said Bray.

"Most probably you're right but it doesn't stop my knees from aching, it gives me the chill." He gave Elora a wink. "What's your name then love?"

"Elora," said Bray before she had chance to answer herself. "She'll be here until Diagus comes back. Then … " He shrugged his shoulders. "Is Prince Dylap in?"

"Yep. He's been hanging about down there for the last week or so. He's got his little knickers in a right twist over something," answered the man as he removed a chain from around his neck and handed it to Bray. The chain had an old iron key attached to it.

Bray took the chain and without giving her a second glance descended down a dark staircase that led from an opening to the left. Elora watched him leave and shook her head.

"Don't take it personally love, he's like that with everybody. He's got a hard job; it makes a hard man. But I think his heart's in the right place. I just wouldn't say it to his face." He smiled at her and held out his hand. "I'm Norgie."

She shook it, "Elora."

"Let's get you settled in. Are you hungry?"

"Starved," she answered, having not eaten anything since yesterday's dinner.

"Good, we've got plenty in the kitchen. Hope you like roast lamb," he said, taking her by the arm and leading her down the dusty hallway.

She looked at the floor again as a final wisp of the strange black mist curled into the letterbox and disappeared.

"What was that black smoke that followed us in? I've never seen anything like it before," she asked, taking in the rest of the house. At one time it had been a proper home with rich furnishings and a feminine decor. Even the tiles on the floor had, at one time, an elaborate pattern but was now missing more than a few tiles. Still, it was clean, which was more than could be said from the outside.

"Don't know what it's called. It's something the fairies have done with the place. Makes it so people don't want to come too close. Kind of freaks them out and they go back the way they came."

"Fairies?" Elora raised an eyebrow.

They arrived at the kitchen door and Norgie was about to twist the brass knob when he paused.

"How much do you know? I mean, I take it those eyes of yours aren't contacts, so I'm guessing you're not Earth-born."

Elora shook her head "Apparently I was born on Thea."

"And you've only recently found that fact out. Talk about baptism by fire. Thought I might have let the cat out of the bag and gone blathering to an Earth-born, but … well, Bray wouldn't have brought you here if he didn't trust you."

"So you're not from Thea either?"

"No, I'm from Yorkshire. Only got myself tangled up with all this stuff by accident. Now I live here, kind of a caretaker."

"But fairies actually exist?"

Norgie nodded. "Come on, let me introduce you to Gurple."

He pushed the door open and ushered her into a cosy kitchen, the smell of freshly roasted lamb, mint and vegetables tickled her nostrils, causing her belly to cramp up in anticipation.

Thick gravy simmering in a saucepan sat atop a hob on an iron Aga; cabbage and chopped carrots boiled beside it, the steam drifting towards an open sash window above a Belfast sink. An oak table took up the left portion of the kitchen with seats enough for six but only two plates and two sets of cutlery were laid out.

"Gurple? I told you to keep stirring the gravy. It'll stick to the bottom of the pan," said Norgie to the empty kitchen. "Come on out, she won't harm you."

"I don't see anybody," Elora said as she glanced beneath the table: about the only place in the kitchen to hide.

"Gurple's in here. It's just that he gets a bit shy," Norgie put his hands on his hips. "Come on out, Gurple."

Elora heard the clattering of metal pans and trays from inside a cupboard. Then the door slowly crept open and swung towards her. A pair of feet, as small as a toddler's, – but covered in dark brown fur, appeared beneath the door and childlike hands with the same pelt grasped the top, sharp black nails digging into the wood.

"That's better Gurple. Now say hello to the young lady," said Norgie encouragingly.

Pointy ears slowly rose above the cupboard door, like that of a koala bear but dark brown instead of grey. Then the top of a head appeared, followed by large brown eyes that stared at her, showing signs of fear. Slowly its eyes softened and it shuffled from behind the door until it was fully revealed. It was roughly the size and shape of a four-year-old child, but there the similarities ended. The large brown eyes sat above a dark flat nose surrounded by wrinkles that formed around a large mouth. Elora thought it had a kind of a pug quality: ugly but in a cute sort of way. Brown fur seemed to cover its entire body although she couldn't see beneath the denim dungarees it wore. She couldn't decide if it was a type of bear, dog or hobbit. Perhaps a strange mixture of the three yet she was even more astonished when it spoke.

"Herro," it said gruffly.

"Hi," she replied awkwardly, not entirely sure if it could understand her.

He stared at her a moment as if unsure, like a frightened puppy, his huge brown eyes regarding her with trepidation. He sniffed the air and shuffled closer. She put out her open hand towards him, inviting him to take a sniff, showing that she meant him no harm. "It's ok" she encouraged. "I won't hurt you."

He frowned causing the wrinkles on his face to furrow even deeper, then opened his mouth wide in what Elora thought might be a smile and placed his small furry hand on hers.

"Erora," he said and grinned, his large canine teeth protruding either side of his mouth.

"Elora," she corrected, pronouncing her name slowly.

Gurple nodded enthusiastically. "Erora."

"Come on now Gurple, let's finish off the dinner and lay the table for our extra guest," said Norgie. "Might have to do with burnt gravy, though."

Elora watched Gurple's ears droop as he turned to look at the pan he should have been watching. "I like gravy with a bit of a burnt taste – adds flavour," she said and smiled as Gurple's ears pricked back up. Then to Norgie she said "We'll need two extra places making up, one for me, the other for Bray."

Norgie shook his head. "He'll be talking to Prince Dylap until the early hours most likely. We'll plate him a dinner and he can have his later."

Elora wondered who this Prince Dylap was and if she was ever going to meet him but didn't ask anymore questions. Her belly was cramping for food and she didn't want to delay the dinner anymore.

<hr />

ooooooooooooooooooooo

Bray left the dark cellar and locked the heavy door behind him. He felt weary as he climbed the stairs but years of harsh training ensured that he still moved in silence. Instinctively his feet touched the parts of the steps that were less likely to creak whilst his mind worried over the grisly task ahead of him.

Prince Dylap had warned that there was an extreme unbalance between Thea, Earth and even a shift in the Shadowlands; the likes of which hadn't been witnessed since the great rift which split the worlds. And he would have greater knowledge than any other, being the only creature who could freely move between them. Something had happened which had started a change, a catalyst of some kind, the starting of the end. Elora's appearance couldn't have been merely coincidental, things had been in balance since the time of the small gods, hundreds of thousands of years ago and he believed she was the catalyst. That might explain the reason how the bulworg had arrived. If the barrier that separated the worlds was becoming unstable then all kinds of nasties could be coming through. He also worried about the lack of communication with the Shadojak.

Diagus wasn't the best at handling the technologies of this world and he may have broken his mobile phone again. The Shadojak was on the western coast of Ireland, investigating the strange sightings of a huge sea-beast that had apparently destroyed a North Sea oil tanker and pulled it beneath the waves. A handful of survivors had reportedly told the coast guard that a gigantic creature had wrapped octopus-like tentacles around the ship, crushing the hull and foredeck before pulling the vessel and crew into a watery grave. The descriptions they gave of the monster were uncannily like a leviathan of Thea. A fearsome creature of the deep oceans, created by older gods for their ability to sing under water. He had never seen one himself, but Diagus had. His master doubted that what the survivors witnessed was such a creature as the leviathan, yet it was his duty to find the truth of it. He'd left three days ago and Bray thought he would have been back by now.

The hallway was in darkness, the only light flickered through the bottom of the lounge door where somebody was watching the television. He guessed it to be Elora as he could hear the tuneless humming of Norgie coming from the kitchen.

His hand hovered above the door handle, his mind set at what he must do. Best to do it quick, no suffering, no pain. He resolved his mind to the task and as he pushed the handle down the kitchen door suddenly swung open. Norgie's tall body silhouetted against the light, dark features regarding him.

"Come grab your dinner before it gets cold, Bray. I can't reheat it a second time."

Bray's hand dropped by his side, his resolve to do the task evaporating in an instant. If he was true to himself, he had realised that he was glad for the distraction. But he didn't want to believe that, for if that was the fact then he was losing his grip on his emotions and that would stray him from his path to become the Shadojak.

Briefly he glanced at the door handle, the silver plating long ago tarnished by wear and fracturing the reflection of light from the kitchen. Then drew his eyes away, it wouldn't hurt any to delay the task while he had something to eat.

Stalking passed Norgie into the kitchen, he took a glass from the sideboard and filled it with water before sitting at the table.

"Nice girl, that Elora," offered Norgie as he closed the door and took a chair opposite him.

Bray didn't answer, his attention diverted to cutting up the meat.

"Gurple's taken a bit of a shine to her too," continued the old man. "Think she needs a friend right now, though. It can't be easy; you know, what she's gone through."

Bray could feel him staring at him as he stirred the fork of meat into the gravy and wished he would shut up. He was in no mood to talk and most certainly didn't want to discuss the girl. But his wishes were rarely granted and Norgie wasn't about to break the tradition.

"Poor lass. A good night's sleep is what she needs. She's dog tired but insists on staying up until you had finished your business with Prince Dylap. She wants to speak with you."

Bray put the fork in his mouth and forced himself to chew, his appetite lost before he even swallowed.

"Might do you both some good, you know, to chat. You're both about the same age."

Bray dropped the fork on the plate. "What makes you think I need to chat?" he said, coldly.

Norgie scratched his head and finally glanced away. "Well, it's just. In your line of work." Bray glared at him, willing him to stop. "You know, judging people; all that killing. It's got to play on your mind hasn't it?"

"Does the sea care when it drowns a sailor? Does fire need to talk after burning a village? Will a sword shed a tear after taking a husband, a father, mother or child?"

Norgie shook his head. "They don't think or mull things over. And a sword is simply a tool, an inanimate object until somebody picks it up. They don't have feelings."

"I'm a Shaigun. I don't have feelings," he said, keeping his tone level although wanting to scream it at the old man.

"That's not true Bray," argued the caretaker as he rose from his chair and wandered to the oven, taking a pan from a cupboard and pouring milk into it before placing it on the hob. "What about Gurple? Diagus ordered you to kill him, didn't he? If you were just his tool and had no feelings, he wouldn't be breathing now."

"His judgment was that he couldn't be seen by human eyes. Is that not what has happened?"

"You know how the Shadojak works. If it can't be sent back it must be terminated. Don't tell me you didn't persuade him to let Gurple stay here with me. I was there, remember? I saw the look in your eyes when he told you to kill him."

Bray remembered it well. They'd found Gurple in a skip outside a supermarket; cold, scared and alone. His fur was matted and stained with the rotten food he had been living off. It had been pity he had felt for the defenseless creature. But their orders were simple. Terminate anything that didn't belong. They had killed many beasts and nasties that had penetrated the barrier. Judging, executing and sparing only the very few that were of some use. And hadn't he done some dark tasks even before becoming a Shaigun?

There were reasons he was trained to suppress feelings, becoming like the wind passing through a village, empty and uncaring. That's what it was to be Shaigun, to be Shadojak. Yet he had suggested that Gurple, a harmless wood troll, could serve his life out with Norgie. Aiding him with keeping the house secure and stocked with supplies. He had expected Diagus to disagree with his suggestion, but thought he caught a softness to the Shadojak's good eye. His other was dead, a pure white pearl that replaced the eye that had been torn out in a long ago fight.

The Pearly White was a name he had heard whispered about the barracks as he grew up. A name to put fear into young boys that misbehaved or threats to new recruits that if they didn't look sharp they'd have the stare of the Pearly White upon them. A threat that would bestow a coldness to the blood and dread in the heart. He had felt the stare himself plenty of times after becoming Shaigun to him, yet came to realise that there was a gentleness to the man beyond the blind pearl and it had shown that day when he relented to his wishes. Maybe there was something to Norgie's words then. But could he afford to delay her judgement until Diagus returned? Prince Dylap didn't think so. There was a link between Elora and the ever weakening barrier and there could only be one outcome, one judgment.

A painful gasp from Norgie brought Bray out of his contemplation as he watched the old man splash himself with boiling milk.

"Damn it. That's the second time I've done that today," said Norgie, running his wrist under the cold tap. "I'm getting too bloody old."

The act wasn't lost on Bray as he watched a bead of hot milk trail down the front of the iron Aga. He had seen that pattern somewhere before, but it hadn't been milk.

"She can't live here Norgie. The reasons go beyond your knowledge but she must be judged and soon. And you're not so old that you can't clean up after your accidents."

Norgie's brow raised. "Will you not wait until Diagus returns? Give the poor girl a chance."

"If Diagus was here she would be dead already. No. It has to be soon, has to be this evening." Bray turned his gaze from the spilt milk.

Softly, Norgie's voice eased from the sink. "For a Shaigun that doesn't feel, your fist is clenched tight enough."

Bray looked at his fist, the knuckles turned bone white and willed himself to open his fingers. He spread them on the table and pushed himself up. Once you've made up your mind to do a difficult task, you simply had to act it out.

He reached the door before Norgie's hand fell on his shoulder.

"Give her this," he said, putting a steaming mug of hot chocolate in his hand. "And don't do anything that can't be undone. You may come to regret it later." Bray didn't reply as he left the kitchen, closing the door behind him.

The door to the living room swung open with an ominous creak, the noise startling Gurple who had been curled up at Elora's bare feet. She appeared fresher, having taken a shower, her dark hair hanging loose to her shoulders and now dressed in a pair of his jeans and an old shirt. Norgie would have found these for her earlier.

The wood troll regarded him suspiciously as he entered the softly lit room, his eyes following him to the fireplace where he took the poker in hand and pushed the glowing coals about.

"It's time for bed, Gurple," he said, throwing a log onto the coals and sending a burst of sparks up the chimney. Gurple sat up, rubbing a paw over his wrinkled face.

"Stay," he grumbled.

Bray put the poker back on its stand and tickled the troll behind his ear, making him lean against his hand, a grin spreading wide in pleasure and showing his large sharp teeth.

"No Gurple. It really is time for bed," he said, adding more authority to his voice. Gurple reluctantly rose and gave Elora's leg a squeeze before wandering across the room.

"Goodnight Gurple, pleasant dreams," said Elora as Gurple closed the door behind him. Then her deep violet eyes rolled to him, narrowing with mistrust. Bray saw the flames reflected in those eyes and realised that they shone with fury. "Is that hot chocolate for me?"

He nodded, feeling a pang of uneasiness under her gaze and held the mug out for her to take, turning it around so she may take it handle first so as not to burn herself.

She took it, but didn't drink. "So are you going to kill me now?" she asked, flatly.

The question took him off guard and he took a step back feeling the tinge of shame burning through him. Had he come in here to kill her? Only a few moments ago he would have said yes. But now, here, stood in front of her, he realised he wouldn't go through with it but had no inkling as to why. Maybe it was Norgie's words "don't do what can't be undone", or maybe it wasn't. Just a certainty that it wouldn't happen. He was as sure as the emotions that he had been feeling earlier in the day. Feelings he had suppressed for a long time and that had been sparked somehow by the girl in front of him.

"No," he finally answered.

"So this isn't poisoned?"

He shook his head no. And when she still didn't drink he knelt down and placing his hands around hers, he raised them and guided the mug to his own lips and swallowed a mouthful of the hot chocolate. Her gaze never once left him, the fire it held didn't diminish as he leaned away from her, feeling an awkwardness at the close contact.

She lowered the mug so it was resting on her lap, still not committing herself to take a drink. And now that he observed her he could feel what her intentions were: the heels of her feet tucked underneath, pressing against the legs of the chair, her feet bent, toes going white against the oak floor poised to strike. Elbows bent and hands grasping the mug of hot liquid, ready to fling it at him. Bray grinned. This girl was a fighter, even though she could probably guess that she was no match for him in combat, she would go down fighting, struggling to the bitter end.

"Why are you grinning, killer?" Elora asked him, her voice sharp and icy.

"You've been talking to Norgie haven't you?" And he could tell by the giveaway twitch to the corner of her mouth that he was right. "What did the old guy say?"

She took a sip from the mug, gently blowing the steam away before putting it to her lips. Bray rocked back onto the balls of his feet, ready to spring back should she decide to hurl it at him.

"That you're a killer. An assassin apprentice who will murder people without feeling guilt, without remorse. And that you haven't the capacity to feel any emotion. A cold, heartless killer. Am I wrong?"

"No," he answered, not seeing any reason to lie. Yet he felt ashamed for admitting what he was to her. Who was she to him, to a Shaigun? Why did he care what she thought about him? "Elora, I won't kill you."

"You will if the Shadojak orders it," she said, then averted her eyes to the fire, the log snapped and crackled, filling the silence. What could he reply to that fact when it was true.

"Then why stay. You could have left when I was in the cellar?"

"Because Silk still has my uncle and you're the only hope of him being freed." Her shoulders dropped as she relaxed back into the chair. "I will forfeit my life for his."

Bray studied her intently as she blew on the steam rising from the hot chocolate before drinking it down and laying the empty mug on a side-stand. She meant every word she said. Giving her life for that of her uncle, even though his would probably be met with the same outcome as hers once the Shadojak judged him. These were not the actions of a dangerous being yet that was what she was. Dangerous. Was she telling the truth when she told him she didn't know what was going on?

"You look tired; you need to sleep," he said.

Elora sat up. "I can't sleep. Not while my uncle is still imprisoned," she said whilst stifling a yawn.

"The Shadojak will be back soon, maybe tomorrow. I can't act until he returns. But I can find Silk and where he's keeping your uncle."

"Take me with you," she blurted out, getting ready to stand. Bray put a hand on her knee to make her stay seated.

"No, it's too dangerous," he said, but really meant that she would slow him down and be a hindrance.

"Please. I can't stay here. I won't sleep."

Bray didn't reply but moved closer, gently placing his hands to either side of her face and tenderly stroked her cheeks with his thumb. Her violet eyes gazed at him with what appeared to be shock and he could sense her heart quicken in fright.

"What are you doing?" she asked, placing her own hands upon his but not applying any pressure to remove them.

He gently shushed her, letting a thumb stray over her delicate lips, the other hand lowering, his fingers tracing over her jawline to rest upon the nape of her neck; feeling the rapid but steady beat of her heart as it pulsed through the artery beneath her soft skin.

Her onyx pupils dilated as her gaze fell to his lips, teeth biting her bottom lip, her face an expression of confused wanting.

Bray brought his face closer, their noses almost touching, her pulse quickening, beating harder against his fingers – then he tapped the artery at the nerve junction with his index finger, forcing her heart's rhythm to double-beat and she fainted.

Her head dropped forwards onto his shoulder as she slumped against him. Gently he picked her up off the chair and settled her on the leather sofa, placing a cushion beneath her head and putting a blanket over her. She would sleep now until her body was fully rested. Most likely until midday tomorrow.

He stared at her for a moment, listening to her gentle breathing, her face looking relaxed and innocent. She was beautiful. He had a strange impulse to kiss her. Even taking a step towards her, but thought better of it and strode purposefully to the door. He had work to do.

8

Spliceck

Reuben felt uncomfortable as he waited in Mr Silk's reception room and not only because of the hard leather chair, or the fact that his body felt battered and bruised, especially his face. No, there was an uneasiness to the vast but simplistic room, with modern glass, chrome and plastic furniture that put him on edge.

The hairs on the back of his neck prickled, his palms sweated and his body was on the alert, ready for flight or fight. He was in crap, as deep as this glass building was tall and couldn't take an easy way out. At least he still had his gun, holstered beneath his blood stained suit, cocked and readied.

Leather creaked, echoing around the silent room as he sat back, rubbing his temple and wishing his headache away. It throbbed like a bitch. Pulsing pressure behind his blackened eyes, the result of a head-butt that had broken his nose. That skinny little prick with the boil and acne had done him over royally. An easy mark, caught up in Pinky's grasp and pleading for his life. He couldn't quite remember how the mechanic moved – it was a blur. All he recalled after flicking his lucky coin was the huge mass of Pinky's body being spun over in the air, his gun going off and the boy's face in front of his, giving him a wink before the lights went out.

His next recollection was of being helped to his feet by a copper and worrying that he was going to be arrested for the possession of his gun. He'd been surprised when the copper handed him his gun back and told him to wait in the cruiser outside. From the police car he watched an ambulance arrive and the unconscious bodies of Pinky and Kitch get stretchered to the back before it departed for the hospital. When the copper returned to the car, he asked if they could follow the ambulance to the hospital but was told to be quiet.

The copper answered a call from his phone, speaking in the creepy clicks and clacks that Mr Silk used before hanging up and staring at him in the rear-view mirror.

"You will come with me. You've an appointment with Mr Silk," he said harshly, the corner of his lip curling in a sly grin. Reuben didn't argue.

That had happened hours ago and he had been in this soulless reception room ever since. The only company was an attractive receptionist who sat at a desk watching monitors. Reuben guessed they were fed live feeds from security cameras around the building. Her gaze only left the screens to bear him with a stern glance now and again before returning to her vigil. She had greater discipline than any security guard or soldier Reuben had ever known.

When he couldn't stand the pain in his head anymore he approached her.

"Hello darling. I don't suppose you know when Mr Silk wants me up there do you?"

She looked him up and down, her face taking on a pinched expression at the sight of him and not hiding the fact that he was distracting her from her job. He had to admit he must look a picture with a blood stained suit, twin black eyes and a broken nose but she was just a receptionist for God's sake. Attractive maybe, but he had met better and thought himself well above her league. That was before his face got messed up. If he ever got his hands on that prick mechanic, he would carve his nose off.

"He will see you when he is ready," she said, narrowing her eyes as she glanced at his hand that was resting upon the desk and invading her space. Reuben put it in his pocket.

"I don't suppose you have any painkillers behind your desk? I've a headache that would drop an elephant."

"No."

"What about a drink? Something with alcohol. At least that might numb the pain a bit."

"No." Her tone was cold and dispassionate.

"Really? You're telling me that there's no tablets or drink in the whole building. What a-load-a crap," he said, the headache causing the words to throb in his head.

"Mr Silk will not permit drugs or intoxicants in the building. If you're in pain or discomfort." Her face softened for a moment in mock sympathy, "then tuff, deal with it."

"Screw you, bitch," snapped Reuben, realising that he sounded like a petulant teenager being refused beer at a bar.

The receptionist grinned. "Screwing me is something that you can only dream about. Now sit down and be quiet like a good little boy." Her attention returned to the screens, ending the conversation and dismissing him.

He returned to the chair feeling like a naughty school boy which was probably her intention. Bloody bitch. If he'd been feeling himself, he would have had a witty response ready to shoot her down. Folding his arms, he relaxed into the chair and tried to appear nonchalant. When this was over and he had Pinky beside him, he might pay her a little visit. In the large glass walls he watched her reflection as she studied her screens. Acting as if he wasn't even in the room. Bitch.

The glass entrance suddenly slid open and two men walked briskly in. A tall man in a police uniform, Reuben didn't know much about their rank system but judging by the large crown and pips on his epaulette he guessed he was high up, strode in front of the other who was dressed in a plain grey suit and appeared to lack the confidence of the first as he ambled behind him. Reuben sat up, hiding the bulge of his gun under his arm and tried to make the movement seem natural.

"I'm not sure why I'm needed here. This is your jurisdiction Sir," said the shorter man, struggling to match the pace.

"Calm down Gerald. You know the mayor wants MI6 to work closely with the Met. This is the perfect opportunity," replied the copper as he knowingly eyed the receptionist. She smiled mischievously in response as she picked up the phone.

"But shouldn't our superiors be here also? I don't even know who this Mr Silk is."

"You will soon enough, Gerald. Stop worrying." Then nodding to the receptionist he opened his mouth and spoke in the harsh clicks and clacks tone.

"Tak … tak … tak," she replied and must have pressed a hidden button behind her desk as the lift doors suddenly opened and the copper lead the suit by his elbow inside.

Reuben noticed the man's face as the doors closed behind them. Full of worry and confusion. Then the receptionist starting speaking in that creepy insect-like tone, into the phone. Her eyes sought him out and she smiled, putting the phone down. A second lift that was positioned beside the first, suddenly opened.

"Mr Silk will see you now," she said, the smile curling into a smirk.

Reuben walked to the open doors, his feet feeling heavier than normal as if his body was telling himself that it might not be a good idea to get in. The doors slid silently, closing him off from the world as the lift carried him up to Silk.

When he arrived at the top floor the doors slid open, revealing an opulent-styled corridor full of rich colours. Mahogany and gold guilt lined everything from the ceiling fixtures to skirting boards and even matched the frames of the expensive paintings that adorned the walls. A vast improvement over the reception room. Further up the corridor a man in a butler's uniform held a door open to the policemen and his companion, he smiled pleasantly as they entered the room then turned his attention to Reuben.

"This way sir. Mr Silk will arrive soon," the butler said, in a clipped upper-class accent. Reuben nodded and headed towards him.

"What are the chances of you getting me some painkillers for my head?" he asked as he arrived at the opened door.

"None, sir," replied the butler. Reuben was expecting that so shrugged his shoulders as he entered the room. It seemed

his headache would be with him for the foreseeable future –
bloody marvelous.

The room was vast. As rich with furnishings as the corridor
and had a large oval table taking up most of the floor with as
many as twenty people sat around it, talking in hushed voices.
Sat upon the table was a huge red silk blanket that covered
something huge and lumpy. He couldn't guess what was beneath
but was sure that whatever it was, it was the main topic
of conversation.

The people were an odd group, mainly dressed in expensive suits and shirts. But Reuben also saw that several of them
dressed in high-ranking military uniforms sitting next to police
men and women in their formal dress. The copper he had followed up showed his friend to a chair at the narrow end of the
table where the oval shape naturally singled him out. A fact
not wasted on Gerald as his face took on an awkward look. The
copper sat next to him but started talking with the person to
his other side, obviously old friends by the way they spontaneously burst into conversation, ignoring his companion that he'd
brought in.

The butler followed Reuben in and ushered him to an empty
chair between an army Brigadier and a middle-aged cougar
dressed in a high-powered suit. They both acted as if they didn't
realise he was there, carrying on talking to their neighbours at
the table. In fact, nobody gave him eye contact or showed any
interest in him at all. But what did he expect amongst these
high-ranking and powerful individuals? He was a mercenary.
Beaten up and battered and didn't belong amongst them. He
would have felt as odd and as out-of-sorts as Gerald was if his
headache hadn't been throbbing, pulsing wave after wave of
pain into his brain.

Massaging his temples as he looked at the red silk once
again, he thought he saw movement beneath. Then he caught
movement at a different part of the lumpy mound bringing a
memory to his mind of when he was a small boy, visiting the

coast and watching fishermen hauling in the netted catch of the day. He had been distracted by a canvas sheet that had been thrown haphazardly over a small row-boat, covering fish heads and waste. The sheet had been moving as if strange creatures scurried about beneath it. Curiosity made him lift the corner of it and take a peek beneath, revealing several crabs scuttling amongst the offal, tearing off chunks of rotted flesh with sharp mandibles before skittering away. The strange movements beneath the silk blanket were similar to that, although more rapid than that of a crab and less clumsy. Perhaps rats amongst the silverware? Whatever it was, he brought his gaze away and his eyes settled on the rim of the table where he noticed strange symbols, maybe runes, had been carved crudely into the wood.

They were perhaps two inches in size and ran entirely around the table and were filled with a white powder that stood out starkly against the dark wood of the table. Why hadn't he noticed it when he came in?

He touched one of the symbols with a finger and snapped it back after feeling pain. It wasn't a white powder, it was frost. His brows furrowed as he realised that there was an icy chill settling over the room. As he tried to work out what was going on the door opened, causing the room to fall silent.

Mr Silk's huge bodyguard sauntered in followed by Mr Silk himself and another person clad in a grey robe and cloak. A hood covered its head as it shuffled in behind, face hidden beneath a dark shadow.

Everyone in the room stood. Only himself and Gerald remaining seated, unaware of the custom. He got to his feet just as Mr Silk told the room to be seated and felt foolish at being caught half rising from the seat and slowly sat back down with the rest. Thankfully nobody seemed to notice as their attention was given fully to Mr Silk who casually wandered to the head of the table, his huge bodyguard standing behind him.

He was immersed in conversation with the cloaked figure, talking in whispers yet Reuben could hear them perfectly.

"And you're sure it's the Shaigun? Why not the Shadojak?" asked Silk.

"The Shadojak is out of the city. Besides, all it seems his Shaigun is doing is watching the building. Maybe gathering information for when his master returns," replied the figure. Its cloak appeared damp although the weather had been dry for days. Due to the subtle shape of the creature, a slight bulge at the hips and breast area, Reuben guessed the cloaked figure was a female.

"Perhaps you're right. But his involvement complicates things. I'll have a team go down and take this Shaigun out. Maybe even take him alive and take his body."

"No. His mind is too strong. You'd kill him before breaking his mind. Besides, if he has the girl then there is another way we can use him to bring her to us." She produced a small bottle from inside her sleeve and handed it to Silk. "Attack him with only a handful of men. Make it hard, but don't kill him. Have one of your fighters douse a dagger in this and rake it across his skin. It would only take a small scratch for him to ingest the poison."

"I don't follow."

"There is only one place in which you can get an antidote. We'll meet him there in his weakened state and if he's protecting the girl he'll want to keep her close."

Silk took the bottle and handed it to his bodyguard. He spoke in the spine tingling harsh clicks that they all seemed to know. The bodyguard nodded and wandered from the room. Silk forced a smile to his face and regarded the crowd before him.

"Ladies and gentlemen. Brothers, sisters, warriors one and all. Thank you for coming."

Reuben watched the old man as he spoke to the table, looking each of them in the eye, except himself. He didn't know if that was a good sign or a bad one.

"The barrier between our worlds is diminishing by the day and very soon the reckoning will be upon us. We need to be ready for this day. Our ranks grow stronger and the time is nearing when this world will be ours for the taking."

Mr Silk stared at the police chief and spoke in the clicking tongue for a moment. The chief grinned, clicking a response.

"Yes, Mr Lord. This is Mr LeBron. Secretarial Chief of MI6." Then with a snake-like quickness, flicked a pair of handcuffs over Gerald's wrist and secured him to the chair.

"Whoa … " began a startled Gerald, his eyes going wild as the man to his other side grasped his other wrist and shoulder, holding him firm.

"Calm down. This will only hurt for a second. The honour will far outweigh the pain," chuckled the police chief.

Reuben watched Gerald struggle against the man that pinned him but it seemed his hold was as strong as the handcuffs. What in hell was going on? Brothers, sisters, warriors; this world will be ours? The heads around the table grinned eagerly at the handcuffed man as he pleaded to be released.

Reuben remained silent and tried to make himself small and unnoticeable. He would make a getaway soon, fake going to the toilet or something. To hell with this creepy stuff, he wanted none of it.

"And now my friends, we will welcome some newcomers." He smiled before nodding once to the cloaked woman and in one fluid movement she grasped the red blanket and yanked it from the table.

A rapturous gasp escaped the people around the table as Reuben struggled to believe what he was seeing.

Two bodies lay on their backs, pale faces starring at the ceiling with empty gazes. One of which was a fractured mess of broken flesh and blood but Reuben still recognised the green fist, tattooed on the cadaver's head. Both Pinky's and Kitch's necks had been cut at the artery and their blood had been drained down channels that ran to the centre of the table, where it formed a large circular puddle in which hideous insects crawled.

Some of the hand-sized creatures had climbed onto the carcasses of his friends, nibbling at the skin and tearing away flesh with sharp mandibles. He had never seen such hideous things before, they appeared to be something between a praying mantis and a dung beetle.

Reuben turned his head and was violently sick onto the floor. The puke slapping down on the hard oak boards and splashing up the neatly pressed trousers of the Brigadier. He felt hot and clammy. White dots flashed at the corners of his vision, the room suddenly drifting out of focus.

Laughter and snorts of giddiness issued from those around him, pierced by the screams of a man. For a second he thought it escaped from his own mouth but as his heart pumped him full of adrenaline he realised that it had been Gerald.

Fighting down the urge to throw up again, Reuben sat straight and shoved his hand beneath his jacket, grasping his gun. Sweat and tears from being sick clung to his eyes as he readied himself to shoot the first freak that came at him. But he paused as he realised that everyone's attention was on Gerald who frantically wriggled against his restraints. His face a mask of panic, eyes wide and staring at a huge creature that scampered across the table towards him.

"Get that thing away from me," Gerald squealed, now throwing his body to either side and trying to wrench his arm from the handcuffs, but only succeeding in ripping the sleeve of his white shirt. Blood began to soak through from the damage he'd inflicted on himself.

The laughter around the table was aimed at the MI6 secretary, all eyes watching with glee.

Reuben kept still, fighting down bile that burned his throat. Maybe Silk didn't intend to kill him. Butchering his friends may have been punishment enough. All he needed to do was get through this hell, pretend to be one of them and then get away at the first opportunity. He'd toast his fallen comrades when he was well clear of Silk.

Something suddenly caused the puddle of blood to ripple, the insect-like creatures paused and turned to face it, as did the people around the table. All laughter hushed yet they still wore wide eager smiles.

The woman in the cloak inclined her covered head and Reuben thought he glanced a chin, only for a split second as the shadows shifted, revealing that her skin was dry and cracked to the point where it flaked like burnt pastry.

"The Spliceck has arrived," she said, her voice matching the dryness of her skin.

Movement from the circle of blood brought Reuben's gaze back as he watched, transfixed, as another insect-like creature emerged from the blackness.

Twice the size of the others, its shape was more like that of a scorpion with large claws and a needle sharp stinger arching over its armoured back. It crawled from the blood, its fellow insects taking a step away, some raising claws of their own either in defence or to warn the bigger creature away. It paused to shake blood from its legs, its vicious mandibles working to loosen the congealed fluid that clung to them.

"Welcome brother," said Silk, his hook nose creasing as he grinned. The new creature turned to face him and made the clicking sounds that sent shivers down Reuben's spine. Was he the only one not bloody clicking?

"What in damnation is this? I demand you release me at once." Gerald's voice attracted the scorpion's attention and it began to crawl towards him. Its sharp legs tapping the table with every step.

The entire room followed its progress as it got level with its smaller brother who had already taken an interest in the bound man. The smaller insect stepped in its path and raised its own claws. Formidable and deadly as they were they paled in comparison to that of the lobster-sized scorpion. Yet it seemed it had staked its claim and wouldn't be frightened off by the spliceck.

Reuben gasped in surprise as the scorpion shot one of its huge claws out and pincered the praying mantis. It lifted it high above its own body and appeared as if it was going to fling it away until Silk spoke again.

"No, brother. That human is not the one intended. I've got better plans for you," he said and Reuben couldn't help but get the feeling that the other plans involved himself. He needed to get out.

The scorpion opened its mandibles and made a high pitched screech, snapping its claw shut and severing the mantis in half.

It had a temper.

"Calm yourself spliceck," chuckled Silk. "I promise you a fresh body soon." He made several clicks from his mouth and a second mantis crawled past the scorpion. Deep set black eyes followed its progress, Reuben sensed that it was less than pleased with the situation.

The mantis reached the edge of the table and leapt onto Gerald's knee. Gerald frantically shook his leg in an attempt at dislodging the creature but its prickly legs with tiny hooks on the end meant the shaking was futile.

"Get it off me," Gerald screamed, but Reuben only saw excited anticipation on the faces of those around the table. He wondered if the mantis was going to bite him, could it be poisonous? Did those sharp fangs contain venom?

He didn't want to watch, he wanted to be somewhere else, somewhere a thousand miles away but his only chance was to appear to be one of these freaks and to not draw attention to himself.

Excited clicking came from the mantis as it crawled up the defenseless man's arm and onto his bare neck.

Gerald had gone as white as a sheet, beads of sweat ran from his face and he shivered in the way a child does when waking from a nightmare. Then the mantis struck.

It bit into his neck, blood oozing around its small triangular head as it locked itself in place; like a leech taking its fill. Gerald let out a blood-curdling scream and arched his back, stretching painfully against the restraints, veins bulging to the extent that Reuben wondered if they might rupture.

Then the mantis dislodged from his neck, falling limp to the floor with a thud and Gerald began to convulse. Shaking violently, his eyes rolling back in his head, he began to froth at the mouth.

Reuben gritted his teeth and forced himself to watch whilst fighting the urge to throw up again. By the time he regained control of his own body, Gerald had stopped convulsing and was sitting straighter in his chair. The man to his left released his arm and the copper unlocked the cuffs.

"Welcome brother," said the copper and slapped Gerald on the shoulder.

The blood stopped oozing from the bite mark as Gerald opened his eyes and surveyed the room. He turned his head left to right as if stretching his neck, the tendons showing clearly through the skin as they pulled taut. He opened his mouth and the terrible clicking noise came out. Tak … tak … tak.

Silk leaned forward placing his hands flat upon the table. "You will need to practice speaking in your body's language. Read his mind and be the man who you've taken. Like all of us takwich around this table, you will only be valuable if you fit into the life of Gerald."

The 'not Gerald' nodded. "Understood," it said, sounding clumsy as if using an unfamiliar language.

"Good," said Silk as his eyes roamed over those around the table before settling on Reuben. "You," he began, his voice full of disappointment. "You have failed me."

Reuben squirmed in his chair under Silk's glare. His bowels loosened as he began to tremble – this was bad. He watched, horror-struck, as Silk pointed a bony finger at the dead bodies. "This is how I deal with problems. I warned you about that."

"But … " stammered Reuben, but was cut short by Silk who silenced him with the same bony finger. Although he had no idea what he intended to say anyway, just that he needed to try and argue his way out.

"Silence you fool," Silk shouted. Reuben' s face burned as he felt all eyes on the table turn to him. The new Gerald even seemed amused with his plight. "Yet you may be of some small use to me."

"Anything, Mr Silk. Just name it," he said. He would agree to anything to get out of this nightmare.

Silk leaned closer, staring down his narrow, hook nose. "You are the only one here who has actually seen the girl, who knows what she looks like."

Reuben nodded enthusiastically. "Yes. I could spot her a mile off. I could find her again. Mr Silk, give me one more chance."

"Oh, you will find her; I have no doubt about that Reuben. And to make sure you don't fail me again, I will give you a – gift."

Reuben saw the evil grin curling Silk's lips and got the strangest feeling that he wouldn't like this so called gift. Others around the table also smiled as if they were all in on a practical joke. He let his eyes fall to the table, resigning himself to whatever fate Silk had planned and clung to the thought that at least he wouldn't die, not yet. Then his gaze settled on the hideous scorpion. The lobster-sized spliceck stood on the table, barely a foot away and staring at him with black soulless orbs. It tapped the polished table with one of its sharp pincers as if impatiently waiting for an order.

Then realisation hit Reuben. "No!"

Silk opened his mouth and made a single clicking sound and the spliceck shot forward with incredible speed, launching itself off the table and landing on Reuben's face with enough force to knock him to the ground.

Reuben thudded onto his back and felt the weight of the creature pushing down on his bruised nose. The sharp points of its feet digging into his cheeks. He wanted to scream but with the creature securing itself over his mouth he daren't open it.

Sharp pain pricked the back of his hand as he gripped the armoured shell in a futile attempt to pull it away. Its scorpion tail flicking its lethal stinger in him and piercing his skin as he struggled to locate the gun.

He opened his eyes in time to watch the spliceck's head drop towards his face and its fearsome mandibles bite down into the open cut of his broken nose.

An explosion suddenly erupted in the back of his head as tears mixed with the blood that streamed down his face. A death curdling scream drowned out all other sounds, seeming far away as if he was in a separate place; removed from his body yet he recognised the voice to be his own.

His body violently shook. The scream cut off and was replaced with the banging of his head and limbs against the wooden floor. Yet blessedly there was no more pain. No suffering, as if his body simply switched off its own nervous system.

When he finally stopped convulsing, like Gerald had done before him, he felt a sensation of weightlessness, as if someone was lifting him. No, that wasn't right. His body picked itself up and clumsily rose to its feet. His feet, like he was a passenger in his own body. His eyes swiveled towards Silk who was grinning maniacally.

Clicking noises echoed through his mind. Strangely he knew that it issued from his own mouth, yet he wasn't the one speaking.

"Welcome brother," said Silk.

9

Moon Daisies and Fairy Circles

Elora awoke on the sofa and stretched the stiffness from the crick in her neck that she had acquired from sleeping in an uncomfortable position. With the back of her hand she wiped the grit from her eyes, focusing on the red glow of smouldering coals in the fire place: the only light in the cosy room, yet through the closed curtains she could see the outline of a grey dawn. Or was it a bright dawn failing to break through the veil of blackness that hovered around the building? She couldn't tell which but guessed it was morning.

A mouthwatering smell of bacon and eggs drifted through the door, causing her belly to grumble in anticipation and erase the grogginess she felt from waking. She smiled as she crossed the corridor and entered the kitchen.

"Morning," she offered, stifling a yawn. Norgie was at the Aga with his back to her but turned as she entered.

"Morning, Elora. Hungry?" he asked. She nodded, as Gurple appeared from beneath the table and came running towards her, his feet padding frantically on the floor. She laughed as he collided with her legs and wrapped his furry arms around them.

She ruffled the thick fur on his head. "Morning Gurple," she said as he took her by the hand and lead her to the table.

"Erora, sit. Bekfast," he said in his gruff voice before padding towards Norgie.

"Think he likes you," said the old man, chuckling. "How'd you like your eggs, runny?"

"Yes please. I haven't had a good fry-up in ages," she said, trying to remember when Nat had last made breakfast for them. It must have been a few months back and everything was burned around the edges. She did most of the cooking aboard the *Molly* . Nat's skill in the kitchen was experimental at best. The memory made her sad.

"What time did Bray come back?" she broached, expecting that he returned earlier and was now asleep upstairs.

"He hasn't come back yet," replied Norgie, as he set down a huge plate of food.

Two eggs sat atop a slice of fried bread with crispy bacon curling up beside thick sausages that were smothered in baked beans. Two tomato halves, singed black with their skins peeling, were set amongst a variety of grilled mushrooms that had been dressed with basil and peppers. Black pudding slices were arranged around the golden hash browns that partly hung over the edge of the crowded plate and threatened to fall onto the table.

"There's plenty more if you've an appetite for it. Would you like juice or a cup of tea?"

She stared at the breakfast. "There's more?"

Norgie let out a laugh. "Sorry lass. It is a bit much isn't it? I'm used to feeding Bray and Diagus. Now those lads can eat."

"Maybe a glass of juice will help wash this down," she chuckled as Gurple climbed onto a chair next to her, his furry little feet just clearing the edge of the cushion. Norgie slid him closer to the table and placed a smaller plate containing a couple of sausages and a rasher of bacon in front of him. He was so low to the table that he was eye level with his breakfast, yet it didn't hinder him any as he enthusiastically reached up and grasped a sausage and rammed it into his mouth.

"Where's your manners Gurple? Use a fork," rebuked Norgie.

Gurple stopped chewing and looked up at him apologetically, half the sausage hanging loose, ready to fall. Elora couldn't help but laugh as she watched him try to stab it with a fork, but the motion of his arm caused the sausage to swing out of the way. Norgie was chuckling too.

"Just use your fingers before you stab yourself in the chin," he said, placing down a jug of apple juice and an empty glass on the table. Elora poured herself a drink and took a deep gulp, wetting her throat before she attacked the plate.

Gurple had long ago finished his breakfast when Elora decided she couldn't eat another mouthful. She set her knife and fork down leaving almost half the plate.

"I'm going to blame you Norgie, if I have a heart attack this afternoon from blocked arteries," she said, smiling.

"No, that would be from the beef in ale pie I'm going to make for dinn– " began Norgie but the words died on his lips as he looked towards the doorway. Elora followed his gaze and gasped.

Bray leant against the doorframe with one arm across his stomach clutching his side whilst his other, slick with blood, dangled limp.

A deep jagged gash ran the length of his forearm, wide enough to expose the muscle beneath and so deep that the white of his radial bone glistened under the kitchen light. More blood stuck his t-shirt to his chest and more spread across the legs of his jeans but she didn't think it was his.

Elora went to him, frightened that he would drop to the floor at any moment. The paleness of his skin showed that he had lost a lot of blood and must be feeling weak. The whites of his eyes had turned pink, the veins showing bright against his green irises, yet he gently pushed her away before taking a step into the room. Blood dripping from the fingers of his injured arm and splashing onto the tiled floor.

"I'd hate to have seen the state of the other guy," remarked Norgie, concern etched upon his face.

"I need the key," growled Bray through clenched teeth.

"Sit down lad, before you collapse," said Norgie, pulling out a chair from the table.

Bray shook his head and held out his hand. "The key." Reluctantly Norgie pulled the chain from around his neck and dropped it onto Bray's open palm.

"What the hell happened to you?" he asked. Bray ignored the question and put his back to them. Walking down the corridor on unsteady legs, trailing his arm along the wall for support and leaving dark red hand prints along the aged paper.

Elora followed, noticing that he favoured his right leg, somebody or something had attacked him with the intent to kill.

"Bray?" she said to his back. He neither stopped nor acknowledged that he had heard her. "Bray, please."

He stopped, head lolling to one side, yet he didn't turn.

"What happened? Did Silk do this to you?"

Bray's head dropped forwards. "Got careless."

She was now in front of him, placing her hands against his shoulder worried that he would slump onto his face.

"Bray, you need to go to the hospital." She felt the sticky wetness beneath her hands and was thankful the shirt was black and not white. "You've lost too much blood."

"It's not all mine," he replied and Elora felt pressure against her arms as he leaned forwards, losing his balance.

"You need to stop. Look at yourself, you can't even keep upright."

"I'm fine," he argued and tried to step past her but his knee gave way and he fell, pressing her against the wall; sweat running down his clammy pale face. He didn't only look injured she thought, he looked like he was dying.

She gently swung his good arm over her shoulder and supported his weight, attempting to guide him back to the kitchen.

"No. I need to get to the cellar," he said, his face grimacing with the immense pain. Somehow he found the strength to push against her and took a step towards the cellar's staircase.

"Ok," she relented. "I'll help you down there but you're going to need medical treatment before you pass out."

The staircase was dangerously steep and narrow, leading down into darkness. If he fell it would probably finish him off. She eased him down as gently as she could but noticed him wince with every step. Once they reached the bottom he attempted to insert the iron key into the lock but couldn't stop his hand shaking. Elora took the key from him and unlocked the door.

"You can't come in," Bray warned her as he grasped the brass door knob and pulled the door towards them.

Daylight shone through the gap, filling the confined space with a warm yellow glow as if the door opened onto a bright spring day and not a dark cellar. Elora also recognised the sweet aroma of wild flowers and the soft sounds of birdsong that lay on the edge of her hearing, bringing to mind a lush meadow in the Cotswolds.

"I mean it Elora. Don't follow me," he said, then slipped through the gap, using the door for support and blocking her from gazing within.

The door pulled closed behind him with a snap, leaving her once again in the gloom. But it wasn't too dark to notice that he had left the key in the lock.

She plucked it from the key hole and placed it in her pocket, ready to give to Norgie. Yet she didn't head to the kitchen right away. Instead she put her ear to the door, attempting to listen to whatever was going on in there. It had to be important, she guessed. Why else would Bray refuse to sort himself out before going in? And why all the secrecy?

An overwhelming sense of interest told her to open the door; just a little, just to have a quick peek. But she decided against it. Things were happening that went far beyond her knowing and everything lately seemed 'out to get her'. Maybe it was best to leave things be. Bray knew what he was doing.

Norgie had a steaming mug of tea sat on the table when she returned to the kitchen. She went over to the sink and washed the blood from her hands before slumping into the chair. Norgie was down on the floor on his knees, cloth in hand next to a bucket of bleach and was scrubbing Bray's blood from the tiles.

"Does he come back in that state often?" asked Elora before taking a sip of tea. Norgie paused mid scrub.

"Never. Don't get me wrong, he comes back with ripped clothes, bruises, the odd cut or two. He gets in bigger scrapes after sword practice with Diagus, but not like that. Not to that extent. Something sure as hell roughed him up some."

"Roughed him up? His arm was torn open and he was drenched in blood," she exclaimed.

"Don't worry about him, lass. He heals quicker than most. You'll see. He's got some kind of elf genes in him or something."

"Elf? Bray's an elf?" asked Elora, scolding her tongue on the hot tea as the revelation caught her off balance.

"Aye, not a true elf though. Think his mother was an elf. He's what you would call a half-blood. Don't know the full truth of it, mind. Bray won't talk about it and Diagus is a man of few words."

Elora stared into her drink, mulling over what Norgie told her. She had always thought elves were creatures in fairy tales, short with pointy ears and brightly coloured hats. But then again, Norgie had let loose about the fairies that lived in the house. Not that she had seen any. Bray was definitely not what she thought elves looked like although it went some way to explaining how he could move so fast and heal so quickly.

She couldn't stop her imagination putting a bright red pointy hat on Bray's head. The image almost made her choke on the tea a second time.

By mid-morning, Elora had taken a shower, changed into fresh jeans and top and was back in the kitchen helping Norgie prepare the dinner. Bray still hadn't returned from the cellar and she'd begun to worry. Even Gurple kept going back to the cellar steps, sitting on the floor and fretting with a button on his dungarees.

"Don't you think you should go and check on him?" she asked Norgie, whilst skinning carrots.

"No. I won't go down there," he replied, dicing up a thick beef steak and dropping the chunks into a frying pan.

"Why not?" she asked and noticed that his chopping suddenly became heavier, hacking hard into the chopping board.

"Something happened to me down there a few years ago. Frightened the life out of me. Almost died." He paused chopping and stared into the pan with a vacant look.

"I used to be homeless. A 'free man' as I used to call it. One night the rain came down something terrible and I knew these houses were empty. So, I broke into the cellar to get out of it and stumbled into some weird ritual or something. Was almost killed in the bloody ritual too. If it hadn't been for Bray and Diagus turning up when they did, I'd have been bled dry. They told me it was the rum I'd been drinking that saved me. Apparently, takwiches can't possess a body that has alcohol in the blood. I haven't been able to go down there since."

"That's awful. But what's down there now?"

Norgie shrugged. "Don't know. The ritual opened up a gate into the Shadowlands. It couldn't be left open: you don't know what might come through and the only way to re-seal it was to bless it with a fairy ring. I've never seen it myself but there's fairies down there."

"Shadowlands?" Elora set the knife down, not trusting herself to keep chopping when her mind was elsewhere.

"Aye. Between Earth and Thea there's a barrier. Don't ask me how it works or why it's there – my mind isn't built to understand the likes of other dimensions and things. But as I understand it, the Shadowlands is another place that is attached to the barrier. A place that never sees the sun, where even time has no effect. Apparently that's where a lot of demons, half-gods, monsters and other nasties get banished to. No room on Thea for that kind of evil. And it certainly doesn't belong on Earth. So … " He stabbed the chopping board leaving the knife sticking up at a right angle. "I suppose you could call it hell."

"Oh," was all Elora could say to that, thinking that the Shadowlands was a place that was missing a takwich or two.

"Do you mind if I rest for moment? Think the events over the last couple of days have taken its toll on me," she lied, an idea forming in her mind.

Norgie nodded. "Course you can lass. I'll finish off in here then I'll be going out anyway. Need to get to the butchers before he shuts. Do you want anything whilst I'm out?"

"No, thank you."

"Right you are then, get some sleep. I'll bring you in a cup of tea when I get back."

Elora smiled at him. She really liked Norgie, he was a nice person and felt guilty at what she was going to do.

Shutting the kitchen door, she walked to the living room and placed cushions on the sofa, throwing the blanket over them and arranging them to appear as if she was sleeping beneath. It wouldn't fool anybody who actually came in but somebody poking their head around the door would get the impression that she was asleep.

Once done she closed the door and slipped down the staircase to the cellar, taking each step as softly as she could. Holding her breath, she grasped the door knob and pulled the door open, wide enough for her to slip through then swiftly shut it behind her.

A gasp escaped her mouth as she took in her surroundings. Pressing her back against the door to steady her suddenly weak legs, she blinked several times as her mind processed the scene before her.

Tall, rich grass covered the floor, surrounded by large flowers that formed a circular wall around the perimeter where the grass ended and the concrete began. The flowers themselves appeared to be a kind of moon daisy although they were perhaps twice the size of the moon daisies she was used to; their petals so vibrantly white that they seemed to radiate from within, from golden centres shining like tiny suns.

The flowers swayed to a breeze that she couldn't feel and when their stems touched each other, it caused the air between to crackle and shimmer as if filling the space with static.

The circle almost covered the entire cellar, raised perhaps a few inches above the ground and forming a kind of lush green dais. She took a step towards the phenomenon, her eyes unable to recognise a large object that lay at the centre as the very air within the circle oscillated like the waves of a mirage above a hot road.

Another step and she could make out the beautiful twittering of song birds and the bubbling of a brook that seemed distant yet she was sure it came from within the dais. So this was the fairy circle Norgie had mentioned. She found it beautiful as she took in the bright colours and rich smells. Her eyes gazing about the edges, seeking out the fairies themselves.

A high pitched caw, like that of an eagle, suddenly screamed above her and she caught rapid movement in the shadows above. A large black object darted between the bright shimmering air and the dark dusty ceiling.

It moved swiftly, darting from above, too fast to make out any detail other than it was the size and shape of a large bird; a flash of sharp talons as it passed her face. It let cry another caw and she felt a sharp sting on her bare arm. She looked down but saw no cut or scratch to indicate an injury.

The bird passed her face again, causing a wind that ruffled her hair. She stepped back bringing her arms over her head defensively and felt further stings on her arms, as if being repeatedly stabbed with a needle.

She stared through her fingers and watched as the bird banked behind the fairy circle; momentarily going out of sight behind the curtain of blurred air before flying high and then diving directly at her.

Blue light, like the tiny spark from a lighter, flashed from the bird's back and she received another sting to the elbow. She retreated until she felt the door press against her, she found the handle and twisted it but a second flash from the bird's back caused her hand to jolt, releasing her grip.

The pain was more like that of an electric shock, reacting with the nerves in her hand, making her release the handle. Another jolt to her leg and it gave way, her teeth jarring as she hit the ground. The bird cawed another time and Elora curled her knees up and placed her arms over her head.

"Leave me alone," she shouted at her attacker whose answer was to hit her with another painful shock on her bare neck. Her eyes sought out a way to escape or an object to hide behind but instead they found the bird flying across her vision, its sleek body silhouetted against the bright fairy circle.

As it passed once again she noticed something small dislodge from its back and glide swiftly towards her. She attempted to roll out of the way but it was too quick, landing hard on her knee and sending another jolt of electricity into her leg. She swiped her arm towards the object, attempting to knock it off but felt another sting dash through her hand. When her eyes finally focused she ceased struggling.

"Stop. Please. I don't mean you any harm," she blurted out to the tiny little creature.

It was three inches tall and in the shape of a man. A silver helmet adorned his head, blue eyes scowling from beneath the pointy peak. He held a long javelin, cocked back in his arm, aimed at her face and ready to throw.

Astonished, she watched as he opened a pair of wings, their span spreading at least a hand's width each side and pulsing with electricity, like tiny lightning storms forking across the fine membrane. A fairy. Elora felt a giddy excitement rush though her. She was actually seeing a real fairy.

"I'm a friend of Bray's," she said. The fairy cocked his head to the side as is if he was considering her words yet didn't lower the javelin. "Please. He is injured, I came to help him." But the fairy didn't seem to understand. He shouted at her in a strange language, his voice high pitched and barely audible. Then the moon daisies parted and a tall figure stepped from the dais.

"Bray," she said, relief easing the tension. He limped towards them. His face a pale alabaster, sweat clinging in sticky beads and blood still dripping from his arm. How much more could he lose before he fell unconscious?

"I told you not to follow," he whispered through clenched teeth. The fairy watched the exchange between them and lowered the javelin, resting the point on her knee.

"But your injuries. You look ready to fall at any moment," she said, wanting to rise from the floor but not wanting to upset the fairy who stood in place, eyes shining with the electric blue of his wings. Then he opened its mouth and made the cawing sound of the bird. Within a heartbeat the large bird landed on her other knee, long talons hooking into her jeans. It had a sharp but slender beak, its body sleek yet muscled like that of a falcon. It surveyed her with an intelligence greater than any bird.

"Elora. This is Prince Dylap of the Farrosian Forest," offered Bray, nodding towards the fairy. "Prince Dylap, this is Elora Delermere of the Minuans."

Elora gazed at the fairy as he climbed upon the back of the black falcon. "Pleased to meet you," she said. The fairy regarded her, his handsome features fixed in a firm expression. Then nodded once before grasping the feathers behind the bird's back and kicked his heels into its flank. It jumped into the air and disappeared into the dais.

"I thought fairies could fly by themselves," remarked Elora as she rose to her feet.

"Humans can walk. Doesn't stop them riding horses or driving cars. Besides he's not a fairy. He's god created."

"Oh. It's only that Norgie said there were fairies in the cellar and …" Elora brought up her arms and caught Bray's upper body as he collapsed. She couldn't hold his weight but eased his falling body to the floor, shifting a hand under his head to prevent it striking the concrete.

"Bray?" she said, urgently, placing a hand on his chest and feeling relief when she felt it rise and fall. "Bray, can you hear me?" He didn't reply, as she guessed, he had lost too much blood.

She shifted her hand to his forehead and found that it was hot. He needed help soon if he was going to live.

"Prince Dylap?" she shouted at the fairy circle, hoping that he could hear her. Her heart felt heavy in her chest, this boy needed to live if she was to get her uncle back. "Prince Dylap?" she shouted once again and was sure she heard a caw in answer. Then she watched as a dark dot appeared in the blurring air within the dais. It grew in size before breaking through the flowers.

Prince Dylap banked around before landing beside them, his face glaring up at her as if he thought this was her doing.

"He collapsed. He's lost too much blood. Please, can you help him?" she said but it was clear that the fairy couldn't understand. He shouted something at her and pointed his javelin towards the fairy circle.

"You want me to take him in there?" she asked, but it was obvious that was what he was trying to explain. "Ok. I'll try."

Gently, she lowered Bray's head to the ground and grasped his hands in each of hers. Her back muscles strained as she fought to pull him into a sitting position. He was a dead weight, head flopping forward and upper torso teetering over on the side.

Jamming her feet in front of his to prevent his body from sliding, she yanked him up, hissing through her teeth with the effort. She held him up in an awkward embrace, gripping him around his waist, his head against her shoulder as she half dragged him towards the fairy circle, taking a shuffling step one at a time.

When she reached the dais, she carefully pushed one leg through the moon daisies, her foot treading on something soft but strong enough for her to transfer her weight.

With her attention focused on not dropping Bray, she caught her heel behind his foot and fell backwards through the crackling flowers.

She landed on her back, the wind driven from her lungs as Bray landed on top of her. He mumbled something incoherently as she wriggled out from under him. Rising to her knees she glanced about and saw that she was no longer in the cellar but on a circular glade that would struggle to fit in a tennis court. Wild flowers lay in abundance and covered the majority of the grass bed that gently sloped towards a turquoise stream. The bottom half of a dark tree, its roots as thick as human limbs, clung to the side of the bank, the upper half disappearing, roughly where the ceiling of the cellar would have been, into a light blue haze that surrounded the entire circle forming a dome. It was like being inside a large snow globe, without the cheap plastic snowman, or indeed the snow. And even though she couldn't see any sky she got the impression she was outside, with the sun touching her face and her hair being tussled by a soft breeze.

Butterflies danced upon the exotic wild plants that floated on the water like lilies, sipping liquid from lilac petals. Others flapped about the many different flowers before her, fluttering from golden buttercups to blue crocuses and weaving between tall blades of grass to the strange magnolia coloured fruit that hung from the trees branches.

Prince Dylap emerged through the oscillating air at the fringe of the circle, his bird glistening in the sunlight as he landed on a low tree branch. He shouted at the glade in general and the butterflies paused what they were doing and flew to him. That's when Elora realised they were not butterflies.

Fairies circled towards the Prince, landing deftly before him, their tiny cherub faces seeming eager to please. Prince Dylap gave them orders in a language she didn't understand before directing his attention to her. He first pointed his javelin at Bray and then directed its point towards the stream. She understood and keeping on her knees rolled the unconscious Shaigun onto his back. The gentle slope made dragging him towards the water's edge easier than she thought it would. In no time at all she had him positioned how the fairy wanted him. His body an inch from the turquoise water, his head resting on her lap as the fairies danced about him, their little faces an emotional mix of worry and concern before setting about different tasks, delegated by another fairy that had arrived.

The newcomer was a female, dressed in a white silk slip and appeared different to the others. Where they had large wings with fine rib bones to allow them more movement, she had two sets of thinner wings like those of a dragonfly.

Once she had finished speaking to the others she flew towards Elora, hovering for a moment in front of her face before gently landing on Bray's injured arm. She bent low to the wound, sniffing the torn flesh and recoiling in disgust. Then, she began to pace up and down the length of the arm, her own slender arms crossed in front of her, dark hair hanging to the side and catching the sun. Elora wanted to pinch herself to make sure she wasn't dreaming.

A group of fairies returned carrying what appeared to be a white cotton handkerchief but to the small fairies it was more like a huge blanket; one fairy to each corner. They lowered it upon Bray's leg and under the double-winged fairy's orders, gathered lily petals and lay them upon the blanket. Then two corners were folded over trapping the golden petals within.

The white-slip fairy turned to face Elora once again and held her hands towards her. She pointed at the blanket containing the petals then made a dipping motion with her hands and pointed towards the stream. Elora nodded that she understood and gently picked the blanket up, careful not to let any petals fall out, and dipped it once in the cool water. The fairy then pointed at Bray's wound and made a stroking motion with one hand over her arm. Elora nodded once more and placed the wet cloth over Bray's wound and carefully wiped away the blood. The fairy, who Elora took to be a healer of some kind, smiled encouragingly.

It took several wipes and the cloth needed dipping in the stream twice more before the healer held up her hand; satisfied that it was as clean as it was going to get. She then pointed to the cloth once more and lay her palm against her forehead, tilting her face to the side and pointing once again at Bray. Elora soaked the cloth and held it to his brow. A murmur escaped his lips as she did so but he still remained unconscious.

More fairies returned carrying red bundles which they dropped into the gaping wound. Elora watched as the bundles turned out to be fat-bodied spiders which began to weave a silvery web inside the gash, halting the escaping blood. Once the inside of the wound was mostly silver the healer stepped closer and staring at Elora pointed at the wound and pinched her fingers together.

Elora left the cloth against Bray's brow and laying her hands either side of the gash, pushed her thumbs towards each other, closing the wound. The spiders set to work, weaving intricate webs up the length of the dark line, the skin puckered like a long thin mouth. In no time at all the spiders had finished and scurried away leaving the nurse to inspect their work. She smiled at Elora and spread her arms out indicating for her to move her thumbs away. Elora was reluctant at first but as she released her grip she was relieved to see that the binding weave held.

The healer's wings began to buzz, moving with such speed that they appeared as a blur, propelling the fairy as she flew to Prince Dylap who watched everything from the back of his bird. He nodded towards her and spoke several words that were unintelligible to Elora. The healer smiled as she nodded then flew away. Disappearing through the oscillating dome wall and vanishing from view. The other fairies also vanished through the vale until only the Prince remained.

With his silver javelin he pointed at her and then at Bray before pointing at the dome in general. Elora got the message. She was to stay here until Bray awoke. If he awoke. She nodded that she understood and watched as he followed the other fairies out of the glade.

Alone, Elora absorbed her situation: Bray breathing gently, his face looking peaceful on her lap. Something which his face rarely did. The half-elf was handsome. Beautiful even, she mused as she withdrew the cloth so she could re-soak it in the stream.

Elora let out a laugh. Here she was, resting inside a fairy circle, a half-elf resting on her lap and feeling like a princess in a fairy tale. At some point she would surely wake. She didn't know why the moment grasped her, maybe it was the scene she had just witnessed or the longing for somebody to share it with, but she began to sing. It was an old song that Nat used to sing to her in the early years on the *Molly* .

When her singing trailed off to a gentle hum, she gazed down and saw that she had absent mindedly twirled Bray's dark hair between her fingers. Her humming stopped when she noticed his green eyes staring up at her, full of wonder.

She unpicked his hair from her fingers. "Sorry," she said, feeling a blush coming to her cheeks. "Are you feeling any better?"

"Beautiful," came his whisper. Eyes staring unblinking into hers.

"Err … thanks," she said, not knowing whether he meant her or the song. She decided on the latter. "Do you want a drink?"

"Yeah." His voice came out croaked and dry as he tried to sit up. Elora placed her hand on his chest to still him, then leaned over to the stream and plucked one of the brightly coloured heads from a floating lily. She put the petal to his lips and slowly tipped the water into his mouth.

"Thank you," he said, after taking a swallow.

Elora couldn't decide what to say next so remained silent. Biting her lower lip and gazing up at the blue haze above which she noticed had gone a few shades darker. How long had they been in the glade? Maybe it was time they headed back although she thought she could stay here all night if the need arose. This private little glade was so peaceful.

"Do you think you can stand?" Elora asked. Bray shifted, then stopped. Wincing at the movement.

"I'm still weak. I think I've been poisoned." He raised his damaged arm, a thin line of red glistened along the wound. "It should have closed up by itself by now and be no more than scar tissue. When I was attacked I'm sure that the blades they used were laced with knoll sap." He struggled into a sitting position and stretched his neck. "Will you take my sword from me. It'll make me lighter. Don't think I'd get to my feet otherwise."

"You haven't got a sword," Elora replied.

Bray grinned. "It's in my smuggler's pouch. Out of sight."

Elora watched as he turned his hand on its side so his palm faced the ground, then touched the pad of his thumb to the tip of his middle finger and slid it part way down to the inside of the knuckle joint. When he pulled his thumb away it seemed that he ripped the very air between, causing a black oval hole to open up. "Reach inside."

Gingerly, Elora pressed her finger into the blackness and found no resistance yet watched unbelieving as first her finger then her hand disappeared from sight. She could feel an object inside the pocket, it felt solid, like cold metal. The handle of Bray's sword. She grasped it and pulled it free from the hole, needing her other hand to aid her as the weight took her by surprise. No wonder she struggled to lift him into the circle. It was the same weapon she had seen Bray produce from thin air in the garage yesterday. She lay the sword on the ground next to him, a smile playing on her lips. She now knew how he did that seemingly impossible trick.

"Now, try to stand up." She pulled him onto his knee and tucking his arm over her shoulder, heaved him to his feet.

"There's only one place that will have an antidote for knoll sap," said Bray as he stooped to recover his sword. Using it as a walking stick he allowed her to shuffle him from the fairy circle and into the dark cellar. "Norgie will need to take me into town."

"Norgie's out. He's got a few things to do," said Elora, helping Bray to sit down on the bottom step of the staircase; a fresh film of sweat coating his forehead, his skin a waxy yellow. "Can't I help you?"

"Think you're going to have to," he replied, his bloodshot eyes regarding her curiously. "How are you at stealing cars?"

10

Knoll Sap

Elora held out the arm she wasn't supporting Bray with and flagged down a London cab; feeling relief at not having to steal a car. She'd convinced him that it wouldn't have worked as she couldn't even drive let alone break into a one.

It hadn't been easy struggling out of the house or as they made their way to another street. The dark cloud that clung to the small row of terraces caused the hairs on the back of her neck to rise and seemed to extract what energy Bray had left from him. The darkness didn't distinguish between friends or strangers. But once through, her courage lifted with the feel of the sun on her face although it had begun to sink in the evening sky. It was probably getting on for eight o'clock.

She pulled open the cab door and helped Bray sit down, noticing that he placed his sword, now wrapped in a woollen blanket, across his lap.

"West Ferguson," Bray instructed the driver using his London accent. The effort seemed to drain him and he sat back, resting his head against the window. Elora hoped that where ever he was taking her, had the right antidote. She doubted he would last much longer and knoll sap antidote isn't well stocked in hospitals.

West Ferguson took them south of the Thames, a quiet area, devoid of traffic and pedestrians. The street ran alongside a brick-walled industrial area to either side of the road with no shops or dwellings.

The cab pulled in and Elora paid the driver the last of her money before helping Bray onto the flagstone path. He leaned against the wall, using his sword for support.

"Your friend alright?" asked the driver. "Looks a bit ill if you ask me. Not a lot down here love, are you sure this is where you want to be left?"

Catching a subtle nod from Bray she replied to the driver. "He's fine, just had a few too many last night. Nothing a good two-minute walk won't clear." The driver chuckled before pulling away.

Elora watched him disappear down a side street before placing Bray's arm once again over her shoulder, taking most of his weight.

"Where to?" she asked.

"You see that bridge?" Bray nodded towards a red-brick railway bridge that arched over the road. "On the other side of that you'll find an alley. That's where we need to be."

Bray's breath came in fast short bursts as if he had completed a marathon and not the few yards which they'd done to reach the alley. Elora put a hand to his pale forehead and felt the fever burning beneath. He wouldn't last long. She gazed down the narrow alley that ran between a huge brick building and the tall footings of the bridge.

"How much further are we going?" she asked.

"The alley leads to another street. There's a shop that sells Asian medicines and herbal remedies."

"Why couldn't the taxi drop us off directly outside it?"

Bray began to cough violently, bending over as he struggled to regain control of his chest. Elora patted his back but wondered what good it was actually doing.

"You can only find the shop from entering the street from this alley," he finally said, speaking through coughs.

They struggled down the narrow path, Bray striking the ground with his sword with every step, the sound echoing around them. It gave way onto another street, emerging onto a tight bend. Across the road was a row of four shops and a hair salon that had seen better days. They were all closed and appeared locked up. Elora saw no sign of any other shops and the rest of the buildings, the ones she could see before the street vanished around the bend, were houses and maisonettes.

"There, between the hairdressers and the pawn brokers. You see it?"

"No" And at first glance she saw that only a narrow brick wall lay between the two; red, crumbling and nothing of any interest. Then, as if some trick were being played on her eyes, she watched as an outline of a doorframe shimmered upon the wall. The longer she watched the more focused it became until it was a solid door, as bold as if it had always been there. "I see it," she whispered. Fairies, elves – why not a magic door.

They crossed the street as slowly as they'd progressed down the alley. Bray leaned against the door for support, sweat shining across his brow as he knocked heavily on the oak paneling. He looked ready to slide to the floor, Elora gripped him by the upper arm and readied herself to catch him.

There was the sound of a sliding bolt and a small hole appeared in the door at head level. A large brown eye peered out at her and then flicked across to Bray. She thought she saw recognition in that stare before it disappeared and the door opened inwards on creaky hinges.

A tall elderly lady stood before them, dressed in a flowing dark green gown over which she wore a brown apron. Dark brown hair that matched her eyes, was tied up in tight buns and out of the way, overly long arms on hips, fingers drumming the top of her thighs as she surveyed them.

"Tut – tut – tut. What have you done to yourself now, Shaigun?" she asked, creases forming a heavy scowl. "Bloody fool keeps on getting himself messed up and expects me to be the one to patch him up. And where's the Pearly White, may I ask? Told the Shadojak last time he was here that I wasn't a healer."

"Hello Grendel. Diagus is out of town," stammered Bray, barely keeping his eyes open.

"I thought Shaiguns were supposed to be with their Shado-jaks. Or are times changing? You can never tell with that one."

Bray suddenly flopped forwards, sinking to his knees, it was all Elora could do to guide him down.

"Please. He's been poisoned with knoll sap," she said.

"Knoll sap? Nasty stuff. It's a wonder he hasn't croaked already. Come on then, don't dawdle outside all day. Bring him in, bring him in," said the old lady, standing aside to allow Elora to half carry, half drag Bray over the threshold but didn't help in any way other than to tut and mutter to herself.

Inside was a large shop-floor that must have taken up what room the salon had but instead of sinks, mirrors and comfortable chairs, there were row upon row of shelves, cupboards and drawers. What light there was, splintered through a dusty window where there should have been a large glass fronted wall with the salon's name emblazoned across its front. The fractured light cast many a strange shadow from the thousands of stranger objects that festooned the shelves and cupboard tops: small glass vials, dusty boxes, jars containing pickled body parts, dried bones, powders, bowls overflowing with what appeared to be crushed insect shells and parts of plants, littered several shelves that made up one wall. Against another were hundreds of tiny square drawers, labels stuck to the front with unfamiliar symbols scrawled upon them. A few of the drawers were left partially open and Elora saw little stones or jewells glistening from inside; in another there were seashells and in a third she took a second glance at a what appeared to be dried out eyeballs.

"Lay him down there," said the lady, nodding towards an antique chaise longue. Elora gently lowered Bray onto the low furniture, he was barely conscious. The elderly lady began to root through drawers, pulling something out of one, slamming it shut before opening and taking another object from a second.

"Can you help him?" Elora asked, hearing the worry in her own voice as she watched the woman gather up the strange things. She turned to answer and placed something in Elora's hand.

"Put this under his tongue but make sure he doesn't swallow it," she said before scurrying from the room. "And don't touch anything," she shouted from the corridor.

Elora opened her hand, the object was a stone or seed, the size of a peppercorn but with bright red and dark green dappling. She bent down and used her fingers to open Bray's mouth and wriggled the stone beneath his tongue before resting his head on its side so he wouldn't choke.

"She said not to swallow it. Bray, can you hear me?" Elora guessed that he couldn't. His eyes were closed, his breath laboured and when she touched his skin it felt hot.

Grendel suddenly returned, flanked by two huge men in dark suits. Each had a gun drawn. One pointing at the back of her head, the other on Bray.

"I'm sorry child. They arrived a few hours before you did," said the woman, before she was roughly shoved to the floor. The man who shoved her raised a phone to his mouth and made strange clicking sounds into it. The same teeth chattering noise which Mr Silk had used to speak to his bodyguard. Elora guessed they were takwiches. They had found her again, but how?

A cold fear wrapped its icy fingers around her heart as she stared into the dead eyes of the man on the phone. Dark, calculating and void of emotion. He put his phone away and a third man sauntered into the room.

"Reuben?" exclaimed Elora.

He smiled, dimples showing as he displayed white teeth yet his eyes had lost the glint they held on their last encounter, instead they were as dead as his companions. Elora felt a small amount of satisfaction at seeing the ruined nose, broken and crooked.

"My child? I've done what you wanted. Please, let him go," said the old woman frantically as she rose from the floor.

"Your boy is untouched," replied Reuben, as he stepped closer to Elora. He glanced down at Bray, his grin growing wider. "Is he dead?"

"Yes," said Grendel "I gave him a rutworm seed." Her eyes found Elora and she thought she saw a subtle shake of the head.

Bitch! She wanted to scream at her but it seemed that Reuben held her child hostage. No mother would risk the life of her child over another. She couldn't blame her for what she had done. No, this was Silk and Reuben's doing. But was the old woman right? Was Bray dead?

Reuben placed his fingers against Bray's neck. "The Shaigun is truly dead, so it appears these highly trained balancers are not as hard to kill as you're led to believe. Shame, I wanted to test myself."

"He made a mess of your face before," spat Elora as she watched the woman leave the room.

Reuben took Bray's sword and let the blanket fall to the floor. He held the dull blade up, testing its edge with his thumb, making a soft scraping sound.

"You may have been in the presence of this body before, little girl but we've never met. And I'm damned sure no mere Shaigun would have done this to me," he said, pointing to his nose.

Elora found it hard to believe that Bray was dead. His face looked smooth of wrinkle, at peace as if he was simply asleep. Now, it seemed he would be sleeping forever. She felt a tear run down her cheek; her throat tightening up.

"Take her out to the car," ordered Reuben as he deftly swung the sword about his body, flourishing the blade with the expertise of a master before bringing the point in front of her face. "And watch her. She's slippery as an eel in oil."

The closer man took her roughly by the elbow and propelled her towards the door, the other one followed behind, his gun pressing into her spine. She turned her head in time to see Reuben raise the sword above Bray's neck, about to bring it down.

"No!" she screamed, hands flicking out and gripping the door. "Leave him alone. Isn't killing him enough for you?"

Reuben's cold black eyes regarded her, the grin returning to his face as the blade hovered above Bray. "Don't worry little girl. He won't feel a thing," he said and brought the sword down.

Elora scrambled to get back into the room but froze when she watched the blade stop a hair's breadth from Bray's neck, his dead hands holding Reuben's as his eyelids flicked open. Moss green eyes shimmered with a fierce fire as he glared up at the man about to take his head.

"Yield in the name of the Shadojak," said Bray, his voice little more than a dry rasp but sounding all the deadlier for it. Elora couldn't believe her eyes. Had he faked his death? But how then did he still his heartbeat when Reuben checked for a pulse?

The shocked expression on Reuben's face fell as he pushed harder onto the sword. "I never yield, boy."

"Thought you'd say that," replied Bray, before pushing the blade away from him and rolling from under Reuben. As he spun he swiped the legs from under his attacker.

Reuben fell backwards as his other hand came up and caught Bray a hard blow to the head that sent him sprawling into the shelves.

The takwich that had been pressing his gun into Elora's back shoved her to the side and aimed his weapon. She brought her hand down onto his wrist and shoved it away. The gun went off, the bullet smashing through a glass jar and spilling its gruesome contents onto the floor. He elbowed her in the stomach, causing her to double-over with pain, the breath knocked out of her. But his companion grasped a handful of her hair and wrenched her back up before putting his meaty arm around her neck and pulled her out of the room.

She struggled to stay where she was, fingers digging into the doorframe once again and gripping on with all her might. Not having the strength to pull herself back into the room, she found that at least she wasn't going any further.

More shelves were knocked down and a cupboard shoved over as Bray's body slammed into it before he crumpled to the ground. Elora noticed that the wound in his arm had split open once again, blood now freely flowing.

Reuben towered above him, sword held in both hands, the knuckles of his fingers bone-white as he plunged the blade down. Bray shifted his head a fraction of a second before the steel struck the floor where it had been. The Shaigun flipped back to his feet, striking Reuben in the face but he saw it coming and ducked, the blow glancing off the side of his head and doing no more than forcing him back a step. He glanced at Elora, their eye's locked for a moment before he shouted at his men.

"Get her out of here! I don't need any help with this runt. Go"

Strong hands yanked her back as the other takwich grabbed her around the legs and lifted her up. She struggled like a cat in a pillow case, thrashing her legs, throwing her shoulders about in a vain attempt to free herself but the men held fast. Carrying her briskly through the strange building to the back door.

There was a scream of rage from the room where Bray and Reuben fought, followed by a scream of pain. The former belonged to Reuben, the latter, Bray. Elora felt sure that Bray should have bested him with ease yet this new Reuben seemed different, as if a demon had possessed his body. That and the fact that Bray was still sick. She needed to get to him.

As they reached the back door, the man holding her upper body momentarily let go with one hand so he could slide the deadbolt open. Elora took the opportunity to sink her teeth into the arm that held around her neck.

She bit as hard as she could, the hot tangy taste of blood filling her mouth.

The arm released, letting her fall. Her shoulders struck the tiles hard, jarring her back, yet she didn't let it hinder her as she drew her knees in then kicked out as hard as she could.

The second takwich stumbled back but kept on his feet, drawing his gun and aiming at her. She knew he wouldn't shoot, Silk wanted her alive, so clinging to that hope she rolled onto her front and sprang to her feet. Dipping her shoulder low, she drove her body into the man she had bitten, knocking him clear of the door. With him out of the way she grasped the handle and pulled. Thankfully the bolt had been slid before she was dropped and she rushed out into a small courtyard.

Clicking sounds from the men inside spurred her on and she crossed the yard in a few easy strides to the gate and shoved it open, spilling into the alley beyond. But, just as she found her footing she ran straight into a tall man that had been walking towards her.

Yelping with surprise, she stumbled into the wall, fighting to keep on her feet but the alley was too narrow for her to pass the man. He didn't make a move to grab her; just watched, half his face hidden in the shadow of a building, regarding her with a menacing look.

He had a slate-grey beard, the same colour as his hair which was shaved to a whisper above stubble. His face was mean, weathered, full of hard edges – high cheek bones and deep crags. A nose that looked to have been broken a good couple of times and a scar over his icy blue eye that took a notch from his eyebrow. He wore plain khaki cargo pants and a grey shirt. Not something you would expect a person of his age to wear. He was surely one of Silk's men but as her two pursuers crashed through the gate they stopped to survey him. The one she had bitten, bringing his gun up level – so he wasn't one of them.

"Turn around and leave old man," ordered the takwich with the gun. "This is of no concern to you. Leave or regret staying."

The old man gazed at him, his lip curled back in a menacing grin. "Happens I might make it my concern." He took a step closer, the shadow falling away to reveal the other half of his face.

Elora was shocked to find that this side had an even meaner look. A savage scar forked across his jaw, ending above his hairline. An ugly red mess that pulled the skin in some places and puckered it out in others. And where his eye should have been, was a bright white stone that reflected the scene before her.

"It's the Pearly White," exclaimed the man with the bleeding arm.

The grin vanished from the newcomer as his arm whipped out lightning fast, striking the takwich in the throat. He collapsed to the ground, clutching at his Adam's apple; his gun forgotten.

His comrade clicked loudly. The sound escaping his mouth like an old wooden clacker. He drew his weapon on the old man who sidestepped the bullet and brought his hand down on the gun, twisting and squeezing, releasing another bullet that exploded into the takwich's chest. His body fell through the gate, the gun dropped to the floor.

Elora rose unsteadily to her feet, regarding the tall man warily. This was Diagus. The Shadojak. He stared at her, his white eye seeming to pierce her very soul.

"Where's the boy?" he asked, sternly.

As if to answer his question, Bray's body hurtled backwards through the kitchen window and fell to the floor in a shower of glass.

"Bray!" shouted Elora and made to run to his unmoving body but the old man grabbed her arm and yanked her back.

"Stay behind me," he ordered. She wanted to tell him to go to hell but something in his command rooted her to the spot. And so she followed him as he prowled into the courtyard.

As she passed the man clutching his throat he collapsed onto his side, his hands falling limp beside him. Dead, Elora realised. The Shadojak had killed two men with no more remorse than swatting a couple of flies.

The kitchen door swung in and Reuben stepped out, holding Bray's sword. He spied them approaching and smiled.

"Today I get to kill a Shaigun and the Shadojak. Your blade will make a handsome gift for my Lord. Unless of course, I keep it for myself," he said.

Diagus approached him, opening a smuggler's pocket and drawing out a sword that was almost identical to Bray's although its blade had a dark green hue to it.

"Now I'm supposed to offer you the chance to yield but I'm guessing that you would refuse, so I won't waste our time with that nonsense," said the Shadojak, raising the sword before him.

"Clever man," said Reuben, bringing Bray's sword to bear.

Elora went to Bray and rolled him onto his back. He gazed up at her, his breathing sounding worse than it had before the attack, but she saw no mortal wounds on him other than the one on his arm which had opened up afresh. She tore a sleeve from her shirt and wrapped it around the large gash, staunching the flow of blood the best she could, then rested his head upon her lap like she had in the fairy circle although now they lacked the fairies.

Reuben circled the Shadojak, sizing him up like a cat deciding how it was going to kill a trapped mouse. Diagus remained still, poised yet motionless. His eyes, both blue and pearl, gave away no hint of his intentions.

Suddenly and without warning, Reuben struck out with the sword, it swung low making a whistling noise in the air. The Shadojak parried it easily, blue sparks flashing where the metal met as he danced away with the fluidity of water. Twice more Reuben slashed towards the old man, first aiming high then low yet each attack was met with the slightest of movements, the blades touching for the briefest of moments.

Diagus tiptoed around Silk's man as light as a ballerina compared to the bull-like aggression used by his opponent. Elora wondered why the Shadojak didn't strike back. Each calculating movement was one of defence, there was no offence to his dance.

Bray weakly grasped her hand and squeezed. "What's happening?" he croaked.

Elora gazed into his face, his skin as pale as snow. "The Shadojak is here. He's fighting Reuben."

"Diagus," he whispered, his eyelids slowly closing. Elora thought that his body suffered too much and that the poison had taken its ugly grip once again. He needed the antidote immediately.

"Shadojak," she shouted, hoping that he could hear her above the ringing of clashing steel. "Bray will die soon if we don't get him inside."

The Shadojak gave her a quick glance, raising an eyebrow. Then simply ducked beneath Reuben's next blow and brought his sword up as he stepped towards her.

Reuben paused mid-swing, legs locked in place, arms still gripping the sword but didn't turn around. Elora was expecting him to strike Diagus in the back now that it was exposed, yet he didn't so much as twitch. It was like he was playing his own game of musical statues and the music had stopped.

The Shadojak put his sword away into his invisible pocket and crouched down, placing a calloused hand upon Bray's head.

"What about Reuben?" asked Elora, her eyes still on Silk's man.

Diagus glanced at her, a wicked grin spreading across his face, the ugly scar pulling his skin tight against his jaw. "He hasn't the mind to fight no more."

Elora frowned, her gaze switching back to Reuben in time to watch his head slide sideways from his shoulders and tumble to the ground, making a dull thumping sound. His body teetered forwards then collapsed beside the head. Elora's mouth fell open, she suddenly felt sick. It was the Shadojak that finally drew her attention away from the mutilated body.

"Grab his legs, girl," he ordered.

Between them they carried Bray's body into the kitchen and lay him down on the chaise longue.

"Grendel!" shouted the Shadojak. "Grendel, if you don't get your skinny arse in here I swear by the Blessed Mother I'm going to judge you here and now."

Grendel burst into the room carrying a silver syringe. A small boy with the same dark eyes, at her heels.

"I'm sorry my Lord. They said they would take my child's head if I didn't do what they asked," she cried as she knelt by Bray.

"I'm no Lord, wench. Now fix the boy with the draught. And if he dies you'll share his fate."

Elora watched Grendel administer the antidote, then grasp his wrist and count his pulse. "He needs rest."

"How long?" growled the Shadojak.

"A couple of days. Maybe a week. The longer he rests the better he will heal. Knoll sap is a hideous poison."

"We can't spare that long," spat Diagus, running a hand through his hair.

"I've done all I can. Its rest he needs now."

"Then you are of no further use," he said and dismissed her with a wave of his hand. She rose to leave the room, steering her son out before her, but as she made to close the door the Shadojak spoke once more.

"Tell me Grendel. How did those three manage to better my Shaigun. Is it possible you aided them? What did you have to gain from those takwich?"

Grendel halted at the door, her shoulders slumped in resignation. "I did what I could for your Shaigun but they arrived much earlier. They held my son hostage and forced me to admit Bray and the girl. I was to let them in here then leave the room. Nothing more."

"An act of treason."

"No my Lord," she begged, kneeling before the Shadojak, tears running down her face. "They had my son."

Diagus appeared indignant. "The reasons don't matter. You committed treason."

"I did my Lord."

"Order your son to leave the room," said the Shadojak, as he pulled his sword free from the invisible pocket. Grendel stared at her son, eyes red and swollen from crying and offered him a sad smile.

"Go to your room, Darrion." The boy looked at her, fear in his eyes but did as he was told. When the door was closed she lowered her head, barring her neck to the Shadojak. Elora struggled to understand what was going on, surely he wouldn't kill her.

"Grendel Tracathion. You've been judged on account of treason. The Shadojak has found you guilty." He lifted the sword above his head. "May the Mother have mercy on your soul."

"No!" cried Elora. "You can't just kill her," her legs felt like jelly as she stepped in front of the Shadojak.

"Silence girl," said Grendel. "Or you will share the same fate as me. I made a choice and must suffer the consequences."

Elora glanced up at the dull green blade that loomed above her, ready to fall "No," she enforced. "I won't move. If you're going to kill her, then you'll need to strike through me."

The Shadojak stared at her for a moment. "So be it."

"No," came Bray's voice from behind him. "The girl must live."

"Why? You know our mission. I will be judging her next anyway."

"Master please. There is something happening. Something big unfolding and somehow she is at its centre."

"Then tell her to stand aside."

Elora folded her arms. "I won't move. I won't let you kill her."

"Master. Grendel does not deserve to die. She aided me. She helped as much as she could."

"Did she tell you that you were being led into a trap. Did she conceal the takwich?"

"Yes. But she also gave me this," he said as he sat up. He opened his palm. Elora saw the rut worm seed and didn't understand Bray's meaning. Surely, showing the Shadojak the rut worm seed would seal Grendel's fate.

"Tryella stone?" asked the Shadojak.

"Yes, my Lord," said Grendel. "The girl told me he had been poisoned with knoll sap. I had the ingredients in here to make the antidote but it would require me boiling the grimrot root and grinding down the spalding claw. I didn't have time to do these things immediately and so I hid them in my apron so I could make the draught once I satisfied my captors. I knew he wouldn't last much longer without help and so I gave him the tryella stone."

"I thought if taken whole it would boil your blood," the Shadojak said.

"Only if swallowed. But if placed beneath the tongue it will give enough energy to the blood to revive somebody close to death."

That would explain why Bray managed to recover enough to fight Reuben, thought Elora.

"Once I was out of the way, I made up the antidote."

The Shadojak lowered his sword although his face was still set in a less than satisfied grimace. "You're free to go, Grendel. But you have been marked as a traitor. See to it those bodies outside are eaten by carrion spore," he said, sliding the sword away where it vanished. Elora didn't think she would ever get used to seeing things like that.

Grendel stood up and surprised Elora by wrapping her long arms around her and squeezing her tight.

"If there is anything I have and could do for you, anything, just name it. It will be yours, sweet girl."

Tears ran freely from her eyes as she let her go. She smiled and gave Elora's hand a final squeeze before her son came back into the room. He gave them all a puzzled look before racing to his mother where she embraced him.

Elora smiled at the pair, it was a lovely sight. But the smile dropped from her mouth when she saw the Shadojak's thunderous expression as he stared at her.

"There is some explaining needs doing," he said.

It was midnight before Bray felt well enough to stand by himself, albeit with the frowns and curses, from Grendel.

Elora had spent the time telling the Shadojak who she was and of all that had happened over the last few days. He listened intently, frown set throughout, a frown that grew deeper the more she spoke. She even showed him Nat's journal but like Bray, he couldn't read it. Neither could Grendel.

After she had finished, the Shadojak only spoke to ask her to leave the room so he could speak freely with his Shaigun.

Grendel took her by the hand, like an old friend, saying that she could help her make tea. But instead of leading her into the kitchen she led her up a flight of stairs to a dark room full of strange objects, even more obscure than those in the shop. Maybe this was where she hid the things she didn't want the Shadojak to see.

A circular table adorned with a purple velvet cloth sat in the centre of the room. An oak chest inlaid with fine gold straps and hinges lay open at its centre; dark shadows swam from within, reminding Elora of the swirling darkness that surrounding the house where Norgie lived.

The curtains were made from the same material as the tablecloth. Drawn across the window the fine velvet gleamed in the flames from wall sconces. To either side of the room lay huge glass cabinets with rich ornaments and jewells sat upon the glass shelves within. Necklaces, brooches, gold and silver rings, jewell encrusted daggers, drinking horns; goblets, jugs and cutlery of ivory and jade. Elora gazed about the Aladdin's cave of treasure.

"I meant what I said earlier. There are things in this room which are priceless. Choose one and it is yours," said Grendel, gesturing about the room with her arm.

"There is no need Grendel. I don't want anything."

"Hush, Elora. Choose something. I always pay my debt and I owe you my life, so please."

Warily, Elora paced the room, gazing at the opulent objects and wondering what it was that she actually needed. Any of the treasures were worth a fortune, but her life aboard the *Molly* had taught her that you could live quite richly without having riches. She paused at the chest in the centre of the room. Black wisps curled like smoky fingers above the opening, never probing further than the shadows and retreating when the warm light touched it.

"Djinn smoke. It's yours if you wish it. It's more valuable than everything in this room combined, but may cause you more trouble than pleasure," said Grendel, tracing a slender hand along the rim of the chest, fine tendrils of the smoke intertwining with her fingers.

"What does it do?" Elora asked, intrigued.

"It's what's left of a powerful Djinn or genie, whatever your language names the magical deliverer of wishes. Some say that the smoke has power enough to grant a man anything his heart desires. Others, tell of wishes granted, born of trickery where the wisher is given more than what he wants and ends up forfeiting his life. His own soul given to the smoke."

"My uncle used to warn me; be careful what you wish for because it may come true."

"Your uncle is wise," said Grendel as she closed the lid of the chest. "Then perhaps a gold bracelet? The metal was mined in the mountains of Valaria, far beyond the reach of the Empire. Or its sister necklace or both."

Elora eyed the bracelet and necklace, red fire from the sconces dancing along the polished metal. They were riches far beyond anything a girl like her would ever dream of owning. But what good would they bring her? Would they keep her safe from harm, would they bring her uncle back?

"Both Bray and the Shadojak have an invisible pocket, a smuggler's pocket to hide their swords," said Elora.

Grendel's eyes narrowed. "Argh. Smuggler's pouches. Worth kingdoms, can't be bought for love nor money and banned by the Empire. If it's detected that somebody entering any of the cities has one, they would lose the limb that bears it. Only the Balancers may have them."

"Oh," was all Elora could mutter, feeling disappointment. Then watched as a cunning smile played on Grendel's lips.

"But a small price to pay, I think, for what you did for me," she said. "Wait here, I'll be back."

Elora waited, her eyes drawing back to the chest. It was surreal to think that a genie resided inside that small wooden box. A tiny part of her wanted to open it but she knew it would be foolish. Luckily Grendel returned before the temptation grew beyond control.

"Are you right-handed?" asked Grendel. Elora nodded, "Then give me your left."

Elora did as she was told. Grendel took her hand in hers, turning it palm up and rubbing something soft against her skin, yet she was unable to see what it was.

"Do you feel it? That's the rim of the smuggler's pocket."

With her other hand she produced a silver dagger with a sharp blade. Without warning she pierced the pad of Elora's thumb and made a fine cut down into the web of her hand and up the length of her index finger.

"Ouch!" exclaimed Elora, pulling her finger back; blood dripping from several places along the cut.

"Hush girl. Pain is a minor thing compared to the gift you're receiving. And I can heal the wound up after."

Elora gave her the injured hand back and braced herself for more pain. But it appeared that Grendel had done with cutting and placed the dagger on the circular table. An itching sensation tickled along the cut as Grendel traced it with her finger and thumb, chanting in a foreign language as she did so, until she reached the tip of her injured finger.

"Done," she said.

Elora tipped her hand this way and that but couldn't see or feel any difference except for the pain that smarted along the cut.

"Let me show you how it works," said Grendel holding her own hand up. "Place your finger and thumb together like so. Gently rub them until you feel the ends of the pocket."

Elora copied her actions but still felt nothing. Maybe Grendel had put it on wrong. Then suddenly she felt it. Her thumb snagged against a light raise on her finger.

"Now gently pull them apart. Not too fast, until you've gotten used to how it works."

Elora did as instructed and found the minutest of resistance and watched as the space between thumb and finger became a round black hole. It spread wide enough for her to put her other hand in.

She laughed. "This is brilliant." Her arm disappeared to the elbow yet she couldn't feel the bottom. "How deep does it go?"

"It has no length nor depth. Its only limitations are of weight and by that I mean how much you yourself can carry. Although the pocket is hidden from sight and touch you must still bear its burden. It's not unknown for people to be hidden inside. The perfect place to smuggle somebody across borders. Although it would be a giveaway for somebody seeming to struggle, huff and grunt whilst appearing to be carrying nothing. Do you see what I mean?"

Elora nodded, feeling thrilled with her new gift.

"Perhaps something to put in it?" continued Grendel as she opened the glass cabinet and retrieved an elegant dagger.

"No I couldn't," began Elora but was shushed once again.

"Please. Dark times are coming I fear. And ill outcomes come to those ill prepared."

The dagger was slender with a silver handle, a large sapphire set in the butt, matching another, set in the silver sheath; polished to a high gleam they refracted the light from a hundred angles. She pulled it free, a pleasant ringing sound followed the blade out which appeared to be silver with a light blue tinge to the metal, the sharpened edge, a deep azure.

"It's goblin silver. Smithed in the Valiciern hills with dragon fire and folded over a thousand times. It can cut through steel and will never lose its edge."

"It's beautiful" said Elora, if such a word could be used to describe something designed to kill. She slipped it back into its sheath and placed it inside the smuggler's pocket where it vanished.

The Shadojak suddenly entered the room, the flames in the sconces shimmering with the wind from the door. He stared at them, a frown forming upon his wrinkled brow. "What's gone on here?" he asked.

"Nothing my Lord. I was only showing Elora some of my finer wares," replied Grendel, whilst offering her a wink.

The Shadojak eyed the objects in the room, his gaze falling upon the chest at its centre.

"I think I may have to return here for closer inspection at some point. I dare say some of these ... may have gone by then."

Grendal's lips drew tight, her face a still mask. "I dare say you're right." Then she embraced Elora, wrapping her long arms around her. "Goodbye Elora. I hope you get your uncle back. And if you should ever find yourself friendless; you are always welcome here."

Elora thanked her and followed the Shadojak out of the room, wondering if she would ever see her again.

11

Sea Witch

Bray flexed his injured arm, the ugly gash now reduced to a fine silver scar that pulled the skin tight. Rid of the knoll sap, his body healed itself quickly and he was feeling his usual self. So why was he frowning, why the tightness in his belly and why, whenever he let his concentration lapse for even a moment, his gaze drifted towards Elora? Thankfully she had gone to bed, leaving himself and Diagus alone in Norgie's kitchen, sharing a bottle of red wine while they discussed the best course of action for the girl.

"So you believe the beast in the North Sea is truly a leviathan?" asked Bray.

Diagus nodded. "Couldn't be anything else. What was left of the ship was a twisted wreck, crushed flat and chewed up as if made from paper instead of thick steel." He drained his glass and filled another. Offering the bottle to Bray. In truth he had only sipped to swill the taste of the vile stone that Grendel gave Elora to put under his tongue. Potent little thing – left an equally potent taste.

"You think the girl's involved?" He avoided using her name – attempting to distance himself somehow.

Diagus took a swallow, leaving a crimson stain on his grey beard. It jostled as he spoke. "I'd stake my blade on it. Five years I've spent here in this mother forsaken realm. Took over from old Driffen and him from Fogmell Dan Bunt. And the Shadojak before him all the ways back since the time of the Romans; hasn't never been anything the likes of a bulworg, takwich or Minuan in all that time. Not to mention a god created sea beast like a leviathan. That pretty little girl is at the centre of it. Maybe the sensible thing to do would be to judge her now and have done. Before we see grumpkins skinning children and dragons in the sky."

"No," said Bray, more forcefully than intended.

"No?" echoed the Shadojak, an eyebrow arching above the staring pearl. "Do I detect a fondness for the girl?" A hint of amusement in his deep voice.

"No, Master. But until we know who the girl truly is, it would be prudent to keep her safe. This Silk has clearly marked her as his and wants her badly."

Diagus took another drink and rocked back so his chair was balancing on its back legs; his own he had crossed and placed upon the table. This was a position Bray had seen him in many a time before when mulling things over. Slouching back whilst draining a glass of wine. Something that the other seven Shadojaks would never do.

Calm, calculated discipline. Control over every action, every situation and all emotions. That was the bare bones of being a Shadojak. Diagus was different. Having become a Shadojak without ever being a Shaigun, he lacked the training and discipline. But once he had the soul blade he couldn't give it up without forfeiting his life. But that didn't stop other Shaiguns from trying to take it from him. The trouble was that nobody could. Even the half-god that took his eye and left an ugly scar only strengthened his ability: as the special blade of the Shadojak absorbed powers from those it slayed through the heart. This caused other Shadojaks to seek out his blade and attempt to take it from him and drive it through his heart. And for everyone that tried then died, it made Diagus stronger. As a Shadojak he went through dozens of Shaiguns. Each either quit or died within a year under his service until nobody wanted him as a master.

His reputation grew amongst the Shades that branded him the Pearly White, a living Legend and a threat on the lips of every drill sergeant and sword master in the Shades. That's the reason he ended up on Earth. A place cut off from Thea where he was kept out of the way. Bray had been his Shaigun for three years now and thought that the Shadojak Supreme had sent him here to keep out of the way also. What better place for a half-breed?

"Maybe you've got the right of it boy. And quit that Master crap, you're not a dog."

Bray often fell into old habits. His training had been harsh as he soldiered with the Imperial army, harsher still when he became a Shade. Yet both paled in comparison to the torturous path of becoming a blades master. They broke you down to nothing before rebuilding you harder than the steel you danced with.

"It was a trap. They knew we were coming," said Bray, absently rubbing his new scar. "Silk's cleverer than I first thought. When I was attacked, one of the blades was laced with knoll sap. They knew I would seek out the hedge witch Grendel."

Diagus nodded. "It would seem so. This girl Elora, whoever she is, can never slip into their hands. Even if to do so will mean killing her ourselves."

Bray felt his gaze upon him, was he judging his loyalty to the girl? It is said that the Pearly White can stare into your soul. If that's what he was doing now, what did he see?

"That sigil on the bulwarg you described to me; eight tentacles surrounding an eye. That belongs to Neptula."

"The sea witch?"

Diagus nodded. "Happens, she's in town. In the Thames to be more precise. Do you think you can root her out?" He drained the glass and set it on the table.

"Yes," replied Bray, "It shouldn't be too hard."

"Good. Get what rest you can, I want you hunting before first light. And take a jar of nip-crasters with you."

"Nip-crasters?"

"Yep. I don't think she'll take too kindly when you ask her how she smuggled the leviathan over. Those little nip-crasters will help loosen her tongue."

A jar of those little creatures could devour all the fish in the river in the time it takes the tide to go out. Ripping and tearing the flesh of anything that swims, stripping life to bones faster than piranhas yet so small a shoal will fit in a jar. Grendel would keep them for trading, he would need to visit her first thing and with plenty of coin. They weren't cheap.

"You think the leviathan is the sea witch's doing?"

"Could be no other."

"Won't you be joining me?"

"Nope. I'll be taking the girl out of town. Happens I know someone who can read Minuan and get that journal of hers deciphered. Find out who she is."

"Who?" Bray found it hard to keep the question light, masking the concern that had jolted his stomach at his Master's words.

"A Minuan, as it goes. If I can find the slippery weasel."

Will you be bringing her back here? He wanted to ask as he calmed his thumping heart. Would he really harm her if she turned out to be something dangerous? He knew the answer to that; the Shadojak wouldn't think twice.

Bray was about to retire to bed when Diagus spoke again.

"Be careful with Neptula, don't take any chances. She found the last Shaigun delicious."

"I won't," replied Bray, trying not to think of the Shaigun in the belly of the sea witch.

"Get what information you can from her but don't get lured to the water's edge, she's a devious creature, especially in the water." Diagus's voice deepened, taking on a more serious quality. "When I return we're going to judge Silk and his takwich army. Do not make a move without me. Understand?" Bray nodded and noted the 'I' return, not 'we'. "Good, now get some rest."

The sun was a pale ghost. A silver circle barely visible through the overcast sky, casting neither rays nor shadow against the glass fronted salon which disguised Grendel's shop.

Nobody observed Bray enter the herbalists but as he left he almost bumped into a blonde woman who was entering the salon. She looked surprised to see him appear suddenly, as if stepping out of a wall, but quickly recovered, her eyes regarding him hungrily; a playful smile on her lips. Bray stepped passed, ignoring the woman and cursing himself for not checking if there was anybody outside before leaving Grendel's.

Elora was clouding his mind; his judgement and being at the forefront of any thought or lapse of concentration. He'd already had a near miss with a bus as he'd crossed a busy junction earlier.

He swung a leg over Norgie's old Triumph and jammed his foot down on the kickstart. It thumped to life, coughing out a cloud of black smoke which cleared as he revved the engine. He slipped the clutch and made his way across London, heading for Tilbury docks, as good a place as any to begin the search for the sea witch.

Grendel had given him the nip-crasters, a way of trying to get back into Diagus's good books, although the Shadojak couldn't be bought by favour.

The jar felt clumsy inside his jacket pocket, pressing against his ribs with every bump the old bike found, if the glass shattered the nip-crasters would kill him a whole lot faster than the knoll sap would. And this time he didn't have Elora to help him. Great, there he went again, thinking about the girl.

Never before had somebody filled his thoughts the way she did. And it wasn't as if he could do anything about it. Even if she was an innocent Earth-born there could be nothing between them; Shaiguns, like Shadojaks, forsake love. Love! Was that it now, had he gone and fallen in love? Impossible.

The traffic lights in front suddenly turned red, taking him unawares and he braked harshly, coming to a stop three feet over the white line. He checked in his mirror and noticed the driver of the car behind shaking his head. Bray held his hand up apologising and berated himself for being an idiot. Love? That was stupid. The lights turned green and he accelerated away as fast as the old bike would go.

Tilbury docks was busy. Huge container ships were docked; monolith like cranes reaching into their holds and moving cargo straight onto lorries, waiting to transport the loads to the far reaches of the country.

Bray stayed a while, watching the murky grey water sloshing around the steel vessels until he was satisfied that the sea witch wouldn't remain somewhere so busy.

He turned his attention inland and followed a narrow road that skirted along the mouth of the Thames estuary and then parallel with the river. It was a slow job, especially since he needed to stop every so often when he lost sight of the brackish water and abandon the bike to scramble through gardens or over buildings. But if he was to find Neptula then he needed to be methodical: if he missed one vital spot he would need to restart the search.

Night began to draw on as he neared Elizabeth Docks, a small yet busy yard on the north bank. Two ships were being unloaded in the quay as he paced around the steel wire perimeter. She wouldn't be here; he knew that but perhaps some of the workers had noticed strange 'goings on' along the river.

Procuring a hard hat and hi-vis vest from an empty cloak room, he began to question the dock workers. Speaking with the local accent he posed as a health and safety officer. Within an hour he had spoken to the majority of the staff but had found nothing of interest. He was about to give up and head back to his bike when he came upon a young teen at the water's edge, taking pictures of the ships.

"What you doing here?" Bray asked, putting on an authoritative voice. The boy started and almost dropped his camera in the water.

"I was only taking pictures. I like the ships," he answered, staring at the ground. "I got a thing for ships, like others have for trains or planes. I'm really sorry if I was trespassing."

Bray held his hand up and smiled. "It's ok. Is it just here you come to take pictures?"

"No. I try to go to as many places as possible, you can get the best pictures from Tower Bridge though, but you don't get the bigger ships all too often."

"Have you seen anything strange lately? Anything out of place or unusual?"

The boy cocked his head. "Like what?"

Like a huge bloody sea beast big enough to pull an oil tanker below the waves and crush it like it was a plastic scale model. Bray might have said. "You'd know it if you'd seen it."

The boy shook his head and was about to leave. Bray placed a hand on his shoulder. "The water's edge isn't really a safe place at the moment. Not yet anyway. If I was you I'd keep clear of the Thames for a while."

"Ok. I only came here because some businessman bought the old King's Dock further down. You could get some really good pics from the roof of the service dock, as long as you didn't mind heights. It's a long way down to the water from up there. Mind you, the service dock was well deep. Supposedly a ship had once sunk there, went deep enough for the mast to sink below the water. But some rich business guy bought the whole yard and now I can't even get close."

"Do you know who bought it?"

"Nope, sorry. Was somebody with a lot of dough though. Put up huge fences. Got security guards, dogs the lot. I've even seen a helicopter fly in and land a couple of times. Don't know what he's got planned. Hope it's one of those super docks like they got in the States but I doubt the politicians would … "

"Was it a black helicopter by any chance?"

"Yep. Could have been. I didn't take much notice. Like I said, I'm into ships, not aircraft."

Bray had heard enough. "Thanks for your time. Oh, and take my advice. Stay away from the water."

Bray hid in the shadows of a doorway at the back of an old paper factory, watching the entrance to the old King's Dock. The ship enthusiast had been right. A twelve-foot steel fence had been constructed around the perimeter of the yard, blocking the view inside although it seemed quiet from within. Two security guards stood beside the gate, appearing unarmed but showed the bulges of hand guns beneath their black jackets. They were statue still, more like professional soldiers than hired security. More like takwiches than humans, Bray guessed.

It wasn't long before a car pulled up, one of the security guards opened a back door and a cloaked figure stepped out. It didn't say a word as the other guard opened the gate, bowing his head as it passed through. The tips of the grey cloak swished as it walked, leaving wet foot prints on the dry cobbled street. It was the sea witch. Was she working for Silk? Or was Silk one of her pets?

He waited until the car had gone then prowled along the side of the building, out of the guard's vision. Then, he shimmied up the drain pipe of the building next to the fence. He climbed onto a window ledge that was a story higher than the fence, crouching low whilst balancing on the balls of his feet.

From this vantage point he watched Neptula enter a large square building that sat beside the river. Probably the service house the boy had mentioned. Scanning the grounds, he saw no further threat and so launched himself from his perch.

Clearing the fence by a foot before hitting the ground, he flowed into a forward roll. The jump had been silent but he still checked for any signs that he had been spotted. When it appeared that he hadn't, he crept to the door the sea witch had gone through, hugging the walls and keeping to the shadows.

The only sound he heard from the other side was the steady drip of water but the cause of that could be anything – he was on the docks. Carefully he opened the door as wide as he dared, then slipped through, silently closing the outside world behind him.

Darkness enveloped the inside of the service house, only a faint gloom reflected from the water that almost filled the room, casting ghostly pale fingers around the brick walls. Bray edged closer to the mouth of the service yard and leaned down into the blackness. Maybe Neptula had already gone below and was at this very moment watching him as he sought her out.

The words of Diagus came back to him. 'Don't go near the water, she found the last Shaigun delicious. Warily, he took a step back, then another and slowly drew his sword from its sheath.

"Steel can't hurt me Bray but keep the blade out if it makes you feel safer," came a voice from the corner of the room, its throat sounding dry and full of dust.

From the blackness the cloaked figure stepped out, closely followed by a takwich, his gun drawn. As she came closer to the water she let her hood fall revealing a hairless head, the face bone white, skin cracked and sagging with deep crags down both sides. She stared from dark pits, a smile causing her flesh to crack further, skin pastry thin floated down to the water's surface like fish flakes.

"How do you know my name?" Bray asked, his mind already working on a course of action to take the takwich down. He watched Neptula lower herself to the floor and submerge her legs in the river, her back to him. She let out the kind of sigh he imagined a person would make after sinking into a hot bath.

"I know quite a lot, Shaigun," she said, her voice sounding more seductive and less dry. Bray watched as her face filled out, the dry and dead skin turning to fine silver scales that shimmered with the colours of the rainbow when the light touched it. Thin spikes ran in a single line over the top of her head and down her neck following the line of her spine. An azure blue membrane linked the spines together that she flexed back and forth.

"This water is disgusting, full of poison and man dirt. I can't drink it, eat from it or even get clean. It's good for the rats, good for the dead and nothing else."

"Then why stay?" asked Bray, slowly circling the takwich which was dressed in a police uniform.

"Needs must. But not for long. Keep close, he tells me. But the sea calls to me, singing from the deep blue but I've a song for myself to sing before I leave."

Bray looked down on the black, shark like eyes of the sea witch and forced himself not to shiver as death stared back. "Would it be the song of the leviathan?"

She smiled showing rows of triangular teeth, small yet razor sharp. "A haunting song indeed, the sound of a leviathan. It carries through the depths, stretching across oceans and echoing for days after, beautiful; haunting but beautiful." She patted the space beside her. "Come sit with me Bray, put your feet in the river, feel its motions, its rhythms. For I believe you've a more important question to ask than that of the leviathan."

"You don't deny that you have a leviathan then? You know it brought down an oil tanker killing hundreds of men."

"My children must eat. Oil draws them like bees to nectar. If man left it in the ground they'd dig down for it themselves."

"Children, so there's more than one?" He spared a glance at the witch, her legs swaying in the water, webbed feet bobbing below the surface.

"Sixteen children have I. Swimming in this realm's seas and oceans, surrounding every continent, every landmass."

"Why?"

"To sing of course, humans can't appreciate the beauty of the song in the water. They may appreciate it when they sing out of it. By dawn tomorrow their song will smother this planet entirely. Changing it for the better. Now come, sit." She beckoned him closer with a finger.

"I'm not stupid, Neptula, right here's fine by me," Bray said, returning his attention to the takwich, its face an unreadable mask.

Diagus needed to hear this. Sixteen huge sea beasts roaming at will, the effects would be devastating and that would be before they sang.

"Let's play a game of trust and truths shall we?" asked Neptula, playfully. "I'll go first as you are my guest."

Bray noticed movement from the shadows; long tentacles weaving towards him, he ducked and was about to roll when the takwich suddenly screamed. He glanced up, sword raised but was surprised to see a thick blue tentacle, slick with river water wrap around the policeman's neck, another curled around the arm that held the gun. A heartbeat later the scream was cut short as the tentacle tightened, followed by the snapping sound of the takwich's neck. The body fell to the floor and was dragged into the water, disappearing into the inky blackness.

"A token of trust, Bray," said Neptula, smiling wickedly. "Now one from you. Put away your steel and come sit." She patted the spot next to her again. "I won't bite."

Bray hesitated, then re-sheathed his sword and sat beside her, if she was going to kill him she would have done so already. Besides, he still had the jar of nip-crasters.

"Good. Now that you can see I mean you no harm, we can play. A trust for a truth. An answer for an answer, yes? So ask."

"Why did you kill the takwich?"

Neptula hissed playfully through her teeth. "I was expecting a bigger question, Shaigun. Like I told you already, a token of trust."

"So you don't work for Silk?" he asked.

"Another question wasted. Tut … tut, you're really not good at this." She let out a disappointed sigh. "Silk is merely a puppet who dances to his master's strings. I … provide a service for the master."

"Who's the master?"

Neptula laughed. "A better question, but it's now my turn. A truth for a truth." Her black eyes sparkled in the moon's reflection, deep black circles without any whites. "You know, you've an elvish look to you." Her cold hand traced his face leaving a wet trail behind.

"My mother was an elf. My father a soldier," he said.

"Half-breed. It's a truth I suppose but not one I hadn't worked out for myself. The master's strings are long. Long enough to reach from his prison on Thea."

163

"Who is Silk's master?" he asked again, feeling impatience.

"For that information I will want more than just knowledge of your parentage. Where is the Shadojak?"

Bray shook his head. "He didn't tell me."

"But the girl Elora is with him yes? I can see by the sad look on your face that you are less than happy about that. It is a dreadful shame."

"My master does as he pleases. It's not up to me to question him." The sea witch was far too knowing, a fact that irked him to irritation.

"The Pearly White has his reasons I'm sure. Reasons for not keeping his Shaigun close. Does he fear that when he judges the girl you might stop him? Does he know, I wonder, that you have feelings for her that may compromise your loyalty to his blade? It makes sense then, does it not, that he leaves you behind because he wouldn't leave such a threat alive, would he?"

Bray felt his heart clench, a sudden wave of heat pulsed throughout his body as he realised Diagus' s intentions. He will kill her, regardless of who she is. Simply because his Shaigun shows feelings towards her. Before he could suppress his anger he slammed his fist into the floor, cracking concrete and sending bits into the water. He thought it strange at the time, being sent on a separate mission whilst his master travelled elsewhere with Elora. Could he stop him? Was she dead already?

Neptula grinned slyly, her eyes narrowing in pleasure at his obvious discomfort. "Poor little elf man. Tasting the forbidden love for the first time, then have it ripped away from you before you even realise what it was. Her expression changed to one of mock sympathy. "Please feel free to cry. Nothing tastes sweeter than the tears of a broken heart."

Bray was inwardly hurting but he wouldn't give her the satisfaction of seeing it. Instead he drew on his training, the months spent learning how to suppress emotions, losing your body's reactions to what, when all is said and done, is a mere chemical reaction in the brain and take a mental step away. Becoming rock, becoming Shaigun.

He slipped a smile of his own upon his face, curling it into the most menacing grimace he could muster whilst drawing out the jar of nip-crasters.

Holding it up to the moonlight he slowly turned the glass showing its contents to Neptula. The creatures inside were tiny; bright green fish the size of pinheads, millions of them clustered together with sharp red teeth.

The pleasure dropped from Neptula's face when she realised what he held.

"The girl is nothing to me," he lied. "Now tell me, who is Silk's master? Tell true and I'll give you a minute's head start before I drop my little friends." He suddenly dropped his hand to indicate he wasn't messing around.

"No, don't. Please," pleaded the sea witch, the playfulness vanishing from her with the threat; her eyes locking on the jar. When she didn't answer Bray began to unscrew the lid.

"Solarius," she blurted out, raising her hands towards the jar. "Solarius. The God of Chaos."

"Don't lie to me witch," said Bray, removing the lid entirely and tipping it towards the water.

"No, please. I tell you no lies, Solarius lives."

Bray heard the truth in her words but struggled to believe them. Solarius was slain by the original eight, the founding fathers of the Shadojaks. His body torn apart and his dark knights killed, their swords destroyed and broken into the eight blades which the Shadojaks still hold, thousands of years after the event.

"Impossible. If he was alive we would know," he said.

"He lives and has been plotting his own return for decades. Weaving webs, raising an army, controlling his puppets. As the barrier weakens he grows stronger. Soon he will be free of his bonds and will break both Earth and Thea, bending them to his will."

"You are one of his puppets?"

Neptula nodded. "My last task is to let my children sing. By dawn I will have played my part. Even if you kill me now it won't stop the task from happening."

"Why? Solarius is nothing of the sea. Why are you his?"

"Fool. The God of Chaos won't be content at ruling the lands of both worlds, he wants it all and will spread chaos until it is his. By bending the knee now, I will save my people, my world below the waves."

"He's been beaten before, when the great rift happened. That war is over, finished," Bray argued.

"He was defeated, the battle won but not the war. He returns to get what he believes is his. And this time he's created another beast. A weapon, equally as powerful as himself, a creature spawned from his own loins. It is already here among us, right under our noses."

Bray took in all that was being said, finding it too unreal but beginning to believe the words. If such a thing was possible, then chaos and war would ravage everything breathing on both worlds. It would go some way into explaining why there were so many takwich on Earth. An army.

He needed to contact Diagus and warn him. As he thought of it a mental picture of Elora lying dead at the Shadojak's feet, flashed across his mind. Gritting his teeth, he screwed the lid tightly on the jar.

"Why are you telling me this."

"Let's just say I'm hedging my bets. You may still defeat him. If you take his weapon and use it against him."

"Tell me of this new weapon, this beast he's created. If we kill it, we may slow his plans."

Neptula relaxed her shoulders as Bray lowered the jar to the floor. A token of his trust. "Tell me where this beast, this son of Solarius is. I'll kill him before his father can use him."

"Son?" Neptula smiled. "Solarius didn't spawn a son, he had a daughter. Her name is Elora."

12

Flames and Champagne Cognac

The dark arms of night nestled over the clear sky, smothering another day away. An early star; bright but alone, shone enthusiastically above Clifford's Tower, a medieval circular building near York's city centre. Standing on a small grass mound in the middle of an empty car park; flood lit and on display, one of many stone built relics that lay scattered about the richly historic city.

Diagus parked the car across two spaces and switched off the engine before climbing out. Elora watched him slam the door and wondered if he wanted her to follow. He didn't say much – no, that wasn't right. To not say much would indicate that he had at least said something; which he hadn't. The last words spoken to her were from Norgie.

"Take care," he had said, giving a reassuring squeeze of her hand before closing the car door. Elora had already said bye to Gurple who seemed too upset to wave her off and remained in the house. She had wanted to say a farewell to Bray but the Shaigun had left before she awoke and the Shadojak was of no mind to wait.

They had travelled north for four hours, stopping only once at a service station and Diagus had not muttered one word to her, a frown constantly etched upon his brow as his one eye concentrated on the road ahead. Yet the silence suited her. Her mind was a muddle, juggling with a heavy weight of emotions from worrying about her uncle, to a sense of loss at not knowing if she would ever see Bray again.

She stared out of the window, watching the world pass by but her mind often wondered back to the fairy circle, Bray's head on her lap, twirling his hair through her fingers. Had it been only yesterday? It seemed so far away, so distant but it would be a memory she would take with her to the grave.

York was alive with music, people walking by, men dressed in trousers and shirts, the women, short skirts and tight tops. Couples, small groups, big groups, hen parties, all heading for pubs and clubs that lit up the city, oblivious to the new world which Elora had been introduced to. Did she envy their ignorance? No, she liked to know what was happening, what was real, all of life's details in all its colour, including the darker shades; the perilous parts that wanted to fight her, wanted her dead. It was those that made her feel more alive, even though she was scared witless at the time.

She watched the Shadojak as he stalked towards the tower, heading for a small group of people that sat on the grass mound and decided that she would rather be with him than stay. Whether he wanted it or not.

The small group consisted of two girls a little older than herself, kneeling in front of a lavishly dressed man who sat on the grass his back against the stone wall of Clifford's Tower, playing a seven-string lute and singing with a beautiful voice that was on par, if not better, than her own.

The song was jaunty, sweet and light hearted. His slender fingers picking softly at the strings, teasing each note out perfectly. The girls leaned in close, intent on the song and the comely man and didn't notice them approach but the musician's eyes tracked them; one pale blue, the other green. As he sang, the corners of his mouth grew wider showing perfect white teeth.

> "And what a ferocious sight,
> That on this particular night,
> From a man so bold and feared,
> The stare of the Pearly White."

Diagus stood behind the girls, arms folded, glaring at the man. But the musician didn't appear intimidated, finishing his song with a flourish. He stood and bowed to the girls, his locks of blonde hair almost touching the ground.

Pushing the lute behind his back he took a hand from both girls and kissed the back of each, causing them to blush.

"I fear my little larkings that my songs tonight have ended. But Otholo will rise again on the morro and I will sing you the song of the 'Glen Maiden and the Broken Bell of Arimath'." He kissed their hands once more. "Sweet dreams Cathy."

"I'm Kelly," she corrected.

"So you are my dear. And pleasant dreams to you … "

"Sophie," the girl said, before Otholo guessed the wrong name. They both gave a nervous curtsy before hurrying off. Otholo watched them leave with a cat-like grin. When they had rounded the tower and were out of sight he descended the grass mound until he stood before Elora and the Shadojak.

"This is unexpected, Diagus. I thought I'd never have the pleasure of your amiable company again. You know what your last words were to me?" Otholo cleared his throat and fixed a scowl upon his face. "The next time we meet, you puffed up peacock, I'll take your big dandy head from your shoulders and ram it up your powdered arse." Elora tried to conceal her smile and failed. Otholo had mimicked the Shadojak's voice perfectly.

"Yep," said Diagus. "Sounds like something I'd say. And maybe I still will at that. Unless you can make yourself helpful."

"Of, course," replied Otholo, bowing theatrically. Elora got the sense he was mocking him. "Anything for the Pearly White. And who is this gorgeous young rose you've brought me?" His odd-coloured eyes roamed over her body lustfully before settling on her own odd eyes.

"Does the sweet rose have a name?" he asked, taking her hand and raising it to his mouth. She pulled it back before it touched his lips.

"Elora," she answered, raising an eyebrow at his hurt look. He seemed friendly, in a sly way. She guessed him to be in his early twenties although the way he held himself and acted suggested somebody older.

Otholo smiled. "This rose has thorns. Let me introduce myself, Elora. Seeing as manners are something the Shadojak is lacking. I am Otholo of the golden lute: roaming bard of the southern nations, the morning songbird of the north. I've sung in every city and free town, from the snowcapped peaks in the Valarian Mountains, to the wild dusty villages of the travelling desert people. Personal singer to King Rionstark of Gromland and one-time lover of his daughter Princess Dalana; she wanted to make a prince of me, but alas." Otholo held his hands over his heart, shaking his head, a sorrowful expression drooping his face. "My heart belongs to all, slave to the song and master of music. I belong to everyone and not to just one. I am the whisper in the wind the … "

"Pipe it, you puffed up peacock," growled Diagus, cutting him mid-flow, "We are short of time and I am short of patience yet have temper of plenty."

"Of course, Diagus. So what is that you will have of me? I don't think you've come to seek me out for my voice."

"No. I need you to read a journal for me."

"Whose? And why?" asked Otholo.

Diagus nodded towards Elora "Hers. And because it's written in Minuan."

Elora now understood why he had brought her here. It wasn't to find help in getting her uncle back from Silk. It was to find out who she was. Her eyes roamed over Otholo again, dressed in tight fitting leather trousers and shiny boots with a Cuban heel – a white silk shirt, full of lace at the cuffs and down the button line. About his neck he wore a purple cravat, pinned through with a golden broach in the shape of a lute.

"How can you read Minuan?" she asked, feeling a rising excitement rush over her. This might be her chance to find out who her father was.

"I'm Minuan. Or was before they cast me out." He cocked his head to the side, blue, green eyes puzzling her out. "Tell me why your journal is written in Minuan."

"It's my uncle's. He was also Minuan. He took me from Aslania when I was a child and brought me here."

"But you can't be Minuan. You've the wrong colouring," said Otholo. "I was cast from God's Peak for having a green eye and this." He turned his head, his fingers finding a dark lock of hair amongst his blond curls. Finger thick, it was braided and held together with ivory beads. "They're a strict race, Minuans. Anything more than silver blonde hair, blue eyes and you're out. You think Hitler was bad, he's got nothing on them. These differences I had, made me an outcast. Characteristics from a time when Minuans were less than pure, a throwback. I was given the choice to leave or stay on as a servant with no prospects. To be free, never to return or stay and be castrated. Not much of a choice really. I was glad to be rid of the bleeding lot of them.

"But you Elora, I'm afraid would have been killed at birth. I mean, your hair is raven but your eyes, they're … so un-pure." He bent down to retrieve a bottle of wine that was by his feet, held it up to the light and grinned when he saw the last few mouthfuls of the red liquid. He put it to his lips and upended the bottle.

Once finished he dropped it to the floor and dabbed his lips with a handkerchief that he flourished from his sleeve.

Elora had never heard of her eyes been described as un-pure before. Strange, freaky and on a couple of occasions evil but never un-pure. At least she now knew the reasons she was hidden as a child and why Nat had smuggled her away from Thea.

"So where's this journal of yours? You have me intrigued."

"We need to go somewhere quiet, away from prying eyes," said Diagus.

"Very good. But first I need a drink," said Otholo and putting one arm through Elora's, led them away from the tower, his Cuban heels tapping against cobbles and echoing down the street. She let herself be led, although felt wary of the Shado-jak following silently behind. Was it his intention to take her somewhere quiet so he could give her the final judgment? It's not something he would do in public. Would Otholo try to stop him?

She spared a glance at the bard. Tall and rangy, striding with his chin held high, swaggering confidently-if not a little camp-as if he owned the city. Even if he did stand up against Diagus, she doubted that there was much he could do. Otholo didn't have the look of a fighter.

They passed through the main street, people spilling from several pubs or queuing for the night clubs; laughing, shouting or making out. Otholo weaved passed them, nodding at burly doorman who nodded back, waving out to people he knew who seemed thrilled to see him and winking at random girls, a mischievous grin on his face. It seemed to Elora that the whole of York knew him.

"This way, if you please," he said, leading them down a darkened side street that ran away from the pubs and clubs then down a narrow path that came out onto a lane, a number of shop fronts lay to either side. Dark and quiet, they had long ago shut for the day and so Elora was surprised when Otholo stopped outside a wine merchant shop.

"Frog snot!" he exclaimed, when he pushed on the door and found it to be locked. Then began to pat down his shirt and push his hands inside the pockets of his tight trousers.

"What are you doing?" growled Diagus, glancing up and down the street.

"I've got a key somewhere; I know I have."

When it became apparent that the key wasn't on his person, Otholo scanned the floor, even pushing a plant pot aside with a polished boot.

"Otholo, come on, forget the bloody wine." The Shado-jak shook his head, agitation written hard upon his already hard face.

Otholo paused, bent over and grasped a house brick that lay beside the plant pot he had moved. "Here it is."

Elora thought it was a stupid place to leave a key, under a brick beside the door. But soon realised as Otholo pulled the brick back over his shoulder – that the brick itself was a key.

Before Diagus had time to react the brick passed through the door. The glass imploding, scattering shards of the broken window but the shattering sound was barely audible above the shrieking alarm that forced Elora to cover her ears.

She turned wide-eyed to Otholo and was surprised to see him grinning at her before placing his finger to his lips.

"Shhh," he whispered. Then kicked the remainder of the glass from the door and stepped inside.

Elora watched as Diagus's granite face went a shade of puce and stormed in after Otholo, murder written in his good eye, death in the other. She followed, careful not to snag her arm against any shards left in the frame, hoping that the Shadojak would keep his cool.

Otholo was pulling random bottles of wine from shelves and scanning the labels before tutting and replacing them, perusing at leisure as if the alarm wasn't blaring with the threat of the police at any moment.

"Tsssk, no," he said replacing another. "Is there no decent spirit in the place?" Then his gaze fell upon a shelf at the back of the store. He sauntered across the room and picked up a bottle, removing the cork with his teeth. He spat the cork out, placed the bottle to his lips and took a long pull.

"Much better. Champagne cognac, the only thing worth drinking in this poor establishment. Now ... " He grabbed two more of the bottles and shoved them into Diagus's arms. "Make yourself useful, you can do more than just glare." His attention then turned to her, "Fancy anything, my sweet. Don't be shy, I'm paying."

"No," she replied, feeling angst at the situation. After all, she had broken into a wine shop and the bottles he handed her were worth sixty pounds each. He placed another bottle in her hands and gave her a mischievous wink.

"Right, let us venture forth into the night, I've a wicked thirst that needs quenching." He took another bottle and stuffed it beneath his arm before striding purposefully out of the shop.

The Shadojak shook his head but followed him out all the same and Elora noticed that he still held the cognac. She gripped tight to her loot and hastily went after them.

An hour later saw them on the edge of the city, a small park that sat beside the old city wall, dark and empty. Otholo led them to an empty bench that sat beneath a large oak, its thick branches filtering the amber glow of a street lamp, casting them in a patchy shadow that swayed in the breeze.

Wood creaked as the bard sat down sideways on the bench, crossing his legs and placing them atop the worn arm, making himself comfortable. He took a swig of cognac then placed the half empty bottle on the ground, replacing the drink for his lute. Slender fingers began to pluck at the strings.

"A fine young buxom maid, was she … "

Diagus kicked Otholo's boots from the bench arm, making him pluck the wrong strings and stop singing.

"The Farmer's Seven Daughters' is not to your liking Diagus? Then maybe … The Old Sea Goat?" Otholo began to play a different tune.

"Do you really think I dragged your skinny arse halfway across York only to hear your wind-filled bladder bleed upon the night? No, I want you to read this." He slung the journal at the bard. It bounced off his lute and landed in his lap.

Otholo raised an eyebrow. "My wind-filled bladder has filled palaces; had people crushing into colosseums to hear me sing. My voice has been handpicked by king … " He stopped when he saw the Shadojak's grim expression. "I suppose my voice sounds just as good when reciting from books." He picked up the journal and began to skim through the first few pages.

"What is it I'm looking for?" he asked.

Elora, sitting beside him, stared down at her uncle's swirling writing. "Anything to indicate who my father is. It would be in the first few pages," she said, forcing herself to stop fretting with the scab on her finger from where Grendel cut her for the smuggler's pouch. Instead, she concentrated on Otholo's face, his mouth moving as he read the words to himself, a frown increasing upon his brow, growing deeper with every page until he stopped.

His eyes suddenly locked on hers and she thought she saw fear in them.

"What is it?" she asked, biting her lip. "Does it say who my father is?"

Otholo nodded and took a long slug of the cognac before turning the journal back a page.

"*'Athena hid her pregnancy well,'*" Otholo began to recite, "*'I, her own brother, never knew the truth until the day she gave birth. And only then because the babe came screaming into the world.*

"*'Shock, like none I felt before, took me as I ran to her chamber and saw the tiny pink creature swaddled up in her arms. Shock was soon replaced by fear as I noticed the knife in her other hand, poised above the new babe's neck.*

"*'Had I not taken it from her that instant, I'm sure she would have ended that life before it began. I took the child, a girl, in my own arms, demanding the father's name. My sister became hysterical and through sobs told me how she had, several months ago, felt a dizziness take her whilst praying alone in a quiet sanctum within the High Church. She collapsed and fell into a dream state, neither awake nor asleep. Visions had played in her mind, lustful wants releasing as she felt another presence, holding her, touching her – using her.*

"*'When she finally awoke, it was dark and so she hurried home. Whilst bathing that night she found scratches and bruising on her body where she had no injury before. She told nobody of her dream state in the church and only when she missed her third moon's blood did she realise that she was with child.*

"*'Nightmares had plagued her nights ever since. Terrible dreams of the demon that took her in the church, a dark creature with eyes like the burning embers of coal, fire-kissed blood that ran through his veins. An evil so strong that it could ravish a woman without ever being present. I didn't want to believe her but the facts were wriggling in my arms.*

"'Solarius, God of Chaos and the prisoner in the Well of Redemption had brought a daughter into the world.

"'I found the child to have eyes the colour of burning coals and the fine veins under her thin skin were as red as the fire in the smith's forge. I took the knife from my sister and made a small cut on the back of the baby's fleshy hand and the moment the blood was exposed to the air it caught aflame, scorching the knife I held and forcing me to let it go. The cut healed before my eyes. Further proof of the father's claims.

"'But for all the evil that child should have been, I felt only a babe's innocence. I could no sooner kill her than kill my dear sister.'"

Elora felt icy fingers working through her chest as she struggled with what she was being told. Could it be true? Was she the daughter of a god?

She caught movement beside her, then felt the cold taste of metal against her neck. Whilst listening intently to Otholo she hadn't noticed Diagus slip silently behind the bench, now his sword was drawn and pressing against her neck.

"Do you yield?" he breathed.

"It's not like I can go anywhere," she replied, careful not to move her neck as she spoke; having seen firsthand the sharpness of the Shadojak's blade.

Somehow, unknowingly, maybe on a subconscious level, she had slipped the dagger Grendel had given her from its sheath within the smuggler's pouch and now concealed it beneath her forearm.

"Does the journal speak true, Otholo, does Solarius live?" asked Diagus.

"Solarius never died. How can you truly kill a god? The founding Shadojak's broke him, destroyed the physical form and left it for the crows. It was his sister Minu who took his remains and hid them in the mountains."

"That impossible. The Shadojaks would have known."

"Would they? She was as powerful as her brother although she devoted her energy for the greater good. She was the bringer of light, not a child of darkness like Solarius. Minu healed his body and brought breath once again to his lips. Or so the legend goes.

"When the dark Lord recovered enough to speak, his first words were of vengeance. Swearing by the Mother that he would tear the Shadojaks apart and using his armies would crush mankind from the world. Minu had taken precautions against this and cleverly placed her brother deep inside a cavern within a mountain.

"There, while his body lacked the strength to oppose her, she buried him within rocks too big to be moved by mortal man. She lulled him into a deep sleep by singing him a lullaby, taught to her by the blessed Mother herself. Singing while she buried him deeper and leaving only enough space for her song to echo down to him. That's the reason it's called God's Peak. Years passed as she worked, hollowing out the mountain and turning it into an echo chamber, not once ending the song, for to do so would wake her brother. When she finished her work, Malou, her daughter, took up the song, allowing Minu to build the High Church above a deep well that sank to the bottom of the mountain. This became the Well of Redemption. Once finished, Malou's daughters also took up the song, leaving their mother and grandmother to build a town for the High Church, for what is a church without people? It was named Aslania and populated with followers of Minu. Malou's daughters were also blessed with daughters and took their mother's places, singing the verses that held Solarius. And on it went for thousands of years, daughter replacing daughter, the song never stopping."

"Eversong." The words whispered passed Elora's lips before she could hold them back.

"If this is true, then how did Solarius get free to put his seed in this Athena?" asked Diagus.

"The singing has never stopped but the bloodline grows weaker with every generation, the potency of the song with it. They keep it as pure as they can, hence the reason I was banished – no room for impurities. But the blood still gets watered down with each generation."

Elora felt the sword at her neck bite a little deeper.

"And his spawn will end the song and break his bonds," spat Diagus.

Elora instinctively rolled her neck to the side and leapt from the bench, using it as a barrier between her and the Shadojak. She never actually said she would yield.

"I am not Solarius' s daughter," she yelled at him, trying to stop the rising tide of anger that pulsed through her, quenching her fear.

"Mother damn you, girl. This could have been quick, painless. Yield to me and it will be over in a heartbeat," said the Shadojak as he stalked around the bench.

"Yield? So I can make it easier for you?" Elora growled, circling around the bench, keeping it between them. "I am not that girl. My blood does not catch fire."

Without thinking she brought her dagger down on her own hand. The blade cut deep into her palm, blood welling around its point. She didn't mean for it to sink in so far but like Grendel had warned her, Valerian steel had a sharp edge. Yet the wound hurt no more than a simple paper cut.

"See? It doesn't burn, it's normal blood," she said, holding her palm up, the blood flowing around her fingers in dark streams.

Diagus paused but didn't lower his weapon. "You may have lost your powers Elora, but it's too dangerous to let you live. What if he returns and awakens your abilities? I've got to make the balance. Is your life worth more than all the lives on Earth? On Thea? Because that's what it comes down to. Your life for theirs."

She hadn't thought of it like that. He was right of course. And now she understood why her uncle had kept her hidden. There were those who would kill her, those who would use her. If she hadn't sung that day in Gloucester, none of this would have happened. But she had, the damage was done and there was no changing that now, no going back. She doubted she could live with herself if anybody got hurt or died because of her.

"I yield," she said, dropping the knife. She wouldn't risk the lives of anybody, let alone two world's worth.

Slowly she stepped around the bench and made herself kneel before Diagus, bending her head low and exposing her neck. "Make it quick," she said, feeling too stunned, too numb to be scared, or feel any emotion at all. Perhaps it was for the best. Shutting her eyes, she waited for oblivion.

"No," said Otholo. "She could be useful."

"I've judged her and the balance doesn't way up. I don't want this any more than you but the girl can't live."

"But she maybe the only person who can stop him."

Elora let out breath she'd been holding – was there a hope she may live after all?"

"Explain," said the Shadojak, sword still hovering above her neck.

"Solarius maybe her father but she still has the purist Minuan blood of anyone alive today. As pure as Minu's daughter's blood. If she were to sing the Eversong at the well in the High Church, it would strengthen the barrier that binds him. Making it as strong as it was over a thousand years ago."

Silence engulfed them and Elora could almost hear the Shadojak's brain working as he mulled Otholo's words over.

"Can it be done?" Diagus demanded.

"Well, you would need to get to Thea, travel to Aslania and pass … "

"If she was to get to the well in the High Church, would it work?" Diagus asked more firmly.

"Yes."

Elora glanced up and stared straight into the grim face of the Pearly White.

"Would you do this Elora? Would you sing this … Eversong that binds your father?"

"Yes," she answered.

Diagus put his sword away and offered the empty hand to Elora, "So be it. But crossing me will be the undoing of you."

She took his hand and allowed herself to be pulled to her feet, her legs feeling weak now that her life had been given back. She nodded to the Shadojak, showing that she understood, then slumped next to Otholo on the bench.

He offered her his bottle and this time she took it, putting it to her lips and taking a big gulp, then choked on the foul-tasting stuff.

"The second drink always tastes better," laughed Otholo.

She tried a second time and swallowed the liquid, feeling it burn as it passed her throat. "Thanks for saving my life," she said to him, passing the bottle back.

"Don't thank me just yet. Chances are you'll die before reaching Aslania," he replied before up-ending the bottle and dropping it to the ground. He then shuffled closer to her and took her injured hand in his and delicately wiped the blood from the cut with his handkerchief. "That's some knife," he said, placing the blood-soaked rag on the bench arm.

"Valarian steel," put in Diagus, picking it up from the ground and handing it to her, handle first. "And I see Grendel gave you a smuggler's pouch."

Elora was about to plea for Grendel, not wanting her to get into trouble when Diagus held up a hand. "It's fine. only don't get caught by any city guards on Thea."

Diagus's phone rang before she had chance to ask why.

"Did you find the sea witch?" he asked, the reply deepening his scowl. Elora couldn't hear the person on the other end of the phone but guessed it was Bray. "Sixteen leviathan? Why? … They sing at dawn? That will be anytime now … Elora? What's the girl to you? … Solarius is alive, she is his daughter. I'll explain more when we next meet … I've judged her already

… " Diagus removed the phone from his ear and checked the display before placing it back. "Hello? Bray?" He shrugged his shoulders and placed the phone away. "Lost his signal."

"Was that your She-girl?"

"Shaigun," Elora corrected. Then caught Diagus's glare.

"That boy seems too interested in you," he said.

Otholo laughed. "That boy thinks you've killed her," he explained to Diagus. "The line went dead right after you said you'd judged her."

Again Diagus shrugged his shoulders. "Probably for the best. He'll be taking my blade over before too long. Then he will have no time for girls."

Elora felt suddenly cold. Did Bray have feelings for her? The Shadojak seemed to think so and nobody knew Bray better. But now he thinks she was dead. Would he care? Would he shed a tear for me? She wanted Diagus to ring him back and tell her she was alive but couldn't think of a good enough reason to ask him, other than for her own emotions.

"Sixteen leviathan," Otholo said. "So when do they sing?"

"What do you know about leviathans?" asked Diagus, taking the cognac from the bard and drinking deeply.

"I know they are god created. By Solarius of all gods. And why would he want them? – Because they are weapons."

"I thought Neptune created them. Making beasts that could sing underwater and communicate great distances across the oceans."

"Oh, they can do that. Under the water. But Solarius also made it possible for their song to be heard out of water, and for a very different purpose."

Diagus scanned the horizon. "Well we're about to find out what. Dawn approaches."

Elora searched the same place and saw nothing but the lights and sounds of the city. Music still drifting from a distant night club, a couple of cars and a truck driving along the ring road.

All of a sudden she felt the ground shake, as if a tremor ran under York.

Birds suddenly broke from surrounding trees, squawking with fright as they fought one another to get away from some unseen force. Two deer ran across an open field, leaping as they raced away from an invisible threat. Then the lights went out, throwing the entire city into darkness and a deathly silence settled over the whole area. Even the cars and truck rolled to a stop, their engines cut out and headlights off. Nothing.

Elora's body suddenly lit with an internal fire. Every nerve in every cell sparking with painful bursts of electricity. The pain was so great she fell to the ground, hugging herself. Then as abruptly as it began, it stopped, leaving her feeling weak.

Smoke erupted from her hand, she glanced down to see a red flame flicker along the cut, then fizzle out leaving unblemished skin, the cut healed. Impossible, she thought as she struggled into a sitting position.

The handkerchief, soaked with her blood, suddenly burst into flames on the bench arm, the only light seen from anywhere.

Otholo, sat next to the burning rag, eyes gleaming in the firelight.

"Looks like daddy's little girl has his powers after all."

13

Leviathan's Song

Captain Furghan held tight to the foredeck rail of his trawler. The old vessel listed low in the water, engine dead and at the mercy of the currents. It drifted in and out of the troughs created by the harsh North Sea, taking on more of the brine with every wave that washed over her.

Hugging the rail tight as it dipped once again, the sea slapped his face, soaking his beard with salt water and drenching him to the core. His eyes stung with it, his skin raw, wind whipped and burning, but he couldn't pull his gaze away from the beast that had damaged his boat.

She was sinking and there wasn't a damn thing he could do about it.

It happened moments before dawn. Midge had woken him, shaking him awake in a wild panic, practically dragging him from his bunk.

"You've got to come quick, Cap'n. It's that sea monster that sank the oil tanker last week. It's outside Cap'n. Come on."

Midge had been with him nigh on fifteen years. A solid bloke, plenty of saltwater in his veins, plenty of experience. Like himself, he had seen most of everything the deep blue had to offer. But when he pointed out the colossal beast before them his eyes were wild with panic.

"It's a goddamn kraken," he shrieked.

Furghan craned his head up, searching for the top of the monster, tipping back as far as he would if stood at the base of a skyscraper wanting to see the roof. Tentacles as thick as tube trains, corded with muscle and dripping sea water reached up into the night. They waved and fluttered, curling and slamming back into the sea, sending up plumes of water big enough to sink battleships.

Eight crewmen, the trawlers full contingency, were out on deck staring at the rising creature. The youngest, a lad of sixteen had been gripping a rope with one hand whilst recording footage on his mobile phone.

"Fossy, get your bloody life suit on," Furghan bellowed above the noise.

"Aye Cap'n," Fossy replied and rushed below deck. The other crew members including Fossy's father hadn't been wearing life suits either. But they were all experienced men and it was up to them whether they chose to wear the suit or not. Yet Fossy Junior was the Captain's responsibility.

"It's still rising," shouted Midge.

Furghan watched as the tentacles appeared to reach further up, a large squid like body following with yellow eyes as big as a truck. The black pupil was flat and horizontal like that of a goat.

If the kraken existed in real life and not just Greek mythology, then this beast was surely it.

"Must be a kilometer high, at least," said Fossy Senior.

"Aye. And it's not swimming either. Its fins or feet or whatever it has must be planted in the sea bed, else it wouldn't be able to reach up like that."

oooooooooooooooooooo

"Midge. Bring us about and head for shore. Full throttle," Furghan ordered, wishing he had done it the moment he saw the monster.

"Don't think it even knows we're here Cap'n."

"Now Midge!" he shouted. "If it decides to dive, it's going to have half the sea displacing above it, sucking us down into whatever hell it came from."

That seemed to change his mind.

"Aye, Cap'n," he said and hurried off to the wheelhouse.

"And get hold of the coast guard, see if they can get a helicopter out. They need to see this."

Furghan held tight to the rail, watching as the beast's tentacles seemed to move with a kind of pattern. Swaying to a rhythm and no longer striking the sea.

"What's it doing?" asked Fossy Junior, rushing back on deck, now wearing his rubber life suit. He went to stand by his father, taking his mobile phone out once again.

Nobody answered as they watched the creature, its long appendages now locking out straight, then slowly curl down forming an upside-down bell shape.

Furghan got a nasty feeling in the pit of his stomach. He felt so insignificant staring up at the monster. It was like god's way of showing you how pathetically small you actually were in the grand scheme of things.

The old diesel engine began to pick up pace, chugging loudly and coughing out fumes from the large chimney above the engine room as Midge brought the boat about. The captain winced and expected the big yellow eyes of the kraken to swivel onto his tiny vessel. Thankfully it didn't, having not heard or not taking any interest. It seemed totally immersed in what it was doing.

"It's getting bigger" shouted the boy and Furghan witnessed it for himself. Although he wouldn't have said it was getting bigger, expanding as if huge lungs pushed against its sides as it sucked in air.

The tentacles flattened in that bell shape, the sides of each extending to meet the next and forming a tight seal. It was gearing up for something, but only itself and God knew what.

He gazed off the starboard bow and saw the flickering light from Flamborough Head's lighthouse and wondered if they were witnessing what they were. Most probably not, the creature was a dark object against a dark backdrop. Only the lights of Whitby Harbour, further down the coastline, could be seen sparkling on the water.

To the opposite side above the sea line he watched the first appearances of dawn touching the sky with a deep blood-red hue. 'Red sky in the morning, sailors warning', went the old saying – damn, but that was true.

The bell shape that formed above the kraken widened as the squid-shaped monster drew it towards where its mouth would be. Then it drove it forwards, exhaling its sides with it; causing a deep grumbling noise that shook the boat and rattled every man down to the bone.

Pain ruptured from Furghan's ears. He clamped his hands over them, crouching low to the deck and curling up, expecting the world to implode. As he opened his eyes the world appeared in a blurred vision, where everything vibrated with the creature's sound waves. He spared a glance to his men, they were all doing the same save for Foss senior who lay face down on the deck, motionless.

All the lights on the trawler suddenly blinked out and the engine ceased its chugging. Furghan pulled his hands from his ears, they came away bloody as if his eardrums had popped. They hurt like hell but he ignored the pain as he crawled towards Fossy.

"What's up with him? Has he been knocked out?" shouted one of the crew who joined him. It was Derek, one of the older crew members. Furghan noticed that he too had blood dripping from his ears.

Together they rolled the man on his back and Furghan lay his face against his chest. Nothing.

"Heart attack. Fetch me the defibrillator and the first aid box," he shouted as he began CPR. Derek ambled away while he began pumping pressure, hands laced together over Fossy's heart. He spared a glance at the creature that was still bellowing into the sky as if singing, letting the world know it was there.

The rest of the crew gathered around, watching with shocked expressions. All except Fossy Junior who knelt by his father's head holding his hand.

Derek returned with Midge in tow.

"There's no power, Cap'n. No lights, no radio. Nothing. Even the bloody torches are flat and I replaced the batteries myself last week," Midge said as he stared down at the scene.

Derek dropped the defibrillator beside Fossy. "That thing's flat too. Bloody useless."

Junior stared down at his father, tears running down his face. "Wouldn't have worked anyway. Dad's got a pace-maker – thing would have fried it."

Furghan stopped the CPR, sat back on his haunches and put a hand on young Fossy's shoulder.

"I'm sorry lad. I wish I could do something more."

Junior nodded, but didn't look up. "Stay with him" he ordered Derek, who he knew would be more compassionate to the lad than the rest of the crew. Then turned to Midge. "Come on, we need to get that engine going again or we'll go down with the kraken."

No sooner had he spoken than a rogue wave washed over the boat, the force strong enough to knock every man off his feet and tip the vessel at such an angle that Furghan saw more sea than sky.

He slid into the wall and almost went overboard, only just managing to lock an arm around the rail and hold fast.

Quickly he craned his head around to check his crew, they were all on the deck, gripping ropes, sheeting or the steel supports. Thankfully no more injuries.

When his vision panned back to the monster he saw that its tentacles had disassembled from the bell shape and were now curling about as the creature began to sink, slapping the water and causing massive waves that smashed his boat.

"Brace yourselves," he bellowed, as a vertical wall of water rose out of the sea, blocking his vision.

He gripped tighter to the rail as it struck, rocking the boat a second time. The trawler let out a painful groan, then something smashed the hull and Furghan realised that he could hear water gushing into the boat from below.

The vessel never righted itself, instead it listed to the side. He counted his men once again. Then he shouted for Midge.

"Get the lifeboat in the water. We're abandoning ship." The dreaded words left his mouth, tasting salty and sour. Something a Captain hoped he had never need to command.

Midge nodded and crawled on hands and knees to the steel container box that contained the inflatable Zodiac. He grabbed Derek on the way and together they dragged the bright orange bag to the edge. He held the cord while Derek hauled the lifeboat overboard.

Midge glanced back at Furghan and nodded. The job done, the crew slid to the rope ladder and climbed down into the inflatable boat.

The kraken was going down faster now, the sea following in a great mass, pulling the broken boat towards it. Furghan watched his men disembark until only junior and himself remained. He crawled over to the lad who still held his father's hand.

"Come on son. We need to leave," he said, as softly as he could under the extreme circumstances.

Junior wiped his wet face with the back of his sleeve. "I'm not leaving him."

"We don't have a choice. This boat's going down and soon. We need to abandon ship."

"No. You go, I'm staying." The determined youth stared him in the face, jaw clenched.

Furghan put a hand on his shoulder and squeezed. "I've already got to tell your mother that she's lost a husband. Do you think she wants to lose a son too?" Junior thought it over for a second then rose to his feet and let himself be led to the lifeboat.

Once in the Zodiac, they began to row. Six men, six ores. The outboard motor hadn't started but that didn't surprise Furghan. It appeared that whatever the creature screamed, it had knocked the life from everything electrical, including batteries – including Foss senior.

"Row lads, row. Our lives depend on how much water we get between us and that sea beast. Pull, pull. Come on stick your backs into it. Pull … " Furghan screamed the words over and over, willing his men on until faces were red with the strain.

They were several hundred meters away when the beast had fully submerged, taking the trawler with it. Leaving a dark empty sea, still and calm, the red dawn sky shimmering atop its surface and showing no sign of the monster that sank his livelihood with one of his crew.

He scanned the coast, searching out the lighthouse but saw no light, nor did he see the lights of Whitby Bay. The damage the kraken had done had spread to the mainland, he wondered how far it had gone.

∞∞∞∞∞∞∞∞∞∞∞∞∞

Bray threw his mobile phone against a building in a flash of temper. Smashing on impact it fell to the ground in a thousand pieces.

"She's been judged." The last words Diagus spoke to him before the line went dead. She's been judged. Dead, in other words. Neptula's warning came too late and now Elora had paid the ultimate price.

He had rung as soon as he could but it wasn't soon enough and he couldn't even call the Shadojak back because his phone lost power. As did the street lights along with Norgie's motorbike. A passing lorry engine cut out at the same time and glided to a stop, the driver looking baffled as the city fell into darkness.

The leviathan had sung.

Anger, raw and all consuming, boiled through Bray's core. An emotion he hadn't felt in years, yet one he could control if he wished it, but did he wish it?

His foot connected with Norgie's motorbike the instant before his mind registered what he had done.

The old Triumph clattered over, wing mirror shattering against the road, handlebar buckling and denting the fuel tank. As its rocking stopped Bray put one hand against the building and taking a deep shuddering breath he forced himself to gain control. Elora was dead.

He had only known her for a little over two days, so why was he feeling this way? Was the sea witch right; had he found love and lost it without ever knowing what it was? Was it even possible to fall in love in two days?

Bray stamped his foot into the ground, cracking the flagstone he stood on. He wanted to fight something, he wanted to destroy, to damage. To kill.

Dawn had arrived. A blood-red dawn that bathed London's tall buildings in an angry glow, reflecting from windows that should have been lit from within.

No electricity. No sounds of engines, the roads eerily quiet, cars and trucks parked haphazardly where they came to a stop after the Leviathan song. There were no planes in the sky, no helicopters, no boats on the Thames. It was like the city had died.

Bray let his feet carry him randomly through the quiet streets, along roads and paths, not really thinking where he was going, not even caring. He passed people, not giving them much notice but got the impression that they were lost without the lights and sounds of the city.

One man was trapped on the inside of a building, banging on the glass, the automatic door not being so automatic anymore and he didn't have the common sense to find the emergency exit. Bray ignored him and carried on.

Down another street he startled a cat that emerged from an alley. The ginger tom had a dark lizard-like creature hanging limp in its jaws, black blood dripping from webbed feet.

The cat eyed him suspiciously, watching him pass before disappearing back into the alley, his teeth still clenching its prize.

Bray recognised the dead thing it carried to be a plugrin, a venomous reptile that usually lurked in the shallow ponds and swamps in the river lands on Thea. Lucky for the cat he'd caught only a small one, he had seen much bigger plugrins, but it shouldn't have been here in the first place. He watched the ginger tail as the cat disappeared from view and wondered what other creatures would begin to break through the barrier.

By the time the sun had risen above the cityscape, Bray found that his legs had brought him near Canary Wharf. In front of him, looming high and dominating his vision was Silk's building. He had just enough time to register where he was and hide from view as the entrance swung open and row upon row of soldiers marched out. Each carrying a rifle and wearing combat fatigues.

Bray counted at least twelve platoons, separating as they met the road, half going one way, half the other. At the head of each file, rode an officer on horseback, shouting down at the men in that rattily clicking tongue of the takwich. It was clear that they were to head into the city, but for what reason he didn't know. He doubted it was to keep law and order.

Bray debated whether to draw his sword and cut them down from the rear, letting his steel sing and taking as many down as he could before he was taken down himself. It was a foolish suicide mission but the black mood he was in made it tempting.

He waited until they were out of sight and crept back to scan the main entrance. Two guards stood beside the glass door. Armed with rifles, they would see him coming before he could get close enough to take them down. He guessed the exit at the rear of the building would also be guarded. Silk wouldn't make a mistake like that. Not when he had done so much planning already. So this would be a waiting game, then.

Bray crawled beneath an abandoned a car that had broken down near the gate and kept vigil. Silk had all this planned out. His army was taking the capital and with no electricity, not even battery life, there would be no communications to mount a defence.

The glass door swiveled round and four policeman marched out, an elderly prisoner cuffed and blindfolded being forcefully led between them, two to each side. They made their way across the car park and loaded the prisoner into the back of a horse-drawn carriage, two of the policeman climbing in the back with him, two in front.

The carriage itself was modern; made from a light metal with slender spoked wheels and tyres. He wondered how many of these Silk had. With the death of electricity and the combustion engine, horses would become the best form of transport and it seemed the takwich had more than a few.

The driver whipped the horses and the carriage wheeled out onto the street and began to make its way toward the city centre. Bray waited until they passed the car he was hiding beneath before rolling out and following.

The horses travelled at a steady trot, metal shoes striking tarmac and replacing the sounds of rolling rubber. It wasn't hard for him to keep pace, crouching behind parked cars, vans, sprinting the gaps between and avoiding being spotted as the carriage weaved through the vehicles that lay abandoned in the road. If the leviathans had sung at the time of rush hour, the streets would have been a solid block of metal. Maybe that's why they chose a dawn attack.

As they approached a junction, Bray saw that a bendy-bus had stopped across it and made an impenetrable obstacle, forcing the carriage onto the pavement. He waited until they were at a choke point, the back wheels catching against the curb and holding them momentarily. Then he leapt upon the bus, ran along the roof in a crouch, drawing out his blade and as silent as cat he launched himself onto the back of the carriage.

He landed beside the prisoner and drove the hilt of his sword into the takwich beside him. Anger pulsed through his veins as he punched the other man in the throat, collapsing the windpipe while his blade cut deep into the skull of the takwich in front. Blood spraying up as he wrenched his sword free.

The motion startled the horses and they began to buck, one of them kicking the chest of the driver and knocking him off the carriage. The remaining takwich made to grab the reins as the horses bolted forwards, pulling them off the curb with a bang.

Bray grabbed the back of the seat before he fell out, the horses now in full gallop, hurtling down the street now it was free from the bus. Londoners who had been wandering like lost sheep in the middle of the road, dived out of the way as they raced by.

Bray righted himself as the last takwich took the reins with one hand and levelled a gun in his face with the other. He twisted his head to the left and felt the bullet brush the hairs on his scalp before it thudded into the takwich whose throat he had punched.

Before his attacker had time to fire another shot, Bray grasped the top of the gun, twisted it around and yanked it back.

The hammer fell and connected with the firing pin. The bullet entered through the takwich's temple and exited the back of the cranium, pulling grey chunks of brain and splintered fragments of skull with it.

The body fell from the carriage and Bray took the reins.

"Woah, easy now," he spoke soothingly to the horses, pulling gently back on the reins.

They slowed to a trot but he didn't stop until he was sure that the takwich that was kicked from the carriage wasn't going to catch them up.

Guiding the horses onto a quiet road he halted. Climbing back into the rear seats he put a hand to the prisoner's shoulder and pressed the tip of his sword to the man's exposed neck. In one fluid movement he pulled the blindfold off and studied the old man.

He was of an age with Norgie, with long greying hair that still held a hint of blonde and the bluest eyes he had ever seen in his life.

"Who are you?" Bray asked, relaxing the grip on his sword.

"My name's Nathaniel."

Bray nodded. He searched the takwich's body and found the keys for the handcuffs. "You're Elora's uncle." It was a statement, not a question. The fact that he resembled her brought a fresh jolt of heartache.

Nathaniel's shoulders seemed to relax. "You have her, is she safe?"

Bray clenched his teeth and willed the emotion from his voice. "Climb in the front," he ordered, climbing into the front himself and taking hold of the reins.

From the alley beside him, a large black reptile padded out on webbed feet. A limp tom cat hanging between sharp teeth, blood dripping from the end of its ginger tail. Its head bounced as the adult plugrin scurried away with its prize in its jaws.

"We need to get out of the city," Bray said as Nathaniel sat beside him. He snapped the reins and got the horses into motion.

14

Drink a Spirit to Trap a Spirit

Elora shifted uncomfortably in her saddle but no matter how she positioned her legs or bottom, it was impossible to avoid a sore spot. At least her mount had stopped trying to bite Diagus's horse; her Gypsy Vanner had a temper, almost as bad as her own. Her ears seemed to be permanently pulled back, eyes bright and alert, waiting for any opportunity to bite the heavy set cobs Diagus and Otholo rode.

"Your arse sore, girl?" asked the Shadojak, whose mood seemed to lift as they began to ride although it was still a long way from being happy. "Give it another hour and it will go numb."

They'd been riding all afternoon, steel shoes clip clipping against the tarmac of a dual carriageway that led away from the vale of York, yet it seemed an age ago that she had first mounted her horse. Intimidated by the mare at first, as it bit her when she first put her foot in the stirrup, she asked to swap with Otholo whose grey cob, like the Shadojak's, seemed calm and amiable.

"No, sorry Elora. The dealer said that your mare didn't like men riding her," said Otholo, who looked amused.

"She doesn't want me riding her either," she replied, pulling her arm away and narrowly avoiding another bite. She lost her temper then and tapped her horse on the end of its nose.

"Quit it or I'm going to bite a chunk off your own stupid ear!" she growled, glaring at the mare and baring her teeth. Otholo was laughing behind her, she turned to him about to give him a piece of her mind when he saw her face and laughed louder.

"You suit each other. Give Daisy a carrot and make friends," he said through sniggers.

Elora snatched the carrot he offered and turned back to the mare. She was the best looking of the three with a long flowing white mane and tail. Large chocolate brown patches on her white body and another over half of her face covering one of her dark eyes. She would have had a warm handsome face if she wasn't screwing it up in anger all the time.

She held the point of the carrot to the horse's mouth but pulled away when she opened it. "We can be friends Daisy." She kept her tone soft, keeping eye contact and allowed it a nibble. "Don't show me up in front of them." Again another nibble. "Now I'm going to climb on your back and you're going to be a good girl." She gave it the rest of the carrot, took a deep breath and put one foot in the stirrup and hauled herself up.

Daisy turned her head to bite, baring her teeth over Elora's leg, but before the mare had time to bite down, Elora leant forwards in the saddle and sunk her teeth into the horse's neck. Daisy whinnied and reared up yet Elora held fast, keeping her teeth firmly planted but not biting so hard as to draw blood – the taste of horse was bad enough.

Hooves slammed back onto the ground, the mare snorting loudly through flared nostrils. Elora increased pressure on her teeth before letting go then glared at the horse as it turned its head as if ready to bite again.

This time she pulled back, stamping a hoof in frustration and whinnied once again but Elora thought she had gotten the message.

On the journey since, she thought the two of them had come to an understanding, albeit reluctantly.

The dual carriageway seemed to go on forever. Stretching out into the distance, cars and trucks were left abandoned with just enough space for them to weave through. For the first few miles she noticed that the majority of people stayed with their vehicles, waiting for the authorities to come and fix the problem. But the further on they travelled the steadier the flow of people, ambling down the hard shoulder; growing until there were more people walking than staying in cars.

"Like sheep," remarked Otholo. "It only takes a few bright individuals to realise that nobody is coming to help and that they need to fend for themselves. But once people notice that others are joining the ones walking, they'll follow on like sheep."

Elora found that Otholo was right. The further they rode the more people walking towards them, until they reached a point where the number of people on the road began to dwindle until only a rare few still sat in vehicles. This seemed to be the very old or immobile, watching them ride past and wondering what to make of three horses riding the wrong way along what should be a busy road.

"We should help them," suggested Elora, after seeing an elderly man, reclined back in his driver's seat, mouth wide open and snoring loudly.

"No, we keep moving," replied Diagus.

"It will start to get dark soon. How are those people going to get home?" she asked, annoyed at the Shadojak's lack of compassion.

"What would you do, give them your horse? Carry them back to York? Then what? Help the next person, then the next?" He gestured with his arm to the world in general. "One leviathan rid this entire country of electricity, power, communications. With sixteen of them your father has plunged Earth back into the dark ages. You can't help any one person, but you can try and save them all. And the longer we delay, the worse it will get."

"What do you mean?" she asked, forcing herself to look away from the elderly man.

"They'll band together to start with. Community spirit and all that. Help each other out. But after a few days with no electricity, no running water, they'll start to look out for themselves. Even if the authorities, the police, the army, had sufficient resources to help the population, do you think that they would just sit at home waiting? No, it's not in their nature. Panic will set in soon enough, they'll be no control and they will turn on each other. So you may save a handful of them today, maybe tomorrow, but you can't save them all, one at a time. You want to help the old man, best thing you could do for him is run that pretty dagger of yours across his throat. Better to die in your sleep than have days of suffering and die anyway."

Elora stared into his back, mulling his words over. No doubt he was right. But that didn't stop her feeling terrible over it. Especially since it was her father, Solarius, that was the cause.

Night came on swiftly and with no lights it seemed a darker kind of night. Elora followed Diagus as he left the road, leading his horse across an empty field. She kept far enough back so that Daisy wouldn't bite his cob's rump. He led them through another field, then up a small hillock to a copse of trees that stood black against the dimming sky.

"We're stopping here for the night?" asked Otholo, who'd turned his nose up as if experiencing a bad smell.

"If it's not to your liking, then take your pampered peacocks arse, somewhere else," said Diagus as he dismounted and tethered his cob to a tree.

Elora climbed down, her legs feeling like jelly from the day's ride and began to tie her reins to a tree.

"No, leave them to graze. They won't go far. There's a stream at the bottom of this hill they can drink from. I'm going to the next town to get supplies. You two stay here and get some sleep."

Otholo looked about, his face pinched, "How delightful," he said, but dismounted and removed his saddle from his horse. Elora did the same, smiling as Daisy sped off.

"I'll be back in a couple of hours," said the Shadojak, glancing down at Elora's trainers. "What size feet are you?"

"Six, why?"

"You're going to need a pair of boots. Those things won't last." He nodded towards her footwear, then glanced down at Otholo's feet and shook his head, making a tssk sound through his teeth.

"Don't think you're going to be choosing me any boots," said Otholo, scowling at him. "I've seen your dress sense and I find it lacking my rich qualities."

"Whatever, peacock. Make sure one of you keeps awake at all times" he said and re-mounted his cob. Then putting heel to flank he rode away.

Otholo dropped his saddle onto the ground beside a tall birch and lay back on it, the lute across his stomach. Fast fingers picked gently at the strings as he spoke.

"So what does it feel like being a demigod?"

Elora copied him, placing her saddle against the birch beside his and sat on the soft grass. "I feel the same as I did before. Out of my depth. I'm the same girl, but then, I've always been a bit different than most. My blood catching fire is something new I suppose. It's never done that before."

"That's because Earth's magic has suppressed yours. That's why your uncle brought you hear, expecting that you wouldn't be able use whatever he thought you'd inherited from your father."

"Earth has no magic. None that I've felt anyway." She could hear Daisy snorting somewhere below, probably at the stream Diagus mentioned.

"Of course you have. It's called electricity. You don't get that on Thea. And not because it's yet to be discovered. It's that it doesn't exist. People have tried to create it and have failed. Thea has its own kind of magic. A force that wouldn't work here, just like electricity won't work there. You know, there used to be a little magic on Earth that spilled over from Thea. Every now and then, something slipped through. Only small, say the odd fairy, pixie or even a unicorn. And sometimes something sinister came through, say a goblin, troll or takwich. It used to be common to fear the dark, to not travel alone at night or enter strange forests. But they became old wives' tales, maybe a couple of hundred years ago. Around the time that men on Earth started to play with electricity. It's only recently that the barrier has weakened and allows once again, magical creatures through."

"But now electricity doesn't work here either," she said.

"And that, my little demigod, is why your blood catches fire." He paused, resting his slender fingers against the strings and grinned wickedly showing his perfect white teeth. "So I wonder what other powers you have."

"I don't know if I have any. What was Solarius capable of, what powers did he have?" She didn't want to call him father out loud, she felt too ashamed of who he was.

"The same as most gods I suppose; he's immortal, he can fly, he can manipulate elements but mostly, he burned things. That's what he was best at, his legacy. He tore through Thea and left it blackened, scorched and smoldering."

"Then maybe it's better that I don't try. I don't want to damage anything."

"Probably wise. It was said that he razed the city of Tilanis to the ground. Burning the place with enough heat to reduce it to a molten river." He lay his lute down and retrieved a bottle of cognac from his saddle. "Try to sleep, I'll stay awake."

Elora doubted sleep would find her, but she lay back and closed her eyes. "Otholo, why did you come? You'd made York your home."

"My home is anywhere; a bard shouldn't linger too long in one place. Oh, they try to keep me, some cities. Some people. Did I mention that I was one-time lover to the princess of Rosland? She would have made a prince of me, you know?"

"I know; you've told me that already. So why come?"

Otholo took a deep pull from the bottle. "Because I feel a story unfolding. A big story that songs will be made of and it will be my words, my lips that will craft this adventure. I'll be with you to the very end, whether it's a bitter one or no, I can't say, but I will be the one to make a song of it. Now sleep, your thighs are going to be as sore as a dock whore's … " Otholo paused, struggling to find a better word for a lady and failed. "They will be sore, demigod or not."

Elora said goodnight, thankful that she felt so tired that she barely gave a thought to how uncomfortable she was. Yet her mind was plagued with the death her father bestowed upon the Earth. No electricity meant that everyone in a hospital on life support would be dead, anyone on dialysis or with a pacemaker also. All those who would be killed in the near future either from starvation or as an act of direct violence, like the Shadojak predicted. All those lives, gone.

Guilt rose with the numbers that she tallied in her head and tears ran down her cheeks, but she remained silent, swearing to herself that if she had the powers to help, she would use everything which she had for the greater good or die trying.

Sleep must have found her at some point as she jolted awake with a not too gentle nudge to her leg.

"Wake up girl, we've got plenty of ground to cover and you've yet to catch that damn mare of yours," Diagus grumbled as he dropped something beside her.

Pain throbbed through Elora's neck as she sat up, gritty eyes adjusting to the predawn sky. Her side joined in with the pain in her neck, an ache that stretched down one side of her torso and as she clambered to her feet her inner thighs screamed at her, drowning out the other pains.

"Put those on and grab your nag," ordered Diagus, nodding to the boots he had dropped in front of her. "We'll have break-fast once we're on the move."

By the time the sun had risen above the fields and trees, they were making their way back to the road. They would have been well on their way already if Daisy hadn't kept running off whenever Elora got within a few feet of her. Much to the amusement of Otholo who had easily caught and saddled his horse, laughing as Elora stumbled through the thick grass. It was only when Elora growled at the nuisance mare and threat-ened to send her to the knacker's yard that Daisy let her put the bridle over her head. But not before painfully nipping at her shoulder.

Breakfast consisted of dried bread and a large wedge of cheese which Diagus cut from the wheel he had stolen.

By the afternoon they had swapped the road for a country lane with tall hedges to either side, broken occasionally with steel gates leading to fields. The stiffness in Elora's legs had finally abated and with the sun warming her face she found the gentle motion of Daisy, mixed with the creaking of the leather saddle, pleasant. Under different circumstances she may have enjoyed the ride, even with the moody mare attempting to bite the other horses, whenever their rumps came within reach.

"So where are we heading?" Otholo asked.

Diagus stretched his neck to the side, making a sharp clicking sound. "Rams Keep."

"Never heard of it. What awaits us at Rams Keep?" asked the Bard.

"Why would you have heard of it? It's a secret place, a bolt-hole that the Shadojaks have been using for centuries. There'll be food, shelter, supplies."

"Girls?" cut in Otholo, excitedly.

"A girl, and one that you'd best keep your hands off or she's as like to take them, along with your stones."

Otholo produced his bottle of cognac that never appeared to be too far from hand and swallowed a mouthful. "We'll see what she does with my stones after she's heard me sing. Maybe the ballad of the piebald swan – it never fails to get the ladies swooning." He gave a mischievous wink to Elora. "Did I mention that I was the personal songbird to King … "

"Yes," Elora and Diagus said together, much to the detriment of Otholo.

"Sing what you will peacock, but you've been warned."

Otholo took another swig of his drink, feigned indifference and picked the pace up, trotting in front of them.

"Will Bray be there?" asked Elora, trying to feign indifference herself but felt her face grow warm when she said his name.

"Like as not, if the boy's got any sense that's where he'll be."

Otholo suddenly stopped, his cob's hooves scraping against the road, steel upon asphalt. Elora looked passed the bard to see why he had halted and saw a large white strip of plastic, scorched and smelling of petrol, laying above the hedgerow.

She thought it a kind of long flat roof at first, an unusual thing to see across the road, sleek and paneled with tendrils of smoke billowing from its edge. Then she recognised it for what it was. The wing from a large aircraft, but where was the plane itself?

Steering her mount about, Elora cantered to the last break in the hedge and opened the gate. Daisy snorted and shook her head to either side, not wanting to ride into the field but as Elora patted her neck, giving her reassurance, the horse reluctantly trotted on.

The scene before her was straight out of a disaster movie. The crushed fuselage lay crumpled and smoldering in the centre of the field, the cockpit having broken off entirely and lay on its side, the nose crushed; blackened glass scattered about the long grass. It was huge, not a jumbo but big enough to carry over a hundred people. The other wing and tail were gone entirely.

Elora sat rigid in the saddle, taking in the horrific sight; destruction on a scale she found hard to comprehend.

"Where are all the passengers?" The words tumbled past her lips, barely audible to herself. The breeze carried them away as she realised that the passengers were still in their seats.

Charred blackened lumps that molded into the fuselage, nothing recognisable as human, apart from the odd shape of a cranium here, an elbow joint there; nothing to distinguish between bodies and the seats they were strapped to. Just blackened lumps.

She didn't hear the Shadojak approach, her eyes fixed on the bodies but became aware of him only when her horse tried to bite his.

"Come now girl, nothing we can do for them," he said, wheeling his horse around. His face was grim. "We need to keep going."

Elora tapped Daisy's flank lightly with her heel, setting her in motion, but not in the direction Diagus wanted. She set off towards the wreck of the plane, whispering words of encouragement to her horse to keep her moving, not knowing if the Shadojak followed and not caring.

A crow took flight as Elora neared the mass grave, startling him from the meal it was making from a blackened corpse. It screamed at her as it circled above, now joined by two others – black eyes staring down dark beaks, upon darker feathers. They'd be others joining the feast soon, other carrion birds and scavengers; plenty for everybody. She drew her gaze away from the carnage, feeling bile at the back of her throat. Her father did this.

Movement pulled her attention towards the cockpit, an arm waved from within a shattered window. Bloodied, weak but moving. She jumped down from Daisy and ran towards it, stumbling over strewn baggage and almost losing her footing in her haste to get there.

The remains of the cockpit rocked as she climbed in, scrambling over torn seats, broken plastic and bits of people. A wheezing gurgling sound brought her attention to the pilot's seat, the pilot still in it. His head slumped back and struggling to breathe.

Elora crawled over the debris to reach him, he must have sensed her coming as his breathing suddenly became more erratic as he attempted to turn in the seat but was trapped – his legs crushed into the controls and switchgear.

"Don't move, ok?" she heard herself say. "Try and keep still or you'll do yourself more damage." If that was possible.

As she slipped alongside him she got a better view of his injuries and gasped. It was a wonder he was alive at all. A shard of glass was embeddedin his forehead, narrowly missing an eye, his vision blocked from the blood that flowed from the wound. The steering wheel was pinning him in place, pushing into one side of his chest, his clavicle protruding, broken and white through his torn bloodied shirt.

"Water," he said, the words sounding wet as blood bubbled from his mouth.

"Keep still. I'll bring you water," she said, taking his hand gently in hers. "Help's coming," she reassured him, but guessed that even then his chances of survival were slim to none.

Diagus crept up beside her, scanning the pilot's wounds.

"He asked for water," she offered, hoping that the Shadojak could help him.

His face fixed and expressionless, he produced a flask of water. With a tenderness that belied anything that Elora knew of Diagus, he tipped the man's head back and rested it in one hand whilst putting the flask to the pilot's mouth.

The injured man sipped the water at first, then took a bigger swallow before coughing some back out. Then with a swiftness that almost went unseen, the Shadojak leaned forwards and slipped a small dirk between the pilot's ribs.

In – out, without a sound. He gently lowered the man's head to his chest, silent now that the painful breathing had ceased, almost peaceful.

"What did you do that for?" demanded Elora, shock causing her to tremble.

Diagus looked at her grimly. "I gave him mercy. This plane came down over a day and a half ago. Nobody has come to help, nobody will. A quick death is better than a prolonged painful one." And with that, he crawled out of the cockpit leaving her with the dead pilot.

He was right of course, nobody would come but it didn't stop her feeling shock, the cold way in which it happened, in – out and that was that.

When she felt the strength return to her legs she climbed out of the cockpit, leaving the pilot in his tomb. Diagus was already mounted, Otholo at his side, Daisy's reins in his hand.

"Mount up girl, we've got ground to cover," said Diagus and began to swing his horse around.

Elora wiped cold sweat from her brow, feeling a tide of anger rise from deep within her chest.

"You're a heartless bastard." The words echoed around the field.

Diagus halted and looked down at her, then simply shrugged his shoulders. "I've never pretended otherwise."

"And you're a complete … arsehole!" She shouted the last word, hearing it again as it echoed back.

Otholo's face paled as he made his horse sidestep away from the Shadojak whose mouth turned up in a grin.

"Happens you might be right there, too. But it doesn't change anything. Now get on your horse and get moving."

Elora watched him ride out of the field, hatred burning fierce inside her, making her clenched fists shake uncontrollably. But the raw emotion wasn't directed at Diagus, it was at her father and at herself for not being strong enough to deal with the fact.

Daisy eyed her suspiciously as she approached. Taking the reins from Otholo, Elora expected the mare to attempt to bite her but she must have sensed something in her that gave her a change of mind.

"You know; nobody has ever called the Shadojak an arsehole before," remarked Otholo. "Especially the Pearly White. I think there's a song in that somewhere."

They rode for the remainder of the day in silence and spent the night beneath the canopy of a shallow wood that bordered farmlands. By the third day in the saddle Elora thought she had bonded with the Gypsy Vanna. No longer did she try to bite her, nor did the mare run away when approached to saddle up in the morning. She ruffled the long forelock that hung in front of the horse's face, thick white hair blocking her vision. Daisy snickered at the touch, ears forwards and walked with a calm steady stride. Elora decided she would keep her, if they both survived the ordeal ahead.

They covered a lot of ground that day, mostly fields of crops yet to be harvested or sparse woodland that lay scattered about the farms. But no people, not one. Until early into the afternoon.

They rounded a lane that crested a thick wood, a small farm-house sat in the shade of large conifers. A woman, dressed in an apron, carrying a baby rushed to them as they came into view.

"Please help me. My little Danny's run off into the woods and won't come back. Please help," she said, through sobs. "He's only five. He said he found a magical friend in there that plays games with him. I told him he wasn't to go into the woods but he ran off with his ball and now won't answer me when I call. I just know something's happened to him." She pulled the baby closer into her arms as she cried.

Elora watched the granite appearance of Diagus as he shook his head. "Dark times have arrived, my dear," he said, placing a hand on the woman's shoulder. "Woods are no longer safe. If your boy hasn't returned, then more likely than not he never will. There's nothing we can do, I'm sorry. Don't go into the woods after him, or you'll share his fate."

His hand fell from her shoulder and he nudged his cob on. He spared Elora a glance, a slight shake of the head. "We keep moving."

She understood. You can't save them one at a time, a lesson she'd learned the hard way in the plane wreckage. Her heels touched Daisy's flank and the mare walked on, tears forming in Elora's eyes as she put her back to the sobs of the mother that they left beside the woods.

By the time they'd descended to the bottom of the lane the sobs were out of earshot, the farm out of sight although Elora heard them in sharp clarity, heaving in her heart. What that poor mother must be going through.

Several strides later and Elora let go of the reins; her arms falling by her side, head tilting forwards. Daisy slowed then stopped, the other horses plodding on unaware that she no longer followed.

To hell with them, she thought.

Elora gathered up the reins, turned the mare around and kicked her on. The horse responded without hesitation, racing into full gallop, hooves slamming into the worn tarmac as she charged back towards the farmhouse, her long white mane swaying behind her and whipping Elora in the face.

She found the mother where they had left her, weeping in the road, baby clutched tight in her arms. At Elora's approach she lifted her head, hope written in her face.

"Thank you, thank you," she cried, as Elora jumped down and tied Daisy to the nearest tree.

"Stay here, don't follow me in," she said to the mother, as she ran between the trees.

There was a wrongness to the woods that Elora couldn't put words to. Maybe it was the lack of noise, the stillness in a place that should be teeming with wildlife, or the cold air that seeped into her, making her breath visible. Or maybe it was the realisation that the deeper she went the darker the woods became; but not because of the canopy blotting out the sun; it was more like the light itself pulled back, too timid to penetrate to the soft earthy floor.

"Danny?" she yelled, remembering the boy's name. "Danny? Your mother wants you home." There was no echo to her voice, as if the thick oaks and elms soaked it up. "Danny?" she screamed.

Her foot suddenly caught beneath thick bramble and tugged at her ankles, she had just enough time to raise her hand and prevent her face being pricked by a thorn bush.

As she scrambled back to her feet she heard a childish giggling.

"Danny, is that you?" she asked, pulling a thorn from her palm, the puncture wound flamed for a heartbeat before healing up. She doubted she would ever get used to that.

Giggling again. Elora marched through the thick foliage in the direction it came from. She pushed away sticky ivy that had somehow grown between the trees, forming dark green curtains, and stumbled into a clearing.

A small boy sat at the centre, rolling a bright red ball into a black space in front of him. The space was a strange phenomenon. Filling the gap between an elm, its roots and a branch that had fallen against the trees trunk, forming a triangle.

She watched as the ball rolled into the black triangle and disappeared, a moment later it rolled back out again as if somebody from within the inky darkness was playing a game with the boy, who laughed and clapped his hands as the ball reappeared.

"Danny," Elora offered stepping closer. The boy turned his head, his plump little face staring in puzzlement. "Danny, come with me. Your mother's been worried about you."

Danny looked at the hand she offered him and shook his head.

"You have funny eyes," he said, pointing a chubby little finger at her face.

"It is dangerous here, Danny. Come with me and we'll go to your mother together."

"No," he said, folding his arms and frowning, lips drawn tight in the determined way of a five-year old.

A large green hand, ending with sharp yellow claws, extended out of the black triangle. It turned over, index finger curling, enticing the boy nearer. Danny watched, his face full of wonder and began to shuffle closer, the hand slowly drawing back as the boy neared.

"Danny, no!" Elora shouted, dashing towards the boy. She grasped his arm and pulled him into her as the green hand shot out and grabbed his other and yanked back.

Danny screamed in fright as she spun away from the dark space, lashing out with her foot and kicking the thick arm attached to the boy's other hand. It let go and she fell to the soft earth hugging the boy close. He cried into her shoulder as she scurried away from the blackness.

A heavily muscled arm re-emerged from the blackness, then a meaty shoulder followed by a huge head. Small red eyes stared down a pig-like snout, large tusks jutted upwards from its mouth like that of a wild boar.

Elora put her arm around Danny, preventing him from seeing the monster.

"Stop, you stupid oaf," came a voice, echoing around the clearing.

A creature stepped barefoot from around an oak. He was old, skin loose and sagging, maybe a foot shorter than herself and dressed in torn britches and a black tattered waistcoat. "Grimbles can't fit in the upsies, stupid oaf. You will break the gate."

The boar-like monster halted and gingerly craned his head about to inspect the branch that formed part of the triangle. Seeing that it was undisturbed he relaxed, letting out a breath but advanced no further.

"Go back into the downsies, stupid oaf. You can't be in both the upsies and the downsies or you'll find that you'll be split asunder. Stupid oaf," continued the little spindly man who moved far too fast for something looking as old as he did.

"She took my dinner," replied the oaf, his voice sounding so deep Elora could feel it rattling inside her chest.

"Nope, nope. Little girl is your dinner, stupid oaf. The boy is for this grumpkins. Sweet little boy likes to play with grumpkins," said the man padding closer to them.

"Leave us alone," growled Elora, clambering to her feet and clutching the boy.

"The girl is sour. I want the boy, sweet young and juicy," boomed the boar's head.

The old man skipped forwards like a child and slapped the beast around his head. "Stupid oaf. This grumpkins tells you what's you having. Grumpkins in the upsies, you should be remembering, stupid oaf. The boy is for this grumpkins; the girl is for you."

Elora carefully crept back, placing her feet down gently so as not to make a sound as the two creatures argued over which of them they wanted to eat.

"Elora?" She heard the Shadojak shout, causing the argument to stop and attention brought back to her and Danny.

"We're here, Diagus. Over here," she shouted, feeling grateful that he had come back for her.

"Elora?" came his voice once more, sounding a little further away. He hadn't heard her.

"Diagus!" she bellowed. Her voice echoing around the trees and bouncing about them. It was the ivy curtains that did something with the sound. Her voice still resonated when the little man snatched his hand out and seemed to grasp an echo in his fist.

He tipped his narrow head back and hawked up phlegm from the back of his throat and spat it into his other hand before clapping them together. He rubbed them, whispering something she didn't understand then opened his hands. A small yellow sphere appeared, made from the spit. The grumpkin threw it out of the clearing.

As it bounced off a tree she heard her own voice shouting Diagus, and with every tree the sphere struck after, the name echoed again and again as it ricocheted further and further away.

It would lead the Shadojak away.

"Stupid girl. This grumpkins cleverer than you are," said the creature, a wicked grin forming on his overly large mouth, revealing sharp pointy teeth.

He drew a jagged knife from his belt. It was rusty with age but still carried a sharp edge. Elora pulled Danny behind her and drew her own dagger from the smuggler's pocket.

"See, little girl wants to play with grumpkins," he laughed, waving his knife around as if it was a playful game, taking light steps as he came closer.

Danny was sniffling now, whispering for his mother, clutching onto her jeans. He must he frightened out of his wits, thought Elora, narrowing her eyes at the advancing grumpkin. It wasn't fear that pulsed through her heart, it was anger.

Waiting for the grumpkin's hand to swing to the right she sprang into him, driving her dagger into his chest, mimicking the move Diagus used on the dying pilot. Quick in – out.

The blade disappeared to the hilt before she jumped back, expecting blood to flow freely from the wound. Yet as she gazed upon the small cut that parted the creature's ribs, none came.

The grumpkin chuckled. "You can't ends this grumpkins so easily. This skin I borrowed." He pushed one of his fingers into the hole she cut and wiggled it around so she could see it was baggy. "Will need a new one now. This grumpkins will take little Danny's once I've eaten him up. Nice and fresh, will fit this grumpkins with no baggies."

Elora backed away, dagger still held in front, Danny crying by her side. How do you kill a grumpkin when stabbing it in the heart doesn't work?

"Will you play some more, little girl? Come, play with this grumpkins." The monster that was half in, half out of the black space was laughing too, a deep rumble that shook the ground.

Then a figure stepped into the clearing and the laughter died.

"I will play with this grumpkin," said Otholo, striding before it.

Elora used the opportunity to scoop Danny into her arms, thankful for Otholo's timely arrival. But as she watched the Bard advance on the grumpkin, she thought something wasn't right about him. He didn't move right. Gone was the camp swagger, replaced by a purposeful no- nonsense stride, and even his voice had lost its sing-song quality, now sounding deeper and edgy.

The grumpkin backed away, hands rising and warding him off. "No, not you. Not you!" he pleaded, sounding petrified. "I didn't know, this grumpkins is sorry. Take her. Take them both, this grumpkins is sorry, he didn't know."

Otholo strode into him, bowling him over with his shoulder, then picked him up by the ankles, heaving him upside down.

"No, no, no," the grumpkin protested, as Otholo swung him around and around, lank hair flying out horizontal with his saggy body. Then his head connected with the oak, making a sickening crunch.

Otholo let the body drop and advanced on the other monster. Snarling menacingly, his eyes dark, appearing a polar opposite of the Otholo Elora had ridden with for the last few days.

At the last moment before Otholo could grab him, the monster pulled back into the darkness and disappeared. Otholo screamed in rage, spit flying from his mouth and in his anger he threw his arm into the triangle and pulled the boar's head back out, a fist grasping it by a tusk.

The creature struggled to pull itself back but Otholo dug his heels into the soft earth – yanked hard and kicked the branch that created the edge of the triangle. The blackness suddenly vanished.

Otholo fell back, the monster's head in his hands, mouth silently working as dark green blood oozed from its stump of neck. The rest of it vanishing with the blackness.

"Otholo, are you alright?" asked Elora, letting out a breath she didn't know she had been holding.

The bard snapped his head around and seemed to notice them for the first time. He hurled the severed head against a tree, spreading green gore as it spun in the air before thudding to the ground.

Otholo's menacing grin returned, his eyes alight with violence; hands clenching and flexing.

"Otholo, it's me. Elora," she said, but the words fell on deaf ears as the bard stalked towards them, thick veins pulsing in his neck – he meant to kill them. Elora backed into a tree, Danny squealed and buried his head into her neck.

"Stop," she shouted, bringing her dagger up in front of them. His gaze found hers and there was no recognition in them, only hatred.

Beside her face, a grey blade appeared, pointing at the bard. It lengthened passed her, a long sharp edged sword, then a hand, aged fingers wrapped around the hilt.

"Take the boy back to his mother and wait for us by the horses," Diagus whispered into her ear, as he stepped cautiously on; the point of his sword pressing into Otholo's chest. "Now," he growled when he realised that she hadn't moved. With his free hand he lifted a bottle of cognac. "Time for a drink,

Otholo." The bard's eyes shifted to the Shadojak, then to the bottle, confusion creasing his brow.

Elora pushed through the ivy curtain and ran as fast as she dared whilst carrying Danny. Before long the trees grew less thick and she broke from the woods. Her lungs screaming for her to stop – heart pounding inside her chest but she didn't slow until she reached the farmhouse.

Danny's mother was sobbing anew, eyes red-raw from all the tears. She took her boy in her arms, trying to speak but losing the words with the emotion.

"It's ok, he's safe now, just don't let him go back into the woods," Elora warned. The mother nodded, choking back the tears. "It might be best that you take him inside, he's seen some nasty things." She ruffled Danny's hair. "Take care" she said and left them there, hoping they'd be gone before the Shadojak came back.

Daisy nudged Elora with her nose, snickering as she untied the reins, the first sign of affection her horse had given her. She stroked her slender neck, leaning against her body as Diagus paced out of the woods – alone.

"Where's Otholo?" she asked, when he came to untie his cob.

The Shadojak glanced back to the woods. "He'll be out soon. Now mount up."

She climbed on her horse, aware that Diagus was still staring.

"Do not disobey me again girl," he growled through clenched teeth. "If you'd have died, Earth would have fallen into Solarius's lap and there'd be more than one boy dead."

"He would have died if I didn't intervene. Don't you care about that? He was a little boy," she argued, struggling to keep her temper at bay.

"Is one boy worth risking the entire world for?"

"It was to his mother; it is to me. My father has taken millions of lives already, just by destroying electricity. Well that little boy is one life I took back. And I will save the next life and the life after that if needs be. You can judge people how the bloody hell

214

you like, but while you're out 'balancing', I'll be doing my own judging." Her face felt hot now, the anger rising and not caring as she witnessed Diagus's face grow red; casting the pearl in his eye into stark contrast. He wanted to say more but Otholo chose that moment to stumble out of the woods.

He appeared drunk, swaggering towards them and humming a merry little tune. The Shadojak gave her a glare to let her know this wasn't finished, then went to help the bard onto his horse.

Once Otholo was settled in his saddle, Diagus led them off down the lane at a steady trot, while Elora held back to ride with the bard.

"What happened to you, back in there?" she asked, nodding towards the woods. "I thought you were going to kill me."

Otholo smiled at her apologetically and took a deep pull on the cognac. "I would have torn you and the boy apart before finding something else to destroy." He stared ahead, not meeting her eyes as he continued. "When I left Thea and crossed the Shadowlands I payed a heavy price. I was tricked into a bargain with an evil spirit, a demon. That beast is inside me now – always and forever. He possesses my body when he can, usually when I'm not expecting it, taking control of me when I least expect it. Or if I feel threatened."

"Like just now?" she asked.

He nodded. "Pops right out and starts destroying. The demon loves violence. Only thing that seems to keep him at bay is alcohol." He took another swallow from the bottle then held it in the crook of his arm as if it his child. "So I drink a spirit, to trap a spirit."

Elora watched as he left her side, trotting up to Diagus and ending the conversation. At least now she knew the reason why he drank so much.

15

Kiss of a Ghost

The morning was dark and overcast, greeting the group as Diagus led them through a green landscape of tall hills and deep valleys. A range of mountains stood grey against the lighter greys of clouds in the far distance. Elora thought they might have travelled as far west as Wales in the last few days, the Shadojak had kept them in the countryside, avoiding towns and villages and so she couldn't be sure where they were. But now that the few roads they crossed had sign posts written in Welsh as well as English, she knew they were in Wales.

They followed a narrow trail, no wider than a deer track that weaved around trees, skirting a shallow brook that led them deeper into a forest. It wasn't long before they were swallowed by the thick green foliage, blocking out the hills around them. She trusted that Diagus knew where he was leading them, even though the track kept breaking and he needed to scout ahead to locate it again. Otholo made more than one comment of the fact, they had passed the same spot several times and that they were going around in circles. Elora agreed with him, a feeling of déjà-vu, sure that she had spotted the same pointy rock that jutted from the bubbling water at least three times. She was about to suggest to the Shadojak that he was lost when a man stepped from behind a thick elm, startling the horses.

"That's far enough," he said firmly, stepping in front of Diagus and setting the shaft of a huge war hammer into the dirt, rested his meaty hands upon the heavy head.

The hammer was tall enough for the large man to rest his chin upon his hands, a brown beard, braided into three tails, hanging over the top. Similar braids were woven into his shoulder length hair, framing his round face. He wore grey fur skin trousers and boots and a leather vest tied together with cord – a pot belly poking out beneath it.

"Why didn't you stop us the first pass we made?" Diagus asked.

The large man shrugged his shoulder. "To tell you the truth, Shadojak; I was snoozing. Gets me all kinds of tired, sat around waiting. Didn't figure the fairy glamour would work so well on you and besides, your Shaigun told me you would be here days ago and alone. So I let you pass a second time to be sure. The third time was for fun." He let out a laugh, brown eyes sparkling with mischief. "But it's good to see you, Diagus."

"Aye, you too, Ragna. So the boy's here then?"

"Came a few days ago, riding in on a fancy carriage, would you believe. Him, two old men and a wood troll."

"That would be Norgie and Gurple. Who's the other?"

The large man gave another shrug of the shoulders. "Says he's a Minuan, name of Nathaniel."

Elora almost jumped from the saddle. "Nathaniel. He's here?"

"And who might you be, pretty one?" asked Ragna, absently curling a braid on his beard around a chubby finger.

"I'm his niece, Elora," she answered, watching his eyes widen and a grin form on his face, large teeth shining through the beard.

"So you're the one they've all been maudlin over. Gonna put a thunder clap over em when you turn up. They think you've gone back to dust," he chuckled as he swung the hammer over the back of his neck, one arm draping over the shaft, the other over the steel head as if it was a milk-maid's yoke. "Come on then, follow me."

They were led along a track wide enough for the horses to ride side by side, so Elora wondered how they had missed it before, but overheard Ragna explaining to Diagus that the fairy glamour was working stronger since the Earth's magic had disappeared. Maybe it was similar to the darkness that shrouded Norgie's house in London. That would explain why they had been walking around in circles.

The track ran alongside a ruined castle; its stone walls mainly lay in piles of broken masonry. A few of the moss covered walls and the odd staircase covered in creeping vines remained, giving the overall impression of a huge building, long ago reclaimed by the forest.

"That's Rams Keep?" asked Otholo, not appearing impressed.

"Aye, what's left of it. Most of it's below ground now. A castle originally, predates anything that anyone knows about. The keep was built on those ruins, then rebuilt again to make it stronger; walls built upon walls and tunnels created amongst floors and more hidden vaults and ways hidden and forgotten than I'd care to know. A lot of the keep below the ground is still there; passageways, cells and dungeons carved out of the caves and caverns. There's even a tunnel that comes out at a gorge in the next valley."

Elora watched Otholo's face grow a shade paler. Ragna must have noticed it too.

"Don't worry yourself none though, you'll be sleeping at the inn," he said.

Sunlight broke through the clouds and shone on a break in the trees as they rounded a bend, opening up onto a small cornfield above which Elora could see a thatched roof, smoke rising from a chimney.

The horses were forced to travel in single file down a narrow path that wound through the tall corn before a clearing opened up revealing a large grey stone building beneath the thatch.

They crossed a courtyard, passing a stone well at its centre, the horses kicking up dust from the dry ground as they passed.

"Jaygen?" Ragna bellowed, then turned to them, smiling. "Welcome to Rams Keep Inn."

A boy of maybe fourteen or fifteen, ambled over from the side of the inn, rubbing his sandy coloured hair and regarding them curiously.

"Jaygen, stable the horses, they'll be staying with us for a while," said Ragna to the boy. "Make sure they get a good brush down; they've been on the road for a few days."

"Aye, Da," replied the boy.

Elora climbed down from her mount and handed Jaygen the reins. "You might want to be careful with this one, she's quite mean," she said, giving the boy a smile and causing him to blush. He glanced away, gently stroking Daisy's nose.

"Don't worry yourself Elora, my boy's got a way with the horses," said Ragna.

The oak door of the inn suddenly swung open and Gurple came charging out, his little legs pumping hard as he crossed the courtyard whilst shouting "Erora!" He slammed into her legs and wrapped his furry arms around her.

She tickled him behind his ears. "Hello, Gurple" she said, grinning down at the little troll. When she gazed back up she saw her uncle in the doorway, one arm against the frame for support, his mouth gaping open before he suddenly shut it.

She went to him, Gurple still gripping tight to her leg and pulled Nat into a hug.

"I thought you were dead," he said, gently kissing the top of her head.

She looked into his tear-filled eyes. "Not quite." Then when she saw his face go stern, his gaze falling upon Diagus, she continued. "It's ok. I know who my father is and so does the Shadojak."

Nat let out a deep breath and held her at arm's length. "I'm so sorry for lying to you all these years."

"Hush. I wouldn't have had it any other way, even if there was another way, which I doubt."

Nat nodded and brushed his fingers through his grey hair. "Norgie will be glad to see you, he's in the kitchen helping Ejan."

The thought of freshly cooked food made Elora's stomach gurgle, the noise heard by her uncle who chuckled.

"Come on through then," said Ragna, going ahead of them into the inn.

Elora followed him into the large room, taking in the dark wood of the exposed beams above, the same used to carve the thick window ledges and wall supports. Another thicker piece used for the bar, old and well worn, dipping in the places that had at one time propped up the elbows of many a patron but the highly polished shine to it showed the little use in recent years. Fresh logs had been placed in a stone fireplace, large axes, one crossed over the other, were attached to the bricks on the chimney breast above the hearth. Several tables stood around the room, their tops worn and chipped in places, but like the bar, polished so as you could see your face in them, chairs pushed neatly beneath. Lanterns hung, two to each wall giving the room a warm cosy feel.

Elora could imagine a smoky atmosphere, the laughter of men being served ale, travellers propped up at the bar being served by a burly innkeeper. Somebody like Ragna. The inn had a pleasant 'old world' feel about it.

A door beside the bar slammed open, the smell of freshly baked bread drifting out behind an angry looking woman, hands on hips, as she glared at Ragna.

"How many times do I need to tell you to take your bloody boots off?" she spat. "I didn't spend the morning polishing the floor, just so's you can trample in dirt from outside."

Ragna paused mid-step, his face fixed with the expression of a boy being caught doing something his mother didn't approve of. "Not in front of the guests, wench," he said, then screwed his face up as he realised he had said the wrong thing.

"Wench? Call me that again you five-bellied pig and I'll shove that hammer of yours up your … "

"Ejan," offered Nat, intervening between the bickering couple. "This is my niece, Elora."

Ejan gave Ragna a final scowl before turning her fiery gaze on her. "I thought you'd gone back to dust," she said, then her features softened. "So it's you I have to thank for all the firewood."

"Firewood?" Elora asked, wondering what she meant.

She found the woman before her beautiful, her smile transforming her from the deadly battleaxe, her first impression as she emerged from the kitchen, to a curvaceous vixen with long blonde hair that she wore in a thick golden plait that settled over her shoulder and trailed down into a deep cleavage.

Elora felt annoyance of the fact that Bray had spent several days with this woman. Or was it jealousy?

"Bray's being in one hell of a black mood. Disappearing into the woods at dawn, chopping down tree after tree, reducing them to logs and kindling before hauling it all home by dusk. He's been at it like a mad man, that one; working himself to exhaustion each night and then doing it all again the next day. I think he blames himself for your death, that's what Norgie tells me. He's cut enough firewood to last us until winter, three years from now."

A lump caught at the back of Elora's throat at the mention of Bray. So he did have feelings for her and they must have been deep for what he did to himself.

"It'll be nice to have some female company around the place too," Ejan continued. "But you best get yourself cleaned up, you've got road dirt and dust ground into your hair and you smell of sweaty horse – no offence."

"None taken" laughed Elora, feeling every bit as grimy as Ejan depicted.

"That goes for you two as well," said Ejan, eyeing Diagus and Otholo.

The Bard approached and bowed low before the women, taking her hand in his and was about to kiss it when Ejan snatched it away and flicked out a paring knife, blade wickedly sharp.

"None of that, I'm married to five-bellies there," she nodded to Ragna. "And that man is more than enough for any woman to cope with. Raise your lips to me again and I'll cut them off."

"I warned you," said Diagus, grinning, his white pearl twinkling in the lamplight.

Otholo took a step back, masking embarrassment with another bow before Ragna slipped a large meaty arm over his shoulder, a laugh bellowing from huge lungs.

"Don't worry yourself, lad, she scares the hell out of me and she's my wench." He flinched again, unable to change the word.

Ejan narrowed her eyes on her husband, flicking the knife expertly around her hand and appearing as if she would throw it.

"I'll go fetch the water then," said Ragna, making a quick exit.

Ejan took Elora by the arm and steered her through the kitchen door. "Let's get you freshened up before the men folk make a mess."

Elora was desperate to see the Shaigun but would prefer it if she wasn't smelling of horse and a week's worth of road dust when she did.

The water had been barely above room temperature but felt like the best bath she had ever had. Crystal clear as she climbed in and a greyish brown when she climbed out; clean and smelling of lavender from the homemade soap. Ejan had been waiting outside and showed her to the small room where she would be sleeping.

A simple bed, fresh white linen and a rough spun woollen blanket were luxuries she was looking forward to after spending a week in the saddle, using the hard ground as a bed. Ejan opened a heavy chest that was against one wall and pulled out a pretty silk gown with lace worked into the sleeves and neckline. It was a pale blue that shimmered green when it moved against the light. She held it up to Elora's body, cocked her head then laid it carefully down on the bed.

"You'll find that the clothes in here should fit you nicely. Take what you want, there's britches and shirts if you're not one for dresses, I never was."

Elora peered inside the chest and selected a pair of suede trousers that had been dyed green, and a light cotton shirt. She put them on, the trousers fitting snugly and surprisingly comfortable, but the shirt was large so Ejan found a leather belt to wear around her waist to cinch it tight.

"Were these clothes yours?" asked Elora, as she went to peer out of the leaded window.

"Some of them were, not the dresses. Those were probably stolen in the raids before we settled here."

"Raids?"

Ejan grinned wickedly. "Me and Ragna are Norseman, Vikings. Raiding was in our blood and our way of life, amongst other things." She must have seen the shock on Elora's face and softened her grin to a smile. "We don't raid anymore. We're caretakers now. Keeping this place up and running takes all our time and energies."

"You made a deal with Diagus?"

Ejan nodded. "The Pearly White can be persuasive."

From the window Elora could see the stables, her mare happily grazing on hay whilst Jaygen brushed her down, chickens picking at the grass at his feet. Beyond the stables lay a pigsty, a large pink and black spotty pig wallowing in mud and enjoying the afternoon sunshine. Further out a trio of goats were busily munching apples that had fallen from the trees in a large orchard; fenced in by bramble and gooseberry bushes that separated the orchard from a lush green field where a heavily pregnant cow grazed on the grass. It rose its head as if sensing being watched, green blades poking out from its lips. Next to the cow's field was a flatter ground, the trees of the forest surrounding its perimeter, Elora counted six horses, two of which sheltered beneath a large oak watching the rest playfully gallop about the field.

The canopy of the forest stretched as far as she could see, rising and falling in dips and troughs, a breeze stirring the leaves and giving the impression of waves breaking on a dark green ocean. Above the noise the animals occasionally made, she could hear the thump of wood being chopped, harsh and erratic, chipping away at the peacefulness of the surroundings.

"That will be Bray," said Ejan, joining her at the window. "If I was ten years younger I'd try and steal him away from his Shaigun path myself. Such a waste."

"What do you mean?" asked Elora, feeling another pang of jealousy towards the women who she knew could turn the heads of any man of any age.

"Shadojaks don't feel love, they don't take a wife or father any children. Once Bray was set on the path of becoming a Shaigun he had chosen to forsake the same things. If he can't control his feelings, if he falls in love or strays from the path he'll never be a Shadojak."

Elora suddenly felt a chill – icy fingers clutching her heart and she tried to mask her feelings from Ejan as she realised that the love she imagined with Bray could never be. She inwardly berated herself for being so foolish.

"Why don't you go down there, tell him to come and get cleaned up. I won't have him dirty and sweaty for this evening's meal. And you can put him out of his misery whilst you're at it. He'll probably think he's seen a ghost."

Elora nodded, it would be good to see him, even if only seeing him was all she could do.

Thump, went the axe, growing louder as she drew nearer; thump went her heart, faster and fiercer as she went over in her mind what she was going to say. Before she decided what to tell him, she rounded a fallen elm and stopped.

He was there, arms held aloft, axe in hand and half naked. Sun rays glistened from his back, a thin bead of sweat running down the centre above the dip of his spine. Shoulder muscles bunched, his slim torso twisting as he brought the axe down.

Thwack. He hit a log that stood on end upon a tree stump, striking dead centre and splitting it in two. He threw the halves into a cart and placed another log upon the stump.

Heat pulsed through Elora, her blood becoming hot as she watched him raise the axe again, arms thick with muscle, back arching, abs stretching. Thwack.

Wood chips shot into his dark hair, it went unnoticed, like herself as she guiltily watched him work, her hands feeling sweaty, her breath deeper. Thwack.

Careful not to snap a twig or rustle any leaves, Elora stalked further around to the front of him, her gaze taking in his large chest, pectorals working beneath bare skin, gorgeous face set in fierce determination; moss green eyes, alive, focused and beautiful.

Her heart was on fire; she could watch him chop wood all day.

Biceps tensed as Bray began to bring the axe down, his eyes flicked to hers at the last moment. The axe missed the log and struck into the stump.

Bray's jaw tightened as he took her in, appearing as if he had seen a ghost.

"Elora?" he whispered, his voice sounding hoarse and choked.

She nodded, smiling as she stepped closer, noticing that his hands still gripped the axe, knuckles turning white.

"Hello, Elf boy," she said, her voice coming out deep and throaty. Another step towards him, close enough to touch, close enough to lay her hands against his heaving chest. "I've got a small gift for you," she said. Then placing her hands on his tensed shoulders, stood on the tips of her toes and kissed him on the lips, her chest pressing into his and feeling his warm skin against hers.

"That's for saving my uncle."

Bray stood still as if feeling the aftershock from an electrical charge, green eyes staring at her, alive with what? Fury? Hatred? Lust? An intense mixture of all three? Elora felt foolish and was about to apologise when his arm wrapped around her, his hand at the base of her back, pulling her towards his body once again. His other hand grasped her shoulder as he lowered his head to hers; briefly rubbing noses and the bristles of his stubble grazing her chin before their mouths touched.

This kiss was more passionate than the first, Bray pressing harder, his lips parting and tongue searching. She closed her eyes, kissing him back, leaning further into his embrace, placing a hand on his chest and felt his heart thumping. She had never kissed like this before, had never been kissed like this. His fingers grasped tighter as their bodies crushed as if becoming one. Then he pulled away leaving her feeling light-headed.

His lips curled into a gorgeous smile, the unshaven face giving him a sexy edge. "That's for being alive," he said.

Her fingers entwined into his as she tried to slow her breathing and keep herself from toppling over. Then she noticed the red welts on his chest where her fingers had been. Angry red blisters in the shape of her hand.

"Did I do that?"

Bray chuckled and pulled her close, arms wrapping tightly around her.

"They say you've got fire in your blood. Play with fire and you're going to get burnt." He kissed the top of her head before letting her go and stepping away. His eyes softened, his smile faltering. "I thought you were dead."

"It came close. Diagus judged me but was persuaded to let me live, in case I'm some use against Solarius."

"Neptula had the same idea. She said you're a powerful weapon of some kind."

Elora didn't know what to say to that, she didn't feel like a weapon. Just a girl with an evil lineage. She hoped she didn't let anybody down.

"I better be getting back; my uncle will be wondering where I am." She reluctantly unwound her fingers from his and stepped away. "I'll see you at dinner. Oh, and Ejan said you need to wash before we dine. A shame really, I like you all dirty and sweaty." She gazed at his body once again, grinning at the handprint she had left. "And now I've marked you as mine."

Bray looked down at himself, his grin matching hers. "Might be I'll have to mark you as mine somehow."

"Only if I let you," she teased. "I'm a powerful weapon, you know."

He raised an eyebrow. "I'll see you at dinner. Clean."

She mocked an upturned lip but couldn't hold it for long, she doubted she would stop smiling for the rest of the day.

Her legs felt like jelly as she ambled away, trying to walk naturally; feeling his eyes on her back as she went. Her heart was still hammering as she left the forest, the taste of his kiss lingering upon her lips.

Bray's grin never faulted as he watched her disappear from view, leaving the memory of her behind. She hadn't seemed real, the way she simply appeared. Yet the blistered handprint on his chest was proof it had. He placed his own hand over it, marked as hers, he let out a laugh – could it be that simple?

Sudden silence as animals quieted for an approaching predator, snapped Bray out his reverie and heightened his senses. He moved his head a split second before feeling a harsh blow glance off the back of his neck.

White stars exploded in the corners of his vision as he fell down, tucking his body in low at the last point, using his momentum to propel him into a forward roll – hands wrenching the axe free as he went.

A black shape launched from the stump, a sword held over head, descending towards his face. Bray rolled onto his back, holding the axe in both hands and brought it up to meet his attacker's blade. Steel bit deep into the wooden shaft as the swordsman put his full weight on it, a bristled face snarling as it leaned in close, one blue eye penetrating into his, the other a blind pearl that stared into his soul.

"I don't want the same greeting you gave the girl," said Diagus, applying more pressure.

Before the shaft snapped Bray brought his foot between them and thrust his leg up, throwing the Shadojak over him. The pressing weight suddenly released he flipped onto his feet, bringing his sword out of the smuggler's pouch and adopted a defensive stance.

Steel met steel, Bray's arms jarring as he parried blow after blow, the sharp ringing of swords echoing off the trees. Diagus came in high then low, feigning a leg swipe then driving an elbow into Bray's gut and doubling him over. Another explosion of pain and white stars as the hilt slammed down onto the back of his head.

"You're, sluggish boy," spat the Shadojak, as he kicked Bray in the belly. "Your mind's full of the girl, it's blinding you to your surroundings."

Bray caught the foot as it came in for a second kick and twisted. The Shadojak spun his body in the same direction so as not to sprain his ankle, then dropped his knee into Bray's exposed ribs.

"Sloppy – pathetic."

Scissor kicking his legs, Bray managed to turn his body away from a third kick and swiped Diagus's legs from under him. With his body in motion he flipped back onto his feet, swinging his sword out in a chop to the Shadojak's neck, but it met his sword and with a simple flick of his wrist sent Bray's blade spinning end over end into a tree where it stuck, deep into the bark.

"You've not been practicing, boy," said Diagus, spit flying from the corner of his mouth. "This girl will be the end of everything you've been training for, years of hell to get where you are now."

Bray noticed the Shadojak's knuckles tighten on his sword, was he going to cut him down, unarmed and defenceless? The glare the Pearly White gave him told him he was in the mood for it.

Bray relaxed when Diagus shoved his sword away and took a step back, folding his arms, thunder still chiseled into his face.

"You're good, Bray. Better than good. You're the best Shaigun that I've ever been sent. I've fought countless times, defended my sword and title against the best and nobody ever came close to killing me, not one." He sat down on the tree stump, shaking his head. "I will grow old and die in my sleep before somebody takes my blade, but by then the best of your years will have past and you're the only one who has the ability to take my place."

Bray leaned against the cart as he listened to Diagus, who suddenly seemed as old and frail as his years and not the hardest bastard he had ever met.

"There's a battle coming. One big hell of a battle, the likes of which haven't been witnessed since the great rift. If I fall in that battle, I want you to be the one to take my blade, drive it through my black heart and take my legacy. There can be no other, only you. You're to be the next Shadojak."

"And if you don't fall?"

"If I don't fall then … I'll take the Blade's peace."

Blade's peace … the words rattled around Bray's head making him think that he misheard the Shadojak.

Diagus grinned. "What, you don't think I've had enough, don't think I might be getting too long in the tooth – too damned old? These bones speak otherwise." He clenched his fingers, they clicked loudly, the knuckles seeming bigger than normal: misshapen. "On Earth they'd have shoved me in a home for the old and decrepit. Pills for the arthritis, pills for the pain and more pills to make me sleep. On Thea I'd have been left to rot and I don't know which is better." He rubbed his hands as if easing away a pain, yet his face gave away no signs of discomfort. "Given the choice I'd rather fall in battle, sword in hand, but if not I'll take the peace, I think I've earned that."

Bray nodded slowly. The Blade's peace was a rare thing and only claimed by the oldest of Shadojaks. Old was also a rarity amongst their kind. The Blade's peace hadn't been performed in a long time. It meant that the Shadojak would give his sword to his Shaigun and allow him to drive the blade into his heart, the final beat releasing all the Shadojak's skills, powers and memories into the sword – into the soul reaver.

Every Shadojak, since the falling of Solarius, had passed their experience on, the next Shaigun becoming the master and taking on their own apprentice. It's why the swords were so precious, not only taking on the previous owner's powers but that of any other whose heart it had struck.

Diagus was the most skilled, the most feared and no other could beat him in swordplay, the next Shadojak would be equally as powerful.

"I had no idea," was all Bray could say. Diagus was the meanest person he knew, harder than coffin nails, tough as a tomb gollum. He had seen the legendary Pearly White walk into an illegal troll tavern; two gangs of heavily armed rock trolls following him in, and he'd be the only one to walk out, a layer of rock dust coating his cloak. Was this power truly meant to be his, would he be the Shadojak? Why tell him now though? Bray got the distinct impression that the timing had something to do with Elora and the fact that a Shadojak's path was a lonely one.

"Diagus, I … I love Elora." There, he had said it. Told the big man himself, displayed it right out there on the slab for the world to see. I love Elora.

The Shadojak's face grew darker, losing its vulnerable touch from a moment ago, returning to the cold hard granite that Bray was used to.

"Love. Love is it? An emotion triggered by the brain, nothing more than a chemical reaction. You've had the training, you know how to control your emotions, boy. Love?" he hissed through his teeth. "The girl is the daughter of Solarius, the spawn of Chaos. She will live long enough to serve her purpose, unless she joins the ranks of her father's dark army, which I'm expecting."

"You judged her, you let her live," Bray almost pleaded.

"She lives because she maybe the only chance we have, and a gnat's whisker of a chance at that. But if she turns, she will be re-judged. And if she doesn't, if by some incredible chance, almost impossible chance that we make it to Aslania and make this thing work and if we succeed – she will still be re-judged. Don't you see, boy? No matter the outcome, even if Solarius dies, his dark army destroyed, even then the daughter of Chaos cannot live. The lives of everyone, everything on both worlds is at risk as long as she breaths. And if I fall, maybe the Shadojak that will deliver her soul through the final door, will be you, returning her to dust."

An intense pressure crushed Bray's heart. After days torturing himself over Elora's death, hating himself for losing the girl he loved, then the shock of seeing her alive; holding her, kissing her and realising that she felt the same love for him. And now knowing that she would die, no matter the outcome, no matter what happened her life was already forfeit.

Bray could control his emotions, that much was true, but he didn't want to, he wanted to feel the hurt, the pain. It was what he deserved. He knew that Diagus was right. Elora had no future on either Earth or Thea. Death would be her only reward for giving life to those that survived.

The Shadojak rose and stepped closer to him, placing a hand firmly on his shoulder.

"Hell is rising, Bray, and I need you to be my Shaigun. You need to do the right thing, choose the right path, find the right balance. Earth and Thea, the lives of everyone on both worlds or the girl, Elora?" He applied a touch of pressure before releasing his grip. "Make your choice, judge, balance and see it through. Do the right thing."

Bray watched the Shadojak walk away, leaving him alone with his thoughts, with the choices, with the hurt and the pain.

Darkness had fallen on the forest by the time Bray had come to a decision. His bare skin was cold, muscles stiff and jaw aching he rose from the log he was sat upon and pulled his sword from the tree. He headed back to the inn, determination leading him where his body lacked the strength, willpower driving him, focus guiding his actions as he followed the right path, the only path.

16

Daughter of Chaos

The afternoon passed quickly, Elora occupied herself by helping Ejan and Norgie prepare the evening's meal but her mind was elsewhere – her thoughts belonging to Bray and that kiss. By the evening everyone was sat at the table and helping themselves to roasted venison, seasoned with sage, onion and apple. Elora's mouth was watering as the aroma hit her nostrils, her stomach grumbled yet she forced herself to wait until Bray arrived, unlike the rest who had already filled plates with the rare meat along with vegetables and were busy eating.

She had planned for the Shaigun to sit next to her but Gurple had managed to squeeze up to her right whilst Jaygen had quietly sat on her left. The Shadojak sat at the head of the table, talking with her uncle; Norgie contributing to the conversation beside him. Ragna was on Diagus's other side, draining a large tankard of mead and unceremoniously wiping his mouth with the back of his arm and gaining a mean look from Ejan. Otholo was sipping red wine from a glass, whilst picking at his food, his eyes drifting every so often over Ejan who seemed oblivious to the attention.

Elora finally gave up waiting and began to cut into her meat when Bray entered the room, washed, cleanly shaven and wearing black jeans and t-shirt, along with a deep frown.

The smile on her lips faded as he sat beside Norgie, not even sparing her a glance, not sparing anyone a glance. Had she done something wrong? She put a mouthful of venison in her mouth and chewed mechanically, her hunger vanishing as she realised something had changed. Did he regret what had happened earlier or was he now acting the un-feeling Shaigun, a front for the benefit of the Shadojak? She hoped for the latter but knew that a secret relationship would be all but impossible with the Pearly White's gaze on her at all times.

She set her fork down and picked up a glass of wine. It was dry and bitter, much like the direction in which her mood was sinking to.

Jaygen reached for his tankard, which was half the size of his father's and refilled it from a large jug, sloshing beery foam on the table.

"No more, Jaygen. I said just the one," enforced Ejan, her voice cutting across the table.

Jaygen placed the jug down heavier than he needed to. "But I'm a man grown now, Ma, just one more fill?"

Ejan glanced at her husband who had quieted his own discussion. "What do you think, Ragna? Has our boy become a man?"

Ragna laughed. "Let us see now. My own Da told me that I'd be a man after I can raise the Fist of the North to salute Odin. You do that Jaygen and I'll fill your tankard myself."

Elora watched Jaygen's hope-filled gaze shifting between his mother and father.

"Fine," he said, slamming a fist down on the table and rising with grim determination.

"Fist of the North?" Otholo put his elbows on the table and leaned in close to Ragna, both watching Jaygen pace across the room to the huge war hammer that was resting by the door.

"The actual 'Fist of the North'. Red-Path Bowen's hammer? And Black Owen before him?"

"Yep. Bowen, son of Owen, was my Da; Owen was my Da's Da, but I never met him. Died in a battle, but the story goes he was as black as his name. My Da too, always seeking the red path – earned his name in another battle."

Elora witnessed an excitement build in Otholo, his fingers drumming on the table as he watched Jaygen carry the hammer awkwardly in both arms, face a bright red, either from the embarrassment of being watched or the effort needed to lift the weapon.

"Your father has a song, your grandfather too. They can be heard in most taverns in the north but I've yet to hear a song for Ragna."

"You will, Otholo. My time will come and the Fist of the North will sing it for me."

"Of course it will," chuckled Ejan, raising her own tankard. "Ragna of the five bellies." She leaned closer to her husband and slapped his pot belly then planted a kiss on his lips. "My little Raggy."

"Raggy?" Otholo mouthed the name to Elora and she smiled, it was a name unsuited to a warrior Viking.

Ragna laughed, throwing an arm around Ejan. "It's all that delicious food you keep cooking, got me my very own larder in here."

Elora felt a little envious at their closeness, it was obvious to everyone the affection they had for each other. She spared a glance at Bray and was sure that he had been watching her, only averting his eyes when she turned hers to him.

"Go on then lad, salute your God," Ragna bellowed, picking the jug of mead up and bringing it to his mouth.

Jaygen set the base of the shaft on the floor, gripping the handle below its heavy head which was at a level with his own, and took a deep breath.

He grew a deeper shade of red, veins bulging in his neck as the hammer lifted. A moment later and his arm was shaking, his body twisting over to one side in an attempt to compensate for the weight he was struggling with. It was clear he wasn't strong enough even though the effort must have been verging on painful. Elora winced as the hammer thudded back down on the floor, Jaygen struggling to keep it from falling against the table.

Ragna sprang from the table to help, gripping the hammer in one hand and slapping his son on the shoulder with the other. "Nearly son, it won't be long before you're swinging the Fist. You can have half a tankard for half a salute."

Jaygen seemed satisfied with that and slouched back into his chair, sweat plastering his hair to his forehead, whilst Ragna held the hammer high without effort. "Odin!" he bellowed.

Then set the hammer on the table in front of Otholo, his eyes alive with enthusiasm. "You want to try, bard?"

"No, the only god I'd be saluting is the god of good wine." He raised his glass into the air, saluting an invisible deity then swallowed the wine in one go. His mismatched eyes settled on the hammer. "Doesn't look very pretty does it? Quite plain really, how'd we know it's the real Fist?"

Elora agreed, it was only a heavy block of steel: flat at one end and tapered to a point on the other but she wouldn't have put it like Otholo did and not to its current owner.

Ragna settled back in his chair, wrapping an arm around his wife. "It's not supposed to be pretty. Pretty weapons are for fancy kings and princes to wear at the back of a battle; shouting commands and looking like they're controlling their men in all their gold finery and silk pantaloons. Norseman weapons are hard and vicious, straight edged and cruel, like the men themselves. An ugly brutal tool for an ugly brutal job. There's an honesty in that. Why do you think the Shadojak looks so pretty?"

Diagus nodded, an ugly grin causing his scar to pucker out, stretching the skin tight along his cheekbone beneath the pearl.

"And I'm as honest as they come," said Diagus. "But right now Otholo, I need some honest answers from you."

Otholo refilled his glass and lounged back in his chair, hands behind his head. "I'm more of the pretty kind, as you can see. But honesty, from a bard?"

"I'd settle for the truth then. Oh, and if it falls short of the truth … " The dead pearl glinted bright and menacing in the lamplight. Otholo nodded, the threat behind the words sinking in. "So, you came to Earth gaining passage through the Shadowlands, yes?" Otholo sipped his wine, attempting to remain calm yet Elora could sense an awkwardness in the way he appeared. Fingers grasping the glass too tightly, a twitch catching his wine stained lips. "How? Anything without a black heart dies there. Not any animal nor any plants can survive. So tell us how you survived."

Otholo stared at his drink, swishing the red liquid around; dark and rich as blood. "By ship."

"By ship?" repeated Diagus. "There are no seas, no oceans or any body of water in the Shadowlands."

"The ship isn't nautical, it's aeronautical. We sailed on the winds in the sky, on a ship made from bones, harvested from the souls that flame her sails," Otholo answered.

"I've heard a tale about such a ship; the *Necrolosis*, didn't ever think it might be real," offered Nat. "But how did you get passage and at what cost?"

Otholo laughed. "I offered the ship's owner a song, and a pretty little song it was too. And he took me across the Shadowlands as promised. But the parting gift for me was a curse. As I slipped through a gate between the worlds, he slipped into me. And a real nasty bastard of a demon he is."

"The Captain of the *Necrolosis* is inside you?" asked Diagus. "Is there a way he would take us across the Shadowlands to Thea."

Otholo laughed again, slamming his hand on the table, tears beginning to form in his eyes. "He spent the last few thousand years searching for a way out of the Shadowlands, that's the reason he built the *Necrolosis*. I very much doubt he's going to just waltz straight back into the hell he was condemned to."

"What if I was to command him?"

"The Shadojak has no power over a free demon, especially one so strong."

Diagus lowered his elbows to the table, tapping his fingers. "Unless I had the demon's name. With that I would hold power over him, is that not so?"

"Owning his name would give you a will over him, yes. If you have his name. Do you?"

The Shadojak remained silent.

"I thought so. If it's any consolation, neither do I. There must be another way into Thea."

Nat cleared his voice. "Not without a charmed key and none would be charmed on Earth, not with Thea's magic."

"But what about the stone we used to get here. Does that hold any powers?" Elora asked, an idea coming to her.

Her uncle shook his head. "Even if it still held enough energy, it's spent the last twelve years at the bottom of Lake Bled and it would take weeks to get there on foot or horseback. And we would need to make it cross the channel. Time is a luxury we can ill afford."

"I knew a necromancer once," said Ragna, eyebrows knitting together. "Claimed he had a way of dissecting a bull, cutting it up so that it would open doors into another world."

"Is he at hand?" Diagus asked.

"Nope."

"Then it doesn't matter. Otholo, I want to speak with your demon, this ship of his is the only way we're getting to Thea."

"He cannot be summoned. He'll show himself when he wants to and only if I've not been drinking," Otholo grinned wickedly as he raised his glass to his lips.

"Stay your hand, bard. I will speak with this demon."

"You've seen what he is capable of, do you think you can control him?" Otholo lowered the glass. "He will tear your friends apart before you stick him – stick me with that blade of yours."

"We will see. Ragna, how strong are the chains and bars in the dungeons? Have you been down there lately?"

Otholo laughed again, but the sounds faded as he realised that the Shadojak was being serious.

"They've been touched by a spot of rust I suppose, but the iron's still thick beneath. It'll hold out against a rock troll, or two."

"You cannot be serious. You're going to put me, Otholo the Bard, songbird … " He gave up the argument as the Shadojak grinned. "How degrading. A dungeon."

"I'm sure Ejan will sort you out with cushions and blankets, it's only for one night. Unless the demon doesn't show at all. Might be we'll need to tickle you some, come the morning."

Elora wondered what sort of tickling would coax out a demon, then realised that it would probably be the violent kind.

Ragna rose from the table, chuckling to himself. "Come now Otholo, let's get you tucked into your new bed, I'll not clamp the manacles too tight."

"Manacles?" he whispered, following Ragna to the door. "I could have been a prince, you know. A prince."

The door slammed behind them, leaving the sound of the lamps gently burning as they flickered in an unseen draught. It was fully dark outside now; it would be darker still in a dungeon. Elora felt sorry for Otholo and guilt, for the blame lay with her. It was her mission, her quest to bring down Solarius, yet it seemed that it was other people that shouldered the pain.

Norgie rose from the table and began to tidy away the dishes, as did Ejan and Jaygen. Elora began to help, rising from her seat but Ejan told her to sit, telling her that she was a guest and that she should think about sleep after the long day she'd had.

Sleep was something she was looking forward to, a comfortable bed and clean sheets. Rising from the table, she gave her uncle and Gurple a goodnight kiss, her gaze wandering over to the Shaigun. Bray was in conversation with Diagus and either didn't realise she was turning in for the night or didn't care. Maybe it was an act for the Shadojak, unless the act had been with her earlier. She would see him in the morning and wring the truth from him.

Elora awoke to the sound of goat's bleating. She sat up and massaged life back into her neck that was stiff from sleeping in an awkward position. The bed had been comfortable and she had fallen asleep as soon as the covers were pulled up, but she must have slept too deeply.

She peered out of her window, the goats were chasing chickens from the gooseberry bushes while a large red cockerel chased the goats, pecking at their legs. Elora could see her mare, grazing in the field with the other horses, scowling at the goats as if they disturbed her breakfast. She was sure that horse was constantly in a bad mood.

A washbasin and cloth had been laid upon the chest, next to her old blue jeans and shirt. Elora guessed it was Ejan who had washed them and left them out.

Washed and dressed she left the room and found Ejan and Norgie in the kitchen, apparently she was the last out of bed. Bray, Diagus and Ragna had already left for the keep, to check on Otholo and his demon. She had wanted to go with them but doubted they would have permitted it.

Breakfast was cheese and bread; Ejan gave her a basket to carry to her uncle who hadn't eaten yet. Nat had wanted to walk around the lake and so she set off to find him there.

The lake lay beyond the cornfield, hidden from the inn and surrounded by trees. A narrow path led to the water's edge, two large willows trailing branches in the shallows where ducks were feeding and playfully splashing themselves. Her uncle was staring out into the body of water, hands clasped behind his back and humming a familiar tune.

Further out into the lake she saw the white crests of waves rising and falling in a peculiar pattern. Coalescing in circles at the centre, then fanning out in spirals, the ducks bobbing up and down as the ripples passed them by.

"Beautiful," Elora whispered, hoping she didn't startle Nat and spoil the effect.

His humming quieted then he stopped, the swirling water pattern washing away to nothing as he turned her way. "Morning, did you sleep well?"

"Slept like a rock. Here, I've brought breakfast." She sat on the long grass and patted the spot next to her and Nat lowered himself down.

"You were manipulating the elements," Elora stated, staring out into the lake.

"Yes. You've got to keep practicing or else your ability weakens," he said, taking the cheese and bread Elora had cut for him.

"Use it or lose it, right. Can you teach me?" she asked.

Her uncle bit into the cheese, crumbs catching in his beard. "I promised the Shadojak I wouldn't."

Elora felt a familiar flare of anger rise up but swallowed it down with the bread. Diagus would have his reasons and she couldn't go taking it out on Nat. "What did Silk do to you after you were taken from the *Molly* ?" she asked, changing the subject.

"They questioned me, wanting to know where you would have gone, what people you knew. I told them nothing so they tried beating it out of me, threatening torture. When that didn't work they used a takwich; thinking to take my body and memories."

"What? Are you alright? Are you still you?" spat Elora, almost choking on the cheese.

Nat smiled, and leaned in to hug her close. "I'm still me. My mind was too strong for the takwich to cope with. It bit me – it died. Simple as that. Afterwards they left me alone, then when they tried moving me to a different location, Bray came to the rescue."

Elora hugged him tight, feeling anger again at the thought of him being beaten. "And where is Silk now?" After her father, he was the next one she would hunt down.

She rolled a piece of bread between her fingers, making a small white ball and flicked it into the water. The ducks raced each other to get to it first.

"I don't know," he answered, throwing another piece of bread into the lake. He remained quiet for some time, his forehead creasing as if deep in thought. "Can you remember what I taught you about the elements, when you were small?"

"Yeah. They all have a rhythm, subtle waves or vibrations that lie beyond human senses. And that if you know the rhythms and reach for them, they can be altered. Air is the easiest to feel, to alter."

"Good, you remember. So now try."

Elora glanced around to make sure they were alone. "I thought you promised the Shadojak you wouldn't teach me."

"I did. But how can I teach you something you already know. It's the practice that you need. I won't help you there either, but I think you already possess the basics. It should be easier without Earth's magic fudging things up."

Earth's magic? Was that the only reason it hadn't worked before? She snapped a blade of grass from between her feet and held it in her open palm. A gentle breeze, strong enough to tease its edge without blowing it from her hand, played along its length.

Questing with her mind she reached for the breeze, feeling for its rhythm and stumbled upon it so easily she thought it must be wrong. But it was there, a gentle flowing, rising and falling in sporadic beats. Her mind touched the edge of the flow, pausing for just a moment and directed it towards the blade of grass.

A fine tendril spiraled towards her, unseen but felt with her inner eye. It touched her hand and flowed over her skin lifting the blade away from her palm to hover an inch above, spinning in a light whirlwind.

It was working, she had actually manipulated an element. She felt a joy run through her, the thrill of having succeeded in something she doubted she could ever do. The emotion made her momentarily lose the thread, linking her to the wind and the blade of grass settled back on her hand.

"Well done," Nat praised her.

Excitedly, she wanted to try again but she spotted Ragna marching towards them, the Fist strapped to his back and decided it might not be a good idea to show what she could do. She would practice more later.

"Diagus says he needs you," Ragna said, helping himself to what was left of the cheese.

"Has something happened to Otholo?" she asked, worried that the demon had somehow hurt the Bard.

"The demon has yet to show itself. Otholo's been tickled black and blue but the thing won't be summoned. He wants to try something else. He says the demon may respond to you,"

Ragna shrugged his shoulders. "Don't know what, don't know why but the Shadojak wants to try."

It was a short walk to the keep, following the same path they rode in on the previous day. The remnants of a tower reached far enough to penetrate the forest canopy; jagged edges poking through the branches and leaves where the stone bricks had long ago toppled off, leaving only an empty shell. Crows had made nests in its broken, lichen covered walls, staring at them as they passed below.

Ragna led them through a maze of stone debris and shattered masonry, down ancient staircases and along corridors that had at one time been tiled but were now open to the elements, strewn with leaves and animal droppings and home to the mice and rats. Some of the stone archways were still intact, leading into rooms which the forest and claimed back; the outline and general square shapes of vast chambers and rooms were scattered, their ruined floors a network of tree roots and bramble. Elora couldn't quite believe the vastness of Rams Keep, it was colossal. She wished she could have witnessed what it was like a thousand years ago when it was in its prime.

Another tower in worst condition than the last, with a thick circular wall that was half the height, spanned before them. Wide enough to accommodate the entire inn and maybe the stables. They climbed over what was left of a portcullis, now a twisted mess of rusted iron, leaning against the ruined frame; bent and sagging at its centre by weight and time. The ground inside was cleared of debris, and the stone cobbles were intact, only yellow grass having managed to push through cracks and loose bricks.

The remains of some walls still stood, marking out where there were once rooms, probably barracks or guard rooms. Ragna ducked beneath the remains of a door that still clung to the wall and down a short staircase that led beneath the ground. Elora linked her arm through her uncle's as they followed, stepping out of the daylight.

When she'd adjusted to the gloom she found that they were in a chamber with a low ceiling, the lamps on the walls doing no more than casting dull light around them until Nat mumbled something under his breath which made them burn brighter; revealing a plain square room with an old rotted table shoved against the far wall, a broken stool sat atop it.

"Handy trick," remarked Ragna. as he knelt before the table and pulled open a trap door. "Mind how you go, the steps are steep, slippery and they go a long way down."

He took a lamp from the wall and descended into blackness, his footfall echoing deeply as he disappeared. Elora went next, taking Nat's hand as she knew his eyesight wasn't what it once was and trod carefully. If she fell it would be Ragna's hammer that would stop her – most probably with her face.

It was a spiral staircase and so she let her hand guide her around as she followed the circle of orange light down almost three turns before the Viking stopped at a thick door. The staircase carried on down and Elora wondered how deep it would go, then remembered Ragna telling them that most of the ruins under Rams Keep were intact.

The door opened into a dimly lit corridor, a layer of dirt coated the stone walls and cobwebs, clinging to the ancient beams, grey with age and thick with dust. They passed heavy doors, banded with iron and studded with bolts, some standing ajar, revealing darkness within, some bolted closed and two of them padlocked.

"What's inside those?" Elora asked, her voice coming out louder than intended within the tight space.

"I couldn't say, most likely empty. Those with locks were sealed a long time ago and probably for good reasons."

They turned a corner descending several more steps that led into a wider room with what appeared to be cells to either side. Fire flickered from between iron bars, coming from sconces that were in the wall.

Diagus stepped into the light, flames playing in his pearly stare. He motioned them inside where she saw Otholo standing at the centre of the room. Manacles bound his ankles to the floor, his arms stretched out to either side of him, thick iron chains secured by iron bands around wrists. He had barely an inch of play in the chains to move.

Bray stood to the bard's side, arms folded and dressed in the same blacks as the Shadojak. Elora had a sick feeling in the pit of stomach that he'd had enough of playing with her and became the cold emotionless Shaigun again. She took a deep breath and gave him a curt nod, masking her true feelings.

"Ragna, said you needed me," she said to Diagus.

"You may be able to help, yes," he replied, coming to stand to the other side of Otholo. "We've tried our methods of reaching the demon but as you can see, the peacock remains."

Otholo chuckled. "I did tell you. He'll come in his own time and the more he senses that you want him here, the less inclined he'll be."

"But the bard thinks that you being here may bring the demon out. I can't see why but we haven't the time to seek other means. So ... " Without warning, he turned and drove his fist into Otholo's belly.

The bard doubled over as far as the chains allowed, attempting to suck air into winded lungs.

"What are you doing?" Elora shouted. "You're hurting him!" She stepped closer but Bray stepped in her way.

"The demon will come if Otholo is threatened, it's the only way."

Elora flinched away from his touch as his hands came to rest on her arms. "Leave me alone!" she spat, feeling satisfaction at seeing hurt flick across Bray's face.

Another thud, followed by the chains suddenly rattling tight let her know that the Shadojak had struck Otholo again. Elora tried to push passed Bray, his hands again on her arms. She looked to her uncle for help, yet he, like Ragna, only watched.

Another thud, this time harder, the iron snapping tight as Otholo took the punch in the chest; Diagus striking expertly without remorse.

"No!" Elora screamed and shoved hard against Bray's chest. She must have shoved harder than she thought because the Shaigun slammed into the wall, surprise raising his eyebrows as he took a moment to register what had happened, before springing back and grasping her arms. His green eyes ablaze with shock and fury.

"Enough, Elora," he barked, his nose almost touching hers. She had an impulse to sink her teeth into it. Recognising the tide of anger rising, she forced herself to calm down.

"She's right," coughed Otholo, a trail of blood running from a split lip. "It's not working. He knows you won't kill me and is quite happy to let me get beaten up. Perhaps ... " A grin stretched across his bruised face as he looked at Bray. "A kiss from the daughter of Chaos."

"No!" said Bray, before Elora realised that Otholo meant her.

The Shadojak stared at his apprentice, raising a grey eyebrow before turning his attention back on the man in chains. "Will it work?"

"It might," offered the Bard.

Diagus's gaze fell back on her. It was her choice – just a simple kiss. It didn't mean anything and although she wasn't attracted to Otholo in any way, he had a certain charm about him and was pleasing to the eye.

"You don't have to do this," Bray whispered, so only she could hear.

Elora heard the urgency in his words, felt his fingers dig deeper into her arms. He was jealous, the emotion was written plain on his face and it made her feel better – he still cared.

"I want to," she said, twisting out of his grasp and witnessing his jaw clench, his scowl deepen.

Diagus gave her room as she stepped closer to the bard, his mismatched eyes following her advance and sparkling with delight.

Her lips touched Otholo's for the briefest moment, light and warm before pulling away. Nothing happened.

"A bit of privacy please. At least step out of the room," Otholo said. He pulled at the chains, showing how little movement he had. "It's not like I can do her any harm, is it?"

Diagus ushered them into the corridor and closed the door behind them, Bray's sullen face appearing at the bars, angry and hurt.

Elora glanced away, hiding the smile that she knew would give away her feelings, he *was* jealous.

Putting her hands on Otholo's shoulders, she leaned close once again and planted another kiss on his mouth, then pulled back.

Otholo licked his lips. "The demon's all about passion. Your kiss should be more alluring, more exciting. Perhaps if you kissed me like you would Bray."

"How do I know you're not just getting some perverted enjoyment from tricking me into kissing you."

He grinned wickedly. "You don't. I dare say I'll enjoy it, you may do too and you never know, it might work. Now pucker up Elora and kiss me like you mean it."

Elora closed her eyes when she put her lips to his, remembering the kiss she'd had with Bray in the forest, his mouth – his lips. Otholo's tongue darted between her teeth, hungry and wanting. She kissed him back, pushing her body against his, the clicking of chains as the bard's body shifted reminding her of where she was.

This wouldn't work, Elora realised as Otholo groaned, this wasn't Bray. The kiss felt fake and dispassionate, yet it had some effect on the bard. A deep rumbling vibrated from his chest, his groan building, his kiss becoming harsh.

She broke away, stepping back from Otholo, who grinned at her like the proverbial cat that got the milk.

"Chaos shouldn't taste so sweet," he said, a deep rumble to his voice an entire octave below his usual tone. And he appeared different, no taller, no wider but somehow he filled the cell. It was the demon.

Bray realised it too and opened the door about to re-enter the room. "Get out," ordered the demon, eyes alight with violence as he stretched his body against his iron bonds.

Bray ignored him and came to stand beside Elora.

"Get out. Leave us, I'll speak only to the Princess of Darkness" said the demon, stretching Otholo's face into a menacing glare that looked wrong on the bard. The voice was harsh and full of hate, nothing like the sing-song camber of Otholo. It gave Elora goosebumps watching his body being used by another.

"It's fine," she said to Bray, ushering him back out. "He's chained up; he can't harm me."

Bray glanced at the manacles and chains. It was clear the demon couldn't break them but he seemed dissatisfied as he stormed from the cell, slamming the door.

The next face to appear through the bars was the Shadojak's.

"Ask him if he can take us across the Shadowlands, ask him if he still has the *Necrolosis*, ask … "

"Shut it Shadojak. I have my ship but I'll not be going back into the Shadowlands. Not unless my queen commands it," said the demon, eyes boring into hers.

"I command it," said Elora, unsure if she was saying the right thing and not understanding why he referred to her as his queen.

The demon laughed. "You're the daughter of Chaos. I can feel it, see it, smell it on you – but you need to be awakened, need to have that black heart of yours pumping with the darkness you possess. Then you will be my queen and I your loyal servant. Not this girl before me."

"Awakened?"

"You must die, daughter of Chaos," he said, then without warning snapped the chain holding his left wrist, his hand shooting out and locking around her throat. His other hand twisted around the chain binding his other wrist.

He yanked it from the wall, a clump of masonry still fixed to the end as he whipped it at the door. The chain passed between the bars, the links wrapping around each other in a knot before he pulled them tight, locking the door before anyone had chance to open it. She was trapped with the demon as he choked the life from her.

Pain exploded in her head as fingers crushed her windpipe, her lungs screaming for air. She dug fingers into his hand, clawed at his face and kicked as hard as she could but couldn't shake the vice like grip around her throat.

"It will be over soon, princess," whispered the demon, his breath hot against her face, barely heard above the crashing of the door as the men struggled to break in – her name being screamed by Bray and Nat.

The sounds seemed to drift far away as her vision dimmed to nothing, even the pain dissolved, replaced by the dizzy sensation of floating – of falling.

A blackness, all consuming, sank into her flesh, her mind, a darkness writhing with haunting whispers, repeating her name over and over. Elora … Elora. They faded with her beating heart.

Then nothing.

17

The Right Thing

Bray screamed her name as he thrashed at the iron chain links that held fast against the door. He watched through the bars in horror as the demon released his grip from Elora's throat and let her limp body fall; arms lifeless and unable to prevent her head smacking against the stone ground.

"Elora!" he screamed again – please don't let her be dead. But her violet eyes stared at him, lifeless and unseeing from the floor. She took no breath.

He was suddenly wrenched away from the door by Ragna as he slammed his war hammer against the old wood. It splintered and broke apart on the second strike, smashing to pieces; fragments still hitting the floor as they rushed in. Bray went to Elora, leaving the demon to Diagus and the Viking.

She had no pulse, no heartbeat and no breath. Tears blurred his vision as he pushed Elora's body onto her back and placed his hands above her heart. Nathaniel cradled Elora's head in his lap as Bray began the compressions.

"Get air into her lungs," he shouted at him. Nathaniel nodded and began to mumble under his breath. Bray didn't know what he was doing and was about to repeat his request when he felt Elora's chest begin to rise, then fall. Whatever the old man was doing, it was making her body breath.

Peaceful, was what Bray was thinking as he massaged her heart, her face looked peaceful; no more than asleep as if she would wake at any moment. Reality was too hard to bear, but he couldn't think she was dead.

"Wake up Elora. Don't be dead," he whispered, realising that the tears that he was shedding were the first to fall from his eyes since he was an infant, dumped on the steps of a church to the Blessed Mother. But that was in another time, another world.

He spared a glance to the demon. It was on its knees, driven there by Ragna's hammer, its head bent low and the Shadojak's sword held to its neck. Bray felt a hatred for that creature, the emotion running so deep it caused his hands to shake. No, his hands were shaking from sudden movements from Elora's heart, strong and rapid beats.

He stopped the compressions and put his ear to her chest. Thump, thump, the rhythm was erratic but her heart was beating. Elora was alive.

"Elora?" he said, taking her hand in his, searching her face for signs of waking.

Her eyes moved rapidly beneath closed lids as if dreaming, her mouth parted, a deep moan escaping through pale lips. "Elora?"

Suddenly the hand Bray was holding flexed, her grip squeezing blood from his fingers and turning them white as they clicked with the pressure. The pain was excruciating yet he couldn't wipe the grin from his face, she was alive.

Her eyelids flashed open, Elora stared at him through crimson irises and increased the pressure on his hand, her mouth twisting into an animal snarl.

Fingers cracked as she broke bone and cartilage, raising her head in an attempt to bite her uncle. Luckily Nathaniel pulled back at the last moment and avoided his nose being chewed off.

Ignoring the pain in his crushed hand – it would heal – Bray attempted to reach her. "Elora. Calm down, you're safe." Her deep red eyes cast back on him, followed by her fist.

Bray was vaguely aware he had been hit. He was punch-drunk, the room spinning as he rolled onto his back and shuffled against a wall, struggling into a sitting position.

His skull throbbed with pain and when he delicately touched his temple he felt the bone beneath crunch and flex where it had been fractured. His broken hand pulsed in agony; loud clicks and pops vibrating up his arm when he foolishly attempted to move his fingers.

As the blurred image of the cell began to refocus he caught the rapid movements of a fight. Diagus was pushing himself up from the floor, a stream of blood leaking from his nose, his good eye swollen shut and Elora standing above him, ready to slam her foot down on his spine.

"No!" screamed Ragna, swinging the Fist of the North over his head, the great war hammer arcing down on her.

Bray attempted to shout but his jaw felt wrong, as if that was broken too, and all he managed was a garbled groan. Yet she didn't need the warning as he watched her spin towards the Viking, Diagus forgotten and caught the head of the falling hammer in one hand.

Steam spiraled between her fingers as they sank into the steel as if it was butter. Ragna's face had only time to go slack with shock as Elora stepped to the side, grasping him around the arm and flung him into the wall. His broken body fell in a heap, the impact knocking him unconscious.

"Elora, what are you doing girl?" croaked Nathaniel, shuffling towards her with a hand held out before him.

Red eyes turned to him, full of hate, brimming with anger.

"Elora, please. These are friends you're killing." But his words fell on deaf ears. It was clear to Bray that she didn't know any of them and only had a mind for violence.

Elora crouched low, teeth bared, growling like a wild cat, ready to pounce on her uncle. Bray couldn't let it happen.

His uninjured hand found purchase in the masonry and he pulled himself up, supporting his body on unsteady legs as the room swayed – or was that him? He shook the dizziness from his head, took two stumbling steps and dived against Nathaniel's legs; bringing him down as his niece sprung into the air, hands slashing where his neck would have been.

Screaming in anger as she deftly landed, Elora jumped against the wall and pushed herself off again, turning her body in midair and coming at them with the ferocity of a tigress. Bray could do no more than shield the old man with his body.

Bracing himself for the attack. But instead of feeling nails and teeth, Elora fell passed them, slamming into the floor and rolling against the wall.

She hissed in pain as Diagus stepped towards her and laid the flat of his blade against her neck. The hiss turned to a scream before she collapsed to all fours, panting to the point of hyperventilating.

"Calm yourself, girl. Lest I take your head," Diagus said calmly.

Elora sat down heavily and curled her knees up against her chest. "What happened?" she said, between breaths. Her eyes returning to violet, wide and staring around her.

"You died, Elora," said the demon, from the corner of the cell, where he had been hiding as the fight broke out. "I killed you and the darkness brought you back. You've been awakened. Now you are the Princess of Chaos, Queen of Darkness. My queen." He dropped to one knee and lowered his head. "I, Zionbuss, feared demon of the Shadowlands, Captain of the *Necrolosis*, give you my name, I am your servant. Your will is my command."

Diagus stepped away from Elora, seeing that the threat had passed from the girl and now placed his blade above the demon.

"Zionbuss? Were you not a General in Solarius's army?"

"My past loyalties have gone stale from my hell in the Shadowlands. Yet I will go to hell and back again if my queen commands it. With my pledge to her I am free of Solarius."

"I should kill the pair of you and spare this world an unforgiving future," said the Shadojak.

"Kill them and you condemn both worlds to hell," said Nathaniel, as he scrambled to his feet. Bray grasped his arm and hauled himself up. "She is the only one capable of killing Solarius."

Bray saw Diagus hesitate, struggling with his options; his sword poised ready to take either head.

"I did this?" said Elora, as she gazed about the cell. Her eyes settled on Ragna, the huge Viking let out a moan as he sat up, wincing as his hands pressed to his shoulder. "I'm so sorry. I don't know what happened, I wasn't me, I was … "

"Chaos," finished the Shadojak. "You've got command of the demon at least. Will he take us to Thea?"

Elora was ready to collapse, the effort to stand making her muscles shake. Her uncle put out an arm to support her.

"Zionbuss?" she started, frowning at the unfamiliar word. "You will take us safely to Thea. Without harm or trickery."

The demon bowed. "I will my queen. And any harm delivered in the Shadowlands will not be of my doing."

She watched the Shadojak, unsure if she had said the right things. Bray knew the man was hard to read, but he slipped the blade away which could only be a good thing.

Ragna climbed back to his feet and dusted himself down.

"Will you look what she did to The Fist," he said, turning his war hammer over in his hands, displaying Elora's handprint an inch deep in the steel.

Bray moved his jaw, testing the break and found that it was already healing although throbbing like hell.

"Have you seen what she did to us?" he said, his gaze settling on her and watched as her eyes rolled back into her head. Pain screamed in his injured hand as he caught her falling body, yet he put that aside as he lifted her into his arms.

"She needs rest," he said.

Diagus nodded, then turned to Zionbuss. "Can I trust you not to harm us?"

The demon grinned. "Would you prefer the drunken bard to retake this body."

"No. But better the devil you know. Bring the peacock back and I'll keep him dry. You cross us, Zionbuss, and I'll take the girl's life as well as yours, queen or not."

The demon took a final glance at Elora, then appeared to sink into his body. Although it was more of a case that he merely shrank and allowed Otholo his physical form back. His facial features seeming softer if not bedraggled.

"Come, let's get these two back to the inn," said Ragna, striding past and taking a lamp from the wall. "At least that's one problem solved."

"Yes," agreed Diagus. "We only need to solve the other dozen or so."

Rain clouds, dark and heavy, filled the morning sky above the inn. Bray knew there would be a storm later as he swung his sword above his head, grey steel against the grey morning, warming life back into his arm and stretching his back against the well, readying himself for an early practice with Diagus.

He had spent the night pacing outside Elora's room, listening to her breathe – to her murmur random words in her sleep and feeling the rhythm of her heart, the beats reaching his sensitive skin through the oak panel door. It had been the Shadojak who'd finally ordered him to bed, to leave the girl be or else he would probably be still there, waiting for her to wake.

Diagus approached him now, his sword already drawn, face grim, eyes sharp. Bray knew his master was furious for the way in which he reacted to Elora's death, yesterday in the keep. How he had dropped his defence and lacked control over his emotions. He was sure that this morning's lesson would be a harsh one and the Shadojak wouldn't be holding back.

Tendons clicked in his neck as he rolled his head to the left, then the right, the damage inflicted upon his body from the event in the dungeon had healed while he slept, unlike the heavily bruised face of Diagus. One black eye, one a pearly white. He forced the grin from his face and focused on the attack.

The Shadojak gave him a curt nod, the only recognition he would get that the lesson had begun, before launching in with a side-swipe. The dark green blade slicing towards Bray's midriff.

Sparks spat as the blades met, Bray parrying whilst side-stepping around the foot of his master which he brought down, aiming to trip him up. Their bodies danced another step, each turning clockwise, Diagus's elbow angling up into Bray's face and meeting air instead of nose, while Bray flashed a punch towards the Shadojak's kidney, yet touched nothing.

They both spun away and came back, Bray ducking low and swiping his leg around attempting to take his master's legs from under him. They did no more than kick up dust from the floor, Diagus having jumped and as Bray rose his chest met a foot, kicking him onto his back.

A shadow cast over Bray's face as he rolled out of the way of the falling body, his hair brushing against a knee as it thudded into the dirt. He heard his master gasp with the pain of striking the ground but was glad the pain belonged to Diagus and not himself.

He barely had time to register the dagger being flung under hand before his reflexes brought his sword about, batting the old blade away. Bray blocked a lunge on the backswing and took a step back.

Diagus meant business this morning, striking with the intent to damage, the attacks lethal as they were brutal, one flowing into another and driving the Shaigun towards the stables.

Bray caught movement from a window above, his eyes flicked up for the briefest moment and saw Otholo watching him from Elora's room. Why was the Bard in there when they were under strict instructions not to disturb her? The momentary lapse in concentration earned him a glancing blow from the pummel of the Shadojak's sword, connecting with the back of his head and knocking him off balance.

He shook the dizziness from his head before catching the next attack. He caught his master's sword on the end of his and angled it down; the god-created metal cutting into his inferior blade, shearing a layer away as if it was no more than peeling an orange. He would need to do some serious sharpening later.

Diagus's cross-piece met his, just as Bray intended, and wedging his foot against his opponent's, he pulled back and ducked under the Shadojak, flipping the older man over his shoulder and following him down with a left-handed punch to the sternum. It connected and Diagus let out a grunt, hitting the floor hard.

Bray took the moment to cast his eyes back up to Elora's room. Something wasn't right. Otholo still watched from the window, a glass of wine in hand, which was also wrong. The Shadojak had prohibited him any alcohol as long as Zionbuss served the girl. What was going on, had Elora come out of her dream state? Was she well?

By the time his eyes drew back to Diagus, the old man was back on his feet, his blade pointing his way, although clearly winded.

"Good. Finally, a bit of fire in your belly," he said, white eye searching him for the next attack. Yet he didn't advance. Instead, Diagus paced over to a horse rug that had been thrown over a tall object, vaguely the shape of a person, the toes of brown leather riding boots poking from beneath.

"What is this?" demanded Bray, beginning to put two and two together. The boots were Elora's, the height and rough outline similar to her also. Had the Shadojak tied her up, was this some kind of sick test. Was this the reason Otholo was watching them?

"Drive your blade through the beast," ordered, Diagus, pointing his own sword at the figure beneath the rug. "Kill her, Bray. Purge the world of its reaper. Strike the black heart while she's weak, while we still have a chance. You've seen what she can do, what she is."

What? No way. So this was why the Bard was drinking wine, to keep Zionbuss from protecting his queen.

"Do it, boy. Strike hard, strike fast. Kill her, become the Shaigun you are, the Shadojak you'll become."

Bray couldn't believe this was happening, that this was real. He wouldn't have put it passed the Shadojak to bring Elora down to be executed, if he judged her to be too dangerous he would have taken her life immediately. Maybe she was already dead and Diagus was searching for proof that his Shaigun was pure of feeling, in full control of his emotions.

The shape wasn't moving, the chest appeared still beneath the rug but he couldn't be sure.

"Kill her Bray. It's one life. One soul against two worlds. Make your judgement boy. Find the balance."

Bray's arm moved mechanically, pulling the sword back, ready to thrust forward.

"Do the right thing," growled the Shadojak, spit flying from his mouth.

Body tense, jaw tight and teeth locked, Bray moved.

Dropping his leading knee to add weight to his thrust, he slammed his arm forward as fast and as hard as he was able; hearing the scream rupture from his lungs with the effort. He put all that he was into that one motion and did 'the right thing'.

The tip of his sword disappeared two inches into the dirt between the Shadojak's feet. Stopping only when the blade touched the stone foundations beneath.

He let go of the hilt and stepped away from his sword, away from his master and away from his chosen path and the life he had.

Diagus didn't flinch, his stony expression as grim and unreadable as always as he yanked the rug from Elora, revealing a stout wooden post with a stuffed sack tied to the top. Her boots innocently standing to attention against the base of the pole, empty – like Bray's future.

"When the time comes I will kill the girl. If you stand against me, I will kill you. If you run, I will hunt you down." The Shadojak spoke in a single flat tone, the words rougher than a sharpening stone.

Bray turned his back on his old master and walked away, a numbness filling his mind as the clouds above opened up. Rain, cold and heavy spilled from the dark sky, grey tears splattering on his clothes, his face, his hair – yet he barely felt anything. The world would cry for him, but who would cry for the world?

Elora … Elora … Her name was whispered each time the wind blew through the open window to disturb the curtains, each time the material swished against the polished floor. *Elora … Elora …* When the door opened in the night, as Ejan came to check on her, her name creaked from old hinges and again when the Norsewoman left. Every sound in the old inn: footfalls echoing down the corridor, the cork popping from a bottle, even the horses snorting from the stables. *Elora … Elora …* Spoken in a thousand hushed voices, the darkness called to her, sang to her, worshipped her. *Elora … Elora …*

"Elora?"

She opened her eyes and saw Otholo standing by the window, concern wrinkling his brow as he sloshed red wine around a glass he was nursing.

"You were talking in your sleep," he said.

It was morning, and judging by the charcoal sky it would be a wet one. She sat up and rubbed life back into her legs, nerve endings flashing pins and needles through her skin.

"Is everybody ok?" she blurted out, suddenly remembering what had happened in the dungeon. "Did I hurt … ?" Otholo raised a hand to calm her.

"You've hurt their pride maybe. Ragna's a bit stiff, Bray's already healed and is out there sparring with Diagus. Can't believe you gave the Shadojak a black eye. Your life's turning out to be a ballad all on its own."

The events in the cell came back to her in a flash. She had wanted to kill them, destroy them totally. The level of violence that propelled her was so intense it was all consuming, powered by the belief that she, herself, was indestructible. It was the dark voices that had been calling to her, guiding her anger, her wrath and if it wasn't for Diagus touching her skin with her father's blade, she would have killed them all. Somehow that blade held a power that drained her will.

"What did Zi– ... What did the demon do to me?" Something had changed inside her, bringing the whispers that came to her from the darkness, snatching other sounds and energies and shaping them to speak her name. Even now, the duel outside between Diagus and Bray, the clashing together of steel against steel brought her name to her ears; sharp, scraping and deep.

"He awakened you. Stopped your heart so it could sing again to a different beat, to a darker beat. Do you feel different?"

Elora nodded. She felt more than herself as if she had spent her life in a dream-state, drugged and only now waking from her stupor but couldn't shape the words to portray how she felt to Otholo, so she decided to change the subject.

"I thought Diagus ordered you not to drink?"

"He did, although he hadn't needed to." He raised the wine toward his lips but before his mouth touched the glass his hand shook and the arm lowered. "I've not touched a drop, I can't. It's so infuriating to have something controlling your limbs when you're actually conscious."

"It's Zio ... "

"Don't speak his name or you'll call him forward. But yes, the demon won't let me touch a drop." Sad eyes cast down upon the drink in his hand. "I should be grateful really. I haven't been sober in a long time. It just irks me that it wasn't my choice." He set the glass down on the windowsill and peered out. A scowl bringing his blonde brows together.

"That's interesting," he said rubbing his chin.

"What's interesting?" asked Elora as she joined him at the window.

Otholo stood aside, giving her room. She looked down into the grounds and watched Bray walking away from Diagus, his sword stuck into the ground at the Shadojak's feet. "What happened?"

"I could be mistaken but I believe the Shadojak now needs a new Shaigun" replied Otholo. Elora stared at Bray as he walked out of the courtyard and into the developing storm.

"What do you mean?"

"Bray's given his sword back to Diagus, giving his title of Shaigun up. He's now a free man."

Her eyes found the Shadojak's who turned his stare from Bray to her, his expression hard, accusing. Did he blame her for this?

"I need to get dressed," she said, pulling at the clothes she had slept in, the same she had worn yesterday. Otholo took the hint and crossed the room to the door.

"I'll be around if you need me," he said, treating her to a mock bow before leaving the room.

Elora dressed in the green britches and shirt she wore on her first evening at the inn, tied her hair back in a no nonsense way and set off to find Bray.

The inn was quiet as she made her way across the empty barroom, her feet making the only sound, slap slap on the polished floor. She stopped when her gaze fell upon Ragna's great war hammer hung above the fire place. Her hand print sunk into the steel of the Fist of the North.

The memory of sinking her fingers into the metal was fresh in her mind, a thing done so easily and naturally it wasn't worth thinking about. But now seeing the damage she wondered how it was even possible.

"I think you've improved it," said Ejan, approaching from behind, so silent that it startled Elora. "Ragna thinks otherwise but he has no taste. How are you feeling today?"

"Much better, thanks" she replied. Ejan smiled but said nothing. Her eyes hard and unreadable as she wandered over to the kitchen door but Elora noticed that the smile was forced as if the Viking had something on her mind.

"There's bread in the kitchen if you're hungry," she said, pushing the door open, her hand gripping the wood as she turned back to Elora. "Oh, and if you hurt my husband again, I'll kill you."

The door swung shut, the echo it made resonating around the empty room. *Kill her … Kill her … Elora, kill.*

The whispers touched her ears, she felt them drawing her towards the door Ejan had left through. *Kill her.* How dare she threaten her, the stupid bitch. You can't kill the darkness.

Elora took a step towards the kitchen, fingers flexing, imagining gripping the Norsewoman's long blonde plait and curling it around her neck, pulling it tight, choking her. Killing her – No! What was she thinking, this wasn't her? It was the darkness. Those whispers putting evil intent into her thoughts, her mind. Was it because she felt threatened by the woman? Ejan had every right to warn her off, she had tried to kill her husband, after all.

Elora stormed out of the inn, the heavy oak door scraping against the floor. *... Elora ...* She slammed it behind her *... Kill ...* And walked out into the cold rain, putting distance between herself and the inn, worried that she was becoming the beast she was yesterday, worried she would kill everyone inside.

Her bare feet squelched against the wet ground, splashing through puddles, the water throwing muddy droplets up her legs *... Kill ... Kill ...* The words falling from the sky, bouncing from leaves, her blood thundering in her ears, a maelstrom of voices shouting her name. She screamed to block them out as she pushed through the tree line. But under the branches, the thick leaves blotting out any light the clouds gave up, darkness ruled and opened up its wide arms to embrace its daughter.

Soft white ash clung to the skin on the back of Elora's hand, it cracked in dark fissures when she unclenched her fist, making her skin appear aged beyond that of the burnt trees around her. It floated about her like snow, coating the smoldering stumps and wood pulp that were once large oaks, elms and birch. It layered the scorched ground, burying her bare feet ankle deep as grey smoke played off the few remaining trunks, bereft of limbs, no more than charcoal tomb stones spanning away from her in a circle with her at its centre. What had she done?

Elora tentatively stepped through the pristine layer of ash, a serene peacefulness embracing her, relief at being released from something unbearable, a heavy pressure, pain, an intense heat that suddenly lifted, leaving her feeling euphoric and cleansed.

Was the destruction her way of releasing the temper, born of the whispered darkness that had been plaguing her since the awakening? Must she release her anger and reduce everything to white ash to rid herself of the darkness?

She left a black trail in her wake; dark footprints that followed her out, further into the wet green forest. Was it a sign, letting her know that below the calm white surface there was blackness?

The whispers; the thousand voices were gone now, but they would be back and most probably sooner than she had care for to needle at her, wanting her to release carnage, destruction, to kill. If she couldn't find a way of controlling her temper somebody would get hurt. Somebody would die.

The day began to get dark, the patches of sky she could see through the breaks in the trees turning a purplish bruise colour, the storm abating but rain water still working its way to the forest floor from the tall branches and leaves.

She had been wandering aimlessly through the trees, too afraid to return to the inn, in fear of causing harm to others, but knowing that if she didn't they would come in search of her. Elora's mind was so preoccupied she hadn't realised that she'd come upon the fallen tree where she had shared that kiss with Bray. Recognition only dawning on her as her eyes found those of Bray's, so green it was like the forest was staring back as he sat, elbows on knees upon the tree stump he had split the logs from a couple of days ago.

Elora could feel her heart thump once again as she stepped closer to him, beating stronger with what, love, lust, or anger? All three or just something more primal, her black heart's reaction to the sensation of danger.

"Hi," she said, squeezing onto the stump beside him, their arms touching, his wet from the rain, hers oddly dry. The sound of him grinding his teeth, adding to the pluck plucking sounds of water dripping from leaf to leaf, filling the gap until he spoke.

"Diagus is going to kill you," he said matter-of-factly. "Even if Solarius falls. He will kill you. Me too." His warm hand slid into hers, fingers interlacing as his grip tightened.

Elora didn't reply. In the back of her mind she already had thoughts of what the Shadojak meant to do with her but somehow pushed them away, not wanting to think about something that was out of her control.

She looked down at his hand in hers, feeling his thumb gently stroking the tender skin between thumb and wrist. She wanted to enjoy his touch, his warmth, yet didn't know if she could take the pain if he decided to become the Shaigun once again.

"Why would he kill you?" Elora asked.

"Because he would need to come through me to get to you," he answered, turning his face to hers, rain water gathering in his dark hair and causing it to spike up above his brow.

"Why?"

"I love you. Love you more than both worlds, it seems." He leaned closer, their faces almost touching, meaning to kiss her, his eyes intense and alive. Yet when she didn't bring her mouth to his, his expression changed, lips tightened and he planted the kiss tenderly on her forehead. When he pulled back she could tell it wasn't the reaction he wanted, his hand relaxed around hers, allowing her to let go. She didn't.

"I'm scared I'll hurt you," she admitted. The damage she caused in the forest too clear in her mind.

Bray shrugged his shoulders. "I don't hurt like most people."

"And I don't attack like most. I almost killed you yesterday, if you haven't forgotten."

He rubbed his jaw with his free hand. "I remember, but I heal really quick."

"Not if I kill you, not if I tear your head off. Maybe Diagus is right and I'm too dangerous to let loose, once my father is dead." She lowered her head to his shoulder and he put an arm protectively around her.

"We can run away together, hide anywhere on Earth or Thea. We'll go where Diagus will never find us."

"No. I still need to stop my father and to do that I need the Shadojak and my uncle and most probably Zionbuss. If Solarius isn't stopped it doesn't matter where we go, Earth will suffer and I can't let that happen."

"Then we will stop him ourselves. Find a way into Aslania without them."

Elora shook her head, hearing the desperate plea in his voice and not liking it. "We won't make it. We may not even make it with the rest but I won't go without them. If I die trying to bring my father down, then so be it. I gave my word to Diagus and I won't go back on it." Elora's gaze settled on the light limbs of an elm in front, swaying in a breeze, creaking, whispering … *Elora … Elora …*

"You say you love me. So in the name of love I ask that you do one thing for me. And I want you to promise me that you will see it through." Bray stiffened, his hands grasping hers tightly once again. "Anything."

She met his eyes, stared straight into his, holding his intense green gaze.

"If I change, if I can't control my temper and hurt people." She leaned closer. "Kill me."

He leapt from the stump and spun around, flinging his arms wide.

"What? No, I can't. I won't," he snapped, hands balling into fists at his side. Elora looked away for a moment, gathering herself, controlling her temper that seemed to rise with the growing darkness. Whispers born of rustling leaves, creaking limbs and birdsong … *Kill … Kill …* She took a deep breath, drawing in air, thick with moisture. Holding it for a moment before slowly releasing. She gazed back at Bray, still staring at her intensely, oblivious to her struggle with her rising anger.

"I love you too," she said and watched his features soften, fingers unclench. "But this will only work if I know you'll kill me if I needed you to. I wanted to destroy you yesterday, my uncle too. Earlier I wanted to strangle Ejan, I wanted to kill her and I came this close." She held up her finger and thumb an inch apart, "from doing it. I know if I allow my temper to get the better of me I will destroy anything in my path, burning everything to ash, I am my father's daughter in that. So please, if you love me, you will Kill me." She watched his jaw tighten, his head drop, then he fell to his knees before her. He gently took her hand in his.

"I don't know if … "

In one fluid movement she slipped a hand around his throat, lifting his body off the ground and slammed him into the nearest tree.

Winded, he struggled against her grip but didn't attempt to strike her. Elora tilted her head, a wicked smile playing on her lips as she pressed her thumb into his Adam's apple. She held it at a point that must have been uncomfortable for him, grinning with the knowledge that she could just as easily push her thumb straight through his throat until it met the tree bark or simply snap his neck like a twig.

"You better know, Bray. This is me – in control." She took a slow breath and released her grip, letting him fall to the floor. He stared up at her, shock sparkling in his eyes as he rose to his feet. "You don't want to see me when I've lost control." They stared at each other, neither speaking as the darkness crept into the forest.

"So what will it be Elf boy?" She grasped a handful of his black t-shirt and pulled him towards her lips. "Can you kill me, for love?" Bray nodded once, then his lips crashed against hers.

When the kiss finally ended, Bray pulled away and held her at arm's length.

"I need you to do one thing for me, too," he said, voice deep, almost husky. She raised an eyebrow.

"Anything."

"Don't ever lose your temper. Killing you would kill me." He pulled her into a tight hug, arms wrapping around her shoulder. She leaned into him, feeling safe even though she knew that if she allowed the darkness into her heart, she would kill him.

"I'll try," she whispered. "We better get back to the inn before they send out a search party." She took his hand and they walked through the trees, darkness surrounding them but with Bray at her side she felt reassured that she had the strength, the will, to hold the daughter of Chaos back.

"You know, if I'm to keep a close watch over you I'll need to stay in your room tonight," said Bray, somewhat sheepishly. "Just in case you have nightmares and try to burn the inn down or something. Nothing, erm … You know?"

Elora laughed.

"Know what exactly?" she teased, smiling as his face took on a pained expression.

"Anything … less honourable," he said, clearing his throat. She laughed again, letting her face slip into the mask of innocence.

"Whatever do you mean?" Elora elbowed his side. Then dropped her voice and gave it a husky quality herself. "What if I have less than honourable intentions towards you?" Bray's eyes went wide and she burst out laughing. "Come on, Elf boy, your innocence is safe with me. But staying in my room is probably a good idea. You've just got to convince my uncle."

18

Averton

Saddles creaked as they meandered down a dirt track, Elora steering her horse with the lightest touch of her reins, a gentle press of her knee; swaying with the mare and enjoying the moment. Bray rode beside her, face towards the sky and catching the morning sun.

She felt at peace, almost tranquil and the exact opposite of when the arguments had ensued on her return to the inn the previous night.

The atmosphere had been thick with disagreements, raised voices and sullen tempers, herself and Bray holding hands as they entered only took it up a notch. Elora had listened for as long as she could before the whispers came, which hadn't been long at all and excused herself before she was inclined to reduce the building to ash.

Bray had followed her to bed and slept beside her, above the covers. His arm draped over her protectively. If her uncle or anyone else was in disagreement with that, they'd kept silent.

Moods in the morning had been somber, the inn quiet but everybody had a task to do and so was busy. Elora and Bray were to ride to the nearest town and locate a chemist that sold blue contact lenses. All her life she had been telling people that her real eyes were contacts; now she would be wearing contacts to cover her real eyes – the irony. They also needed to procure blonde hair dye, hopefully they would have it at the same chemist, Bray didn't want to spend any longer than needed in the town.

"How much further?" she asked, wanting the ride to last a little longer. They would be leaving Rams Keep this evening, heading into the Shadowlands so this would probably be the last time they would be alone together.

"Averton's not far, maybe a mile," he replied, nodding over to the next valley where Elora could see a column of grey smoke rising into the air. It was hard to believe that over the hill was once a thriving town, now silent, devoid of power and electricity.

"It's been over a fortnight since the lights went out, the town will be a mess, the people hungry, thirsty and desperate," continued Bray, his smile gone as his hand drifted towards the axe strapped to his saddle; a long bearded blade one side and a sharp spike the other. "I'd prefer it if you stayed hidden and let me go into town alone."

"Can't do that." Elora took her lock of blonde hair between finger and thumb and waggled it. "You might get the wrong shade of dye."

"Then we'll have to be swift and careful. Desperate people, no matter who they were before, will do desperate things," Elora nodded, more to put Bray at ease than to agree. They were only people, surely they wouldn't try to harm them.

Hooves echoed down the empty street as they weaved between abandoned cars and vans. Litter scattered across the road and pavements; blown by the wind and left to settle undisturbed by any road-sweeper or council worker. Elora stared into the empty shells of shops, windows smashed and looted, a few still smoking, masonry black from old fires but didn't see a soul. The town appeared dead. A ghost town.

"Where are the people?" she asked, her voice sounding loud as it broke the silence that engulfed the place.

Bray shrugged. "Those that haven't left will be hiding. Those that aren't hiding will be foraging and stealing. The rest will be dying or already dead."

He pulled his horse onto the path and halted outside a chemist, its door shattered and the glass cleared from the frame. "I'll go in and have a look around, you stay with the horses. Any sign of trouble and you take off. Don't stop until you get back to the inn."

"Yes sir!" Elora replied, snapping up a mock salute, then grinned when Bray scowled at her.

"I mean it," he said, tying his reins to a lamppost and taking the axe down from the saddle. The weapon looked out of place in the hands of somebody dressed in jeans and t-shirt, instead of a warrior on a battlefield where it belonged.

Elora watched him disappear and suddenly felt alone, sat upon Daisy in the empty street with only the horses and a few pigeons for company. She watched the birds taking advantage of the lack of people, flying in and out of the shops like they owned the town.

Maybe mankind shouldn't have become so dependent on electricity; relying on a power so totally that its loss meant the downfall of civilization. Something that so many took for granted and now struggled to live without. People were dying, were already dead because they put so much of their blind trust into a technology that her father had wiped out in a single move.

She gazed about the town, the abandoned cars, empty shops and wondered if it was possible to bring it back to how it was, if she could somehow restore the electricity could life go on as before?

Movement to her side made her snap her head around, instinctively she reached for the dagger in her smuggler's pouch.

"I've got your contact lenses but there's so many hair dyes, don't know which one will match," said Bray, striding out of the chemist. "You're going to have to help." She climbed off her horse and tied her next to Bray's then followed him into the shop.

Elora's first thought was that a bomb had detonated inside, reducing the interior to a pile of glass, broken bottles, split boxes and wall trimmings. Shelving had been pulled down and lay in a heap under a pile of white ceiling tiles, the till half buried amongst the mess, prised open and empty.

"What happened?" asked Elora, shocked at witnessing the aftermath of what must have been carnage. Bray stepped over the mess, a ceiling tile snapping under his weight.

"People, is what happened. Blind panic and the realisation that there is nobody in charge." He nodded toward the broken shelves behind what was left of the counter. Small green drawers where prescriptions were once kept were now pulled out and discarded. "The drugs and medicines will have gone first, followed by the baby food, toiletries; then anything else needed to survive. Luckily the makeup, care products and contact lenses are not essentials."

Elora climbed over the mess and noticed a patch of dried blood, clinging to a tub of baby milk, the side dented and white powder spilling on the floor.

"But why the mess?"

"The primal will of survival will bring out the worst – or best in anyone. Who's to say how you would react if you needed food, supplies, had a family to feed and no way of getting these things without fighting for it. Solarius knew what he was doing when he ordered those leviathans to sing."

The people were turning on each other, becoming tribal in an effort to take supplies. Would she have been any different, would she be fighting hand, nail and tooth over things that she wouldn't have thought twice about a couple of weeks ago? She didn't want to think about that, luckily Bray brought her back to the here and now.

"Does this match?" He held a bottle of dye next to her lock of blonde hair, shook his head and took another one. Elora saw the smiling model on the front of the box, all teeth and makeup, hair a glossy sheen and wondered where she was now, if she was still smiling, if her hair was still shining. She doubted it.

Bray tossed it aside and took another one. "Got it," he said, relief bringing a rare smile to his face. Then the smile faltered as several men stepped into the chemists with two snarling Staffordshire bull terriers pulling against leads, teeth bared and snapping.

"What do we have here, bruv?" said a tall youth wearing a baseball cap, the peak sticking out to the side.

"Think they're stealing from my town, which means they're stealing from me. Naughty, naughty," said the youth beside him, Elora put him at an age with her, a thick gold chain around his neck, worn over the top of his hoody. The chain looked to be the heavy-set kind, worn by town mayors; large circles of enamelled gold with the town's crest inlaid at its centre.

Bray stepped in front of her, his axe held in one hand, blade touching the floor.

"We don't want trouble, friend. Just taking a couple of items is all. We can pay," Bray said. Elora noticed his feet slowly stepping around the loose floor, axe subtly twisting as the man holding the dogs stepped closer while another stockier man, his hood fully up, face hidden, worked his way around the side of him; a baseball bat twisting in his hands.

The boy with the gold chain sucked in air between his teeth, a grin spreading on thick lips. "Pay with what, money?" He thumbed the chain about his neck. "Got me plenty of that. Got me just about everything I want. Big house, lots of food, lots of supplies. Anything else I'll take. Isn't that right bruv?" He high-fived the boy in the baseball cap.

"Yep, bruv. We want it, we take it. Averton is ours," said baseball cap, eyes drifting to her and hungrily devouring her body. "Think I know how you can pay."

He stepped around the dogs, his stare never leaving hers until Bray raised the axe between them. "I wouldn't do that," Bray warned, ready to spring into action, muscles tensed for violence but was halted by the mayor, a shotgun appearing in his arms and levelled at his face.

"I'd think twice before swinging that tool of yours. This is our town now, this shop and everything in it is ours. She." He nodded towards Elora. "Is ours."

Elora could tell that Bray wanted to act but even he couldn't out manoeuvre a shotgun, baseball bat and two dogs, not to mention what weapons the other thugs had.

"Your funeral," said Bray and lowered the axe.

Baseball cap chuckled as he passed him. "What she gonna do, blood, bite me?" He snapped his own teeth and laughed. "I like a feisty girl and this one's got a goth thing going on. Nice eyes."

Elora took a tentative pace back, her gaze set on the advancing youth's face as she stepped into the shadows where the daylight couldn't reach, where the darkness began and the whispers touched her ears … *Kill.*

A final glance to Bray, his eyes on her as she let the darkness engulf her, feeling heat pumping into her heart, her blood running hot with the tide of anger.

"Damn girl, your eyes are going red. What the hell?" Baseball's voice came to her above the tortuous whispers, his face grinning with fascination. Elora grinned back, she was going to tear his face off, ram that cap down his throat.

Shadows spread out from her, enveloping the shop in blackness as she placed a hand over her would-be-attacker's chest, her fingers itching to jab between ribs and spread fire into his lungs, searing his heart. But the boy kept grinning, his own hand grasping hers and pushing it down, over his stomach towards his groin, his face leaning closer, breath smelling of stale nicotine.

Elora held her own breath and steadied her hand, hovering above his navel.

"Come on girl, don't be shy," he laughed, eyes alight with excitement. His laugh died the moment he realized that the bones in his hands were snapping.

Knuckles crunched into cartilage, as Elora squeezed. She watched his face contort in pain, a scream leaving his lips as she twisted, the bones in his wrist popping before his elbow locked and she jerked him around … *Kill.*

Elora was enjoying this. She lifted his arm high as if it weighed nothing, feeling his elbow stiffen before it suddenly gave. The boy howled anew as his arm bent the wrong way, the noise filling Elora with excitement as she pushed his whimpering body into the floor and gently placed her foot behind his neck. She pushed his face into the broken glass; her smile widening as she increased the pressure.

"No!" screamed the would-be mayor, bringing the barrel of the shotgun towards her. "You're killing him." His face paled with shock, eyes wide with panic.

Elora winked at him, feeling a thrill pulse through her; the world shrinking to this moment, this place, her and them – chaos, darkness and pain. "That's my intention," she laughed, yanking on the ruined arm and dislocating the shoulder.

The boys pathetic whimpering quieted to a moan, his breath ragged, blood from his face mixing with the glass on the floor.

She drew her gaze away in time to see the gun explode. A blinding flash as the shot entered the ceiling, bringing white dust and plaster down. Bray had knocked the shotgun up with his axe and was now swinging the shaft around into the face of the man behind him.

In the confusion the dogs were released, drool flying from their wide vicious mouths as they ran at her.

Elora dropped the arm and bent low, meeting the dogs at face level and roared, barring her own teeth in a vicious snarl.

The dogs stopped, one running into the back of the other before scampering back, tails so far hidden beneath their legs they were tucked out of sight. They ran out of the door like whippets from a trap.

Elora heard laughing, deep and menacing and only realised it was coming from herself as Bray turned to face her, the two remaining thugs, unconscious at his feet.

Weak, he should have killed them – not to worry, more blood-letting for me. She stalked past him, and crouched down in front of the mayor, cocking her head to the side and wondering how much pain he would endure before dying.

The petrified youth scuttled back, dragging his legs behind him until his back hit the wall; eyes wide, frightened as she stepped closer, making a show of sliding her dagger from the smuggler's pouch.

"Whoa, what the hell are you?" he stammered, hands held up before him as if they could somehow halt her advance.

"Hell's, pretty close," she laughed, as she gripped his tightly curled hair and tipped his head back. He didn't struggle as she brought her blade a hair's breadth from his bulging eye.

"Elora, No," came Bray's voice from behind her, staying her hand and irritating her. She felt his touch on her arm as she was about to skewer the boy's watery eye and for a heartbeat had the impulse to reverse her grip on the weapon and drive it into Bray's arm.

Instead she lay her finger over the cross piece and touched the blade itself, feeling an intense heat leave her fingertip and cause the metal to glow red then white.

The boy's eyelashes smoked and curled back, black eyebrows singed as sweat clung to his forehead.

"Elora," continued Bray, his weak voice meagre against the rush of the darkness, a thousand black voices screaming her name, demanding she kill.

She took a breath and withdrew the dagger a fraction, swallowed the excitement catching in her throat, choked down the fury that had built up over the passing moments and calmed her heart. She focused on Bray's touch like it was a moral anchor in the black storm that she had become.

Her grip on the blade relaxed yet she held the mayor's head back, staring into those petrified dark eyes and seeing her own reflection stare back.

"You own this town, so you bear the weight of responsibility for everyone in it," she said, her voice coming out strained and gravelly and being all the more menacing for it. "You will redistribute your stockpile of food to those that are most in need of it. You will help the vulnerable and the weak and protect them from thugs like yourself. Do you understand?" She felt the boy's head dip, his gaze never leaving her dagger and took that for a yes. "Good. I'll not be far away and will be back soon. If anyone dies while I'm gone, if anyone gets hurt … " She twisted his hair in her hand. "If a child so much as catches a bloody cold, I'll know and I'll pay you a visit. And you don't want that, do you?" A shake of his head. "Good. Then you're in charge. Averton is yours, as is the responsibility."

She withdrew her blade and slipped it silently away, gave the boy a final glance then stormed out of the shop before she changed her mind and razed it to the ground in a pile of ash.

Bray followed her out and they mounted their horses in silence.

They were riding deep within the forest before he spoke to her.

"Are you alright?" he asked.

Elora thought for a moment, feeling cold and exhausted as she struggled for an answer. "I nearly killed him. Killed them all."

"But you didn't," he said, reaching over the gap between the horses and resting his hand atop hers.

"I wanted to," she admitted. "I enjoyed it, making them hurt, making them bleed," she looked away, tears prickling her eyes. "I am a monster."

"No. A monster would do all those things and not care, not stop themselves. You controlled yourself. Walked away and gave the town a chance."

"What if next time I couldn't walk away? I don't know if I could control it again."

"Best not find any trouble then," he said, giving her a reassuring smile.

She blinked away tears and breathed deeply. "Trouble has a habit of finding me"

"Gorgeous," remarked Otholo, as Elora stepped into the inn. "Like the golden nymphs from a Gosland play."

Elora felt herself blush as everyone turned to her, gazing at the new blonde hair and blue contacts.

The dye had needed to be done twice, her stubborn black hair only going auburn the first try but was now matching her lock of hair which still persisted to hang to one side.

"Remarkable," offered her uncle, smiling. "You would easily pass as a Minuan, without question."

She didn't like the attention, but what could she do? They were all gawping at her, only Jaygen seeming to share a red flush to his cheeks.

"One more problem solved," said Ragna, slapping a hand on the table and making a jug of mead bounce.

Diagus nodded approvingly at her, like a man who's cultivated an apple tree and seen its first fruit. He turned his attention to Otholo. "How goes the gate, we ready to find this ship of yours?"

Otholo grinned. "Gate's done, and the *Necrolosis* is on her way. How are we on the rest of the provisions?"

"Provisions?" asked Ejan. "We're going to be travelling light. Carrying our own weapons and wearing decent boots and travelling cloaks. We've got dried meats, bread, oat biscuits and enough water for three days."

Ragna shook his head. "We? You're staying here woman. I thought … " Elora couldn't keep up with the blur that was Ejan in motion, but saw the knife sticking erect from the table, embedded in the wood between Ragna's fingers.

"We," she growled, face like thunder, daring him to disagree. Ragna turned to Diagus for help.

"If she hadn't already demanded that she come, Ragna, I would have asked her anyway. Her skill with the bow will be a welcome asset," said the Shadojak.

"But the keep?" Ragna argued, his shoulders slumping as he resigned to the fact he had lost.

Ejan prised her knife out of the table and flicked it into the sheath below her wrist. "Jaygen's staying, along with Norgie. With any luck we'll be back in time to harvest the crops." She grasped a woven tail of his beard and yanked it playfully. "It'll be fun, Raggy, just like the old days. You never know, you may shave a bit off your paunch and become Ragna four-bellies."

Ragna slapped his belly, smiling. "Never," he laughed and planted a smacking kiss on his wife's lips.

Elora sat next to Bray, his hand rested on her thigh and she grasped it in her own.

"You suit blonde," he whispered in her ear.

"You'd suit a black eye," she replied jovially.

Everyone seemed in good spirits, even the Shadojak as he drained a cup of mead. Maybe it was the fact that he was going back to Thea, or that they were on the brink of an adventure, all be it a potentially violent one but she got the impression Diagus wasn't a person whose top virtue was patience. She had to admit, she felt a certain excitement at the prospect of journeying to a new world. Seeing Thea with her own eyes, travelling through dangerous lands like a hero on a quest. There was a closeness to the people around her, more than friends, their lives all pitted together in a kind of fellowship and she felt humbled at being a part of it.

Bray's hand suddenly tightened on her leg and she felt his entire body stiffen as Diagus slid a sword onto the table. It was Bray's sword, the one he gave up when he left the path of the Shaigun.

"I can't accept that," said Bray, shifting uncomfortably away from her.

The Shadojak sighed. "I'm not asking anything of your boy. It's a lump of metal, is all. Yet one you've been used to for the last few years." He inclined his head towards the axe that was leaning against the empty chair beside Bray. "Think your hands would feel more at ease grasping your old sword than that tree splitter."

"I dare say they would," Bray replied, still not convinced.

"And I would feel more at ease knowing you was at my back holding it."

"I dare say you would." And now Bray was smiling as Diagus squeezed his shoulder.

"Afterwards, I'll want it back, you understand?"

Bray nodded as he lifted his old sword and smoothly slid it away into his smuggler's pouch. "Of course, afterwards."

Elora witnessed a look they shared between them, some understanding she wasn't privy too but thought no more about it as Ragna got to his feet and raised his large tankard, foam brimming from the rim.

"Odin!" he bellowed and almost drowned himself attempting to empty his tankard in one go, managing to slosh a good quantity of it down his leather vest. After draining it, he threw it clattering into the fireplace, sending a plume of sparks up the chimney.

"Odin!" Ejan shouted, joining her husband and downing her cup before throwing it into the flames.

Diagus raised his own cup, then drank the remains of the mead before slinging it over his shoulder to join the Vikings' drinking vessels. Norgie and her uncle followed suit as did Jaygen who muttered Odin, although his eyes kept darting to Elora. And even Gurple threw the bowl he had been drinking from although it fell somewhat short of the fire.

Otholo raised what looked to be a glass of water. "To Thea and the ballad I will create," he yelled and threw it into the fireplace, glass smashing as the flames dampened for the briefest of moments.

"Aslania," shouted her uncle, raising a fist.

Bray clicked his cup of mead against hers, drank the liquid in one and threw that into the fire. "Elora," he yelled, a huge grin spreading across his face.

Elora noticed that once again, all eyes were on her, all faces beaming in anticipation.

Grasping her own cup of mead, she tipped her head back, swallowing it down in four huge gulps; spilling some down her chin and wiping it with the back of her sleeve.

"Eversong!" she yelled and sent it hurtling into the flames with the rest.

"Good," said Diagus, placing his heavily calloused hands on the table and pushing himself to his feet. "If we're all ready then there's no reason to stay here getting any older. Time is an enemy we'd best make a peace with." And with that he strode out of the inn.

A quiet pause followed his wake, the others around the table only staring after him, probably as shocked as she felt, thinking they had at least a few moments to gather themselves before the voyage. Diagus had other plans and she knew he was right. Time was against them. Ragna was next to rise, pulling Ejan up with him.

"Got a right prickle up his arse hasn't he?" he said, lifting the Fist from the wall.

"He's right though," Elora said, surprised at herself for defending the Shadojak. "The sooner we're gone, the sooner we're back, right?" Her eyes caught Bray's as he looked away, doubt written plainly in moss green.

Otholo led them through the courtyard to the edge of the forest, as the sun began to fall, turning the long clouds pink. They were only a few trees deep when he halted them.

The large oak before him had a thick limb partially hacked through at the joint where it grew from the trunk. The limb had been pulled down until it touched the dirt and held in place with a wooden stake, driven against the branches where they forked. It formed a large triangle, big enough for even Ragna to walk through.

Otholo reached into a pocket and began to sprinkle salt along the branch and down the trunk, then along the ground beneath. As soon as he completed the triangle, the salt touching the salt where he had started from, the mineral began to hiss and crackle, like static on an old radio.

Then all at once a sheen of darkness, onyx black, shimmered across the triangle, like the one Elora had seen when she found the grumpkin. A shiver passed through her at the memory.

"Might be a good idea to have a blade or two ready," said Otholo taking a step back. "No telling what could come through." He gave Elora a wink and passed her his lute. "Can you hold onto that for me? Zionbuss has no respect for the arts." She took the instrument and felt a change in him as the demon possessed the bard once again. He bowed before her, wicked grin appearing strange on Otholo's face.

"My queen," he said, rising. "I'll enter the gate first, clear any unwanted beasts. I suggest that you all have something sharp and pointy in your hands before you follow. Remember, if it moves, it'll want to kill you." He gave them all a menacing stare, grinning like a skull before stepping into the blackness and vanishing from view.

Ragna gave Jaygen a tight hug, leaving the boy a little dazed. "Make sure you keep the pig away from them apples, the goats too. You know it gives them the shi … "

"Right Da," replied Jaygen, sparing them all the profanity. He watched his father duck under the limb of the tree, careful not to knock the heavy sack against the edge of the triangle as he vanished. Ejan then hugged him just as fierce as her husband did and gave him a kiss on the cheek.

"You do what Norgie tells you, make sure you listen to him." She gave him a final hug, smiled at Norgie then followed Ragna, drawing her short sword as she went. Bray drew his blade, clasped hands with Norgie and playfully mussed up Gurple's fur, gave Jaygen a wink and jumped into the blackness. Her uncle was next, saying a quick farewell before following Bray, leaving only herself and Diagus.

"You're next girl," said the Shadojak, pulling his soul blade free, the setting sun glimmering along its razor edge. Elora nodded, she expected he would make sure she went through before he did.

"Good luck, Elora. We'll see you soon enough," said Norgie, embracing her, whilst Gurple wrapped furry arms around her legs.

"Take care," she said, hoping that she would see them again. She gave Jaygen a hug as she passed him, causing him to blush all over again.

She pulled her dagger free and stepped through the gate, giving herself up to the darkness.

19

Ship of Bones upon a Sea of Souls

Red dust coated the terracotta rocks Elora stood on, falling away into a deep gorge. Its bottom a dry crack that swept down onto an arid plateau that stretched away as far as she could see. Black peaks jutted up on the horizon, like fallen teeth, or tombstones, too far to judge their height or the vast distance between. The plateau itself, an immense bed of cracks, rocks and fissures, was different shades of reds and oranges, like the vista seen through the lens of a Mars Rover. Apart from the fellowship that stepped through the gate, she saw no signs of life, animals of vegetation. Not even a bird or cloud in the dark red sky.

Elora turned about, expecting to see the gate they'd stepped through but it had vanished, leaving only the same view of the empty red wasteland, a rotten egg smell or sulphur, maybe brimstone catching her nostrils.

"Where are all the beasties?" asked Ragna, gripping his hammer and appearing disappointed that he wasn't swinging it.

Zionbuss gave a throaty laugh. "They'll be here soon enough. Like bees to nectar, they know we're here for the taking. Come, we need to reach higher ground and reach the *Necrolosis* before we're found. And Elora." He stepped closer, so he was directly in front of her and using the slender hands of Otholo he gently lifted the hood of her cloak over her head. "Keep your skin hidden. In the Shadowlands your flesh will be like a flame in the dark. And the moths you'll be attracting will want to tear it from your bones."

Elora watched him turn and march up the ridge, the others parting and giving the demon a wide berth whilst pulling hoods on themselves. Bray slid an arm around her waist, giving her a reassuring squeeze.

"You alright?" he asked.

"Yep," she replied, looking about her. The others seemed nervous, knuckles turning white on sword hilts, Ejan now had a bow out, an arrow notched and her uncle was mumbling something too low to hear. Even Diagus appeared apprehensive, spitting on the ground before himself and muttering under his breath to the Blessed Mother. Yet she felt fine, like staring around a place that was familiar, a childhood haunt with fond memories although she couldn't quite tease them to mind.

Bray planted a kiss on her cheek, having to hold the hood aside to do so. "We won't be in the Shadowlands long, don't worry," he said, as they began to climb the rise after Zionbuss.

Elora didn't mind how long they stayed here but sensed the uneasiness in the others so kept that to herself.

Above the rise were tall stacks of rocks, maybe twice the height of Ragna, sticking up like fingers with smoke rising from the top.

"Don't get too close to the chimneys," warned Otholo as they passed. "The vents go down to the fire pits, deep in the belly of this world. The rock down there runs like water and occasionally gets spat out of these."

The group passed warily, careful not to come too close to the smoking stacks. The whole place appeared to be baking, the air dry like the inside of an oven, even the rock was blackened in places, streams of lava long ago dried and stuck to the sides of the chimneys like dark thick veins.

Beyond the stacks the rise gave way to another gorge, Zionbuss led them along its edge, head frequently peering over as if searching for something.

"I thought there was no water here," said Ragna, staring behind them. "Looks like there's a sea down there."

The group halted. Down on the flats where moments ago there was nothing but a dry cracked desert Elora could see a huge black lake. Above the water was a huge cloud, a dark black shape hovering above and spreading out before them.

"Seems it's going to rain as well," he grumbled looking up at the approaching cloud.

Elora watched Zionbuss's reaction and knew that it wasn't good.

"Time to pick up pace. That's not a rain cloud, it's a dust cloud created by the thousands upon thousands of soldiers that are charging this way."

"I don't see any soldiers," remarked Ragna, as everyone drew weapons.

"No? That big black mass which you took for the sea is a tide of heavily armed men, demons, trolls and grumpkins. Every little beastie which you've been looking forward to flattening with that big steel Fist of yours, is coming our way."

"That's an army? But there's got to be millions of them," said Elora, her eyes only now picking out the faint shapes of men amongst the dark mass. Then she felt the ground beginning to tremble as the weight of a thousand, thousand soldiers rumbled up through the rock.

"Not the entire army, just a small portion," replied the demon. "Best find the *Necrolosis* and make for the air – they'll be on us in no time."

They ran, Elora and Bray keeping with her uncle at the back, Nathaniel clenching his teeth as he pushed his ageing limbs into a task they probably hadn't done for decades. She linked her arm through his and bore some of the weight, his breathing coming out hard and laboured as the gap increased between them and the rest.

Gravel crunched under foot, kicking up sand and dust as they pumped their legs for all they were worth. It clung to Elora's clothes and got into her mouth, scratching against her teeth. She pulled Nat with one arm whilst protecting her face with the other, attempting and failing to cover her mouth. Peering through narrowed eyes, she hoped they would reach the ship soon, she didn't know how much longer her uncle could take.

Ragna paused, bending over double, hands on knees and panting like a dog in the sun. Ejan, took his hand and pulled.

"Move it, you great five-bellied lard," she yelled at him.

Diagus came back and took the pack from the huge Viking, slinging one strap over his shoulder. "It's the air, it's too thin. But we can't stop now, look, they're getting closer."

Elora risked a glance behind and saw that the swarming multitudes were closer and as she watched two ranks darted from the front.

From this distance they appeared to be no more than a pair of thick black lines racing ahead of the rest. The creatures which formed it were roughly the shape of men, only bigger, wider and running on all fours. The speed in which they came was startling, they'd be on them in minutes.

"Bulworgs!" shouted Zionbuss. "Now run, we can't be far, she's around here somewhere."

Bray took hold of Nathaniel's arm and hoisted him over his shoulder into a fireman's lift. "Sorry, Nathaniel," he said, as he lumbered on, keeping pace with the others.

Elora ran on at a better speed now she hadn't the burden of her uncle who was now bouncing on Bray's shoulder, face red and veins bulging from the side of his temple. But he kept quiet even though he must have felt shame at being carried.

The bulworgs were close enough to hear, deep throated growls and howls carried on the wind; quiet at first, hidden behind the erratic panting and boot scuffing on rock as the group clambered on. Yet unmistakably the sounds were bestial, snarls and grunts of huge predators that were hunting them down like prey.

She tried desperately to block the threat out and concentrate on running, keeping with the group even though her lungs screamed for her to stop; Otholo's lute banging into her hip, threatening to fall to bits with every bounce.

Zionbuss suddenly skidded to a halt, his boots sliding towards the edge of the gorge where it ended in a cliff, another flat plain before them.

Elora's heart thumped against her chest as she sucked in the thin air, looking down at the vast landscape before them, covered in huge black squares that stretched off into the distance. Horror forcing more adrenalin into her veins as she realised what the shapes were.

Each square was made up of rank upon rank of soldiers, each row numbering about a hundred, arranged in hundred-long columns that stretched to endless thin lines in the distance. This was the dark army, her father's army.

Elora's mouth fell open – they were trapped.

"Don't fancy the odds much," muttered Ejan, as she took an arrow from her quiver that was strapped to her back.

Elora watched how she slowed her breathing, a quiet and determined calm settling over her as if being sandwiched between two colossal armies of killers was something she did on a regular basis. Even Ragna stretched his head from side to side, working the tendons in his neck as he cocked his hammer onto a wide shoulder.

Bray set Nat back on his feet and drew his sword and took a couple of practice swipes, blade cutting the air and making faint whisping sounds. "I'll take the million on the left," he chuckled.

"Aye, I'll start on the wedge on the right, after I've done some bulworg tickling," laughed Ragna.

Elora wished she felt as brave as them, they were hardened to battle and had a wealth of experience when it came to fighting, where as she, had none.

Sweat broke out on the palms of her hand as she fidgeted with the ends of her cloak, Bray placed his warm hand in hers and gave a gentle squeeze. It was less than reassuring but she was glad for the contact.

The bulworgs split formation as they filtered through the rock chimneys. Long white teeth, razor-sharp and bared in a rictus snarl as the wolf-like heads snapped at each other in a race to reach them. Claws sank into the rock as they scrambled up, the leading bulworg striking a chimney with his shoulder and smashing it to rubble. Elora couldn't tell if he had meant to do it or didn't care, the stack of rocks fell away as if it was nothing more than cardboard.

Diagus stepped in front of her, blade drawn before him. Her eyes drifted along the strange green metal, the lethal edge sending a shiver down her spine, her bones tingling. She found it hard to look at that sword for long, it scared her in a way she didn't understand, putting her already frayed nerves on edge and making her teeth itch. Perhaps because it was her father's or because the Shadojak had hurt her with it when she had awakened in Rams Keep.

"Stay behind us. I don't want you turning into that devil spawned creature again and end up tearing us to pieces and helping the enemy." He stared at her for a moment, white pearl seeming to burn straight into her soul before stepping beside the huge Viking.

"If we all die; feel free to turn into what the hell you like. As long as you take as many as those bastards down with you before you join us," said Ejan, giving her an uncharacteristic wink before pulling her bow string fully back, fingers brushing her ear.

"They're out of range," said Bray, seeing what Ejan was about to do. Yet she released her fingers and let the arrow fly.

Elora watched as it arced up into the red sky before gently falling; so graceful it was hard to believe death was on its tip in a sharpened head of metal. It struck the leading bulworg in the neck, just behind its skull. The creature ran for a few more steps before falling sideways and taking the legs from under another. Both crashing in a mess of grey fur and red dust.

Bray whistled through his teeth. "Impressive."

"Told you she was good," said Ragna, face beaming with pride. Even Diagus nodded.

"See if you can take some more down," he said.

Ejan notched another arrow, eyes already narrowed on the next target. "I'll make it rain death," she said, the bow string thrumming as she released her fingers. Her arm was already reaching back for another arrow and putting it to bow before the string stopped humming. Two more bulworgs died before they reached them.

"Here they come," growled Diagus, as he took a step towards the advancing bulworgs which were now within spitting distance.

The creatures slowed to a walk, spreading out and surrounding them, blocking any route of escape save from jumping off the cliff. They appeared huge close up, almost as big and wide as a horse, thick with muscle and sinew, hackles raised and snarling, eyes alive with hate and evil.

One took a step towards them and raised up on its hind legs. Standing taller than Ragna it howled into the air, a long and haunting tone that carried back the way they came, the noise repeated further away and again until it reached the main body of the army where other voices joined it, creating a noise of an entire army of blood thirsty beasts enticing violence. The message was clear. They had them trapped.

Another bulworg reared up, its mouth opening wide to join the howl but an arrow suddenly appeared sticking out of its throat, Ejan's bow humming with the after-shot. The Viking woman then placed the bow over her shoulder and drew out her short sword as the wolf like beast fell dead to the floor.

"That's four to me," she said, pointing her sword in front of her and making slow circles with the blade.

Bray leaned closer to Elora, his words whispered gently into her ear. "I love you." Then before Elora had chance to reply he went to stand beside his old master, rolling his shoulder and loosening his muscles.

'I love you', Elora wanted reply but it was too late. Instead she pulled her dagger from the smuggler's pouch, determined that she would go down fighting.

Behind her, she heard Zionbuss laughing, the sound unnerving in the situation. She turned to see him simply drop off the cliff. One second he was there, the next he was gone. What the hell had he done, did he fear bulworgs so much that he would rather die than face them? Or was he simply abandoning them, leaving them to a gruesome fate? Her eyes locked on the ground he dropped from, wanting to peer down but the wolf-like beasts chose that moment to attack.

They came on fast, large claws striking the ground as they leapt, teeth bared, growls barking from deep chests. The group stepped in to meet them, Ragna's hammer connecting with a head which cracked making a sickening crunch; the skull crushed flat, spitting black blood into the air as its body fell lifeless into the ground.

Diagus spun to his side, ducking below a swiping claw and slid his blade into his attacker's belly, opening an ugly wound and exposing the shiny guts which spilt to the floor; its owner howling in pain as it frantically tried to catch them in its paws. The Shadojak thrust his blade through its back to finish him off.

A severed head spun through the air, tumbling end over end, spraying blood. Its muzzle still set in a snarl as it bounced once, twice, before rolling over the edge.

Elora felt acid burn the back of her throat and fought the bile down as she watched Bray kick the headless body over, blood squirting from the gaping neck. He quickly glanced her way, his eyes catching hers before another bulworg was on him, attacking with a vicious swipe to his chest which he caught on his blade, reducing the limb to a spitting stump. Elora pulled her gaze away from the gore in time to see Ejan pulling her short sword free from the chest of a fallen beast, its paws gripping the blade, now slick with blood, as she drove her boot into its neck, screaming insults into its face.

The Fist of the North swung high then low, the sounds of crunching skulls and snapping bones closely following. Bodies falling in a mess of grey pelt, blood and gristle; steel stained red as they split open beasts revealing the inner workings that should never have touched the outside air but now spilt to the dust in a steaming carnage. But for every bulworg that fell, another took its place and she could see the sweat and pain her friends were enduring – they wouldn't last much longer. Somehow her free hand had found Nat's and she realised she was choking the life from it.

"What shall we do?" she screamed at him, feeling totally defenceless. Nat could only shake his head, his mouth opening and closing like a goldfish, unable to give her an answer, yet she already knew what she must do. They could not take her alive, that's what the Shadojak said, that's what her uncle said.

The grip of her dagger felt slick with sweat, her fingers shaking with the pressure she held it with. Releasing Nat's hand, she held her weapon with both of hers. It couldn't be that hard could it? Surely it was only a case of sticking the pointy end into flesh, a quick in and out and make sure you don't get stuck yourself in the process.

She took a deep breath, attempting to still her shaken nerves and tried to be calm like Ejan, staring across the melee and singling out a target. There, a bulworg was creeping around Ragna, padding slowly out of reach of the hammer, evil eyes set on Bray's back as it stalked closer.

Elora let go a scream of her own and leapt forwards, feeling her uncle's desperate fingers raking against her arm as he tried to hold her back. But this little girl wasn't going to wait for death to come to her, she was flinging herself headlong into its snarling face.

The dagger felt light in her hands as she drew it overhead, ready to strike down into the creatures back, but it somehow sensed her coming and spun at the last second; thick tail whipping about and hitting her in the face as he caught her wrist. He twisted her arm violently and the blade flew out of her grasp to bounce along the ground.

"No!" she spat, as she watched it slide over the cliff's edge.

Yellow eyes stared deep into hers, she pulled her face back as his muzzle came close, saliva dripping from sharp fangs, breath rotten. Elora had never felt so scared, so horror-struck knowing that death was only heartbeats away. Yet she had never felt so alive, adrenaline pulsing through her veins as the world seemed to slow down, to shrink until it was just her and the wolfman.

Her eyes refocused on the bulworg, seeing it not as a lethal killer, but as a pathetic creature to be killed ... *Kill.*

Her blood ran hot as she twisted her hand from its grasp and slammed her fist into its throat, feeling the cartilage beneath give under her knuckles. Its eyes widened in shock as it toppled back, its limbs flinging wildly out and Elora suddenly felt pain burn down her arm, a wild claw finding flesh and tearing it open.

Blood gushed from the wound that had split wide below the elbow, she pulled the torn sleeve away as her blood caught fire, searing the gash closed.

The pain was immense, white heat pulsing up her arm as she watched the flesh heal. It had happened in an instant but was long enough for the bulworg to have regained its balance and its feet, claw pulled back ready to strike again. Elora could only scramble back as the beast came at her, the brief moment of that other girl, that darker being was gone.

The bulworg's hind legs bunched up, hackles raised as it prepared to launch itself at her. She willed herself to be brave, to be ready, her hand grasping enough dust to throw in its face. But as she prepared to hurl, a dagger, thrown from behind her, struck the bulworg in its flat forehead, sinking to the hilt. She recognised the dagger to be hers but how was that possible when she watched it go over the edge?

She whipped her head around and watched the riggings and thick mast of a ship rise above the cliff, Zionbuss, gripping onto rope and grinning whilst the huge vessel rose higher and higher. The *Necrolosis.*

As the side of the deck came into view she saw men with skeletal faces, peering at them, torn and weathered clothes blowing in the breeze and revealing dry yellow skin and bones beneath. Each of them had longbows, the strings pulled back with lethal black arrows notched.

"Now might be a good time to come aboard," Zionbuss bellowed. Elora didn't need telling twice as she scrambled to her feet and slapped Ejan on the shoulder. She was about to tell her that they should get on the ship when she instinctively ducked, Ejan's blade cut through the air where her neck had just been.

"Don't ever touch me in battle," Ejan shrieked, as she gripped Elora under the arm and propelled her towards the *Necrolosis*. "Ever heard of battle etiquette? Now get on the ship, I'll fetch the others."

"Whoa?" Elora mumbled as she staggered, blood rushing through her ears. If two words didn't belong in the same sentence, it was battle and etiquette.

Nat took her hand and together they ran across a plank that Zionbuss had laid across the gap between ship and cliff. As she crossed she saw that the ship floated on green fire, burning without heat and translucent enough for her to see through to the long drop below. She quickly jumped the last stride, giddy with vertigo.

Behind her she heard Ejan shouting for the others to fall back. They came as quickly as they could, Bray swiftly finishing his foe before turning and helping Ragna cut his bloodied opponent down. Diagus was battling two bulworgs simultaneously, dancing between wildly thrashing limbs with the fluidity of a ballet dancer.

On Ejan's command he spun low, slicing both beasts through the knees. As they fell howling he continued his circle, decapitating the pair, heads, bodies and severed legs falling in a gruesome heap. The Shadojak stepped backwards to the ship, keeping his gaze and blade facing the enemy who although vastly outnumbering them, didn't seem as keen to advance.

Diagus paused by a fallen bulworg that was still breathing, the contents of it belly held in its arms. He thrust his soul blade into its heart and Elora thought she saw a tiny green flame rise along the blade before the bulworg relaxed into death.

Once he was level with the others, they peeled off one at a time, sprinting across the plank, wood bouncing with the weight.

Zionbuss, growled something in a foreign language, sounding similar to Latin but with more guttural tones. The skeletal crew immediately set to moving about the ship and rigging as the *Necrolosis* began to rise.

"Wait!" shouted Elora. She'd seen the bulworgs suddenly rush at Ragna, the last man still on the cliff's edge; his blood stained hammer already swinging in a wide arc. There were too many for him to take down alone and now that the ship was rising the plank fell away, slipping through the green fire and clattering down the cliff.

"Raggy!" Ejan screamed, only just realising that her husband wasn't aboard. She brought her bow about, arrow already cocked. She let the string go and was already notching another as Elora spun on Zionbuss.

"Take us back down," she shouted, the panic rising in her chest at the thought of losing the huge Viking.

Zionbuss raised an arm, bellowed a single syllable word she didn't understand and chopped his arm down. All about the ship, the crew which held their bows ready, suddenly released their arrows, sending them down in a black storm. Below she heard the grunts and sudden intakes of breath as they found their marks.

Zionbuss turned to Elora, shaking his head. "I'm sorry my queen. It's too late to go back."

Ejan suddenly turned on the demon, bringing her bow about, the point of an arrow inches from his face.

"You go back or you die," she said, a coldness set in her eyes.

Zionbuss shook his head and shrugged his shoulders as if it was out of his hands. "You kill me and this ship will drop from the sky, killing all of you.

The Viking woman's jaw clenched, teeth grinding in a snarl similar to the bulworgs that were attacking her husband. With a swift motion she spun her shoulders so that the arrow now pointed at the back of Elora's head. "Bring it down or have no queen."

Zionbuss tensed as if about to throw himself at her, only Elora gently placing her hand against his chest stopped him.

"If you hurt her I'll tear your throat out and throw you down for the wolves to finish," he growled in rage.

"I don't care!" spat Ejan. Tapping the point of the arrow against the back of Elora's skull, the pain bringing tears to her eyes.

"She's right Zionbuss. We're not leaving without Ragna. If I am truly your queen, then I order you to get him on this ship. Alive." Elora put as much authority into her voice as she could muster, feeling reassurance that Bray had slipped beside her, his arm rising to push Ejan's arrow away until she stopped him with a subtle shake of her head.

Maybe the Viking really meant to shoot her or was simply bluffing, she didn't know – didn't want to know, but she needed Zionbuss to believe she would.

The demon's eyes flicked from hers to Ejan's, then back. "Fine," he growled, then marched off to the rigging and grabbed a coil of rope. He tossed one end to Bray, took the other end in hand and let the coil drop to the floor. With one final glance at Elora, Zionbuss sprinted for the front of the ship, tying his end of the rope around his waist as he went.

"What's he … " began Bray as the demon jumped off the front of the *Necrolosis*, vanishing from view.

The coil of rope at their feet began to rapidly uncoil. Bray's eyes went wide as he realised why he was holding the other end. Spinning about he quickly wrapped the rope around the mast as the entire length snapped taut. His feet finding purchase against the wooden post as he strained against the weight.

Elora ran to the gunnel and peered down, Ejan now beside her, bow and arrow now trained over the side.

Below the green fire she could make out the body of Zion-buss, swinging on the bottom of the rope like a pendulum. As he passed Ragna he wrapped his legs around the Viking's body, yanking him off his feet and knocking a bulworg off the cliff.

The torturous sound of rope scraping against wood screamed along the ship, Elora flicked her head around to see the rope was sliding along the gunnel, smoke billowing from its strands with friction as it threatened to knock both herself and Ejan over the edge.

Before it touched them she was yanked back, her teeth jarring as she slammed into her uncle's chest. Her eyes never leaving the rope as it whipped in front of where she had just stood. Diagus had pulled Ejan away in the same instant, saving them both from a long drop.

"Need a little help down here," came Zionbuss's voice from below.

Elora returned to the gunnel and peered over once again. The demon and Ragna were now dangling beneath them, both clinging to the rope. Ragna was still clutching his hammer but it was clear he wouldn't be able to hold on for any length of time.

Behind her, Elora sensed movement and two of the demon's crew placed a rope ladder on the edge and pushed it off. It unrolled as it fell, falling within reach of the dangling pair. With the help of Diagus and Bray they pulled them onto the deck where Ragna was instantly throttled in a tight hug by his wife.

Zionbuss pushed passed them and began ordering his crew around, tasking the skeletal beings into setting sail. A moment later arrows began to thud into the ship, striking the wood from below, one of them arcing over the rail to stick into the mast, missing the demon's face by a whisker. He didn't flinch as his eyes traced the wooden shaft to the feather flights.

"Might not be a good idea to look over the edge," he said. "We'll need a good wind to lift us away before they train the scorpions on us."

"Scorpions?" asked Elora.

"They're like crossbows, only much bigger," explained Bray, as he lifted her torn sleeve to inspect the cut but saw only flaw-less skin. She glanced down at the blood soaked into his clothes, on his face and covering his hands. He caught her shocked expression and smiled. "Not mine."

"Think we had luck on our side there. We got away without taking any major injuries," muttered Nat, then turning to Zionbuss. "Set the sails, Captain, and I'll get you such a wind that would knock a dragon sideways." The demon turned to his crew, one of which now wore an arrow poking out of its shoulder, but not seeming to notice, and spoke briefly in that foreign tongue. Within minutes the sails had dropped, the strange material spreading out in twelve huge sheets.

Nat began to chant and evoke the element of air, a gust suddenly appearing from nowhere and snapping the sails out, ropes straining against the force. The ship creaked, the main mast bending but holding as they tilted forwards, revealing more of the landscape and forcing Elora and the others to grab onto the gunnel. Then they were moving, slowly at first but as they climbed altitude their speed increased until they were sailing through the sky, faster than the swiftness of ships in any ocean.

Elora risked a glance down and saw how big her father's army actually was. They were flying above a sea of black, a mass so big that even from this height she couldn't see where the ranks began or ended. If the barrier failed and this army was set loose on the world, Earth wouldn't stand a chance, not in its current state; surviving without electricity.

Ragna approached her then and held out his hand, her dagger appearing small inside his huge grip.

Elora smiled. "You managed to get it back?" she laughed, taking it from him and sliding it away in her smuggler's pouch.

"You can't have too many knives, my Da always said. And that one is quite a knife. Bit fancy for my liking but it's too good to leave in a bulworg."

"Thanks," she said and gave the big Viking a hug.

Laughing, he put his big arms around her, the trails in his beard tickling the top of her head.

"From what Ejan tells me, it was you that got Zionbuss to come back for me, so we're even. Don't reckon much to his ship, mind you. It ain't right: made from bones and stuff. And that crew of his shouldn't be even moving let alone sailing the wretched thing."

Elora glanced around the deck, the mast and sails. Somewhere in the back of her mind she had registered that something wasn't quite right but at the time, what with being in the midst of battle, she hadn't had the luxury to properly look at the *Necrolosis*.

Details in the timber slowly focused into clarity. The porous grain: off white in colour, starting wider at one knobbly end where it interlocked into another joint, before thinning in the middle and then widening to become the shoulder joint and tied into a socket. Bones large and small, packed tightly together, the gaps filled with the smallest of knuckles, even teeth in places made up the deck, the cabin, the hull, everything. The tall thick masts and outer balustrade were made from single bones, poached from some gigantic creature that she couldn't imagine the size of. Perhaps whale bone, or dragon. Even the sails were cut from a dry white hide, stitched roughly together in odd shapes and sizes; thinning grey fur still attached in places. If there was such a thing as a ghost ship, thought Elora, then surely this was it.

She glanced back over the gunnel, into the strange green fire that licked the bottom of the hull and for a heartbeat thought she saw faces, mouths open wide in silent screams, swimming in the flames then dissolve again before she could focus on them. It was similar to the green flame that had run along Diagus's blade when he finished the bulworg off.

"Don't stare too closely, you might not like what stares back," rumbled Zionbuss, as he appeared beside her.

She pulled her gaze from the fire and glared at him. "You would have left Ragna if I hadn't made you go back," she said.

The demon nodded. "Such is life in the Shadowlands. What is his compared to yours?"

"You swore not to harm any of us."

"I swore that no harm would come to them by my hand. I kept to that oath, Elora."

"Well you can damn well make another. Swear by your name that you will protect my friends from harm, whether it's by your hand or otherwise. Swear it now or leave my service and go back to your purgatory. You never know, if my father escapes he may forgive your disloyalty and give you your old rank back, General Zionbuss."

The demon's shoulders dropped as he spat over the side. "Solarius isn't the forgiving type." He dropped to one knee before her. "I Zionbuss, Captain of the *Necrolosis*, swear that I will do everything in my power to protect all aboard this ship." He rose and grinned again, putting his arm through hers. "Come my queen. Let me show you the *Necrolosis*. The ship of bones that sails upon a sea of souls."

20

Necrolosis

Bray leaned against the mast, watching Elora as she was shown about the *Necrolosis*. Zionbuss was explaining enthusiastically about how he had harvested the parts needed for his ship, wielding an imaginary knife as he butchered the air before them.

Bray looked at his own hands, filthy with dirt and dark with blood that clung to the wrinkles in his knuckles and worked deeply into his fingernails. That was the thing about blood; easy to get on, not so easy to get off. Two days since he left the path of the Shaigun and his hands were already bloodied, slipping back into his old role as if slipping on a familiar jacket.

Relief, if he was being honest, was what he felt when the bulworgs came on, and he let his steel sing. Feeling where he should be, what he was trained for and he almost lost himself amongst the battle. But it was seeing Elora's panic-stricken face that brought him back, forcing himself to realise that there was something that he could lose, something that meant more than his own life. That was the price of having somebody to love.

Ragna was equally bloodied up, great splashes of it in his hair, on his face, spattered across his chest and belly, his hammer making fountains of the stuff when it was being worked. Ejan's arms were slick from wrist to elbow as if she had dipped them into a trough of blood. It dripped from her finger tips to the deck, making a polka dot pattern and when she laid her hand on the gunnel it left a red handprint which quickly dulled as it soaked into the porous bone. If those two battle-hardened warriors could make love work between them, why couldn't he and Elora? He just needed to keep them both alive through this ordeal and find some way to keep her alive afterwards.

He followed Elora and the demon about the ship, listening to Zionbuss prattle on about how each and every fibre of the bodies had been used and nothing wasted.

"She's the living embodiment of art," Zionbuss said, proudly, placing a hand on the wheel, a horned, troll skull at its centre. "Each soul enslaved, swimming beneath her and keeping her afloat."

Bray found the entire ship disgustingly gruesome. Its crew no better, even the land beneath them, even the flame lit sky. The Shadowlands, all shades of red and black, blood and death – he hated it. Yet he noticed how relaxed Elora was, the way she smiled whilst the demon spoke, how she seemed comfortable aboard this ship of death. Even before, whilst rushing up the ridge, running from her father's host she was the only one of the group who was at ease with the desolate plains. Then again, this world was created by her father so surely it was in her blood.

"How many have you killed, how many lives have you ended to create this?" Elora asked, gesturing about the ship with her arm.

"How many rain drops make a storm? A lot I think, far too many to count. Souls are much the same, one or two you would never notice. A thousand or so – maybe enough to make a splash, but for a storm? Countless, like the lives spent to create and float the *Necrolosis*." The demon's boastful grin faltered when he saw Elora's scowl. "Is that bad, my queen? But let me put you at ease. I killed nobody that was innocent; black-hearted killers the lot and the worlds will be better off without them."

"When Diagus killed that last bulworg, I saw a green flame flicker along his sword," said Elora.

"What you witnessed, my queen, was the bulworg's soul being harvested by the Shadojak. His sword soaks up the beast's memories, whatever knowledge it had and its final thoughts. That's why the Shadojak is so hard to kill."

"And what of you Zionbuss? Are you an innocent?" snapped Bray, unable to take any more of his bragging and feeling agitated by the demon's knowledge of the Shadojak's soul reaver.

The demon switched his gaze to him, seeing through Otholo's eyes. "No, I've done some pretty bad things. Some ugly bad things too. I'm probably the furthest from innocent you're likely to get. But then, who would sail my ship?" Zionbuss laughed. "Come, let me show you the Captain's quarters."

Bray wanted to know what he meant, but Elora's warm fingers found his, jolting him from his train of thought as she set off after the demon.

The body of the bard held the bone door open for them and they stepped into the dimly lit room. The shape of a circular table came into view, set in the middle of the quarters, papers and scrolls spread about its top in a disorderly fashion. As his eyes adjusted to the gloom he stepped in front of Elora and instinctively went for his sword.

Before them, beyond the table and sat upon a huge throne-like chair made of bone, was a giant black beast. Long claws dug into the human skulls that were set into the chair, thick twisted sinew and muscle made up the meaty arms that ended in huge shoulders. Black glassy orbs stared down at them, unblinking and unseeing from deep sockets, large horns protruded either side of the thick forehead, sharp and menacing.

"Steady there, Bray," spoke Zionbuss, softly laying a hand on his shoulder. "Wouldn't want to ruin its beauty."

The demon crossed the chamber to the seated beast as if it was nothing more than a statue and snapped open the hide curtain that covered the only window.

Enough light spilled through to brighten the room and when it hit the beast, Bray saw that he was mistaken. It wasn't black, its skin was dark red, covered in dark writing and symbols so thick that it gave the appearance that it was black.

Zionbuss went to the huge creature and placed a hand upon its forearm. "Let me introduce you to – me."

He appeared to shrink back a little, his hand snapping away from the beast as he looked about them with fright on his face.

"I hate this ship," said Otholo, the bard taking control of his own body once again.

Then the beast's claws playfully clicked against the skulls. Its black eyes flashed from his to Elora's, at least he thought they did. It was hard to tell when they were totally black with no whites for reference. A grin stretched its face tight, revealing teeth sharpened to points, a forked tongue darting out to wet its thick lips.

"My queen," its voice rumbled as it rose on bare feet. Naked save for a leather skirt that stopped at the knees, it stood a foot taller than Ragna, not including the horns which scraped against the ceiling.

"I hate you," said Otholo, then stormed from the chamber, slamming the door behind him.

Zionbuss laughed, the sound spine-rattling deep. "I can't say I found sharing that little soft body pleasant, either."

Bray surveyed the huge beast, the patterns and writing on his body seeming to swirl before his gaze, constantly swimming in and out of focus as he tried to recognise what language it was written in.

The others came in then. Diagus followed by Ragna and Ejan, weapons drawn and ready to take on whatever was inside.

Diagus lowered his sword when he saw no immediate danger. "Zionbuss, I take it?" The beast nodded.

"No wonder Otholo was so highly strung with you rammed into his little body," said Ragna. "Then again, he does have a rather big head."

Bray watched Elora step closer to the beast before he had time to pull her back. She stared up at the giant whose head sat between the rafters, his height dwarfing her. "You won't take his body again, Zionbuss," she ordered. "His or anyone else's."

He nodded, white teeth shining as his grin widened. "Of course, my queen. Now, please sit." He gestured to the chairs around the table. "Treat these quarters as your own until we reach Thea."

"How far are we?" Bray asked, as they all sat around the table, Zionbuss taking his throne like-chair once again.

"Not far," he answered, shifting through the scrolls and papers in front of them with his claws until he found what looked like an atlas. He rolled it flat and placed metal weights on either side. To Bray it looked like a big red square with patterns scratched in black. But then again, that's what the landscape was.

"We're about here. The gate where Otholo came through from Thea, is here." He stabbed a claw at a small black triangle amongst a crudely drawn mountain range.

"How long will it take us?" asked Ejan, as she dug dried blood out of her fingernails with a small, curved knife.

"Time is irrelevant. Days, weeks, months will pass in the Shadowlands but in the worlds, only a handful of seconds would have ticked by. Those we left back on Earth, Jaygen, Norgie and the wood troll, will probably be still staring down at the gate we passed through. To them we had only just gone over." Zionbuss sat back, placing his elbows on the chair arms and making a steeple with his fingers." It's hard to keep track of time here, where there is no night or day, no sun or moon. Just an endless burning sky."

"That's why it's called the Shadowlands. Trapped between both worlds where the daylight never reaches," explained Diagus, leaning back and making himself comfortable. Bray noticed he was the only one without a drop of spilt blood on him, even though he had probably brought down more bulworgs than the rest of them. "The stillness of time will work in our favour. We need to reach Aslania as soon as possible."

"If Nathaniel can keep up the wind like it is, we could arrive at the gate sometime tomorrow evening. That is if we had a tomorrow, which we don't or indeed an evening."

"No days or nights, think that would drive me insane after a while," said Ragna, twirling his finger in the air near his temple.

"Insane?" laughed Zionbuss bitterly. "I've been trapped here since Solarius's fall. That's over twenty thousand years on Thea. How many lifetimes do you think that is over here in the Shadowlands?"

Bray couldn't comprehend the scale of what that was, if a day here was only a few seconds there, then twenty thousand years there would be; his brain couldn't think of a number so great without a calculator. "You did go insane, hence this ship of death."

"You're probably right. I've sailed every square inch of the Shadowlands a thousand different ways and times. Watched the dust plains crack open and spew mountains from the fire that burns beneath. Seen them crumble away to nothing, eroded by only the wind. The landscape changes shape, shifts itself, creating new crevices, new deserts all the while the Dark Army waits. Madness is my only escape."

"To supply an army of any size, surely you would need provisions. Food, water, the bare essentials yet this land provides none," remarked Ejan, finishing cleaning blood from one hand and beginning to work her knife into her other fingernails.

"It's like I said before. Things work differently here. Solarius is the God of Chaos, but fool he is not. There's no need for sustenance in the Shadowlands, not even water. Think about it. You've been hiking for what must have been hours up a ridge, then chased up the thing. You've fought hard in a bloody battle, in the heat, in the dust and not one of you has worked up a thirst."

They all looked at each other, open mouthed. He was right, thirst hadn't at any point showed itself. Neither were they hungry, and after a fight, even an easy one you always seemed fatigued, your body craving food.

"Your hair or nails will not grow, your skin will not wrinkle and you will cease to age here. Unless somebody opens you up with a blade or sticks you with an arrow, you would live to see the end of days."

Silence descended on the group as they came to terms with those facts. It wasn't everyday somebody pointed out that you were one step away from immortal.

"Still, who wants to live forever?" Ragna said, breaking the silence. "Place is a bit boring to say the least, and the dust –" Zionbuss chuckled at that.

"What's this symbol mean?" asked Elora, her finger pointing to a blot on the map.

Zionbuss leaned over her. "It's not a symbol. It's a name – Grycul," he said, the word sending a pulse of recognition through Bray.

"Interesting," said Diagus. "She's still alive then?"

"Still alive. But don't worry yourself Shadojak, she's chained to a mountain."

"How thick are those chains?" asked Bray, sitting forward.

Zionbuss tapped the map with a claw. "The mountain will break before those chains. The links are forged from Vilarian steel."

"Who's Grycul?" asked Elora, shifting herself closer to Bray and placing a hand on his.

"She's a dragon. God created, by your father, like me," replied Zionbuss. "He rode the fire breathing bitch into battle, reducing men, armies, whole towns to molten ash. When Solarius fell she went berserk and turned on her own. Burning battalions and crushing men between those huge jaws of hers. In the end we took her down by sheer force of numbers. Chained her to the mountain and put her under the protection of an infantry regiment. In the thousands of years that've passed they've become the Dragon Guard. Forging their own armour and shields from Grycul's scales. They've set traps all around the mountain and now none can come close without falling into their hands. Those that try end up as sacrifice to the Dragon."

"She eats them?" asked Elora, lip curling in disgust.

"Eats, burns, crushes. Same difference; whoever steps onto the mountain, dies."

"What if we were to sail over the mountain. We could kill her from above, no?" said Bray, the beginnings of a plan slowly turning in his mind.

Zionbuss shook his huge horned head. "She's god created remember. Only something that is also god created can kill her."

"Like a Shadojak's blade, a soul reaver, for instance," Bray offered, raising an eyebrow as Diagus frowned at him.

"Yes, that would do it. Why, are we taking a small detour?"

"No," said Diagus. Slamming a fist on the map. The weights holding the scroll bounced from the paper and it instantly rolled back up. "Our priority is Solarius. If we waste time killing Grycul, he may have gained enough strength to break his bonds. Then he could simply create another dragon or whatever else he needed to."

Bray nodded, agreeing with his old master. His idea wasn't to kill Grycul until after they had completed the mission. If somehow they all survived this ordeal he would bring Elora back and somehow slay the dragon, hoping that the Shadojak Supreme would grant her clemency for the act and let her live. It was a slim, long chance, he knew. But at least it was a chance.

"That's settled then," said Ragna, rising to leave. "If we're not needing the water to drink, I'm going to use to wash off this bulworg stink."

Bray used the distraction to slip the atlas into his smuggler's pouch, then stood up. "Not a bad idea," he said, brushing dried blood from his sleeve and walking from the room to join Ragna.

Elora stared into the distance, her new blonde hair catching in the breeze as she leaned out over the front of the ship. The plain still spread before them, red dust fractured by black fissures, disappearing into the mountain range which was gradually growing nearer. Her father's army had dwindled to narrow formations, the big black squares of men becoming scattered the further they came until only random pockets of fighters stood alone or in small groups.

Ejan was by her side, leaning out over the rail, staring into the distance. Elora sensed an awkwardness between them, one that had been present since she threw her husband into the dungeon wall and didn't know how to go about mending it. In the end it was the Viking that broke the silence.

"I'm sorry I pointed an arrow at the back of your head," she said, flatly without diverting her gaze from the front.

"That's ok. Don't think Zionbuss would have saved Ragna unless you did. I'm sorry you've got caught up in this … " Elora raised her hands, thinking of the right word. "Quest. It'll likely get us all killed."

"I expect so. Truth is, Ragna's been itching to get his hands bloody for a while. He's an alright farmer, and a great father to Jaygen but he's a Viking at heart. It's not easy living under the names of his father and grandfather. He needs this so he can prove to himself he's cut from the same cloth."

"And you?"

"I'm just making sure he doesn't get himself killed, carving himself a name for the songs."

"The songs are worth the dying for," said Otholo, joining them. Elora could see he was back to himself, cocky as ever as he leaned against the gunnel, strumming his lute.

"What's the point in having your own song when you're not around to hear it?" Ejan asked.

"So that they can live forever in the minds of the listeners. Their daring deeds heard down the ages. Stories sung … "

"But why? What's the point? No doubt the facts will be changed and blown out of proportion."

Elora sensed an argument brewing between the pair so decided to change the subject. "Can you teach me how to hold a sword? Back on the ridge I tried to stab a bulworg with my dagger but it was easily taken from me."

"I saw. But you soon dropped him with that punch to the throat."

Elora shook her head. "No, that was the other me. The one I'm supposed to be controlling. I thought if I were better with a sword they'd be less chance of her showing herself."

"Might be you're right. Ok, I can show you how to wield a blade, maybe a couple of moves and blocks but don't go think-ing you can fight. Until you know what you're doing you could just as easily slice one of us or yourself by accident."

Elora smiled at that and Ejan grinned back "I'll go see Zionbuss, he's bound to have a few spare swords lying around the ship."

It turned out that Zionbuss had a hold in the belly of the *Necrolosis*, full of weapons and armour. Things he said he took from the bodies that made up the ship. Elora found Bray on the way and he helped her find something suitable, nothing too big and heavy. yet not too small. In the end she found a kind of rapier with a curving hand guard. She couldn't stand the thought of losing any fingers if it came down to a sword fight.

"You're ok with me learning? I mean, if you would rather teach me," she began but Bray stopped her with a kiss.

"I'd be a rubbish teacher. Your lips would keep getting in my way," he said, his mouth spreading into a cheeky grin. "Besides, Ejan is as good a fighter as any."

"But not as good a kisser."

"Oh, I don't know?" Bray said, cocking his head to the side and mocking a wistful look. "Maybe I ought to have a few lessons from her myself," he laughed when she punched him in the arm.

"Nobody touches those lips but me. Ok?" she said, pointing her new sword at his chest.

"Fine. They're all yours," he kissed her again before they left the hold, fingers entwined.

"Not bad," remarked Ejan when she returned to the deck. The Viking swung the sword around making whipping sounds in the air. Stared down the blade and tested its edge with her thumb. "Not bad at all. It's good steel, well balanced, light enough to be quick yet strong enough to parry." She passed it back to Elora and drew her own sword. "Plant your feet shoulder width apart, your leading foot slightly in front of the other." Elora did so. "Good. Now don't grip the sword too tightly: you need your whole arm to be fluid. You don't know where your opponent will attack from so your eyes need to be on theirs, watching for any subtle change."

Without warning Ejan stepped towards her. The Viking's arm was a blur of motion as she knocked the sword from Elora's hand. It clattered to the deck as the Ejan flicked the point of her weapon in front of Elora's face. "The grip was too slack. Pick it up, let's do it again," Elora did as she was told and adopted the same position. "Dip your shoulder. Remember, keep your wrist fluid, your sword is an extension of your arm."

Ejan sprang forwards again, Elora only managed to twist her blade an inch before it clattered once again to the floor.

"Pick it up," ordered Ejan. "You're looking at me, but not seeing. My eyes will give away my intention, my shoulder, elbow, dip in the knee, no matter how minuscule, will project my next move.

Elora gritted her teeth ready for the next attack. She watched Ejan carefully, concentrating on keeping her grip relaxed but firm, her wrist supple and free of movement. She stared into the Viking's blue eyes, she didn't know what she was looking for.

A slight narrowing of the lids, so subtle she would have missed it if she wasn't concentrating so hard. Followed by a shift in her shoulder and without thinking about it Elora brought her sword about and met Ejan's. The impact jolted up her arm, followed by her attacker's blade twisting and sending her own sword spinning from her hand.

"Pick it up."

Again Elora bent to pick up her sword, wondering if asking Ejan to teach her was such a good idea. She returned to the same spot and adopted the stance. Before she had her feet planted, Ejan came on.

Elora brought her sword down in time to block the blade, catching the jarring impact yet remembering to let her wrist twist with the it. The moment of joy as she held onto her sword was short lived as Ejan stepped through and tapped her hilt against Elora's finger guard. Her sword spun from her grasp and hit the deck point first, where it stuck.

"Pick it up."

Elora kept her eyes on Ejan this time, although she was still taken by surprise as she came on as soon as the sword was free from the bone deck. Elora quickly planted her feet and spun, her blade glancing off Ejan's as she attacked.

Steel rang in the air, her arm jolting with the impact yet she held on. This time she kept the sword moving, bringing it about again and caught the second blow. Instinctively she took a stepped away as Ejan made a third swipe, cutting the air in front of her. Elora caught the blade, but with her weight now on the back foot she was shoved off balance and fell down, landing hard on her back, her blade skittering across the floor.

Before Ejan had chance to speak, Elora said. "I know, pick it up."

Ejan smirked. "Footwork is the cornerstone of sword play. Without your feet, you will fall."

They practiced for what seemed like hours, but with no sun or moon and the sky a constant unchanging red, there was no reference of time except for the mountains that appeared closer than they were when they began.

Ejan's attacks were harsh, not letting up and never giving ground and the only breaks Elora had were when she was picking her sword up – which was often. At one point she had blocked and parried several attacks in one go, sensing a kind of rhythm with the blades, feeling her arm work instinctively until Ejan hooked her foot around her shin and sent her tumbling. Bray had caught her, giving her a wink before spinning her around to catch another flurry of blows.

"You're getting better," he whispered, as she caught Ejan's blade. She didn't share his confidence but was glad for the compliment. By then the others had come to watch, even a couple of the skeletal crew were pausing in their work, empty sockets staring from the deck or rigging.

Block, parry, duck; dodge, parry, block, swing. Elora kept her gaze on Ejan, almost sensing her next move, a dip of her left shoulder telegraphed her intention she was about to lunge. But instead of meeting her blade with her own, Elora skipped the beat and lunged herself, thrusting her sword forwards.

A sudden flash of pain from her wrist and the world flipped upside down before the deck rushed to meet the back of her head.

Tiny white dots fizzled in the corner of her vision and she could taste blood. Her opponent hovered above, staring down with a smile playing on her lips.

"Not bad," chuckled Ejan, as she tucked the toe of her boot beneath Elora's fallen sword and flipped it up into the air and caught it deftly with her free hand. "You put too much weight into your lunge and over reached." She passed Elora her sword back and pulled her to her feet. "But never the less, a good attempt. That will do today though, I'll teach you more when we reach Thea."

"Which won't be too long," said Zionbuss, staring off into the mountains that were so close now that Elora could make out cliff faces, rocks and boulders on the jagged peaks.

"Looking forward to it," Elora said, sliding her sword into her smuggler's pouch. Bray came up behind her and began to massage the shoulder.

"You ok?" he asked.

"Fine. In fact, I don't even feel tired at all," she answered, finding the fact odd because they must have been practicing for hours.

"Things work differently here. The place isn't right," Bray said.

Elora was about to say that she didn't mind it when she saw movement at the base of the mountain. "What's that?" She pointed at a swarming dark mass which she at first took for vegetation but realised that nothing grew here. She felt Bray's fingers suddenly press tighter.

"Takwiches. It's a swarm," he said, then pointed it out for the rest to see.

Zionbuss hissed through his teeth, forked tongue poking between fangs. "They've sensed there's a gate close by. We'll need to fly above and lower you down directly into the opening. Drop you if needs be."

Elora watched the insectoid creatures as they crawled, squirmed and skittered over each other as they climbed the rocks. "There's so many."

"Solarius's best weapon," said her uncle, frowning down on the swarming mass. "They can crawl silently into enemy ranks. Undetected, it would take a single bite from each takwich and an entire army would suddenly become your father's legion without losing a single soldier."

"So, Silk was one of those originally?" Elora asked.

Nat nodded. "Him and all his men."

"There's enough down there to take control of the entire British army," said Bray.

"And more still. Enough to take all the armies in Europe, Asia and India," said Diagus, white pearl scanning the base of the mountain before turning on Elora. "We cannot fail. Earth will surely fall if we do."

"I remember the last time a swarm came through to Earth. That was a couple of thousand years ago. Somewhere in the middle east," offered Zionbuss.

"Aye," agreed Diagus. "Took a Shadojak and several battalions of Shades to bring it under control."

"But wouldn't something like that have been in the history books?" asked Elora, her mind trying to picture a mass of takwiches back in ancient times.

"Not history books, but it's in the bible," said Bray. "Moses – a plague of locusts, sound familiar? And it wasn't the eldest son of each family they took. It was anybody they could sink their teeth into."

"And the angel of death?" Elora asked.

"A Shadojak by the name of Donifymed the Great. Using the very blade Diagus has now – your father's; carving the rot that would surely of spread throughout Earth and turning the Nile red with their blood. Afterwards, Moses led the

Israelites to their new lands, taking the credit for saving his people and, like a lot of history, the facts were warped in favour of the church."

Ragna spat over the side. "Isn't there a way we can kill this swarm here?"

"Not really," answered Diagus, shaking his head. "Not without going down to their level and start picking them off, but we'd get swamped before we even killed ten score ourselves. And if we get bitten then we'll be fighting each other. Best we avoid them altogether. A swarm that size and there's bound to be a spliceck."

"Spliceck?" This from Otholo.

"Yep. Maybe one in every few thousand is a spliceck. Nastier than the average takwich, they've got the ability to produce another shell after they've taken a body. Unlike a takwich, which will die once the host is killed. A spliceck, given a day or so can move from host to host, even if the body itself is killed and they can take the memories from each possession. Come across one of those then you'll need to kill and burn the body then wait for the creature to escape its host and kill it as well. Never met one myself, but rare as they are, they do exist."

Elora gazed down at the tiny insects and shuddered at the thought of having them crawling on her skin. Bray must have sensed her unease as he slipped an arm around her. She leaned into him and switched her gaze to the bare peak they were rising to. A large rock formation lay scattered around a man-size crater; at first appearing random but as he she stared she found it had a kind of symmetry, almost a pattern.

"The swarm senses our approach, you best not waste any more time. Bard, open the gate," ordered Zionbuss.

Otholo put a foot upon the rail, Cuban heel tapping a beat against the bone as his fingers teased a playful arpeggio on the lute. Then before Elora's eyes a layer of frost sparkled around the crater, white runes standing out against the red rock and at its centre, an onyx black circle shimmered.

Zionbuss shouted at his crew and several of them jumped from the ship and surrounded the gate, swords and axes at hand. The demon then turned to the group.

"Once you're through I'll destroy the gate. Then burn as many of the takwiches as I can."

"You're not coming?" asked Elora. An eight-foot horned demon might have come in handy if they got into any trouble.

"This is where I leave you my queen. I am, after all said and done, still a demon. The barrier prevents me from passing into the worlds unless I take another's body." His black eyes found Otholo and he grinned. "I take it there's no volunteers?" He laughed when the bard leapt behind Ragna. "Don't worry yourself, Otholo. I've work to be doing here." His gaze swung back to Elora "I will meet you again my queen. The Shadowlands are as much your home as they are mine." He nodded at one of his crew and the skeletal mate rolled the rope ladder over the edge, directly above the gate. "Safe journey."

Ragna slapped Zionbuss on the arm and descended down the ladder, closely followed by Ejan who gave the demon a curt nod, but nothing more. After they disappeared through the inky black gate her uncle climbed over the gunnel, took a final look around the ship as if recording it to memory, maybe to write in his journal later, and began to climb down. Otholo swung a leg over the edge next, his lute clattering into his back as he scowled at Zionbuss.

"I still hate you," he said, then made a hasty retreat down the ladder after Elora's uncle. Bray then followed, giving Elora's hand a reassuring squeeze before simply dropping off the ship without using the ladder. Elora rushed to the edge to see his body slip into the hole.

"Now you." ordered the Shadojak, staring at her, hand hovering around his smuggler's pouch.

"Of course," replied Elora, mildly annoyed at his mistrust, but respecting that from his point of view she could just as easily leave with Zionbuss and set off across the Shadowlands.

As she passed the demon she gave him a hug, the top of her head coming level with his bare chest. "Thank you for keeping your word. I hope we'll meet again."

"It is inevitable, my queen." His voice echoing through his chest into Elora's cheek, feeling like an earthquake; the runes and symbols on his skin swirling, making it hard to focus.

Elora smiled at him before swinging her legs over the rail and climbed down the ladder. The sound of a million clicking limbs and claws tapping at the rocks came to her ears as the crew of the *Necrolosis* began striking the approaching swarm of tak-wiches. She dropped into the inky black gate before they were overrun with the body-snatching insects.

21

Bluebell Wood

Elora landed hard, the momentum carrying her forwards onto her knees, hands pressing down into a cold earth. It took a moment to adjust to the darkness, the rich aroma of wild flowers and wet grass reaching her nose as her fingers curled about fine stems of an unfamiliar plant. She plucked a handful of them from the earth as she rose to her feet and brought them closer to her face – bluebells.

She was in a forest of extremely tall trees with dark bark. Fireflies with a soft green glow buzzed about the canopy and weaved between branches, giving the area a magical feel whilst stars twinkled through the gaps above, adding to the atmosphere. The forest floor was covered in a blanket of bluebells that swayed to a gentle breeze, appearing like the waves on a soft ocean, so thick she couldn't see below the pretty flowers to the ground beneath. An owl hooted, further out in the forest, hidden in the darkness; where frogs creaked to a rhythm accompanying the sway of the flowers and in the distance she thought she heard the snatches of a piccolo playing a haunting tune.

The group stood in a rough circle facing out, swords drawn and looking fierce, except from Otholo who was busy singing to a firefly that lazily floated in front of his beaming face.

Diagus suddenly appeared through a large hole in the tree behind her, emerging through the blackness like stepping through a dark curtain. The white frosted runes that surrounded the opening fizzled bright for a second before fading into the tree bark. The gate vanished with the runes, leaving a man-sized hole in the tree.

When they were satisfied there was no threat, they slid their swords away. Ragna scratching his beard as he rested the shaft of his hammer on the ground and leaned his heavy arms over the steel head. Ejan weaved an arm through one of his and rested against his shoulder.

Bray smiled, his eyes catching the glow of a passing firefly and lighting his face. "Welcome to Thea," he said, taking her hand and pulling her into a hug. "Are you cold?" he asked, rubbing her bare arms.

"No," replied Elora, seeing that goosebumps had risen on her skin but that was due to the sudden fresh night air she was breathing, a world of difference to the dusty arid climate of the Shadowlands. The wave of excitement at experiencing this new place only adding to her nerves. "I can't believe we're here, on a different world."

"Believe it Elora," said her uncle, smiling from ear to ear. "This is where you were born. Where magic can happen."

"Where the fairies live?" she asked, her smile matching Nat's.

"Where we've got a bloody job to do," snapped Diagus, the only one of the group whose face was grim. "And we're putting this bluebell wood behind us before we make camp."

"But the place is so peaceful, so beautiful," said Elora, trying to soak up as much of her surroundings as possible.

Diagus snorted his disdain, then marched off between trees, swatting the glowing bugs away from his stern face as he went.

Ragna shrugged his huge shoulders, hefted his hammer around the back of his neck and rested his arms on the shaft, hands dangling. "Can't sleep in a bluebell wood anyway," he said, then followed the Shadojak.

"Or other activities that involve laying above the flowers," laughed Ejan, slapping her husband on the backside. Otholo chuckled as he sauntered after, striking up a soft melody on his lute.

"What's wrong with the woods?" asked Elora as Bray slipped an arm over her shoulder and began to lead her in the direction of the others.

"Even on Earth there is a myth about bluebell woods," offered her uncle. "People go missing, children disappear and sometimes are replaced by strange creatures. There's a kind of fairy magic about them; a mysterious force, playful to them but upsetting if somebody is lost. And it is said that if you were to fall asleep upon the bluebells, you will wake up in a different part of the forest."

"But that's not true, is it?"

"Not on Earth, no. Not yet anyway. But on Thea, there is always some truth about myths. Diagus is right to lead us away."

Elora glanced around the blue forest floor as they followed the others, hoping to catch a peek at the fairies or pixies, but if they were there they eluded her. The only other creature she witnessed in the enchanted woods was a badger that regarded her with its beady black eyes before scurrying down a hole.

Further along she heard the piccolo again, this time playing a waltzing march in time to her footfalls. Otholo fretted a tune to the same beat, the two instruments accompanying each other and Ragna began to hum.

"Who's playing the piccolo?" Elora asked.

"It's not a piccolo. It's a wood knoll," answered Bray, "Each tree has one. Little creatures born out of hardened sap to protect the trees from unwanted fairies. They're singing to each other now, warning themselves that men roam the woods."

He unclipped something from his ear, she hadn't notice he was wearing and passed it to her. It was a small silver disc, no bigger than a five pence coin, with a hole at its centre. Attached to one edge by a silver chain was a cylindrical clasp.

"Here," he said, gently clipping it to the top of her ear so the disc rested above the lobe. "It's a tinker's tongue charm. It changes the language that's been spoken as it hits the disc, so you can understand what's being said. Tinkers use them when travelling through different countries. Merchants too. Listen."

Elora listened as the piccolo sounds faded to a single buzzing tone, then a broken monologue; the buzz becoming the groans and creaks of wood. Then they themselves became recognisable words.

"Danger – men in the wood. Warning – Men in the wood. Flames that devour, steel that cuts. Danger – men in the wood."

"This is amazing," said Elora, touching the tinker's tongue charm with her finger. The wood knoll voices buzzed until she withdrew it.

"It's yours," said Bray, kissing her softly on the cheek. "You're going to need it more than I do. Nobody on Thea speaks English."

Elora kissed him back. "Thank you, it's amazing. But how does it even work?"

"It's charmed. A spell was cast, then the spell was bonded to the disc. It takes two wizards, a caster and a binder to make an object charmed. I don't know how or why, that's for the wizards to know. But it works and now it's yours."

"I love it," she said, wanting to jump up and down on the spot. "I love you."

Bray grinned, taking her hand and leading her on once again. "Love you too."

They trudged for what felt like an hour before emerging from the bluebell wood and entered a clearing with a shallow stream running down one edge. It's waters sparkling silver in the moonlight as it gurgled over worn stones and rocks. Diagus ordered a halt for the night.

"I'll take first watch," offered Bray, taking his bread to a large rock by the tree line.

"Do you want company?" asked Elora.

Bray shook his head. "You need to sleep; we've got a long walk tomorrow."

"I'm not tired," she said, stifling a yawn.

"Get what sleep you can, Elora. We'll be moving off at sunrise and you don't want to miss the sun rising on Thea. It's the second most beautiful sight a man can behold."

"And the first?" she asked, raising a quizzical eyebrow whilst feeling heat rising to her cheeks.

Bray's green eyes twinkled mischievously. "The sunset."

"Wake up," said Nat. Elora felt him gently shaking her shoulder. Grey, pre-dawn light settled around the small camp, the fire having gutted sometime before and was now merely a miserable pile of ash. Otholo lay curled up next to it, an arm over his lute and his head hidden beneath a hood. Ejan was sat on the log, scraping a sharpening stone along the blade of her sword.

Elora stretched, neck and joints stiff from sleeping on the damp ground. "Where's Bray and Diagus?"

"They left earlier, scouting ahead in case of trouble," answered Ragna, taking dried biscuits from his pack and divided them into piles. "They'll be back for breakfast, before we move off."

Yawning, Elora wandered down to the stream and splashed icy water on her face, the mountains which it sprang from looming dark in the reflection. She gazed up at the imposing snowcapped peaks as the sun began to rise above, tinging the few clouds pink whilst projecting golden fingers down the mountain side. Bray was right, it was a beautiful sunrise.

"We've got to climb those?" she asked Ejan, as the Norsewoman joined her at the stream. Crouching low on a rock the Viking dunked her entire head beneath the water, held it under for a moment before lifting her head back, water flying from her long blonde plait.

"Yeah," she answered, shaking the excess drips from her flushed face. "Those are the Gods' Peaks. Aslania is at the top of the tallest."

"They're so big," said Elora, toying with the idea of dunking her own head but deciding the water was too cold.

"They look big now? Wait until we've reached the base and you're staring up at the summit. It's going to make you feel mouse small." Ejan was about to say something else when her head whipped about, her knife suddenly appearing in her hand.

"What is it?" Elora asked, as a tall man stepped from behind a tree on the other side of the stream.

He was dressed in boiled leather, a dull breastplate strapped to his chest and wore a rounded helmet of the same metal. A large crossbow lay heavily in his arms; its bolt levelled towards them. He grunted something Elora didn't understand and Ejan said something back in the same language. She slowly rose to her feet and glared at the man as she dropped her knife.

He smiled and motioned for them to walk back the way they came. When they turned, Elora heard the splashes as he followed.

"Who is he?" Elora felt unnerved at having a huge weapon pointed at her back. She glanced behind and caught him staring at her with hunger in his eyes and an unsavoury grin splitting his matted beard, showing yellow teeth.

"Don't know. But I don't think he's here to chew fat over the weather," Ejan answered.

Elora pushed her cloak open using her elbows to hide her intentions from their captor, and she slid her sword from the smuggler's pouch. She stepped to the side to block his view and placed the hilt in Ejan's hand. The Viking tucked it tight to her body as Elora then pulled her dagger out, holding it against her forearm.

"Ragna will take him down," whispered Ejan. But as they came over the rise Elora saw the huge Viking on his knees, another man dressed in boiled leather, held the point of a long sword against his neck. Nat and Otholo were both perched on the log with a third man holding a drawn bow, arrow notched between the pair.

Two more men rode out of the woods on horses, each pulling other mounts which Elora guessed belonged to the men that had silently crept up and taken them hostage.

"Definitely not here to discuss the weather," said Elora, as another pair of men trotted in from the other side of the clearing, their horses snorting out small clouds of mist. One of the new arrivals, a grey bearded man with a shiny metal breastplate, dismounted and casually walked over to the spent fire and poked it with a stick – attempting to rekindle any sparks that were left.

From the way he moved and from the way the other men watched him, Elora took him to be the leader. After a few vain moments he realised that the fire was truly out and turned his attention to them. He smiled at Ejan and mumbled something.

"Crap," Elora heard her whisper, then dropped the sword onto the ground. "Better drop that dagger, girl. They won't think nothing of putting a bolt in your back."

Elora let her weapon fall to the thick grass.

Grey beard smiled, appearing satisfied with their compliance. Then sauntered over to Ragna, speaking in that strange tongue, Elora guessing that he was being questioned. Frustrated at not being able to understand what was going on she took the tinker's tongue from a pocket in her cloak and slowly clipped it onto her ear. Luckily the men around her were more intent on watching Ragna being interrogated than what she was doing.

"What are Vikings doing this far south?" Grey beard questioned.

Ragna stretched his neck away from the blade as he replied. "Enjoying the countryside. Maybe a spot of fishing."

The interrogator tapped the Fist of the North with the toe of his boot. "Some bloody big fish you're hunting, eh?"

Ragna grinned. "Huge."

"Strange companions though. Vikings and Minuans, if I'm not mistaken." His gaze drifted over Otholo, Nat and Elora. "Didn't think you lot got on with each other."

"Times change. You know how the saying goes; make friends, make friends and never ever break friends."

Grey beard calmly drew a dirk from his belt and placed it against Ragna's Adam's apple, the point pressing an indentation into the skin. "You know the expression; tell me the bloody truth or I'll make you gargle blood with the next lie."

"Wait, wait. There's no need for violence." This from Otholo who attempted to rise from the log, but was roughly shoved back down. "My name's Otholo. These kindly Norsemen were escorting my sister and I, to Aslania."

"Otholo?" Grey beard's eyebrows knitted together as he looked him over. "Otholo the bard? Weren't you the golden harp of Goseland or something?"

Otholo puffed out his chest with pride at being recognised. "I am. Otholo the golden harp. Personal songbird to King Jerome, one-time lover of Princess … "

"I hate bards," cut in the leader. Otholo sagged back, shoulders slumping, deflated at the reaction.

"Rebels, bandits, Vikings or just good honest thieves. It don't matter none to me. You're not going to Aslania. And that's orders that have been sent down from the Emperor himself."

"And who's going to stop us," said Diagus, stepping into the clearing, his hood hiding his face. "You and your rag-tag sell swords?"

Elora heard the man behind her curse, then hiss through his teeth. Gazing over her shoulder she saw that Bray held a knife against his throat.

"I'd be thinking about pointing that crank bow at your feet, about now," his words were hushed, yet the threat was there. His eyes flicked to her and he gave her a wink. Elora felt relief wash over her.

"That's right," continued grey beard, regaining his composure after being interrupted. He pulled his dirk from Ragna's neck as he approached Diagus. "Sellers of swords we maybe, but we're taking the Emperor's coin this season. So we fall into his jurisdiction and hold his law." He folded his arms across his breastplate and stood a foot from the Shadojak, their faces inches apart, and smiled smugly. "There's a battalion of the Emperor's men holding the bridge into Gods' Peaks. Another spread out along its border and he's hired sell swords to patrol the borders for anybody seeking passage into Aslania."

"Who's got command at the bridge?" Asked Diagus, coolly.

"Colonel Debreen. Too young if you ask me, but he's got the rank. That is until the rest of the division arrive."

Diagus leaned closer to grey beard, their noses almost touching. "Never heard of him. I see you've got seven horses. One for each of my group. You will surrender them to us."

The smugness dropped from grey beard the same instance as his dirk came level with Diagus's face. "By whose authority, old man?"

"The Shadojaks," said Diagus, pulling his hood down and revealing his face.

Elora felt a coldness sweep through the clearing. Nobody moved. Then inch by inch grey beard lowered his blade and his mouth opened as if to say something, but no words passed his lips.

"It's the Pearly White," exclaimed one of the sell swords on horseback. The man holding the bow against Otholo and Nat, accidentally let it fly. The arrow disappearing harmlessly into the trees.

"Do you yield?"

Grey beard cowed back and fell to one knee, bowing his head low to the ground. "Forgive me, sir. Had I known … "

"How would you have known?"

Elora noticed a younger man, perhaps closer to her own age, shuffle towards grey beard. A blonde speckling of fluff above his lip, in an attempt at growing a moustache. It bobbed up and down as he spoke. "What? We yielding to this bunch? We could take them easily … ouch!"

Grey beard cuffed the young lad around the back of the head, sending him reeling back, where he stumbled and finally dropped his sword. He turned back to Diagus. "Sorry about that. He's my sister's sprog, full of piss and vinegar, that one. Suppose we all were at that age."

The Shadojak raised an eyebrow, his only reaction to the insult. "Now, about those horses."

Elora was glad to be back on a horse, although the stares they were receiving from the men they had taken them from were full of hatred. As they passed from sight she could hear the young lad whining to his uncle that it wasn't fair, they could have taken them. She heard him being cuffed again and felt a pang of guilt.

"I think Prince Dylap delivered my message to the Shadojak Supreme. He's the only one who'd get the Emperor to move so fast," she heard Bray comment to Diagus as they led the group through the woods, picking their way through the trees until they reached a deer track.

"Might be that the Emperor's reaction will hinder us. It won't be easy getting passed this Colonel Debreen. Might be we'll need to force our way through."

The deer track gave way onto a wider path and the Shadojak quickened the pace. Elora felt invigorated, bouncing in the saddle as they cantered through the woods. Her hood caught in the wind and pushed back, releasing her hair to fly out behind her. Maybe she should ask Ejan to plait it like hers, but then it felt so refreshing having it whipped about.

They stopped only once, to water the horses and let them graze for a spell. By midday they had left the woods and Elora saw that the mountains were a lot closer and a great deal bigger. Snowcapped and incredibly tall, they loomed high into the blue sky. The wind occasionally dusting a layer of snow from a peak in a fine white spray. Between the mountains and themselves lay a camp. Scarlet and gold coloured tents scattered about the flat ground. Men and horses busy between, dressed in the same colours with polished armour glinting in the sun.

As they approached they were stopped by several guards who eyed them warily. Halberds were brought to arms along with crossbows. Diagus steered his horse towards the older man who seemed to be in charge.

"By order of the Shadojak, you will dispatch a runner to the commander, informing him that myself and my companions will be passing through."

"Nobody is permitted to pass," said the guardsmen, but dispatched a young soldier to fetch the Colonel.

About her Elora caught more than once the words 'Pearly White' being whispered excitedly by the soldiers. The hushed voices travelling into camp as the word was spread.

A few moments later the runner returned looking red in the face. Following close on his heel was a clean-shaven man somewhat younger than Elora would have imagined a Colonel to be.

The guard stood erect as he arrived, the guard commander thumping his chest in salute.

"Sergeant, I instructed you that nobody is to pass. Which part of that order did you not understand?" asked the Colonel, clearly irritated.

"Sir, this here's the Shadojak," replied the man who dispatched the runner, his own face going red even though he must have been at least ten years the Colonel's senior.

"Indeed he is, Sergeant. But the order still stands."

"Colonel Debreen?" Diagus cut in. "Am I to understand that you are refusing the authority of the Shadojak?"

Debreen flicked his attention from the guardsmen to Diagus, his face becoming pinched and petulant. "I have my orders, sir. As do my men. Nobody is to pass. The Shadojak you may be, but unless I receive a further order from the Emperor to allow you admittance, you will not cross."

Diagus kicked his mount forwards, stepping close enough to the Colonel to force him back. Jaw clenched, eyes bulging and fingers curling into fists, the commander looked ready to order his men to attack. However, Elora noticed that only the Sergeant seemed determined to stand by his commander: the rest of the guard were already putting space between themselves and the Shadojak.

"You're young for a Colonel. That means one of two things," said Diagus. "Either you're a determined tactician manoeuvering yourself up the ranks with your eyes set on becoming a general. Or maybe you have family connections and you have your father to thank for getting you this position."

The Colonel attempted to argue back but was preoccupied, wrestling to get passed the horse which was pushing him up against the ropes of a pavilion tent.

"Doesn't matter which," continued Diagus, leaning down so his face was inches from Debree's. "You'll get the blame for any tragedy that befalls us from this delay. You see, when it all boils down to high ranks in the army, it's simply a blame game. Shit rolls downhill from on high. When the Emperor learns that this mission failed because we were delayed; even though you're following orders – he won't be impressed. Do you think the General will accept the responsibility for this mistake, or will he use you as a scapegoat, letting the shit roll a little further down?"

"But the General will be here this evening," spluttered the Colonel, his voice rising another octave. If you just wait until then, I'm sure … "

Diagus pulled his sword from his smuggler's pouch. As did Bray. Elora also noticed that Ragna's hammer had found its owner's meaty hands and Ejan already had an arrow notched.

"You misunderstand me Debree. We mean to cross that bridge now. Either with or without your permission. If we are delayed, it is because we needed to cut a bloody path through you. You'll be dead when the General arrives, so you can see how easily he will blame you."

"But, but … " stuttered the Colonel, darting apprehensive glances to his men who were reluctant to draw any weapons of their own against the Shadojak, even the soldiers with the halberds, pointed them in the other direction. Debree's shoulders dropped, his attention drawing back to his Sergeant. "Let them pass," he growled. The Sergeant nodded, relief smoothing the crease from his brow as he ordered the runner to carry the message to the bridge.

Diagus re-sheathed his sword and the rest of the group put away their weapons. "I see you're more of the careerist tactician than a privileged buffoon," said the Shadojak, as he led his horse passed the livid Colonel. "Give my regards to the General, when you see him."

They trotted through the camp unhindered, the guards at the bridge saluting as they crossed the wide river.

The bridge was old. Made from stone it appeared sturdy and just wide enough to take a cart across. A thigh high wall was built to either side to prevent people falling into the vast river. The noise the horses created as they began to ride across, echoed strangely along the huge body of water.

"That went easier than I thought," said Otholo. "For a moment there I was expecting him to order his men to attack."

Two loud blasts of a bugle suddenly pierced the air, startling the horses. Elora patted her mare's neck reassuringly. "Debree's, changed his mind?" she asked, as she stared at the men clambering around the camp, gathering up weapons and mounting horses.

"Clever," remarked Diagus. "Kill us once we've crossed and he can tell the General we broke through his guard. Sparing himself the indignity of informing him that he was bullied into letting us cross."

Elora saw the rush of armoured men and horses begin to cross the bridge, riders jostling to get in front, hooves kicking chips and making dust from the old masonry.

"Yahh!" shouted Diagus, kicking his horse into a gallop.

Elora did the same, as did the rest of the group. Gripping the reigns tightly in both hands, she leaned over the saddle horn, pressing her knees into the mare's flank whilst trying to stay atop. Adrenalin pumped from her heart as they raced down the narrow bridge, only the low brick walls on either side preventing them from plummeting into the fast flowing river.

Hooves thundered and steel clattered amongst the shouts of men as the army took chase. The small group drove their mounts as hard as they could, the four guards at the other side of the bridge jumping clear of Ragna's hammer as they rode through.

An arrow was loosed from a bow, but in his haste the guard missed, the projectile going high above Ragna as he almost fell from his horse; only Bray gripping his arm and pushing him back into his saddle, saving him.

As the grass flatland opened up before them, the horses gathered another burst of speed, lengthening the distance between them and their pursuers. They headed up the open field that gradually grew steeper towards the mountain range which formed the foothills. A copse of tall trees outlined the crest of a long spur that reached down the mountainside like a rocky arm kinking at the elbow.

Elora noticed that Nathaniel slowed, his face creased up in concentration as he chanted a water rhythm.

"Nat, come on. What are you doing?" She risked a glance back and saw that the first few riders had cleared the bridge, close enough now for her to see how sharp their spears were. The rest of the army was a good way across, although some were now stopping to point up river, a few beginning to turn back. When she turned her head in the direction they were pointing she realised what her uncle had done.

A body of water rose twenty feet out of the river in a huge wave. It washed over the bridge with enough force to knock those that were on it over the stone wall. Another, bigger wave crashed into the stonework, smashing it to pieces as it followed its course.

Nat stopped chanting and opened his eyes. He glanced behind him at the destruction and let out a laugh. "Still got it."

"Not for much longer if those riders catch us up," replied Elora, spurring her horse onwards, Nat now keeping pace.

They reached the trees unscathed, the group splitting up as they cut between the low branches, then Diagus raised an arm, bringing them to a halt.

"The horses are spent. It's time to fight," he said, leaping from his horse and rushing back to the tree line. The rest of them followed his example, leaving their mounts where they were and reaching for weapons.

"I count twelve," said Ejan, taking arrows from her quiver and sticking them in the ground at her feet. She put another against the string of her bow and stretched it back.

"Better odds than the last time. I doubt they even know they've been cut off from the main body," said Bray.

In the distance, Elora watched as men floundered on the river, scrambling up the slippery bank away from the lethal current. Others helping them out or calming horses that had gone wild with panic. None attempted to cross without the bridge. Yet the riders thundered towards them, their mounts slick with sweat, bodies glistening in the sun.

"Send them a warning shot," ordered Diagus, crow's feet deepening on his withered face.

Ejan stared down the shaft of the arrow, adjusted her aim and let it fly. Elora watched its graceful flight as it ascended into the afternoon sky before falling in front of the lead horse.

The rider looked up, his face hidden beneath a polished helmet as he slowed the pace. He glanced behind them and slowed again, raising his arm and signalling to the others to halt. They had covered half the ground, appearing no bigger than Elora's fist, if she cared to hold it out in front of her. But twelve armoured men on horseback, were still intimidating.

Dust kicked up from the horses as they stomped around, their snorts audible above the arguing soldiers.

"Reckon they'll go back?" asked Ejan.

"They don't want to look cowardly in front of their battalion," replied Diagus. "Then again, I doubt they'd prefer to die in front of it. Send them another warning shot, remind them they're in range."

Ejan sent the warning arrow and pulled another from the ground by her feet and gave that air before the first had landed. It struck the field an inch from the first. The incredible feat of expert bowman ship wasn't wasted on the men as they steered their horses back towards the river, then galloped away.

"Can't say I blame them," remarked Otholo. "I wouldn't fancy riding against you lot, even with a battalion at my back."

"Still, I think it best to put as much distance as we can between us and the army. When the General arrives, who do you think he's going to send after us?" said Diagus, face as grim as ever.

"Debree, and he's going to be nuttier than a pinbush squirrel," laughed Otholo. "The closest bridge is more than twenty leagues up river and we could probably make it to the pass by tomorrow evening. Once we're there we can block anyone following."

"I want to be there by morning," said Diagus.

"And more likely than not," said Bray. "Debree will have men dug into defensive positions in the mountains as well as platoons patrolling this side of the river."

"So that means, peacock, no more of your irritating songs. It's by stealth we'll reach Aslania," said Diagus. Then turning to Ejan he asked. "Where's Ragna too?"

Elora scanned about the tree line but couldn't see the Viking, which was odd, as he was the largest amongst them. "Did he stay with the horses?" she asked.

"What, and miss a chance to swing the Fist?" answered Ejan, worriedly. She gathered up her arrows and set off back into the trees, concern creasing her brow.

As they neared their horses, Elora saw Ragna still sat upon his mount, one hand gripping the saddle horn, the other inside his cloak.

"What you doing back here, napping?" chuckled Ejan, giving his leg a loving slap.

Elora smiled at seeing the affection, then she saw the trail of blood running from the corner of Ragna's mouth. Ejan noticed it too.

"Raggy? What's happened?" she asked, hands tightening on his leg.

Ragna, winced, closing his eyes tightly as blood began to seep into his beard.

"Got myself stuck. Didn't even know it happened at the time, what with all the chasing and confusion."

"Raggy?"

The Viking lifted his cloak free from his belly, revealing a black patch spreading over his chainmail vest – an arrow sticking out of his side. "Happened when we left the bridge," he coughed; wine coloured blood dribbling from his lips and coating his teeth. "One of the guards, let loose … " He tried to speak more but his words were lost amongst a fit of coughing. When it finally subsided his head flopped to the side and he toppled from the saddle.

22

The Pass

Ejan controlled Ragna's body as it fell, the weight forcing her to the ground. She struggled to roll him onto his back, tears running down her face and made tracks down her dusty cheeks.

"Raggy, no," she cried.

Elora rushed to her side, taking Ragna's huge hand in hers. "Please don't die," she muttered. His fingers twitched in hers, then his eyes slowly opened. They went from hers to Ejan's where they stayed. He attempted to smile but pain twisted it into a grimace.

"Such, beautiful hair," he whispered, trailing his hand down his wife's blonde plait. Her own hands lifting away the cloak so she could inspect the wound. "Leave it. The head's stuck well into my belly." He coughed up more blood then, Elora wincing with the pain he must be feeling. "Didn't think it'd be an arrow that did for me."

"You're not done for," argued Ejan, the words tempered with grit.

"Course I am, wench, nobody lives from an arrow in the gut. Might take days for me to pass into the halls of Valhalla, but that's where I'm heading."

Elora wiped the wetness from her eyes. "There must be something we can do. Are there healers in Aslania?" she pleaded, but understood from the sad look in Nat's face that it wasn't to be.

"You'll be leaving me here," said Ragna. "I'll only slow you down and die anyway. Tell them Diagus, make them see sense."

Elora clenched her teeth as she watched the Shadojak kneel down beside Ejan and place his aged hand upon her shoulder. Her head dropped, she knew what he would say, but before he spoke Elora jumped to her feet, a fury racking her, fuelled by the injustice of it.

"If Ragna stays, then I stay. If you let him die, then I'm going to walk back over to that Colonel and hand myself in. I've had enough of people suffering for the sake of me. I'm not worth it." Bray gently touched her arm and she shrugged him off. "If we make it to Aslania, if we destroy Solarius then there's a chance we can give Earth its magic back – give electricity back to the world. If that happens then the hospitals will be working." She pointed at Ragna's wound, at the shaft now black with blood. "In a hospital that could be treated, with doctors and with antibiotics he would live."

She watched Ejan raise her head, hope mingling with tears as she, along with the rest of the group, looked to Diagus.

"I was about to say before you interrupted, that we'll take Ragna with us as long as there's life left in his body," said Diagus, rising to his feet, but not before Ejan squeezed his hand.

"Snap the shaft and bandage up the wound the best you can. There'll be mountain cats and snow jubbs about, and they'll smell the blood," he continued, then dropped a small block shaped object, wrapped in paper, onto Ragna's lap. "Willow bark, for the pain"

"I'd rather whisky," grumbled Ragna.

Within an hour they were back in the saddle, Bray and Ejan having struggled to get Ragna atop his horse. It was clear to Elora that he was in immense pain, yet he fought not to show it for Ejan's sake.

They began the ride up the foothills, the gradient manageable at first but becoming dangerously steep as the night drew closer. The path became rockier and less sure under foot and every time his horse jolted or made a sudden move, Ragna took in a quickly drawn breath, clutching his wound, a waxy film coating his face.

When the daylight was finally vanquished and the only light came from the waning moon, partly hidden behind black clouds, Diagus brought them to a stop and set up camp. If you could call it that. The Shadojak forbid a fire and the horses were hobbled so it was more of a prolonged pause than a camp. The men took turns to watch in pairs whilst Elora and Ejan kept Ragna as comfortable as possible. Making him sip water and feeding him willow bark. When he finally fell into a fitful sleep, Ejan spoke softly.

"Thank you," she said. "For what you did down there. I was sure Diagus would have left him," she kissed Elora on the forehead, then placed another softer kiss on her husband.

"I was sure he was going to leave him too. But I meant what I said, nobody should suffer because of me. I can't imagine what I would do if Bray got injured and he's got freaky elf genes that make him heal quick."

Ejan smiled. "Yep, he would have healed already from this." She nodded towards the cloth wrapped around the base of the shaft, blood already turning it black. "So what's the story between you two now? Are you an item?"

Elora was glad the darkness hid her reddening cheeks. "We haven't had much time together, but I suppose we are boyfriend and girlfriend." She caught sight of his silhouette, sitting atop a boulder, chatting quietly to Otholo, but felt his gaze upon her every now and then.

"You've found a good one there and he must think the world of you to quit his life as a Shaigun. He's a definite keeper," said Ejan, absently stroking the curls in Ragna's hair.

"I won't let him go without a fight. How did you and Ragna end up at Rams Keep?"

"We were on a raid, coming south of the border – for no other reason than to get one back on the Empire. They'd destroyed most of my hometown, in the winter before, so we wanted retribution. I was swollen with child at the time – Jaygen. Ragna pleaded with me not go with him, but where he went I went." She shook her head, looking longingly at her husband. "It turns out the town we attacked were more than ready for us. They had a hundred score of Imperial soldiers waiting in ambush. When we stalked into the town we were attacked. Everything was flashing steel and fire. Amongst the confusion Ragna and I were separated from the rest of the raiders. And whether it was the panic or blood-lust of battle, Jaygen chose that moment to want out of my belly."

"You had Jaygen in the middle of a battle?" asked Elora, shocked at the revelation.

"No. We fought our way clear, managed to hide out in a cave we found, not too far from the town. But we were tracked by the town's folk. They surrounded the entrance – what was left of the soldiers and the people, armed with pitchforks and the like and waited for us.

"They bayed for our blood, they would butcher us and string what was left on the town's gate as an example to others. Yet none could get passed Ragna. He perched himself between the walls where the cave was narrowest and killed each man that entered, while I was busy screaming to Odin to get this bleeding baby out of me." Ejan slapped the steel head of the Fist that lay to her side. "Ragna held them back all night, must have killed thirty or more, for the dead piled up and blocked the entrance. What was left of the men outside tried a different tack and set fire to huge logs and branches, throwing hay on top and attempting to smoke us out.

"Thankfully, rain put an end to that and realising that smoke wouldn't bring us out – and they wouldn't come in; fearing death as my wailing must have sounded like torture itself, they called for the local warlock."

Elora suddenly felt and arm slip around her and Bray's warm body pressing against her back. He had finished his watch and come to listen to the story. She laced her fingers through his and relaxed into him.

"Jaygen had come into the world by then," continued Ejan. "Kicking and screaming – he had a right set of lungs on him. Ragna joined me, holding his son and cooing in a way that mellowed him, and myself if truth be told. It was the only time I'd seen tears in his eyes, for all the big brute that he is, he was still soft over his son. Or it may have been the fact that we were trapped with no possible escape and feared for both his newly born and myself."

"How did you get away?" Elora sat up, so engrossed in the story.

"When the warlock finally came he sealed the cave entrance with a curse. Sealed and bound by a gate, one that if we walked through would deliver us into the heart of the Shadowlands. We stayed in the cave for as long as possible, maybe two days, could be three but Ragan decided that we should go into the Shadowlands with enough strength to fight. So holding hands, me clutching Jaygen to my chest, him grasping this." She slapped the huge war hammer. "We walked out of the cave. Fortunately for us, the warlock wasn't as good with his runes as he thought because we didn't step into the Shadowlands, but upon a strange land with green fields, trees and sunshine; with noisy buildings, monstrous moving machines and metal birds in the sky and so many people. Too many people. But we felt safe, so much steel about but none of it weapons. We were scared at first, in that strange place – a different world from our own, yet it didn't take long for us to find food, shelter and clothes for Jaygen, even though we couldn't speak or understand the local tongue.

"It wasn't long before we were picked up by the police. Ragna had stolen food and clothes from a supermarket then attacked the officers that arrested him. Luckily the Shadojak turned up when he did, before Ragna began using the hammer. Diagus took us to Rams Keep and we've been there ever since."

Ragna stirred in his sleep, lines deepening into a pained scowl as Ejan brushed his hair back from his face.

"He'll make it," reassured Elora. "I know he will."

Diagus woke them before dawn. Grey light crept down the mountainside, fragmenting into a hundred different shades as it bounced from rocks and crags, making shapes from the darkness into trees and wild bushes.

Elora opened her eyes – Ragna didn't.

"Raggy?" whispered Ejan, urgently shaking her husband, her head resting against his chest.

Elora felt a choke, press deep into her stomach, twisting her guts. "No," she murmured, wriggling free from Bray's embrace, where she'd spent the night.

As she came to the Viking's side, heavy lids struggled open and he peered out through bloodshot eyes, and when he spoke the sound was as dry as sandpaper.

"Feels like I've swallowed an entire horn golem and it's trying to push its way out of me."

Ejan wiped a tear from her cheek, her smile forming from relief while Elora let out the breath she had been holding. She pulled his cloak back to check the wound.

"It doesn't look good," remarked Ejan, peeling back the sticky bandage and revealing the hideous shaft of wood; a yellow puss oozing from the hole in his puckered flesh. "It doesn't smell too good either."

Elora placed the back of her hand against his clammy brow. "He's got a temperature." When Ragna tried to speak again she stopped him, "No, we're not leaving you so you can put that idea out of your head."

He didn't try to speak after that, only groaned as they cleaned and changed his dressing, then hissed as they hauled him onto his horse.

They made slow progress, climbing higher along the winding path, the morning sun touching the grey stone and shining off the pink mica as the wind caressed the Gods' Peaks – picking up strength the further they rose. By midday Elora stopped counting the amount of times that Ragna nearly fell from the saddle, Bray by his side, the only member of the group with the strength to keep him up and keep him moving.

She knew they were going slow, Diagus, ever impatient, disappearing ahead only to come back an hour later to tell them they were weak and slow and that they would never reach Aslania. Yet when she caught sight of the land far below it seemed further away, spreading out before them, the river appearing string-thin and the camp a dark smudge in the patchwork of green fields.

"So bloody slow," growled Diagus as the afternoon came on. They'd rode over a ridge that formed a natural saddle to the next mountain, sweeping over a steep drop to either side. Their mounts scrambling for purchase in the narrower parts and sending stones tumbling down into the scree to cause small landslides.

"It's like herding a rabble of blind slug mammoths. Food for mountain cats and snow jubbs, the lot of you," grumbled Diagus.

The Shadojak spoke less as they began the torturous climb of the next mountain, allowing a rest for the horses and a chance to clean Ragna's wound. They ate on the move, nibbling at dry biscuits and bread, chewing the stale food as they were jostled and bounced in the saddles; the horses struggling to keep a steady gait.

By nightfall the air was thin, Otholo complained of light-headedness and Ragna's wound became too painful to push on.

"Hobble the horses and keep them close. And keep a blade to hand," warned Diagus. "Might be we get an unwanted visitor or two, before sun-up."

Elora thought she would never sleep, fearing that a mountain cat or snow jubb might sneak into camp; Bray had explained, when she asked what a snow jubb was. They were a kind of pygmy. Small wild men, no taller than your knee, covered in a white furry pelt: hunting with spear and net they were not fussy what they ate as meat high in the mountains was rare.

The temperature dropped icily low, her breath visible in the twilight as the wind snatched it away to be buffeted into the rocks. Ragna snorted in his sleep, his breathing sporadic as he fitfully moaned and shook, Ejan pressing her body next to his to share heat. Elora on his other side protecting the huge Viking as best they could from the elements.

The night passed slowly. Elora caught animal noises mingled within the howling of the wind: guttural cat-like snarls that put the horses to stamping and snorting and a strange squealing jib-ba-jubba noise that at first sounded from above, the next below and evoked images of little white men with spears in her mind.

When dawn began to creep over the horizon, outlining the mountains, Elora realised that she hadn't had a minute's sleep. She watched Diagus stalk towards them, ready to wake them up for the day's travel. She dreamed of her own bed back on the *Molly*, literally another world away. The thought of pulling her duvet over herself and sinking into her soft mattress and pillow made her pine for home.

She sat up before he nudged her with his boot, denying him the satisfaction she was sure he felt. "I'm awake," she muttered, her voice thick with the sleep that eluded her.

The Shadojak hunkered down. "Good. How's Ragna?"

"He's hanging in there. Have you any willow bark left?"

Diagus pulled a small block of the herb from a pocket in his cloak, rolled it around his fingers for a moment as if coming to a decision, then dropped it into her hand. "That's all of it, so make it last," he said, rising back to his feet, his aged fingers flexing, his bones clicking. "We're going to get to a point today where we're going to leave the horses. Then … ?"

"We'll walk," Elora scowled at him, daring him to say otherwise, "All of us."

Ragna had tears brimming his bloodshot eyes when they sat him on his saddle. He coped with the pain as silently as he could but it was written in the creases, sat deeply in his face, with the sweat that coated his brow and grimace that stretched his lips. Ejan pretended not to notice but Elora caught her wiping tears from her own cheeks more than once.

They set off without a word, the horses making the only sound as they plodded up the broken track, snorting through flared nostrils, showing disdain at the way they were being treated. Elora couldn't blame the poor beasts, being made to carry them up this giant rock in the cold without any proper grazing.

A fresh wind whipped about their legs and the darkness of the clouds threatened rain. She stroked her mare's neck, curling her fingers around her dark mane, attempting to infuse some warmth into her hands, as she reassured her mount and wishing Bray was here to reassure her. But he was ahead of the group, hunting for obstacles or dangers that lay in their path. Reassurance was a luxury that she would gladly pass onto Ragna or Ejan before taking any for herself. Even her uncle, the eldest amongst them, who closed his cloak tightly about his thin shoulders, set his face in grim determination against the mountain and the elements. She, being the youngest, played the easiest part of this journey, if the others could manage with the hardships then so could she.

When the rain came, it brought with it ice and snow. Large and sharp, it stung any bare flesh, turning skin red and lips blue. Hoods snapped from heads, cloaks whipped about and hooves stomped against the stone earth. Diagus's mount suddenly reared up, ahead of the file, almost throwing the Shadojak and threatening to bolt back the way they came, although there was barely enough room for one horse between rock and the vertical drop. But with a lot of cursing and digging in with his heals, Diagus regained control of his flighty horse and led them on; the sleet rapidly becoming snow.

Bray returned to them by mid-morning, stumbling through a deep snow drift and pulling his stubborn horse which limped on its hind leg. When he got closer Elora saw that Bray had a deep gash down one cheek, and dried blood on the shoulder of his cloak. He raised a weary arm to show he was alright which didn't help the frustration building in her as she tried and failed to squeeze her horse passed the others to get to him.

"Mountain cat?" enquired Diagus, seeming uninterested in his injuries.

"Yeah," Bray said, pointing to the cut on his cheek which had begun to scab over. "A lone rider was too tempting, But the snow jubbs attacked the horse."

"We'd be leaving them soon enough anyway," replied the Shadojak, halting in front of his former Shaigun.

Elora took advantage of the stop and dismounted, flinging her reins at Otholo as she side stepped past the others to get to Bray. He let the reigns of his lame horse drop and the poor animal followed them to the ground. Exhaustion causing its head to drop as it sunk into the soft snow, steam rising from its back.

"That's not all," continued Bray. "Empire soldiers have crossed the river. At least half of the division are at the base of the mountain and making their way up."

Elora finally got to him and kissed his uninjured cheek before turning his face the other way to inspect the gash. The black scab was loose and fresh skin had already knitted beneath. That would be his elf genes quickening the healing process, no wonder Diagus paid his injuries no mind.

"We're almost two days ahead of them. They wouldn't reach us in time, would they?" she asked, not liking the look Bray gave her, which said it wasn't as easy as that.

"There's a hunting party not far behind us, an hour, maybe two. I caught sight of them from the pass. They've got a couple of hounds with them, crank bows and spears. They're travelling light to cover the ground."

"How many?" asked Diagus, scanning back the way they had come, the pearl in his eye socket as white as the snow.

"A platoon or more. Too many to fight," Bray slipped and arm around her. "All they needed to do is pin us down, hold us until the rest of the division caught up."

"Leave me here," growled Ragna, speaking each word between breaths. "I'll slow them some. Make you time to reach the pass."

Diagus raised a notched eyebrow, ready to accept the proposal, until Elora cut him off.

"You will do no such thing. If you stay, I stay. And I've not spent the last two days freezing my arse off for nothing."

Flakes of snow whirled about the Shadojak as he fixed her with an agitated expression. "We press on."

"And the Snow jubbs?" piped in Otholo

In one fluid motion, Diagus pulled his sword from its pouch and drove it into the skull of Bray's fallen horse. It may have been dead already for the lack of movement it made. The sound of metal scraping against bone grated above the wind as Diagus withdrew his sword. Then made a slash across its belly, spilling steaming guts into the open air and turning the snow scarlet.

"This should draw the little snow shits. The rest of you dismount, we're moving out on foot."

Elora watched blood drip from the horse's gaping wound, its large round eyes staring up at nothing. It had been alive only moments ago, breathing the same air as them, probably as tired, as cold and hungry. And most probably, on some horsey level, it dreamed of warm meadows with lush grass. Now it was dead.

Bray's arms tightened about her as he planted a kiss on the top of her head. "It was already dead, Elora. It died the moment a snow jubb cut its tendon," he said, stroking her hair.

"And the rest of them?" she asked, her voice no more than a whisper.

"They'll be glad to run back. Hopefully stamping down our quarry, or at least throw them off our scent."

They made red boot prints in the snow as they passed the dead horse, Diagus leading the way, sword in hand whilst Ejan and Bray shuffled along as best they could, burdened with supporting Ragna, a large arm thrown over each of their shoulders. Elora volunteered to take Ejan's place but the Norsewoman steadfastly refused. Instead she was entrusted to carry the Fist of the North, her chilled fingers locking about its shaft, the hammer's huge head resting over her shoulder and bouncing against her collar bone as she struggled on.

Jibba-jabba noises, echoed from the place they'd just left and as Elora glanced back she favoured her gaze sought out small furry men scurrying over the rocks and through the snow. They blended well with the white surroundings, giving the hint of black lips, pale blue eyes and thick pink tongues. A flash of steel amidst the flakes, teeth and faces turning red as they began to devour the horse flesh. Elora turned her face away, heaving the hammer into a more comfortable position, or one which was a little less painful, and pressed on.

The world near the peak of the mountain was a white one. Snow drifted heavy against the steep rock, it coated the sparse trees and covered the narrow ledge they trudged along. Icicles clung to the overhang above, frozen tears, sharp enough to skewer anything the mountain cared to cry for.

Elora, kept her eyes to the narrow ground, away from the icicles and away from the outer edge, the vertical drop which seemed to lure her when she glanced over, like a moth to a flame.

Both her shoulders burned with the fatigue of carrying Ragna's hammer, she used the pain to drive her forwards, to keep her going – its owner's pain groaning out in laboured breaths with each step. Yet they were still moving. Otholo now carrying the pack, taking turns with her uncle who was now gripping the lute in his aged hands. Diagus, marching out ahead of the group, at a trail blazer's pace in his haste to reach the pass; sporadically halting as he waited for them to catch up. Each time muttering under his breath, whilst fixing them with an expression that said he would like nothing more than to throw each of them from the ledge and watch them tumble out into the white sky.

Then she heard a strange sound above the haunting whispers of the wind. Unclear at first but as it came again her heart struck hard against her chest.

"Hounds," shouted Bray. "They've caught us up."

Diagus rushed to the back of the group, sword already out as he scanned the way they had come.

"Run," he shouted. "The pass isn't far. We can't let them get ahead of us."

Otholo didn't need telling twice as he stumbled in his haste to get away. Elora watched the panic in Ejan's eyes as she realised that Ragna could no more run than lift the mountain. Instead she lowered her husband to the rock wall and unslung her bow.

"Run, I said!" screamed Diagus, but Ejan was having none of it.

"I'll not leave him," she promised, setting an arrow to the string, her countenance cooling to that cold sharpshooter.

"Nor me," said Elora, as she stood by her, ready to drop the great hammer and retrieve her sword.

Men's voices then came on the heels of the baying hounds. Shouting encouragement as they closed in on their prey. The words indecipherable but infused with excitement as armour rattled and heavy boots crushed the snow.

"I'm sorry, Ragna," said Bray, as he gripped the Viking's wrist and bent down to feed his arm through the great man's legs before hoisting him bodily into a fireman's lift. The smooth swiftness with which Bray moved gave little chance for Ragna to protest, instead swallowing the pain as he let himself be carried off at a run, chasing after Otholo.

Elora shifted the hammer once again and followed, her uncle doing the same and finding it a struggle to match the heroic speed of her boyfriend.

The path began to climb at a ridiculously steep angle, twisting around a sudden bend and becoming so narrow that the space between rockface and ledge was less than two feet. Bray showed no signs of slowing as he sprinted up the icy track, momentarily disappearing from view. Elora slowed to allow Nat in front of her, the path only manageable in single-file, keeping her eyes focused on her uncle's back as he ascended the bend and not on the sheer empty drop. If the shouts from Diagus and the sounds of the baying hounds were not at her heels she would have felt better progressing up this treacherous section on hands and knees instead of an all-out sprint; the Fist making her top-heavy and threatening to throw her, unbalanced, from the mountain.

Elora's calves and thighs burned as the path flattened out, yet becoming no less narrow. Before them she could see it wind along the rock face, flowing along its contours until it met an old wooden rope bridge that reached across an abyss.

Thick anchor posts, covered in ancient ice, stood taller and wider than Otholo. Large statues, now hidden beneath snow and icicles, were carved into the old wood. The weather had long ago eroded their faces to noiseless ovals, eyes no deeper than thumb prints yet Elora caught the outline of crowns above and the curving of wings sprouting from their backs – angels, maybe?

The bridge itself reached across an immense gap between this rock face and the next which jutted out from the mountain some hundred feet further away. The snow-laced ropes sagged, dipping incredibly low as it swayed above the void. The planks of wood, maybe half her body length in size, were bound tightly together, although in more than one place she noticed gaps; one of them where three planks had rotten through and leaving a hole she wasn't sure she could cross.

Otholo paused long enough to catch his breath before plunging on, a hand on each rope, which creaked and groaned with the sudden movement. Elora found him to be brave for going over, but realised that he was caught between trusting the reliability of the bridge over the honour of the pursuing soldiers not to kill him.

Bray set Ragna down against one of the posts, his face gone waxy, his features pulled back in pain as he gripped his side. Ejan went to him and breathlessly knelt before his wound but he slapped her probing hands away, shaking his head.

Bray joined Elora and lifted the hammer from her shoulder. The sudden lack of weight made her feel light as a feather, as if she needn't use the bridge at all and could simply float across.

"You're next," he instructed, pointing his sword after the bard. "Go, they'll be on us any minute."

The hounds were yapping loudly now, the men's shouts echoing around the rocks as they rounded the bend. Polished helmets appearing as they scurried up the rise.

"Too late," she said, drawing her sword.

Ejan loosed an arrow which ricocheted off a helmet, making a pinging sound before burying into the face of the soldier behind. He reeled back, blood pumping from the shaft that had imbedded through both cheek and neck.

The rest of the hunting party halted, kneeling low and used the slope as a shield. The leader advanced a step, squeezing to the front where the track was only wide enough to accommodate himself, but still lay hidden, only the top of his sweat-filmed brow visible below the helmet.

"Lay down your arms," he shouted, after quieting the dogs. "You're out numbered and if you try to cross the pass we'll cut the ropes and see how well you fly. You won't make it to the other side. Lay them down now and you'll be treated fairly."

Diagus stepped forwards. "Do you know who I am, soldier?" he growled.

"I do, sir. You're the Pearly White. I dare say you'll take a good few of my men down, but Shadojak or no, I have my orders. And now you've killed one of our own – my men will be more ready to fight." He lifted his head, seeming more confident after saying his piece, a condescending smile curling his lips. "Or you can wait until the main body arrive, they're only a couple of hours behind."

"I'll hand myself in," Elora said, feeling that if she went willingly the soldiers would be less inclined to hurt them.

"No," snapped Diagus. "We have precious little time as it is. The longer we delay, and if we end up in the hands of that idiot, Debree, it will be a long delay, then Solarius gathers strength and more will die."

"But we can't fight them, there's too many and we can't cross the bridge because they'll cut the ropes before we make it to the other side," she argued, not seeing any way out of it. "Unless

… " Elora didn't believe she was even contemplating her next actions, yet she saw no other choice. "Unless I become my father's daughter. Just long enough to … "

"No," said Diagus. "You're as likely to kill us if you become that hell cat. And more than likely burn the bridge down. I saw what you did to the trees at Rams Keep." He studied her face, then observed the group. "You will make a run for it, while I hold them back."

"They'll kill you," argued Elora, gazing to the men at the slope, steel in hand and a violent hunger in their eyes.

Diagus nodded. "I expect so. But I only need to hold them off the bridge until you reach the other side."

"No. Don't you dare," snarled Ragna, pushing himself up from the post he was leaning against. "This is my time," he spluttered through gritted teeth. "My time." Ejan opened her mouth to protest but he silenced her with a glare. "I'm already dead, you know that. Nobody gets stuck in the guts and lives. It was a folly dragging my five-bellies up this frozen rock in the first place. No wonder it took us so long to get here." His bloodshot eyes glared at the Shadojak. "Tell them, Diagus, make them see sense."

"You're not strong enough, Ragna. But if you want to go down fighting then you're welcome to stand with me. We'll go down together."

"If you're staying, Raggy, then so shall I," said Ejan, tears beginning to track down her face.

"No," said Elora, her voice sounding as weak as her legs felt. "Nobody should die."

"I'll be the only one staying," said Ragna, suddenly standing up taller, more sure. "I'm already dead, my fate is sealed. And I want to die with steel in my hand and fire in my blood."

Elora watched Ejan thump the post next to her husband with enough force to shake snow from the top. Ragna pulled her into an embrace and kissed the top of her head. "Don't weep any for me, my love. Tonight I'll be dining in the halls of Valhalla, at Odin's side."

Ejan wrapped her arms around her husband and rested her head against his chest. "You'd better not be wenching in Valhalla."

Ragna laughed, which turned in to a fit of coughs, spittles of blood clinging to his beard. "You're my only wench."

Bray then clasped forearms with the Viking, handing him his hammer. "Black Ragna? Ragna of the red path? Your name is as worthy as your father's or grandfather's."

Ragna handed him the hammer back. "This is Jaygen's now. Can't see how you're going to get it back once you've crossed. Besides." He stroked his wife's hair through his fingers. "I prefer the colour blonde over any other."

Elora went to him next, hugging him tight, tears now freely running down her face. "I'm sorry," she said, resigned to the fact that he was about to die and would never see him again.

"I won't hear it," he said, hugging her back. "Truth be told I should have been dead years ago. Men like me always die young. It's a wonder I've lived long enough to let my belly swell."

There was nothing she could say to that but mouthed the words 'thank you', her tears choked the sounds out but Ragna nodded his understanding. Bray then took her in his arms and led her to the bridge.

"You lot decided what you're about yet?" shouted the leader of the hunting party. "Only my toes are feeling a tad cold."

"My shield," said Ragna, taking a staggering step forwards, scowling at the soldiers. Nat lifted the heavy round shield onto the Viking's arm and Diagus placed a sword in his hand. "This is it then. Better get your arses across the bridge, eh?"

"Wait," said Ejan, placing her hand on his arm. She took a knife from her belt, tipped her head forwards and grasping her braided plait, cut through it. "You will take this with you into the next life. A piece of me so you won't forget."

Ragna took the braid and wrapped it about his shield arm. "I'll never forget you, my love. My dear sweet love." He smiled warmly at her as she cut three strands from his beard. Affection for his wife running from his eyes as he gazed upon her for the last time.

Giving her a final kiss, he ushered them towards the bridge. "Run!"

"Run!" Ragna shouted, blinking the tears away that blurred his vision. Ejan gave him a final glance over her shoulder, mouthing the words 'I love you', as she chased the others across the bridge. "Love you too," he whispered. "More than you'll ever know". But the words caught in his dry throat, choked with tears and strangled by the pain from his wound. He used the pain to fire his blood as he turned to face the Imperial soldiers.

Stretching his neck to the left then the right he lumbered up, swinging his sword arm and tightening his grip on the shield, stroking his thumb along his wife's golden hair that she had wrapped around his forearm.

The soldiers finally moved into action, the leader having realised what their intentions were.

"Charge!" he shouted, spittle leaving his mouth as he pointed his sword towards Ragna. "Cut the bloody ropes, let them fall."

"Come and get some, bastards," screamed Ragna, setting his legs apart and leaning into his shield, feeling the excitement buzz through his body.

The faces on the first two men were unsure, young, maybe inexperienced, yet they ran at him screaming, with their spears raised.

Ragna ducked left, bringing his shield across his body and deflecting the spear on his right – knocking the shorter of the pair against the rock then swinging his shield back, caught the second man against his side, knocking him clear off the ledge.

His death screams echoed from the empty sky beneath as the shorter man regained balance in time to catch Ragna's sword with his face. His lifeless body hit the floor as his partner's scream was cut short by a rocky impact.

Born more out of reflex than thought, Ragna brought his shield about and caught a bolt from a crank bow, the force knocking him back a step. He hated crank bows. The bowman sneered at him as he began to wind the crank, ready to place another bolt.

"Shit!" hissed Ragna, as something hissed past his ear.

An arrow hit the crank bowman in his throat. One of Ejan's. "May Odin grin down on you, my love." He risked a quick glance at his friends on the bridge. They were not even a quarter of the way across the rickety structure.

Ragna switched his attention back to the oncoming soldiers, the crank bowman finally realising that his life had ended, collapsed to the ground, fingers leaking blood as they pressed about his Ejan's arrow; his eyes bulging with disbelief. That's the thing about death; people believe it won't happen to them – that for some reason they were special, that it was always somebody else that got stuck, chopped, thrown from a cliff or pinned to a tree with an arrow in the neck.

Another soldier came on, face peeled back in a snarl, white foam caught in the corners of his pale lips. His body collided with Ragna's shield, his sword reaching over the rim, searching out flesh to slash, to pierce, to gouge.

Ragna snarled back, the shield pressing against his old wound and sending a fresh wave of pain through his body. He lifted the empire man off his feet and rammed his blade against his stomach, feeling the point slide against armour before finding the gap between the buckles. The sword pushed in deep and the soldier's snarl turned to a scream, his eyes going large and round. Ragna shoved him off his shield and pulled his sword back out, letting the body fall next to his comrade on the ground, curling up and whimpering between curses while his body leaked blood.

Within a moment, another filled the gap before him, armour turning white with the glare from the snow as the next victim stepped up to meet his death.

In his youth, Ragna had been huge. A man grown early because of his size, his muscle and strength. He was a lot less slim now, the muscle going to fat over the soft years spent at the keep, but he still had his bulk, dwarfing all of these southern softies.

A spear thrust into the space where his head had been the second before. Ragna slashed it away with his sword and sent the spear over the edge, its owner crashing into him and knocking him against the rock wall.

Ragna shoved him back with his shield, thrusting it into his chest, pushing him away so he had space to bring his sword down, but pain ruptured in his wrist and he was vaguely aware of something metal spinning away at the corner of his vision. His arm abruptly stopped its downwards arc, now lacking his sword and instead gaining a bolt that stuck right through his forearm; sticking out, top and bottom, in equal parts, blood already gushing down his fingers.

"Arrrgh!" he screamed, rage driven into the man before him. Striking him in the face with the rim of his shield, the iron band cutting his jaw open. He smashed it again and again, cracking bone and knocking out teeth.

As the limp body fell another sprung forward, cutting down with his sword, imperial steel chipping chunks from the aged wood. Ragna caught the blows but suddenly lost control of his left leg. Glancing down he saw another bolt sticking out from his thigh, a dark stain spreading from the wound. The strength left him and he fell to one knee, his arm still held aloft, shaking with the effort to hold against the rain of blows.

When the rush of footsteps charged towards him, he knew his time was up. This was the end.

With a final breath he mustered the last of his strength and before his body failed him, his fingers curled about a fallen sword, not caring whether it was his or not, he held tight and growled from the pit of his stomach.

Ragna used the orchestra of pain been played against his body, the wound in his belly, the bolt in his arm, in his leg – the pain of leaving Ejan behind, of never seeing Jaygen again, of everything he should have done, of everything he should have said. He closed his eyes and let his shield drop, but still held tight to his wife's hair, gripping it between thumb and forefinger. He would die with her in his mind, Ejan and Jaygen both and of happier times.

Bringing his left arm to join his right he held the sword and dragged himself standing – shaking with fatigue, with effort, with pain.

Ragna raised the blade high above his head and opened his eyes onto the charging death. With his final breath, he screamed from his spent body as he brought the sword crashing down.

"Oodiiiin!"

23

Aslania

Ragna's final war cry echoed through mountains, bouncing off the Gods' Peaks as Elora's feet thumped down against rock. Her legs buckled at the sudden change from bouncing wood to solid ground. Bray placed an arm around her waist and kept her upright before pulling her behind a large boulder. She was soon joined by her uncle and Otholo.

Ejan was the last off the bridge, dragging her husband's hammer behind her, sparks flying from the head as it scraped against rock. Her own head was hung low, hiding her face as she turned to gaze back across the bridge, seeking out the body of her fallen husband.

"Ejan, get behind the boulder. We need to cut the ropes," said Diagus, ushering her with an arm. The Norsewoman paid him no heed, instead remaining where she was, standing at the posts, Fist of the North held slackly in one hand.

"Ejan," hissed Diagus, more urgently, "They're coming."

From the other side of the void, Elora could see the soldiers stumbling onto the bridge in a race to reach them.

"Let them come" replied Ejan, calmly. Her new shorter hair making her seem like a different person.

Elora stared past her and watched as the soldiers were halfway across the bridge. Perhaps a dozen in all, running as quickly as armoured men could, on a swaying structure that jostled with every step. But coming they were and bringing a lot of steel. At the other side, where she could just make out Ragna's body, laying amongst the men he had slain, came others. A bedraggled line of soldiers that curled back down the mountain side, out of sight. The numbers could be endless, too many to count, too many to fight.

"Ejan, we need to cut the ropes." Bray spoke smoothly, placing a reassuring hand on her arm, but the Viking was having none of it. She shook his hand off and raised her head, focusing on the men stalking closer. One woman against an army.

Elora saw the grief on her face, the tears in her eyes, the tension in her shoulders. Ejan was a loose cannon, hell bent on avenging her husband's death.

"Let them come," she repeated.

The soldiers were closer now. Close enough to see their clenched teeth, to see them pull swords from scabbards, to bring about spears, ready to charge. Elora thought that Bray would need to drag the grief stricken woman back, when the Viking slowly took a step away from the bridge and heaved the hammer onto her shoulders – eyes focusing on the threat. A wicked smile formed on her lips.

Elora watched as she slowly turned away, showing her back to the soldiers and wondered what she was doing but soon realised her intentions. Ejan kept turning, beginning to spin on the spot, lowering her late husband's weapon and having to lean back to compensate for its weight. Three times she spun, picking up speed and momentum, the Fist levelling out like an extension of her arms. As she finished her last rotation she dropped to her knees. The hammer, continued its cycle and struck the anchor post with a thunderous clap that admonished all other sounds as the world seemed to halt.

Nothing happened for several heartbeats, until the silence was replaced with a deep groan as the post Ejan had struck began to topple. Almost lazily at first, yet the sheer size and weight made it continue its path out into the void.

Soldiers shouted and attempted to scramble back, the pursuit now forgotten as they struggled to get passed one another to reach the safety of solid ground. But when the post suddenly came away the bridge jerked and more than half the men tumbled off, screaming as arms futilely sort for something to grasp. Elora closed her eyes, the sight of men dying to much to bear, yet she couldn't block their screams that only death silenced.

When she reopened them she saw that a few of the men that had held fast to the bridge had clambered back to safety on the other side and only one that had been almost upon them was now dangling from the rope – spitting distance away.

"Help him," said Elora, rushing to Ejan's side. But she could tell by the anguished look on the Viking's face that help was the last thing on her mind.

There was another groan, followed by a splintering crack and the last anchor post, now unable to hold the bridge, began to slowly fall.

"Help me. Please," yelled the man as he shakily began to work his way along the rope, yet Elora knew the distance was too great to cover as the post sank lower still.

"The blood that's on your hands, that's clinging to your cloak," said Ejan, coldly as she stepped up to the falling post and placed her boot against it. "Is my husband's." She gave her boot a push and the post fell away with a snap.

"No!" Elora shouted, closing her eyes once again, but not before seeing the image of the helpless soldier, his hand clawing at air, his face screwed up in terror as he plummeted.

The crash of the bridge hitting the rock face on the other side of the void, drowned out the man's screams as it broke to a thousand pieces – as he, most likely broke to pieces. Elora felt cold, and not because of the weather.

Bray must have sensed her unease and stooped down to pick her up.

"We need to keep moving" Diagus said. He eyed Ejan for a moment before turning on them and walking away.

"You alright?" whispered, Bray. Giving her a hug before setting her down.

She nodded, although felt numb as the images of the previous moments, flashed across her mind. Numb at the realisation of losing Ragna. A friend that gave his life for her cause. She spared a glance to Ejan, who stared across the emptiness, seeking out her late husband's body.

"Ejan," she began, feeling tears prickle at her eyes once again. "I'm so sorry."

"It's done now. Can't be undone, can it?" the Viking replied, her voice dry. Then raised a hand to her lips, kissed them and saluted her husband. After staring across the void for a moment she turned, hefted the hammer onto her shoulders and set off after the Shadojak.

She paused beside Otholo. "You will sing him a song, the likes of which have never been heard before."

Otholo, smiled sadly. "I'll create a ballad that will reach him in Valhalla."

Elora and Bray followed, he offered to carry the hammer for Ejan but she refused. The Fist was her burden now, until she placed it Jaygen's hands.

After that they left her alone, letting her grieve as the group, now one short, trudged down a narrow path that wound around the mountain, steadily leading them lower.

By nightfall they had descended beyond the cold reach of the snow and had once again the cover of trees. Diagus halted the group by a mountain stream, where they rested until daybreak. Elora didn't think that any of them slept that night, although their bodies must have been drained, she knew hers was. She lay in Bray's arms, folded snuggly in his embrace, feeling immense guilt as she watched Ejan lay against a tree, her head down and arms wrapped about the hammer. Not moving until Diagus passed water around and harassed them into motion.

The sun had barely risen when Nat halted the group near a rocky outcrop surrounded by trees. His eyes were fixed on Elora when he spoke.

"This is as far as I go. Aslania is less than two hours away and if I'm recognised then my sister may realise who Elora really is."

Elora's heart sank. She was about to protest when he placed a finger against her lips.

"The mission will fail if she finds out who you are, Elora. Remember what I told you back on the *Molly* ?"

"But you can explain things to her, Nat. Tell her that my voice will strengthen the bonds that hold Solarius."

"No, I can't. This plan will only work if she believes you're Otholo's sister. It's the only way she would allow you to perform the Eversong in the church. Even if she did believe us, she wouldn't allow it until she had proof. And how do we acquire that?"

"He's right," offered Otholo. "They're a headstrong race, Minuans. Stuck in their ways and traditions. Eversong has been sung for thousands of years – never stopping, never faltering. They wouldn't allow you to do it. Not without council over council and meeting over meeting, by which time your father will have broken his bonds and be released on both worlds. They'd regret not acting then, but regrets are not worth frog snot."

Elora hugged her uncle tight, wrapping her arms around his frail old frame. "What will you do?"

Nat held her at arm's length, smiling warmly. "This is my land, my home. I'll be quite comfortable waiting here until afterwards. It'll only be for a few days, maybe sooner, then when you can come back for me we'll break the news to your mother, Athena. Besides, I'll have Ejan for company."

"You will?" asked Ejan. "And why am I not seeing this mission through to its bitter end?"

"Because a Viking entering the city would be hard to explain. Otholo and his sister, chaperoned by the Shadojak and his Shaigun would be a strange enough story to swallow, but add a Viking to the tale and you may find entering Aslania a longer process than you want." Nat shrugged, "I may be wrong, you might be able to waltz in easily enough, but can you afford to take that risk?"

Ejan made a shrug of her own. "I'll stay. But I dare say my company will be a quiet one."

"Understandable," said Nat, unable to hide the pity in his smile.

"Two hours," announced Diagus. "We could be there by this afternoon."

Elora tried to sound reassuring, but fell some way short when she told her uncle she would see him again in a couple of days. She didn't know what to say to Ejan. What could she say, no words would bring Ragna back? Instead she wrapped her arms about the Norsewoman's waist and hugged her. It wasn't much, she knew, yet Ejan hugged her back and kissed her softly on the forehead.

The others said their farewells and they set off once again, the group now reduced to four and seeming, to Elora, somewhat more morose for it.

"You're probably best to remain silent," said Otholo after about an hour of hiking. "That tinker's tongue charm allows you to understand what's being spoken but doesn't allow you to speak it. If you talk it will be in your own language and will only confuse them."

"But what should I do? I can't just remain silent," asked Elora, beginning to feel anxious at what was to come.

"Remaining silent is the best thing you can do. If they ask, I will tell them that you are saving your voice for the song. It is known that girls who are about to perform the Eversong for the first time hold their energies in, saving their voices by withholding from even speaking for days, sometimes weeks, prior to singing. When we get there let me do the talking."

Elora was sure she could refrain from speaking, that was easy enough. "But what if they don't believe that I'm your sister. Wouldn't somebody know what she looks like?"

"I doubt it. She left Aslania with me, when she was a toddler. And like any other Minuan she had blonde hair and blue eyes. Like you have. By the way, now might be a good time to put your contact lenses in."

"Where's your sister now?" asked Elora as she fumbled in her pocket for the contacts.

Otholo shrugged. "Last I heard, and that was a fair few years ago, she had settled down in Southern Paquees. Singing for the theatre and for the Duke and Duchess of that country's capital. She may still be there or may have moved on."

Shortly after her conversation with Otholo the track they had been following opened out into a wide valley, becoming a path that led to stone steps that crept alongside a fast flowing stream. The steps became a cobbled path as they ascended the valley where it levelled off onto a grassy plateau. A heard of goats grazed about the flat ground, shaggy grey coats wafting in the breeze. A young man dressed in woolen britches and tunic eyed them warily as they walked by, long blonde hair billowing out behind him, matching the goats he shepherded. Otholo waved out to him as they passed, but the shepherd kept his hand firmly gripped upon his crook, a hostile look dressing his features.

"Are all Minuans as friendly?" asked Bray, sarcastically.

Otholo chuckled. "They don't take kindly to strangers, but once they've warmed to you they're as friendly as any race."

They passed more goats and more shepherds as the path led them in a gentle sweep around the mountain. Elora's legs ached from the hard work they had performed in the last few days and so as the path began to take an upwards turn, her muscles burned with fatigue. As they passed a large stone outcrop they came upon a huge arch, carved out of the sheer rock face. The path leading them to the solid structure, rising up steps to its base where soldiers dressed in silver armour stood to attention; tall spears with blades shaped like leaves, sparkled in the sunlight as they marched towards them.

"Well met," said Otholo, rising an arm in greeting whilst offering them a bow. "I am Otholo the bard. Come home to rejoice in Aslania and to bring my sister Othecna to sing the Eversong."

The guards surveyed them as warily as the shepherds. "Who are these men?" asked the taller, gruffly.

Diagus stepped forwards. "I'm the Shadojak. This is my Shaigun." He indicated to Bray with a nod. "We've come a long way to ensure that Otheena reaches Aslania. It is imperative that she sings in the church of Minu."

The guard scowled, regarding Elora for a moment as he signaled for another guard to come forward. "Bring me a representative of the church, I don't like the look of these men." The guard nodded and hurried away. In a short while he returned with a middle-aged woman dressed in a white and gold gown that flowed to the ground. She was more handsome than pretty, with high cheek bones, the first signs of grey appearing in her blonde hair. She examined them, cool blue eyes looking into each of theirs before settling on Otholo, her brow lifting in recognition.

"Otholo, you've returned," she exclaimed, her stern face becoming bright, decorated with a warm smile.

"I have, Songstress. And you remember my sister, Otheena?" He put an arm about Elora's shoulder, gesturing for her to step forward.

Elora did so, feeling the weight of the woman's stare once again. Did her mother look like this? Could she even be her mother? She was the right age. Maybe not, she didn't feel that she was, surely she would recognise her if she saw her. But Elora couldn't put the thought out of her mind. Was she to judge every middle-aged woman in Aslania as such?

"Why so quiet, child, surely the sister of Otholo would not be shy?"

"Forgive her, Songstress," said Otholo. "For she is resting her voice, she hasn't uttered a word in days, fearing that it will weaken her performance of the Eversong."

The Songstress shook her head. "She does know it may take months before she is ready to sing in the church. Maybe more if she fails the trials."

"She is more than ready, Songstress. If you were but to hear her sing, she would prove to you her quality and you would put her in sooner."

The Songstress gave her another quizzical look. "Well, we shall see. It's rare for someone so young to sing in the church, especially an outsider, but not unheard of. You're welcome in our city."

Her gaze fell on Daigus and Bray. "But these two are not. Please thank them for delivering you through what must have been a hardship and send them on their way. They may wait here for food and drink, but cannot remain and will not pass the city gate."

"What is she saying?" asked Diagus, eyeing the woman suspiciously. Elora wondered why he hadn't heard her himself, but then she realised. The woman was speaking Minuan and neither Diagus or Bray could understand. It was only possible that she could through the tinker's tongue charm.

"Songstress. It is the Shadojak's wish to see my sister perform. He has … "

"Impossible. It is precisely because he's a Shadojak that he cannot enter. Please relay to them what I've already told you."

Otholo shook his head before turning to Diagus. "She won't let you enter."

Diagus folded his arms, his notched eyebrows met together forming a scowl. "Does she know who I am?"

"Yes," replied the Songstress.

"So you do speak the common tongue," growled Diagus. "Why do you forbid the entrance of the Shadojak. Does Aslania not fall under the Empire?"

"It does, but no Shadojak has ever set foot on our lands. There are reasons, none which I can explain to you now but good enough reasons to keep you out." She nodded to the guard who came forwards, their knuckles turning white upon their spears.

Being that there were only three of them Elora guessed that the Songstress had no idea of the potential, Diagus or Bray had in combat.

"Come now, Otholo and Otheena. Say goodbye to your companions and follow me," she turned and began to walk back through the gate when Daigus called her back.

"Does the entire city know that Solarius lives?" he spat. "Or have you been feeding them shit? Letting your bloody song of bonds weaken generation by generation until it is so piss-weak that the God of Chaos breaks free and wreaks havoc on the world. Tell me true, Songstress. Do you hope he'll remain under the mountain for a couple more generations? Just another hundred years. Hoping that maybe Minu will return to strengthen this bond?"

Elora watched the exchange, watched the woman stare open-mouthed either with disbelief at being spoken to in such a way, or with the realisation that the secret was out.

"Well, let me tell you about hope, Songstress. It isn't worth crap where gods are involved. Solarius will break his bonds very soon. He's already destroyed the magic on Earth and has manoeuvred his minions into position."

The Songstress closed her open mouth, her fingers fidgeting together; a vein pulsing against her temple. Yet still she remained silent.

"I don't understand how it works, but trust me. This girl here," he continued, pointing a shaky finger at Elora. "Is the key to rebuilding the bond. She's what's between Solarius and the worlds. Oh, and incidentally, the empire is on your doorstep. We left them at the pass with a broken bridge, but it won't take them long to build another."

The woman's eyes opened wide, she placed a hand against her chest and took a step back.

"They're here for Solarius," said Bray.

"They know not what they meddle with. They'd set him loose in an attempt to kill him." She squeezed the bridge of her nose and stared hard at Elora. "Come with me, all of you. This changes everything. Wait, you can leave your weapons here with the guard. There is no need for weapons in Aslania."

"I don't have any weapons, as you can see," said the Shadojak, opening his arms and turning slowly. "We're on a peace-keeping mission, can't very well keep the peace using violence. Bray?"

Bray imitated Diagus. "No, I'm unarmed."

The Songstress appeared unconvinced. "Search them," she ordered. They didn't find any weapons on the Shadojak or Bray as their swords were hidden in their smuggler's pouch, as was Elora's. However, while patting down Otholo they found a small knife tucked in his boot, the guard holding the small blade up for all to see.

"Tut, tut, tut. I'm shocked," said Diagus, a grin curling his lips. Elora needed to bite the inside of her cheek to stop herself from laughing.

Otholo, shrugged. "A friend once told me; you can never have enough blades."

"You can have it back when you leave," said the Songstress. "Now, follow on. We need to seek council with the Sisters Devine."

Elora followed the Songstress, her white and gold gown flowing around her as she strode through the gates, momentarily bathed in shadow as they passed through the huge rock, before stepping out into sunshine once again. The huge gate was a thick wall of granite that was part of the mountain itself. Once through, the guards closed the enormous doors, needing all three of them to push them together before sliding thick steel bars into place.

The cobbled path they followed led alongside the mountain. a sheer drop once again to the right of them and Elora fought the urge to take Bray's hand. Somehow he felt her worry and stepped between her and the drop, his fingertips gently brushing against hers.

As they came around the corner the path gave way to stone steps, leading down into a small city. Three mountain peaks, taller than the one they were on, were so close together they formed a huge bowl between them. At the bowl's centre was a lake, its waters icy blue, fed from several streams that ran from the snow caps. Slate roof tops, pointed like witches' hats, peppered the bowl and surrounded the lake – smoke trailing from many chimneys, the dwellings themselves were squat and round and made from the mountain granite.

On top of the tallest mountain were the spires of a church, the rest of the building carved into the peak itself with six thickly cut pillars supporting its base – richly carved with sweeping patterns that matched the slope of the mountain. Steps which were also carved from the rock, spiraled down from the church, meeting a central path that wound through the city to a large dome-shaped building, surrounded by lush grass and magnolia trees.

"It's beautiful," remarked Elora. Then clamped a hand to her mouth as she realised she had spoken in English.

"What was that?" asked the woman, descending the steps.

"As beautiful as I remember," offered Otholo, as he himself seemed breathless, his eyes eating up the city below.

"Yes, yes," agreed the Songstress, "It's strange that you forget to appreciate its beauty once you've been here a while. There are subtle differences since you were last here," she said, pointing to a stone aqueduct that ran from the lake to the higher dwelling on the far side. "It took the elemental manipulators years to complete, but now every home has running water.

Nat would have loved that, mused Elora, still soaking up the scenery.

They were led up further steps, along stone passageways between tall round houses; over wooden hump back bridges that lay across streams, before going down more steps. They wound around small courtyards with water fountains at the centre and beautiful trees and plants of all colours growing from pots and gardens along the path.

Faces appeared at leaded windows, the laughter of children carried on the breeze and the voices of adults came to them as they passed through the town. Everyone they met on the way, nodded respectively to the Songstress, a couple may have recognised Otholo for his name was whispered more than once and they all smiled on seeing them. Elora smiled back, feeling almost at home amongst them – well it was her home. This is where she was brought into the world.

They arrived at the large dome, the only building made from wood. The Songstress led them inside and asked them to remain there while she sent for the Sisters Devine.

The building was a kind of arena or amphitheatre. Benches surrounding the room, starting higher around the circular wall and dropping lower as it neared the middle which descended below ground level so the entire room appeared spherical in shape. A raised dais was at its centre, upon which was a font, a crystal ball floating on the water.

Two of the guards remained with them so they were not free to speak to one another without inviting suspicion, especially since sound seemed to amplify in this room. It was not long before the Songstress returned with three elderly women.

"Rise for the Sisters Devine," ordered the woman.

Elora stood up, much to the detriment of her aching legs and sore feet. The moment's sit-down probably did more harm than good.

"My godly sisters, this is Otholo, formally a resident here, as was his sister, Otheena. With them is the Shadojak and his Shaigun." Then the Songstress spoke to Otholo. "These here are the sisters Bethony, Freya and Yolith."

The three woman nodded respectfully before approaching. "Please be seated," said the closer of the three, Freya.

"Miathlin tells us that you are aware of a certain problem that has presented itself over the last few years, yes?"

"A certain problem, sister?" said Otholo. "That's an under-statement. But yes, we are aware, as is the Empire. I have with me the Shadojak and his Shaigun. They also know the 'problem', and have aided me in bringing you the solution to that problem." He placed an arm on Elora's shoulder. "This is my sister Otheena, and her voice is something special."

Elora felt the full stare of the sisters, looking her up and down. Freya beckoned her closer with a bony hand. She felt another blister give on the side of her foot as she stood again, the fluid causing a stickiness between her toes.

The three sisters gathered around her, lifting her hair and pulling it this way and that. Bethony placing cold fingers against her chin and lifted her head up and moved it to the side, then the other – whilst making humphing sounds through cracked lips.

"Do you have any birthmarks or blemishes on your skin?" asked Yolith, her fingers turning over Elora's bare arms as she inspected her. Elora shook her head.

"Her hair is without flaw, her skin pure and those eyes are the truest blue of any Minuan sky," said Freya. "She could be Minu, reborn. Why haven't we seen this child before now?"

"Sister, Freya. After I was excommunicated from Aslania," said Otholo, narrowing his eyes at the three old women. "My parents left soon after. Otheena was barely even walking then."

"Don't sound so pithy, Otholo. You know the Minuan way, our traditions," replied Yolith. Pointing to his mismatch eyes. "And I believe you have a dark lock to your hair."

He does, thought Elora. But my eyes are violet and my hair darker than the night.

"And do you sing as pretty as you look?" asked Bethony. "Come child, let us hear that voice. It is that, that truly counts."

Elora cleared her throat, preparing herself to sing when Freya stopped her with a hand. "Sing beside the font, Otheena. Miathlin, will you demonstrate what she is to do. The first verse will suffice."

Miathlin made her way to the font and placed her hands to either side of the stone rim, then staring at the crystal sphere she began to sing.

Elora couldn't help but smile at hearing the familiar words. The Songstress sung it so beautifully, her voice travelling around the entire dome and echoing back on itself. When the words passed over her she could feel it, like it was something more than sound; as gentle as a sigh that caressed in soft waves.

As it passed the font it caused the water to ripple. A ring of tiny waves flowing towards the centre, causing the crystal ball to turn ever so slightly. A second wave, following the first in succession with the beat of the song, made it turn a little further. By the time Miathlin reached the second line the crystal ball was spinning over and over and began to glow from within. Amber light reflected from the font, portraying the ripple along the Songstress's face, growing brighter until it cast the shadow of the singing woman against the domed ceiling.

When the verse came to an end, Miathlin released her fingers from the font and took a step away, the light from the globe dulling until it was no more and the water became still.

It was the most magnificent voice Elora had ever heard. She doubted her voice would come close to being half as wonderful.

"Thank you Miathlin. Now, Otheena, please step up to the font and try to make the crystal glow," said Freya, who seemed to Elora to be the elder of the sisters and the one taking charge.

Elora wandered between the benches until she was at the font, the globe appeared bigger now she was close up – almost the size of a football. She cleared her throat once again and began the first word.

"No, child. Place your hands on the font, like Miathlin did. But don't be disappointed if you can't make the sphere glow. That only comes with years of experience and Miathlin is one of our stronger sisters." This from Bethony. Elora did as she was told, feeling the cold stone against her fingers as she once again began the song.

Her mouth formed the words, her voice sounding flat as she groped to even find the right key. She glanced at the Sisters Devine, who stared at her solemnly, clearly unimpressed. Yet as her vocal chords warmed to the task, her voice settled into the words, which were still foreign to her even though she was wearing the tinker's tongue.

Nothing happened although her voice echoed back, much like Miathlin's did and the water remained still. She heard one of the sisters mumble to another and Otholo tipped his head to the side, nodding encouragingly. This wasn't working, all this way for nothing. All that pain, all the struggle and Ragna – poor Ragna and Ejan. She felt anger at the thought of the Viking's death and with it came another feeling. The strange fizzing heat that rose from the pit of her stomach, the static energy that had infused her when she sang at Gloucester Cathedral.

The energy seemed to spread throughout the room, first pushing out to the back walls and sweeping along the ceiling and between the benches, then passing through her friends and the sisters, their faces suddenly changing with the effect. When her voice echoed back she felt the hairs on her arms rise, the words felt alive, real enough to touch. Electric.

The water in the font rippled, beating waves working inwards towards the crystal and as they touched it began to turn. It was spinning soon after and began to glow. Warm amber light radiating from within the sphere, illuminating the entire dome. The reflection from the water cast strange moving shadows around them, like spectral angels floating in the air.

Elora sang on, feeling the energy penetrate her skin, sensing the phenomena reach through her heart, beating with her pulse and breathing with each breath. She felt euphoric, the sensation passing from her to the song, caressing the sphere and lifting it from the water, the light growing piercingly bright as it spun faster than her eyes could follow.

When the verse came to an end, she struggled to hold back the words of the next verse, the song wanting to carry on, yet she kept her resolve as Freya only wanted to hear the first. She released her hands from the font and the sphere suddenly dimmed and dropped to the water making a galumph sound and splashing water onto her in the process.

When her eyes adjusted from the bright light she saw that the sisters were staring at her with excited expressions, tears were even running unchecked down Freya's aged cheeks. Otholo's mouth was wide open, imitating a cod and Bray was wearing a wide grin. Diagus was the only person in the room whose face remained unchanged.

"Was that ok?" asked Elora, now unsure with herself. It felt as though it went well and she'd sung better than she had ever done.

Freya approached her, her sisters close behind. When she reached Elora she took both her hands in hers and brought them up to her mouth and kissed them.

"Never in my years have I seen such power. Not from one so young, not from anyone. This changes everything. You, my young sister, will bring us out of these years of woe. The worry these ancient shoulders have had to bear will soon be over. Oh, my child." She reached up on the tips of her toes and kissed Elora on the forehead. "You have surly been blessed by Minu herself."

"So will she do?" asked Diagus impatiently, folded his arms. "Can we get her up to the church and get that song done?"

Miathlin translated for Freya and the old woman scowled at the Shadojak. "Inform him that she is perfect and thank him for bringing her to us. She will sing in the church, but not until dawn. Not until she has rested and fed and slept."

Miathlin translated this to Diagus who seemed bitter about it.

"Why wait?" he asked, rising to his feet. Bray rose with him.

Elora was inclined to agree. The sooner this was done the sooner they could go back for Nat and Ejan -to find her mother and spend time with Bray.

"Perhaps, one night's sleep will do us all some good," said Otholo. "Just think of those steps you've to climb to reach the church. Not to mention that you will be singing for the duration of the day, until they are satisfied the bond had strengthened."

"Wise words," said Freya. "Tell the old fool that he can leave when he wants. Otheena is no longer his concern."

Otholo translated this, leaving the 'old fool', bit out.

"Tell her that I will remain with the girl until the job is done and that she is still under the protection of the Shadojak."

Otholo did so.

"He's a spiky aged prune, with the temperance of a stung dog. Tell him Elora will spend the night with her song-sisters and he is welcome to find shelter with the guards or sit atop the church and let his weathered face become even more like a grimoire that's spent too many harsh winters atop the spire."

Otholo turned to Diagus. "She said Elora will spend tonight with her song-sisters and you can … meet them at the church at dawn."

Diagus looked like he wanted to snap back, yet held his tongue. "Very well. I'll leave her in your care and will be at the church at sunrise." He nodded once towards the sisters, his eyes passing over Elora's, then left.

Bray likewise nodded and gave Elora an encouraging smile before following his old master out of the room.

Freya turned to Miathlin. "Otheena is to sing with you at dawn. She will spend the night with you, if you have room."

"As you wish blessed sister, although I have no bed to spare. My song-sister who will be making up the trio has a spare bed."

"Very well. Make sure she is fed and bathed. Then take her to meet her other song-sister, Athena. It will do her good to spend the night with her."

Elora nodded to the sisters, unable to communicate otherwise as she must remain silent. She followed Maithlin out of the dome building, a giddy sense of surrealism making her feel lightheaded. Athena was her mother's name.

24

The Moon's Twin Moods

After being taken to a kitchen in the back of a large hall, Elora ate meats and breads of the finest she had ever had. Tasting all the better for being so hungry. Once she was sure she couldn't swallow another bite, Miathlin led her to a row of huts by the lake. Here she undressed and lowered herself into a large stone bath. Sighing with relief as she submerged herself in steaming water. She scrubbed raw skin and blisters away with a kind of natural soap sponge that smelled of lavender – her body relaxed, the aches and pains washing away from her muscles with the dust and grime. She was reluctant to leave, but under her song-sister's orders, dried herself and dressed in a white and gold gown, much like Miathlin's. Her other clothes had been taken away.

"Don't worry," Miathlin reassured her, after she looked about for them. "They'll be cleaned and returned to you."

They walked leisurely through the quaint city, winding around buildings, climbing steps and headed to the higher parts of Aslania. As they made their way Miathlin explained more about how the sisters worked together. She learned that song-sisters worked in threes, a trio. If they worked well the trio would stay together for as long as they could sing. The Sisters Devine were the eldest trio, having sung together for over seventy years. Elora found it extraordinary how it all worked. The whole Minuan way was built around the Eversong and the church, and went unchanged for thousands of years. She felt honoured to be a part of it and felt at home in Aslania.

They came to a halt outside a round dwelling that was much like any other they had passed, although the large fountain across the path triggered an old memory.

She had touched it before; she was sure. Only her hands had been small and chubby. Her tiny finger tracing the carved stone fish that poked out of the basin, squirting water from its gaping mouth. This was her mother's house.

Miathlin knocked on the door. It was opened by a lady older than Miathlin, with more grey in her hair. Her blue eyes found the Songstress and she smiled in recognition before they settled on Elora. The smile faded, replaced by surprise, her face paling.

"Athena," said Miathlin, taking her hands and pulling her into an exited embrace. "We have a new song-sister." She beamed when she pulled away and gestured for Elora to step closer. "This is Otheena. Sister to the bard, Otholo. She sang in the trial hall earlier and lifted the sphere clear out of the font. She is what we've been waiting for, what Aslania has been waiting for."

"New song-sister?" Athena repeated.

"Yes. We will be singing in the church at dawn. You will see, she has a voice like the blessed Minu herself. Oh, and Freya wishes for her to sleep here tonight."

"Slow down, Miathlin," Athena said, her gaze never leaving Elora, "Have we ever met?"

Elora shook her head and remained silent – she knows who I am.

"Otheena is saving her voice for tomorrow. But I can't see why you would have met before. She was little older than a baby when she left Aslania."

Her mother didn't seem satisfied with the response, yet said nothing more about it.

"Welcome, song-sister," she said, stepping back and allowing Elora to enter the house she was born in.

It was a cosy home with only three rooms, this main room which was the kitchen, dining room and lounge all in one and two small bedrooms up the spiral steps.

"Sit yourself down Otheena, would you like chamomile tea?" her mother asked. Elora nodded and lowered herself into the chair which Miathlin pulled out for her. She sat at the opposite side of the table.

Her mother was silent as she boiled water above a wood burning stove, her gaze finding Elora every few moments and making her feel nervous. Elora herself, watched her mother, her face was how she remembered although her smooth skin appeared unused to smiling and was empty of laughter lines.

"I've put a spoon of honey in it," said Athena, attempting to smile. It didn't suit her. "It will help soothe your throat and the chamomile will help you sleep."

Elora smiled again, fighting the emotions that were building up in her. She wanted nothing more than to embrace her mother. Instead she drank quickly to cover any signs she may have shown, scolding her tongue in the process.

The honey evoked new memories of a child, running around this small room, climbing on this very table and sucking on boiled honey sweets that Nat had made for her. The emotion brought tears to her eyes which she swiftly blinked away before it was noticed.

Miathlin filled the silence with talk over the day's events, as her mother seemed less inclined to make conversation. Otholo was mentioned and the bullish behaviour of the Shadojak and how handsome his Shaigun was. Elora felt a little pride at that and longed to be with him, wherever he was in the city.

After the tea was drunk, Miathlin excused herself, she had preparations to make for the mornings song: having to rearrange with the trio who was originally scheduled to sing. When she closed the door behind her the house became still, wood crackled in the stove making the only noise to intrude on the quietness.

Athena remained where she was, motionless, her eyes cast down on her hands that wrapped around the empty cup. Elora, feeling awkward rose and went to take her mother's cup so she could wash them in the basin, but as she reached for the cup her mother's hand grasped hers. She held firm for a long while, her head lowered so her face was hidden. Yet Elora didn't mistake the tears that fell to the smooth surface of the table.

After regaining control of herself her mother released her grip and Elora briskly made her way to the basin to wash the cups. When she returned her mother's crystal blue eyes were upon her, red and swollen.

"I had a daughter, once," she said, her words quiet, spoken carefully. "Elora left Aslania with my brother, making the other world a new home." She placed her hands flat against the table. "She was never to return. Never, as death could be her only welcome. Time has passed slowly for me these long years, yet my daughter has remained at the forefront of my mind this entire time. Had I been wrong to send her away? Was there a reason she existed?"

Athena's fingers curled into fists as she strove to hold tears back. "Sometimes, late into the dark hours I find myself talking to her, as if she was here with me. Telling her how sorry I was, how I wished she might understand and forgive me. If Nat could find a way to bring her back to me, he would. But that, I thought, is a dream that would never happen. For the last few years my mind has been wondering if perhaps I should try to find her. Maybe I was wrong to have sent her away. I want her back – want her here with me so much that it hurts and I don't care the consequences anymore. Do you think she forgives me?"

Elora went to her and placed her hand upon her mother's. Emotion was thick in her throat as she smiled down at the person who had been missing for most of her life.

When her mother finally regained control she rose and embraced Elora.

Elora didn't know whether her mother had worked out who she actually was or that she had sparked off emotions because she had seen something in her daughter of this fake Otheena.

"I'm sorry child, you don't need to hear the ramblings of an old woman. You need to sleep. You'll find a bed in the attic room. If you need anything more, please come back down – I don't sleep much these days."

Elora, unable to speak with her mother, smiled and nodded before she departed for the steps. Her mother stopped her as she began to climb.

"Pleasant dreams."

Elora felt a great weight lift from her shoulders as she climbed the stairs to the attic room. Tomorrow, after she had performed the Eversong and strengthened the bonds that held Solarius, she would explain all to her mother.

She opened the door and stepped inside, seeing that her mother had kept it clean and dust free. The bedding was fresh and made as if she had expected somebody to return. Had she done this for the last fourteen years

Elora was still smiling as she knelt on the bed to close the window. The large silver moon that hung above the mountain peaks seemed to smile back, as if it was aware of her happiness and bathed her in its soft light, sharing in her joy.

oooooooooooooooooooo

Ejan scowled at the huge silver moon that grimaced down at her through the branches, as if encouraging her melancholy mood, bathing her in gloom. It even cast a gravestone shadow from Ragna's hammer that she had left against the trunk of the tree she sat under.

The ground was cold, like the mountain air and the water Nathaniel insisted she sip. Her fingers clutched the wooden cup that matched the icy lump her heart had become. Would the soldiers that had killed Ragna bury him or leave his body for food for the snow jubbs and mountain cats? She had a mind to walk back to the bridge to check on him, but she saw that it was folly. No matter what state his body was in or where it was, he was still dead.

Nathaniel approached her, a steaming bowl of food balancing in his hand. "Eat this. It'll fill your belly and help you sleep," he said, placing the bowl down on her lap so she had no choice but to take it.

"What is it?" The grey sludge appeared like bog mud in the darkness.

"I made a porridge from the biscuits we had left. I've put some juniper berries in for the flavour. It'll taste better than it looks," said Nat, lowering himself onto the exposed roots of the tree opposite.

Ejan pushed the spoon around the porridge, green berries semi-floating in the mix. She hadn't the appetite to eat, yet still put a spoonful in her mouth and mechanically chewed. Whatever strength she could gain from this gruel would help her on the long trek home to Jaygen. A berry crunched between her teeth and the bitter juice made a strange fizzy sensation on her tongue. She swallowed it down, disliking the taste and watched Nathaniel watching her.

"Aren't you having any?" she asked, not wanting to be eating all the rations herself.

He made a strange clicking sound with his tongue before speaking. "I'll have something later, it's your body that needs sustenance."

She shrugged and fighting the urge to yawn she shoveled another spoonful into her mouth, all manners forgotten. Nathaniel grinned at her as she ate – a grin she hadn't seen on him before. Was he in pain or worried over his niece and merely putting on a brave front?

"She'll be fine," Ejan offered, her words sounding odd, as if slurred by drink. Another mouthful of the gruel and she felt so drowsy she had trouble putting the spoon in the bowl.

"Oh, I don't doubt she'll be fine," Nathaniel said, the grin widening until he began to chuckle, as if he found the whole ordeal amusing.

Ejan tried to place the porridge down beside her, but her fingers failed to work and ended up dropping the bowl on its side and spilling her meal onto the earth. Why did she suddenly feel drunk? Yet it was more than that, the fizzing sensation on her tongue spread to her lips and cheeks, even her fingers began to feel numb.

"That devil spawn, Elora, will sing sweetly enough in the church of Minu," Nathaniel carried on, as Ejan slid against the tree, her strength failing to keep herself sitting upright.

"Tak … tak … tak. Just like her father planned."

The words sunk into Ejan's mind as she wrestled with their understanding. What was Nathaniel saying? And why the teeth-cringing clicking noises? She attempted to speak, but only a moan passed her swollen tongue. Barely able to raise her head, she swiveled her gaze to follow Nathaniel as he rose and came over to kneel beside her. He shoved her roughly onto her back.

"When … tak … Elora, sings, she will release the bonds on Solarius and he will rise once again. Tak … tak. It's such a shame your husband won't be there to see it." Nathaniel said, as he rose once again to loom over her. "I killed him you know. I slew your Raggy."

Ejan could do no more than moan, her body was totally paralysed. Even tears failed to fall as the frustration boiled in her, wanting to be released.

"He was so brave charging headlong across the bridge at the river, waving his lump of a hammer. Those archers would have missed if I hadn't summoned a wind to alter the course of a stray arrow. I was aiming for the Shadojak but wind is such a fickle temptress." He lifted his aged hands before him, turning them this way and that as if examining them for the first time.

"This is the oldest body I've ever taken. Old and shriveled, yet the power the mind holds to manipulate the elements is incredible. When Silk first suggested that I take this body I refused, after all, Silk is merely a takwich. Yet he was right. After I take your body, I wonder if I can still make the wind blow to my tune, or change the course of water."

All Ejan could manage was to make her leg spasm, a pathetic twitch at her foot. She was trapped inside her own body, at the mercy of her husband's killer who loomed above her, lips grotesquely pulled into a grin that didn't suit the face.

"Don't worry about your lack of movement. That's only the paralysis powder I slipped into your food. It'll wear off in a few hours, but you won't be you, then. I will be.

"Before I took this wrinkled prune of a body I had control of another. A younger man named Reuben. Stronger body, yet weaker mind. I used him to trap Elora and let the Shadojak and the Shaigun kill me. The pompous fools didn't even check that I was truly dead. But then, that was the plan. When they left, I crawled from Reuben's carcass and followed them home. Then made my way back to Silk to tell him where she was. You see, it was never our intention to catch the princess, just to provoke them into moving. Prodding them to take action and guiding her path to where she is now, where she was planned to be all those years ago."

Ejan tried to bite the inside of her cheek, her tongue, anything to try and stimulate a reaction in her nerves. Her mouth failed to move and all her vocal chords could produce was a moan which tapered off into a whimper. All she had was her mind and the spasm in her toe. She didn't even have the luxury of going down fighting; no steel salute to Odin. Would the God take pity on her and allow her into the halls of Valhalla? This wasn't a warrior's death.

"I thought the traitor Zionbuss had me worked out on his ship, that's why I made myself busy with the sails. Even though he mentioned what I was, only feet from me. Spliceck. There's not many of us. Not like the common takwich … tak … tak."

Ejan listened to his words as she worked her toe, putting all her effort into moving it, although it only twitched every few seconds. Not a lot she could do with that, yet it was giving her a way of fighting back, pathetic as it was, she wasn't giving up.

Her gaze fell upon Ragna's hammer, leaning against the tree, steel head uppermost with Elora's handprint facing towards her. Raggy, what shall I do? This entire quest was for nothing. Worse, you died for nothing. It will end with the polar opposite of what they had intended and Solarius will be released to spread chaos and death upon both worlds.

Come on, girl, twitch that foot, she goaded herself. Twitch, you bastard!

"You know – I've never taken a female host," Nathaniel said, eyes alight with excitement as he admired his prey; aged fingers rubbing together as if working out where to begin.

"Tak ... tak ... tak," he clicked, as he stepped closer, raising his hands to his mouth. "You are ripe, like a peach, Ejan. You will do nicely. Now keep still. Tak ... tak. This will probably hurt – a lot."

He put the fingers of each hand inside his mouth and pulled his bearded cheeks apart, stretching the skin so far that Ejan thought it would tear. His Adam's Apple, bobbed up and down violently as if something inside the throat scurried up his windpipe. Then his head began to jerk back and forth, his eyes rolled back in his head so far that only the whites appeared and something dark-shelled, almost beetle-like scrambled from his mouth. Two large claws pushed free of the white lips and yanked the rest of its body through. It dropped to the floor, landing hard on its many pointed legs.

Ejan felt her heart thumping against her ribs, her mind panicking, yet her body immobile as the large scorpion-like creature, the spliceck, crept closer.

"Tak ... tak ... tak."

Nathaniel's body crumpled to the ground in a heap. The aged head making a dull thunk as it slammed against a thick tree root. Small bubbles escaped from his mouth with the blood that ran from a torn lip. Still alive, but would be no help.

"Tak ... tak ... tak."

The spliceck raised a large claw, snapping the razor-sharp pincers together, then did the same with the other. Snip-snip, snip-snip. A row of tiny black orbs stared at her from the top of its hideous head, as wet mandibles worked fast beneath it, strong enough to rip through flesh; her flesh.

She could hear herself whimpering, the only noise her voice could produce whilst her mind screamed 'no'. Needle sharp legs pricked at her own as the spliceck began to crawl up her shin, seeming to take pleasure at her torture, at her pain and nipping her skin with its claws.

"Tak … tak … tak."

Ejan forced herself to stay calm and not show the spiky little shit any fear, she wouldn't give it the satisfaction. Her breath came out in short gasps, plumes of white vapour released from her lips in quickening succession, her chest heaving as she fought to stay conscious. Jaygen, I must escape somehow for Jaygen.

The creature dug its pointy legs into her knee, twisted its body down, flicking its tail into her thigh, the bulbous point on its end striking her flesh beneath her britches. Fire erupted where it had struck, like a thousand hot hornet stings, attacking at once.

"Tak … tak … tak."

It crouched again, its legs preparing to spring itself towards her face. It spread its claws out either side.

'Odin'! Screamed Ejan, inside her head and used the pain in her thigh to power the spasm in her foot. It twitched violently out and struck the shaft of the Fist of the North.

"Tak … tak," began the spliceck, as it launched, like a coiled spring releasing.

The hammer came down, aided by its own weight and struck the creature. The steel head caught against the spliceck's plate armour, snagging it midair, the shadows moving across Elora's handprint and giving the impression that the fingers gripped the creature and brought it down beneath the weight.

The spliceck crunched beneath the hammer, black gore splattering against Ejan's leg as its pincers gave a final violent snap. The hammer then toppled onto its side, pulling bits of shell and leg with it, sticky strings of intestines and blood bridging the torn pieces to the rest of the broken body.

The little orbs still stared at her, a row of tiny moons reflecting back, but lacking any signs of life.

She had done it. Killed the creature that murdered her husband, yet she felt no satisfaction, only emptiness. If she didn't stop Elora from singing in the church, then she may as well have died. Jaygen and everyone on Earth, on Thea, would suffer. But how was she to reach Aslania when she could barely move her eyes. Two hours away, it may have been two years away for all the difference it made.

Ejan tried to move her foot again but now the imminent threat had passed she felt weaker, even the sting in her leg became numb like the rest of her body. Her breath came out slower, reaching the steady rhythm of a sleeper as she fought to keep her eyelids open, but lost the fight; slipping deeper into unconsciousness.

25

God of Chaos

Bray slid off the roof, landing deftly on the cobbled path beside the home Elora had stayed in. He had spent the night sitting beside the warm chimney on the roof of the dwelling opposite, with a clear line of sight into the room where she lay. Watching her chest rise and fall beneath the covers, staring at her peaceful face as she slept, a contented smile on her lips.

"I told you she would be safe," said Diagus, stepping from behind a fish carved water fountain. Bray knew he had been there all night. Watching him, as he watched her. Anticipating them to run away, maybe. The thought had been in Bray's mind too; to make a break for it, but he knew Elora wouldn't go back on her word. She blames herself for what happened on Earth and feels responsible for putting it right.

They waited by the door, ready to escort Elora to the church. Bray listened to the movements from within as the two woman made breakfast and dressed. Elora remaining silent and only a spare word from the older woman.

Bray thought her features were so like Elora's that she could be her mother. But then again, everyone in the city was alike, with blue eyes and blond hair.

He spared a glance to his old master, whose face lay hidden in the darkness, yet his one white eye still found enough light to reveal itself, appearing like a ghostly globe floating in the shadows.

"Don't go thinking I'm not privy to your intentions," Diagus said, his whisper sounding like drawn steel.

Bray remained silent, averting his gaze from the Pearly White to stare up into the pre-dawn sky.

"Do you think I didn't see you steal the scroll on Zionbuss's ship? The chart that leads to the dragon, Grycul," continued the Shadojak.

Bray almost flinched, yet had the strength to hold it together. Then realised that there was no point in denying it. Somehow Diagus had worked it out. He turned to him, feeling an urge to strike the Shadojak down. Maybe taking him off guard was the only way to best him, but then Diagus was always on his guard.

"How did you know?" Bray asked.

"I know you. I've been watching you closely to see what plan you'd come up with. Saw you pocket the scroll; wasn't hard to work out why."

"The plan may work."

"Doubtful. Nobody's ever gotten close to the dragon, not to mention the Dragon Guard you'd need to fight through before finding a way to slay the beast itself."

"It's worth a try."

Diagus snorted through his nose. "Do you really think the Emperor will grant her clemency for killing Grycul?"

Bray began to feel less hopeful about his plan, as Diagus spoke.

"And what of the Shadojak Supreme, do you think he'll let her live?"

"He will have to adhere to what the Emperor commands."

"The Shadojak Superior? I don't think so."

Bray wanted to say more, feeling his temper rising towards Diagus for discovering his plans and for finding fault with them. But the door swung open and Elora and her song-sister stepped out.

Elora appeared surprised to see them there, then her face brightened into a smile that sent his heart soaring. She was dressed in the white and gold gown that she had worn the previous day, her hair curled to shining ringlets that hung to either side of her beautiful face, yet the single natural blonde lock still dangled separate from the rest as if charged with opposing magnetic poles.

"Good morning, Otheena," he said, quickly, anticipating her arms reaching up to embrace him and checked them before the other woman noticed. "Songstress." He inclined his head briefly to the other. She smiled curtly back, then taking Elora by the arm, led her off along the path. He and Diagus followed, keeping in step a few paces behind.

Lamps brightened the way to the church, casting soft amber light along the path. The snow caps of the mountains, barely visible above the city, surrounded them like sentinel observers making silent judgement. They paused briefly outside another dwelling to meet Miathlin, then continued the walk through the quiet city, unimpeded by others as the city slept.

Nobody spoke as they climbed the hundreds of steps that wound up to the church, the only sound was the scraping of slippers and the quickening of breath from Miathlin and Athena.

The sharp spires of the church ran the rest of the way to the summit: tall arches carved from the same side of rock, angled out, sloping down to the base that made the floor, this side of the building rested upon. Underneath them were the colossal pillars that swept down the rock face. Bray found the entire structure a wonder of engineering, made even more wondrous as only half the building was on the outside of the rock face, the other half was inside the mountain.

Miathlin raised a hand to stop him and Diagus proceeding any further.

"I'm sorry gentlemen, this is as far as you may go. Only Minuans are allowed in the church," she explained.

Diagus shrugged. "So be it. We'll stay out here until after the song."

Miathlin raised an eyebrow. "That is your choice of course. But I can assure you that nothing will happen to Otheena. She is quite safe."

Diagus inclined his head and pulled his cloak tighter around him. It was clear to anyone he wasn't going anywhere.

Bray watched the woman pass through the huge doors, Miathlin put a finger to her lips as the sound of the Eversong echoed from within.

As Elora passed over the threshold she glanced at him and mouthed the words "I love you". He began to say them back but the door closed behind her and sealed the sound in.

Diagus shook his head. "Love?" he said, making it sound like a mystery waiting to be solved. "Makes fools of men and ruins women. What's the point of it?"

"What's your point, Shadojak?" Bray snapped, fighting the impulse to follow Elora in.

Diagus raised a notched eyebrow, clearly unused to having his former Shaigun speak to him in such a way. Well, he can stick it up his miserable arse. Yet Diagus's next words shocked Bray.

"Can't say I understand it. Thought I loved somebody once." Diagus puffed his cheeks out, then blew the air threw his lips. "Can't have loved her though, if I gave her up to be Shadojak."

Now it was Bray's turn to raise an eyebrow. He had never pictured his old master ever being doe-eyed over anything. Maybe that was why he was so bitter, his demeanour so grim towards everyone. Had he lived with regrets for most of his life?

They both stared down into the city, where a few dwellings were beginning to show signs of life. Lamps were being lit, wisps of smoke from chimneys rising black against the grey of the slate as Aslania began to wake up. The first signs of dawn appeared above the peaks, a blood-red haze rising against black giant teeth. Bray couldn't help but get the feeling it was a bad omen.

He caught movement on the steps below. It was a gate guard, running at some speed, his silver helmet held under one hand as he came panting up the steps. Sweat clung to his red face as he halted before them.

When he tried to speak his words were lost within his heavy breathing. Bray held a hand up. "Steady yourself, you don't want to get dizzy and fall all the way back down again."

The guard put his hands on his knees and bent over, sucking in air as he calmed himself down. Once he got his breath back he attempted speaking once again but it was clear he wasn't comfortable speaking in the common tongue.

"Two peoples, go gate," he said, holding up two fingers. "Speaking for Shadojak?"

"They want to speak with me?" asked Diagus, pressing his thumb to himself.

The guard nodded.

"Who are they?" Bray questioned.

The guard seemed to consider his words, probably choosing what might sound right.

"One of man, with hair on face. One of woman … " He made a swinging motion over his shoulder, both hands held together.

"A hammer?" asked Bray, holding his hands apart, showing the length of the Fist of the North.

The guard nodded, enthusiastically.

"Ejan and Nathaniel. I thought they were to remain hidden," said Diagus, then glanced at Bray. "We better see what they want. Must be important." Then inclined his head down the steps.

Bray got the message. The 'We', meant himself. He didn't want to leave Diagus here alone, not trusting the Shadojak with Elora, should something go wrong. Yet it was clear from the guard's appearance that they were urgently needed at the gatehouse. It seemed Diagus read his mind.

"Don't worry, lad. I've no intention of taking my blade out, even after the job's done. I think the girl's proved herself to me."

Bray felt a weight lift from his shoulders.

"I'll only take out my sword if Solarius himself raises his monstrous head. Now get yourself to the gatehouse before this lad spontaneously combusts."

○○○○○○○○○○○○○○○○○○○○

Elora stood at the font, her hand pressed lightly against the basin which was twice as large as the one in the trial hall. Her mother and Miathlin stood facing her, their hands also upon the ancient stone vessel; Miathlin already singing the first verse of the Eversong.

The beginnings of the day shone through a large circular window, bathing the large circular hall in red light, mixing with the ghostly white reflections from the sphere that spun upon the font's water with her song-sister's voice.

The font itself stood upon a raised platform that was suspended above a large well, The Well of Redemption – that sank into the ground, disappearing deep into the bowels of the mountain. Runes and symbols were etched into the wall of the well, spiraling down into the depths, glowing with the soft light that seemed to emanate from the font itself.

Elora stared down into the darkness of the well to where Solarius was bound by the song which had been sung perpetually, since Minu had first begun singing it, thousands of years ago. Her father was beneath her, bound in a lost cavern in the mountains – did he know she was above him?

When they first entered the large hall, through a smaller atrium which sealed them from outside noise, Elora was amazed to see another trio already at the font performing the Eversong. She watched as one Songstress began to sing the final verse and her sister began to sing the first so the song was being over-lapped. Word and pitch perfect, the beautiful sound echoed around the circular hall as the sphere spun upon the water in the font.

The Sisters Devine had turned up to observe her perfor-mance, smiling reassuringly at her as she entered. Sat along a row of benches were other trios as they waited for their turn to sing. Elora thought that she would be with them at first but the Devine sister Freya, indicated that they should be next. So when one of the singing trio completed her final verse, she peeled away from the font and Miathlin took her place. Elora was impressed with the practice skill of the movement, so slick and graceful. When the second of the trio peeled away her mother took her place as Miathlin's voice merged with those of the remaining songstresses.

Elora felt excitement as the last of the trio finished the song and peeled away. She gave Elora a curious smile as they swapped places. Her mother had explained to her, as they made breakfast earlier, that new singers slowly blended on with the other trios. Watching from the benches and learning the craft before taking a place at the font and only after many hours spent practicing in the trial hall. This was a way for the other songstresses to familiarise themselves with the new singer and they would naturally find a place amongst them. Athena explained that singing at the font the very next day after only one song in the trial hall was unheard of, so she may expect to receive curious glances from the women about the church.

Her eyes drifted to the spinning sphere of light that glowed in front of her, casting its warm reflection upon her mother. As Athena began to sing, the light brightened, matching the beauty in her mother's voice. Her own turn to sing would be when this verse finished.

ooooooooooooooooooooo

Bray had run through Aslania, leaving the guard far behind. When he arrived at the gate he was greeted with shouts of anger from a commotion happening outside the huge doors. When he investigated he saw that two guards lay on the floor, unconscious – huge dents in their armour, the rest of the guard were shouting at another who was pulled into the corner of the rock, his red face towards them, arms raised and knife held to his throat.

"About bloody time you turned up," came a familiar voice from behind the hostage, blonde spiky hair protruding above his shoulder. "Any longer and things would have gotten ugly."

"You don't think things already have?" asked Bray, as he raised his arms to placate the men. "Easy fellas, she's with me." He pushed the point of a spear away that was being raised against the Viking and took the knife from Ejan. The man who had been held hostage staggered away, a hand delicately probing his neck.

"Where's Nathaniel?" he asked. Then he saw Elora's uncle sat against the rock face, legs drawn up to his chest, his head resting on his knees. "Is he alright?"

"No, not really. But he'll live. Where's Elora?" Ejan asked urgently.

"In the church. She's about to sing, why?" Bray asked, beginning to get an awful feeling that something terrible was about to happen. Ejan's eyes widening in panic only confirmed his suspicion.

ooooooooooooooooooooo

Timing her breathing to coincide with her mother's, Elora prepared to sing. She swallowed a nervous lump in her throat as Athena ended her verse, inhaling deeply then following the song, she sung the first words.

Immediately the sphere brightened and began to pick up speed, spinning fast enough to flick drops of water at her song-sisters. Even the words and symbols that spiraled down the well brightened to the point where the runes all seemed to merge into one. Her mother smiled at her warmly, the light reflecting in her blue eyes.

Elora continued to sing, hearing whispers of astonishment from the benches and then gasps as the spinning orb lifted above the font, floating higher with each word. Light filled the entire church, drowning out the sun's rays which had previously began to fall on the granite walls.

Elora felt weightless and wondered if she would float above the ground as the sphere was. Her words washing back and forth in increasingly heavier waves that had her song-sisters swaying to the rhythm. She felt euphoric, her mind pulsing with a static energy that crackled through every fibre of her body, every cell singing the Eversong.

Then she felt a sudden change.

The air seemed to become thicker, as if charged with a powerful unseen energy, a heaviness that pushed against her, squeezing her chest. Others felt the shift, smiles becoming frowns, tendons appearing on Miathlin's neck, her mother's fingers turning white as she gripped the font.

Elora felt an explosion of pain in the pit of her stomach as if somebody rammed a fist into her guts. She doubled over, hands still remaining locked upon the font as the song was torn from her chest. Her voice dropped an entire octave and a single word was forced from her lips.

"Free!"

The light in the church abruptly went out as the floating sphere turned black and fell into the font. Darkness spread down the well, chasing the light until the entire hall drowned in shadow. Only the red light casting through the window illuminated the shocked faces of the Sisters Devine.

Time stood still – nobody spoke, nobody moved. The only sound came from the bottom of the well; a violent wind, extremely deep, rumbled inside the mountain.

Elora found her mother's stare, locked accusingly on her.

"What have you done?" Her whisper carried about the hall and magnified so nobody failed to hear.

What had she done? Elora tried to speak but no voice came to her mouth, no words passed her lips. She felt stunned as she fought the rising tears. But they came, running from her cheeks and dripping into the font. Her vision blurred for a second and something heavier dropped into the water. The contact lenses.

"Elora?" asked Athena, incredulously. "Is It truly you?"

Before Elora replied, there came a tortuous sound of rock grating against rock. It echoed up the well, followed by a violent tremor that rippled through the ground. She glanced down and witnessed a red ball of light rising up the shaft towards them. As it neared she saw that it was fire; spitting and curling around the circular wall as sharp flames licked the runes, hungry for something to burn.

Without thinking, Elora gripped the side of the font for support and shoved as hard as she could against Miathlin's chest. Then spun about and throwing an arm around her mother's waist she threw herself from the platform.

They landed hard, a wave of heat passing up where they had just been. Crimson flames engulfed the font, scorching the very air as it funneled up to the ceiling, burning through the carved rock. The glass in the round window shattered outwards letting more air in to vent the fire's rage.

Cutting through the screams and shouts in the hall, came sister Freya's commanding voice.

"Sing, sisters!" Elora heard her bellow. "Calm yourselves and sing!" The old lady burst into the first verse of the Eversong and her elderly partners joined in with her. By the time Elora rose to her feet, every woman in the church was joining her own voice to the Sisters Devine. Even her mother, who nursed Miathlin, her head lying unconscious in her lap, was singing, yet she glowered at Elora.

All at once the well exploded, spitting rock and fragments of the font to all corners of the hall and knocking anything in their path to the floor, including several singers. Flames continued to burn the roof and now Elora could see daylight through the black smoke – the fire reaching impossibly high.

Men suddenly burst into the hall. Armoured guards charged in, the blaze reflecting from silver chests and helmets. Bray and Diagus were beside them, swords already drawn and scanning the room for an enemy. When he failed to see a threat, Bray came to Elora's side.

"Are you hurt?" he asked, concern thick in his throat.

Elora shook her head. "I don't know what happened. One second I was singing, the next ... " She held her hand out, pointing towards the raging fire.

"Your voice was the key to unlock Solarius," said Athena, sitting a coughing Miathlin up.

"But, Nat told me ... "

Bray placed an arm around her shoulder. "Nat's body wasn't his own. He had been possessed by a spliceck. Ejan killed it and came to warn us as soon as she could."

"What about Nat, is he alright?" asked Elora, feeling a surge of panic rising in her chest.

"He's hurt, but alive," replied Bray, then protectively stepped in front of Elora as Diagus approached them.

The Shadojak's face said what his words did not. Eyes narrowed to slits, the puckered scar running up his face pulled so tight his cheek turned as white as the pearl in his socket. Elora knew her life had just been forfeit and stepped around Bray's protection. She would willingly sacrifice herself so Bray wouldn't die. It's what she deserved.

As she ducked under his arm his face hardened into a look of anguish. It was then that Diagus struck him on the side of the head, steel pummel connecting with his temple. Bray collapsed to the floor, his sword scraping away from slack fingers.

"Will you make him your Shaigun again?" asked Elora, forcing herself to step over Bray's unconscious body.

"If he chooses it."

Elora nodded and knelt down before him, exposing her neck to his blade for the second and final time. The whispers of darkness, demanding to be heard, niggling at the edge of her hearing. *Kill ... Kill ...*

"Make it quick," she said.

"Elora, no!" shouted Athena, once she realised what was happening. Elora closed her eyes and felt partly lucky for meeting her mother before she died; and partly unlucky for only meeting her before she died. Athena began to say something else but her words were lost amongst another violent explosion.

The entire hall flashed white and a wall of heat lifted Elora off her feet and flung her to the ground atop of Bray. Fresh screams erupted around the room as she shook the dizziness from her head and checked that Bray was still alive. Her shaking fingers found his pulse as she scanned the devastation for her mother.

Athena was on her back, Miathlin laying across her. Both breathing and choking on the smoke that filled the room.

Elora gazed at the rest of the hall and saw bodies everywhere, knocked flat by the explosion. Those that could stand did so, the rest lay injured, unconscious or dead. Daylight spread over the fallen and when Elora sought the source, she realised that the entire wall of the church had been blown out. She could see Aslainia, with its lake and many steepled roofs below her.

The flames billowed out of the vast opening, curling and spiraling as they funneled up into the clouds in a whirlwind of red heat. The red turned momentarily to bright yellow as something black stepped out of the flames and onto the stone floor. It was her father – Solarius.

As tall as Ragna, Solarius stepped towards them. The armour he wore was rusted through in places, decayed through the ages. The leather straps cracked or missing, buckles without pins, gauntlets missing fingers and any sigil that the breastplate once held was now scorched black and unrecognisable. Yet the man wearing it, her father, appeared fresh and healthy as if merely waking from a long sleep.

Glowing crimson eyes stared down over the fallen, a sharp nose and a coal black beard, protruded from a square handsome face. Raven black hair, much like her own, flowed down to his shoulders and shimmered in the reflection of the whirling vortex of fire. She felt more than saw the darkness rush to him, abandoning her to return to the God of Chaos.

A brave guard suddenly rushed forwards, with his spear levelled before him. Solarius watched his advance with a curious expression, not caring to move or defend himself as the guard drove his spear through the ancient armour, the flaking steel offering little resistance as the weapon impaled him.

Seeing that Solarius didn't react to his injury, the guard took a cautious step back, signaling for his men to close ranks either side of him. Diagus joined the men, holding his blade out to the side with both hands.

Elora watched as flames licked from the back of her father, appearing at first like a flaming cloak. But as a grin spread across his face the cloak split and flared out in two huge fire walls in the shape of wings. The spear in his chest simply fell away front and back, clattering to the floor and the metal ran like water from the wound.

Surprise on the guard's face turned to a grimace as the commander ordered them to attack. They ran at the god with spears and swords held before them.

The lead man lunged, driving his spear forwards but Solarius smoothly took it from his grasp and dipped his shoulder, his flaming wings closing around the guard and setting him ablaze.

His screams echoed around the hall as the spear was first spun to the left to crack another guard, hard enough to snap his neck, then to the right and strike a man with enough force to knock him and two others out of the gaping hole, to fall to their deaths.

Diagus spun into the space they left and struck the God a slicing blow to his elbow. The armour parted and crumbled to the floor, yet did no actual damage to the deity. Diagus turned to parry the spear then roll away as huge wings came together where he had just been. They caught another guard instead, engulfing him in flames.

Elora tried to ignore the screams of the dying men as they writhed in agony only feet away. Instead applying her energies into dragging Bray's body free from harm.

The stone basin of the font lay against a bench forming a makeshift shield. Elora dragged Bray's body under it to protect him from the heat and falling masonry, then turned to the fight.

The Shadojak was dancing in and out of the swinging spear, wielded by her father. What was left of the guards didn't intervene, they stood or crouched close by, with spears held ready to throw, yet didn't make a move as the dueling pair moved too swiftly to make a clear target.

Solarius, flashed his spear about, spinning it over head before bringing it down above Diagus's head. The Shadojak brought his blade up to meet it. The steel sparked and Diagus switched his position, chopping his sword across the God's greaves, sending the knee guard spinning in the air. He followed it with a roll and brought his blade back up and knocked the spear from the Solarius's grip. It spun out of the hole and out of sight.

He had done it. Elora thought as she watched her father now weaponless, open his arms out in surrender. The Shadojak gave no mercy and twisting his wrist, spun his sword under arm and drove it into Solarius's chest.

The blade met only black smoke; remnants of the God's flaming wings. Elora watched the confusion set into Diagus as he spun around, searching Solarius out. When his back was turned the God suddenly reappeared in front of him and shoved hard on his shoulder.

Diagus thudded against a stone pillar and crashed to the floor, barely able to lift his head up before Solarius disappeared again, then reappeared in front of the fallen Shadojak. His red eyes cast down on the sword in Diagus's hand.

"Mine. I, believe," said the God, his voice deep and ash dry.

As Solarius's hand came towards the blade, Diagus sprang into action. Hacking an arc in the air, he aimed for the proffered arm, but again, he cut only through smoke.

When Diagus stood up Elora's father appeared.

"Behind you," she shouted.

He spun to her voice and dropped below the swinging fist of the God, cutting sideways with his blade but Solarius dodged the attack and the sword passed harmlessly through the flaming wings. Keeping the momentum going Diagus brought the blade about once more, aiming for the God's head. Solarius saw it coming and simply stepped through the Shadojak.

Elora watched in disbelief as her father passed through Diagus, his body momentarily becoming black smoke, twisting and curling over and between Diagus to transform behind him, once again becoming solid.

How can the Shadojak defeat him when he became smoke at will? With nothing solid to strike, the sword Diagus wielded was useless.

The Shadojak continued fighting in vain, swiping at the God, yet hitting nothing; his target reducing to smoke then materialising to attack Diagus, knocking him onto his front then driving a foot down upon his thigh.

The few of the guards that remained didn't escape the God's wrath. Two were thrown out into the open air and a third was burned, having been enveloped by Solarius's wings. The last fell where he was struck, his face made a ruin by a vicious punch – he didn't get back up.

Elora felt the hatred for her father burning hotter than the fiery pillar of heat that funneled up into the sky. She felt that other being stir inside her as she curled her fingers into fists, letting the anger surge through her blood.

"Elora?" She heard her mother whisper as she shuffled beside her. Then felt a cold hand press against her arm. Elora gently lifted the hand away and placed it upon Bray's rising chest.

"Stay with him," she said. "This is my fault, my mess. It's time I cleared it up." She rose and stalked towards her father; dancing shadows, created by the fire drifted towards her as she gathered her strength.

Elora … Elora … the inferno roared, as the darkness descended about her. *Kill … Kill …*

Diagus fell to his knees, his head hung low and his sword on the ground. He was heaving in broken breaths, his body failing him. Solarius stood behind, his flaming wings spread out either side ready to engulf the fallen Shadojak.

Elora quickened her pace, vaulting over a broken bench and launched herself at her father's back. She struck his spine with her knees, whilst grasping both hands about his neck – digging her nails into hot flesh. She had him, her anger throttling like a volcano as she squeezed his throat. *Kill ... Kill ...*

It felt good, releasing the maelstrom of fury that she, the Princess of Darkness, had built up inside her. She would crush the life out of her father.

She increased the pressure, then all of a sudden it was gone, her fingers gripped nothing and she fell to the floor through a cloud of smoke.

A heartbeat later, she felt scolding fingers about her own neck as she was lifted and turned to face her father.

Elora's hands gripped the armour that surrounded his wrists, crushing the metal to his flesh as he crushed her windpipe. Deep red eyes gazed upon hers, with anger mixed with a touch of curiosity. He stared for a moment, turning her head to the left, then the right, like a butcher surveying a prized lamb he was about to slaughter. Then Solarius let out a guttural chuckle.

"Daughter?" he asked, applying more pressure to his fingers and choking off any air that she tried sucking in.

She applied pressure of her own, trying to crush his wrists, pushing heat into her hands as she had with the Fist of the North. It's only effect was to make her father smile.

"Powerful little creature – fruit of my loins. But I have no need of you. My army, as we speak, already crosses the border between the worlds. It will conquer Earth, then turn to Thea; crushing them both together and making fire and dust, death and ash."

Elora attempted to wriggle free of his grasp, jamming her feet against his chest, she pushed with all her might.

Her father's arms stretched as he struggled to contain her, she almost broke his hold. Then her feet passed through smoke and she fell to the floor beside Diagus.

Rolling onto her knees she sucked in great gasps of air and coughed it back out. The pain in her neck was excruciating.

Fire surged around her and Diagus, forming a blazing ring, trapping them inside.

"The worlds will end," Solarius's voice circled around them, although his body was yet to materialize. "The path that lays before you will be one of punishment, death and destruction. Chaos awaits all." He then stepped through the flames, his greaves momentarily catching fire before dying out.

"You are a tool to me, nothing more. A key to unlock my chains. Yet free me you did."

Elora averted her gaze away from Diagus, guilt breaking through her chest at what she had done. She glared at her father, the cause of so much pain and suffering. The guilt was quickly being replaced by anger once again and she felt a sudden surge of strength, pulsing through her body.

"Killing everything in one fell swoop isn't chaotic. There needs to be room for unpredictability. An imbalance. Wiping the slate clean with life, is just that: clean. Sterile. Not chaos."

Elora listened to his ramblings, but didn't take the words in. She was angry. Her blood boiling with rage with the desire to kill, to destroy. She was her father's daughter, after all. Hadn't she tried doing the right thing? And where did that get her?

"I will let you live, daughter of mine. Spawn of Chaos. You will be at my heels to witness the worlds collide. You will be the imbalance."

The Shadojak had tried to kill her. Cut her head from her shoulders. She looked down on the broken man; pathetic, crippled. Why had she feared him so much?

She didn't intervene when Solarius stooped and lifted the Shadojak from the ground. One arm curling around his neck as he pressed him against his chest.

"I ask but one thing of you, daughter, so as I can trust you to keep out of my way."

"Name it," she said, staring into his face which hovered above Diagus's shoulder.

"Take my blade. The sword which this broken mortal has used as his own and take his head," he said, increasing the pressure on the Shadojak's neck, causing the white of his remaining eye to go bloodshot and the other to bulge so far out that Elora feared it might fall out.

The daughter of darkness retrieved the sword, the dark green blade causing her teeth to itch. It felt alive beneath her grip as if it could think, could comprehend what was about to happen and fought against her.

Diagus watched her approach, lips pulled back in a grimace, teeth stained red. "Kill him," he choked between breaths.

Solarius laughed, his wings folding out, the tips curling in and forming a crescent around them.

"I'm not such a fool to trust in my daughter completely, mortal. Why else do I shield behind your back. Now make your choice, daughter. Watch the worlds end and live forever, or die."

She advanced another step, gripping the sword with both hands as it vibrated within her grasp. She put it to the side of the Shadojak's neck, the blade only inches away from severing its former owners head ... *Kill.*

"Do the right thing, girl," growled Diagus, his eyes never leaving hers, "Do it for Bray, for love."

"You don't believe in love. Just a chemical, remember?" Elora replied, twisting the edge of the blade towards his pulsing artery.

"My life is over now," continued Diagus. "Yet yours and everything on Earth, on Thea, may still go on."

"Enough. I grow impatient," spat the God, yanking Diagus into a tighter hold, "End him."

Elora pulled the blade away, readying to swing the sword, feeling that there was no option left to her. Diagus had just said his life had already ended and she couldn't stop her father. Chaos rules over everything.

"Do the right thing," the words passed the Shadojak's lips, choked from the throat, little more than a croak, but they set something off in Elora. He was sacrificing himself, but how was she to kill Solarius without killing Diagus first. Her father was out of reach; his body behind the Shadojak.

Then she worked it out.

Changing her grip on the sword, she placed a hand upon Diagus's shoulder for support.

His aged hands had already pulled his shirt apart to reveal his chest, his gaze still upon hers, she thought he gave her a subtle nod and clenching her teeth – she did the right thing.

A scream left her lungs as she plunged the blade through the Shadojak's chest. The sword seeming to come alive in her hands as it parted his ribs and punctured his heart; blood spilling out along the blade mixing with the reds of the flames reflection.

Diagus's head sank forwards as a moan escaped his mouth. Elora averted her eyes from his and locked them on her fathers. An evil grin split his beard, his red pupils dilating with pleasure.

"Chaos dies with the Shadojak," she growled, as she thrust the sword deeper, applying all the weight and force she could, feeling the blade pass fully through Diagus and then into her father that hid behind him, slicing through his heart.

The sword was buried to the hilt before Solarius reacted. His eyes suddenly going wide, the centre of his pupils looking like twin red suns, as he tipped his head back and screamed.

Elora held firm to the sword as her father's wings wafted hot air against her as he writhed to free himself.

"That's right father. I was a tool. I was the key that released you. But I am also the tool that will spill your blood."

She couldn't say whether he heard her or not, he was too busy thrashing about and screaming.

The heat before her was becoming intense, as sharp flames erupted from Diagus's heart, his blood mixing with her fathers. Impossibly the Shadojak was still conscious.

Elora attempted to release the sword but her hands remained closed, the blade wouldn't release her and when she stepped away it came with her. Fire crackled along its length, born from her father it licked along its edge, running towards her hands. She was about to snatch her arms away when Diagus shifted and grasped her hand. He slid it over the hilt and onto the flaming steel.

The blade bit deep into her palm and her own blood mixed with that of the Shadojak's and her father's. The instant it did she felt a sudden presence in her mind. A sharp hot presence which she immediately recognised as belonging to the blade itself.

It filled her head, drowning out her other senses, filling her mind's eye with images, with flashes of memories that were not her own. She gave herself to the whispers, to the darkness and to the fire burning and all consuming. She let go of reality and to consciousness, giving her soul freely to the blade – the soul reaver itself – and escaped Chaos.

26

The Emperor Can Wait

Elora became aware of singing. It was a man's voice, his song a soft and flowing melody that she had heard before, yet couldn't understand.

Light filtered through her eyelashes as she gently opened her lids. The long shapes above her focused onto dark wooden beams that she recognised as rafters. A black falcon was perched upon one, preening its glossy feathers, while staring at her with an intelligence greater than any bird. Prince Dylap sat atop him, his serious expression brightening when he noticed she was awake.

Elora was lying in a bed and when she turned her head she found Nathaniel, on a stool beside her, singing softly.

She was in Nat's old chamber, in her mother's house. Daylight coming through the open window, lighting the room and casting gentle reflections on beautiful flowers that sat in a vase upon a table.

Her body ached as he attempted to sit. Nat paused his song and lay a hand upon hers.

"Easy, Elora. You're not quite ready to rise," he said, beaming at her.

She noticed that he appeared thinner than usual and his face had a swollen quality with stitches sewn along a cut at the edge of his mouth.

"What happened?" she croaked, her throat feeling sore and dry.

Nat produced a cup of water and put it in her hands. She took it gladly and sipped the cool liquid.

"You killed him. Solarius is dead and Aslania is now free from the curse that has plagued it for thousands of years."

Memories came flooding back then. Of the church, the fire – the deaths.

"Bray?" she asked, a terrible feeling suddenly gripping her stomach.

"Alive. And your mother also. They've both been taking turns sitting with you. You've been asleep for three days."

Sleep? Elora had flash backs to the nightmares that came to her before she woke. The memories of Diagus and other men unknown to her, working back through time: of the battles he had had, of the men he had killed – even how he lost his eye. And that hateful sword, the soul reaver, being at the centre of it all. Then more images of the man, the Shadojak who owned it before him, stretching back over hundreds of years as it collected the memories and souls of those it had stabbed through the heart. Right back to her father.

The images had been real; they were still there at the periphery of her mind to be called upon when needed. Each soul trapped in the sword along with their skills and abilities.

Suddenly Bray entered the room, her mother at his heel. He looked tired, dark stubble covering his gorgeous face and Elora felt her heart race faster.

"I thought I heard voices," Bray said, a grin causing dimples in his cheeks as he came to her. His lips pressed against her forehead briefly before making way for her mother, who planted an equally loving kiss beside his. She took her hand and sat on the bed while Bray stood to her shoulder, his hand delicately resting on the nape of her neck.

Ejan then entered the room.

"You've finally had enough of sleeping then?" said the Viking ruefully.

"Yeah," was all Elora could manage, needing another sip of water.

"Good, because I don't want to be hanging around here too long. I've got a son to get back to." She leaned against the door frame and folded her arms.

Then Elora remembered what her father had said before she killed him.

"What about Earth? Solarius said the barrier was gone and that his army was now taking the world."

Bray sighed heavily. "It is so. Prince Dylap has seen it. The Dark army has already swept deep into Britain, Europe and is making its way into Asia."

"But we need to stop them. Is there a way back?"

Nat nodded, his face hardening. "Although there maybe more pressing matters to keep you here."

"The Emperor's men are at the gate. They're demanding to see the Shadojak. The Emperor wants answers," Bray said.

"But the Shadojak's dead. I killed him."

"No," continued Bray, taking something from beneath the bed and placing it beside her. It was Diagus's sword, sheathed inside a plain silver scabbard. "The Shadojak never dies." He knelt before her, as did her mother. Ejan joined them, kneeling on the floor as they all bowed their heads.

"What are you doing?" Elora asked, confused.

"You've taken the sword, you've taken the lives and experiences of all it has slayed. You've had the quickening nightmares and you have been blade born." The grin returned to Bray's face. "You are the Shadojak, and we are now under your protection."

The words took a moment to sink in, but when they did she still didn't understand.

"But I can't be. It's you that's done the training, you can have the sword – here." She slid it across to him.

Bray shook his head. "For me to take the sword I must beat you in battle and then run it through your heart. Somehow I don't fancy doing that just now." He rose to his feet and offered her a hand. "Come to the window, let me show you something."

Elora, aided by Bray's arm, shuffled to the window and peered outside.

Aslania was bustling with people and Imperial soldiers. Tents were hastily erected on the green, beside the lake. Brightly coloured bunting was strung up between fountains and roofs and decorations of paper and lace spread on surfaces about the city. People were busy singing together, dancing and merry making. She even saw Otholo, lute in hand, playing under a bright canopy with two young ladies gleefully watching him.

"Looks like they're having a party," Elora said, leaning against Bray's shoulder for support.

"It's all for you, Elora. They're celebrating you. God killer, savour and Shadojak, all in one. Some say you're Minu herself."

"But I killed Diagus," she said, not believing that all the fuss in the city was over her, she had killed the Shadojak for pity's sake.

Bray, nodded and placed something spherical in her hand. "After the fire, this was all that was left of him. I didn't know what to do with it. But don't feel any guilt for your actions, Elora." He hugged her tight. "He was dying – already asked for the blade's peace from me, once this was over. Truth is, Diagus was old; older than old and he'd had enough."

Elora opened her hand and placed the large white pearl on the windowsill. It seemed to stare through her as if making a dismal judgement. Such a small thing to remain from such a powerful man.

"And us?" she asked, turning to Bray and staring up into his moss-green eyes.

"Still complicated," he smiled mischievously. "You are the Shadojak. And the daughter of Chaos, after all." He kissed her on the lips, stubble tickling her cheeks.

She prodded him playfully in the stomach. "And the Princess of Darkness, don't forget," she laughed. "So what happens now? What do I need to do as the Shadojak?"

"Well, you need to seek an audience with the Supreme Shadojak. It's a formality, but an important one. The Emperor also wishes to meet you. Another formality but one that must be observed. In his eyes you're still a threat and he would feel better knowing that you're on his side."

"What about Earth? My father's army is still there, wreaking havoc and causing chaos. Isn't there anything we can do? Is there a way back?"

Bray glanced up at Prince Dylap, a frown forming on his brow. "There is a way back."

"Good," Elora said, picking up the heavy sword which was once her father's, once Diagus's and now hers.

The soul reaver vibrated in her hands, making her fingers tingle. She could hear it whispering to her, singing to her. Its edge, which had lost its green hue had become a dark red, blood red, shimmering in the daylight, the sun playing along the strange metal as her gaze worked up its length.

She returned to stare at the scene outside, at Aslania and at the cold peaks, the Gods' Peaks that stood tall, above everything.

The sword in her hands suddenly erupted in sharp hot flames that licked along the cold blade. It seemed to sense her growing tension, her rising anger and tuned itself to her emotions.

"The Emperor can wait. I'm taking Earth back."

A dark whisper touched the edge of her hearing – *Kill ... Kill ... Kill.*

Acknowledgements

First of all, I would like to thank Paul Manning for the design and creation of the front cover. He has a wealth of knowledge and helped guide me in the right direction and has become a good friend.

Thanks go also to my editor, Elizabeth Watkins (the Typo Sniper), for having a keen eye and helping to spot the typos which have somehow slipped through.

To Genella Stephens who has read *Eversong* (several times) and has been there since the journey began.

To my children who gave me the inspiration, and to my loving wife who had great ideas of her own and has kept me going with her home cooking. Without her I doubt I would have progressed beyond Chapter 5.

And finally to the reader, for taking the time to read *Eversong*.